Dedication

To my brother, David Snell, and to David Shepherd (NTN). Many thanks for all your help with the songs associated with these books.
Here's to their success!

Acknowledgements

I would like to thank everyone who has given me help and encouragement since I formed Albia Publishing to reissue my *Artesans of Albia* trilogy and to publish the next two trilogies, *Circle of Conspiracy*, and *Master of Malice*. I'm not sure what I'd have done without you.

To my husband, Dave, for unflagging encouragement and for getting involved in the 'business end' of this venture. Also for constructive and valuable content suggestions.

To my parents, Barbara and Dennis, for always being interested and supportive.

To Gordon Long, for picking up all my sloppy habits and enabling me to accept valuable criticism.

To Diane Dalton, for expertly editing the final result.

To Mikey Brooks, for another wonderful cover. Sullyan and Drum keep getting better and better!

To my brother, David Snell, and to David Shepherd, for helping make the songs associated with my books so memorable and such fun to write and record.

To everyone who has left me a review, and especially to those reviewers whose words appear at the front of this book. Thank you! I am humbled by your level of enjoyment.

And to all the other fans and readers who I know have enjoyed my books but who haven't (yet!) left a review. I'll come asking soon!

And lastly, very special thanks must go to Janet Morris, for allowing me to use her wonderful endorsement of my *Artesans of Albia* series.

Please do visit my website to hear and download the songs associated with each book. You can also listen to some interviews recorded with various radio stations.

I really hope you enjoy this first novel in the *Circle of Conspiracy* trilogy and, as ever, I would very much appreciate an Amazon review. Reviews really do help authors sell their books.

The Challenge

Circle of Conspiracy

Book One

Cas Peace

Albia Publishing

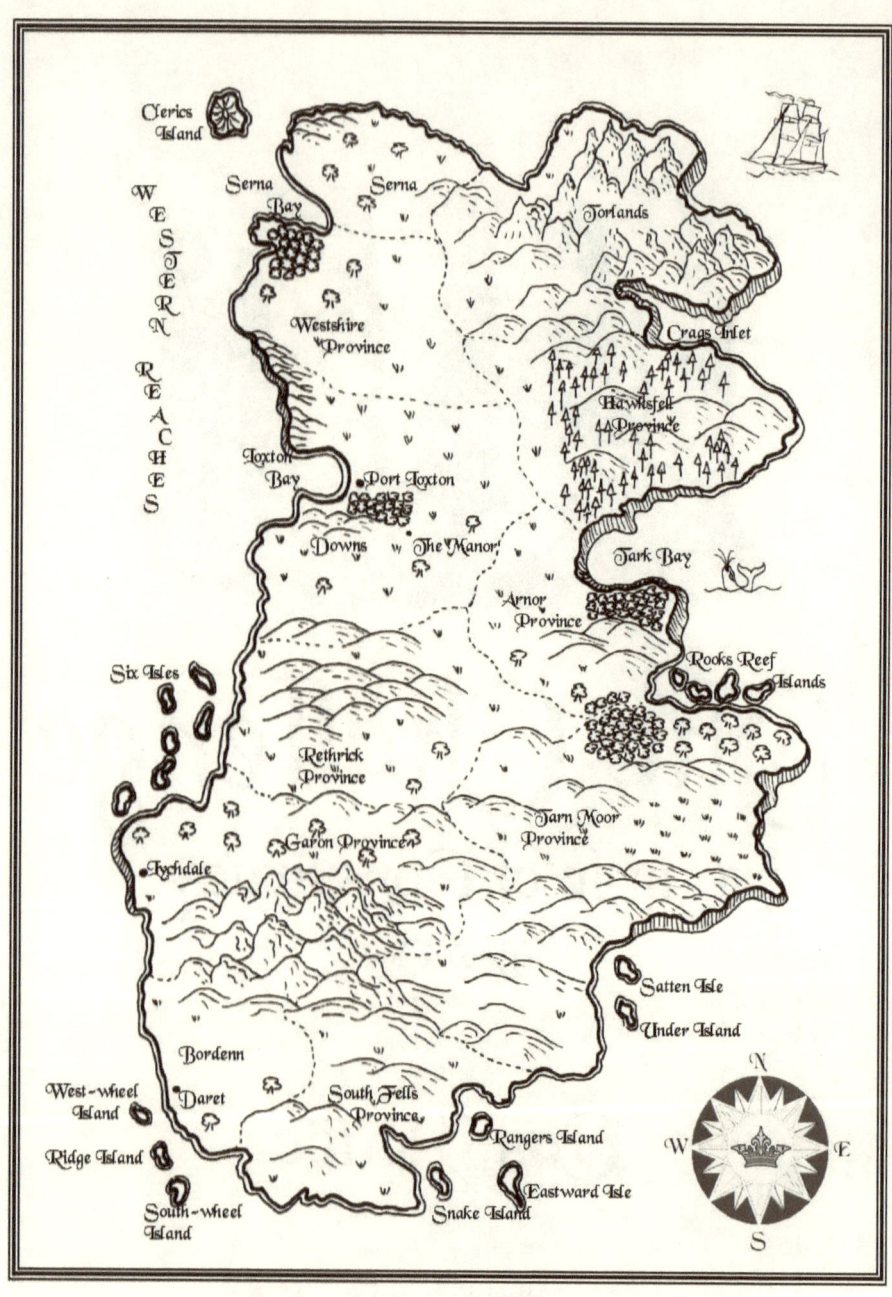

The Kingdom of Albia in the Realm of Albia. (not to scale)

Realm of Andaryon. (not to scale.)

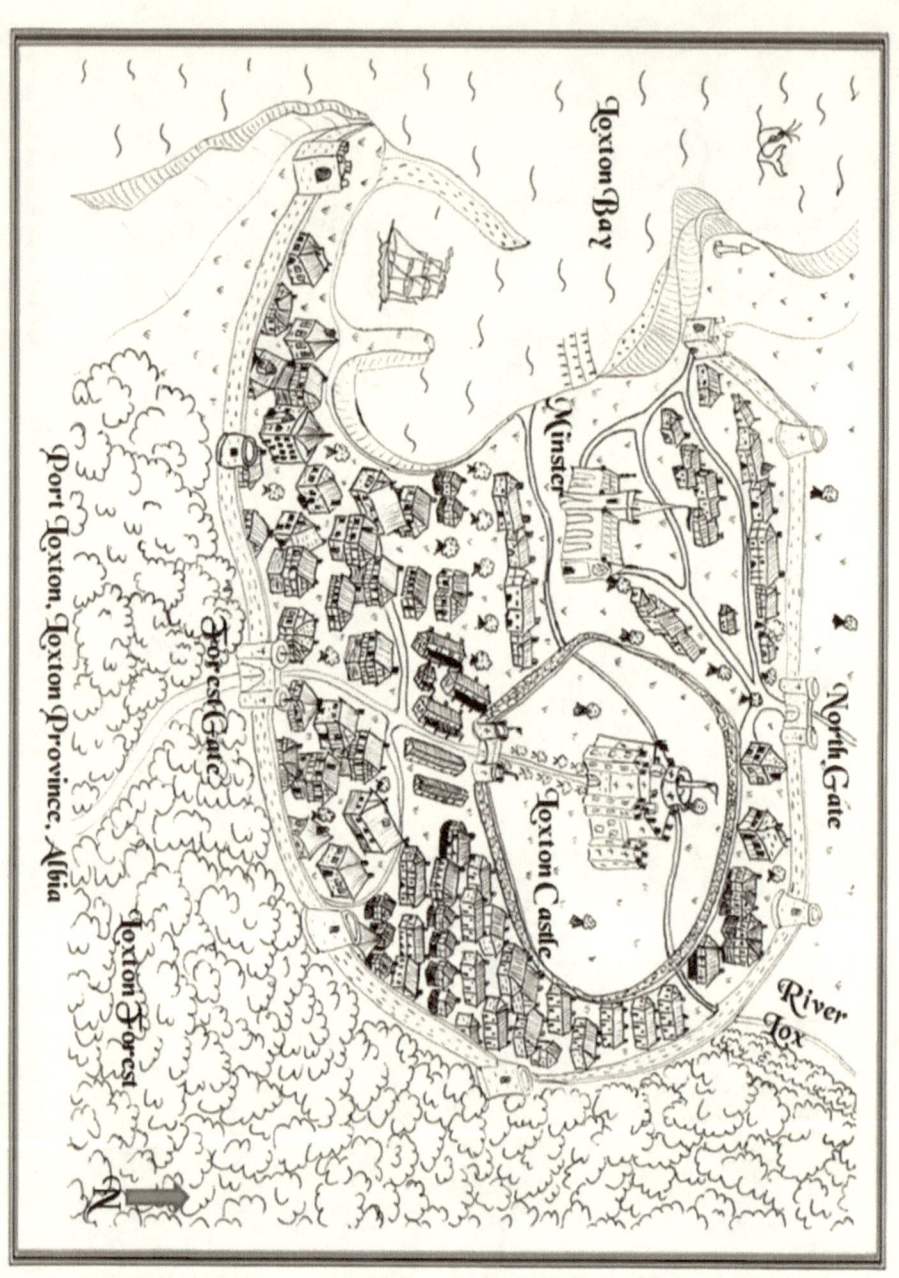

Toxton Bay

Toxton Minster

North Gate

River Tox

Toxton Castle

Forest Gate

Toxton Forest

Port Toxton, Toxton Province, Albia

Chapter One

Taran Elijah stood in the warmth of the evening sun, contemplating the building before him. High King Elias's new Artesan College was finally finished. The Adept sighed in contentment as he watched the setting sun gild the soft gray stone of the College walls.

He still found it hard to believe that a mere fifteen months ago he had been a directionless drifter, desperately seeking the unobtainable. Yet here he was, a founding member of what would hopefully become the foremost center of learning for every Albian Artesan. He knew his good fortune was due to one very special person.

As if summoned by his thought, he heard her musical murmur. "Do you still find it as incredible as I do, Taran?"

He had not heard her come up behind him. The feather-light touch on his arm made him smile, although the contact was fleeting. She knew that the slightest brush of her hand could set his senses tingling with reactions he could barely control, and she would never deliberately cause him distress.

He turned to look at her and the sight made his heart leap, as always.

Since wedding her soul mate, Robin Tamsen, nine months ago, Brynne Sullyan had grown in both presence and beauty. Now that she was back to full fitness after her ordeals in Andaryon and with Rykan's Staff, she exuded a glowing vitality. As usual, her wealth of tawny hair was braided around her head. Her soft, cream-colored shirt was tucked loosely into her combat leathers, and her sword rode at her right hip. Her battle-honors, triple-thunderflash rank insignia, and King's Envoy shooting star glittered over her left breast, catching the sun's last rays. The fire opal at the open neck of her shirt spat red sparks in time with her heartbeat.

Taran's breath caught in his throat and he knew she could sense his desire. She had told him it wouldn't be easy, working so closely together, and she was right. Yet he would bear the pain of knowing she could never be his and take what she could give him: her friendship, her loyalty, and her training. He could bear much for that.

He smiled down at her—her head only reached the level of his shoulder—and replied, "I could never have dreamed things would turn out like this. I only wish my father had lived to see it. It was his dream too, you know, a recognized training center where Artesans could learn in safety. Had it existed when he was alive, I would have been spared a lot of pain and anguish."

She flashed him a knowing glance.

"Ah, but Taran, without that pain and anguish we might never have met. Think what we would have missed."

He grinned.

"True. But I still wish my father had swallowed his pride and told me about his visit here all those years ago. If he had only been able to admit he had asked for help, things might have turned out quite differently."

She gave a small shrug. "We could ponder the 'what if's' all night, my friend. Things have turned out well enough and I for one am happy to accept them. Now, will you help me check that the College is ready for the King's visit next week? The General will have my hide if Elias finds fault with our preparations."

Taran feigned outrage. "He wouldn't dare!"

Sullyan laughed, not bothering to ask whether he meant the King or the General.

Taran followed her into the single story College and they began checking the rooms, enjoying the smell of fresh plaster and new paint, taking in the quiet air of contemplation and study they already seemed to exude. Sullyan hoped that more and more people would get to hear of the College as the King's endorsement of Artesans became more widely known. Maybe then Albians would begin to send their gifted children to the College for training instead of ignoring or suppressing their talents.

"Check the rest of the study rooms, will you, Taran? I want to test the spellsilver in the healer suite. Let me know if you catch any hint of my psyche while I am there."

The College infirmary had been specially designed for housing Artesans. While it was rare for Artesans to be injured in the course of their training, in an environment where students of all ages and levels of experience would be thrown together, accidents were bound to happen. With this in mind, Sullyan had specified that spellsilver should be incorporated into the walls of the healer suite. This should ensure that any inadvertent substrate surges would be contained, protecting the other students.

Taran nodded as she left him, and he continued checking the rooms, finally pausing in the one devoted to the understanding of Fire. This was his current area of study. As Artesan Adept he had mastery over Earth and Water, but if he wanted to raise his status to Adept-elite, he had to learn to influence Fire.

A year ago, he had watched Robin pass his test of Fire to become a Master Artesan. Having felt Robin's strength that day, Taran hadn't believed he would ever wield that much power himself.

Under Sullyan's careful teaching and Robin's guidance, however, he was growing in skill and confidence. He was reaching a point where he felt that mastery over Fire might not actually be beyond him. The technique of creating a Firefield was his next goal.

✣ ✣ ✣ ✣ ✣

Leaving Taran to his musing, Sullyan passed the empty study rooms and moved toward the rear of the building. She trod silently, as was her custom, and so the thin young man standing just inside the healer suite didn't hear her approach. As she stepped through the doorway he seemed to be contemplating the walls, deep in thought.

She frowned. One hand touched the hilt of her sword as she said, "Captain Parren, what are you doing here?"

He spun round. The color drained from his face, making the long scar down his right cheek stand out starkly. Never a handsome man, the scar gave him a rakish air that gained him no favor with the ladies. It was one of many grievances he harbored against Sullyan, and she knew he yearned to exact revenge.

He recovered his composure and replied stiffly. "I was merely indulging my curiosity, Colonel. I was not aware of any restrictions regarding entry."

He managed to look her in the eye as he spoke, although she could sense his courage wavering under the flatness of her stare. She felt him trying to overcome this fear, but it was too deeply rooted, went back too far. The fact that she knew this inflamed his hatred even more.

She regarded him silently before asking, "And have you satisfied your curiosity, Captain? Do you have any questions?"

He flushed. He had clearly not intended to be discovered, thinking himself safe at this hour. Something sly surfaced in his eyes and her heart leaped, wondering if he was going to attack her. But then it faded and he backed down. "I have no questions,

Colonel. I wish you good fortune in this new venture and I hope all goes well with the King's visit. Now, if you will excuse me, I have duties to attend."

He gave the obligatory salute and stalked past her, nearly colliding with Taran in the doorway as he left. The Adept stared after him before giving Sullyan a quizzical look. "What did he want?"

Her eyes narrowed. "A good question, my friend. Who can say with that one?" Her gaze fell on him. "He will bear watching. I fear his dissatisfaction and hatred are growing, especially after being passed over for promotion last summer."

"From what I heard he only has himself to blame for that," the Adept replied. "But why does he hate you and Robin so much?"

Her eyes flickered. "Parren is ruled by ambition and envy, Taran. His animosity is rooted deep in the past and is not something I wish to discuss. Now, will you go outside and close the door and tell me if you can sense any contact through the spellsilver?"

Summarily dismissed, Taran obeyed, but she knew his curiosity had been piqued.

Chapter Two

Three days later, Sullyan was sitting in her office with Robin and Bull. They were drinking fellan and discussing a training mission in Andaryon, involving a joint exercise with a company of the Hierarch's forces.

Since the forging of an alliance between Elias of Albia and Pharikian of Andaryon, traffic had started passing between the two realms, for reasons of both trade and military cooperation. The two forces were getting to know each other well and racial prejudices were fading, gradually turning to respect. The respect might be grudging at times, and there was still outright hostility from one or two factions, but little by little relations were improving.

Bull, lounging comfortably in one of the room's few easy chairs, had given his opinion on which company would benefit most from the planned exercise. Sullyan watched in silence as Robin, between sips of fellan, argued the various points with his old friend. His handsome features were animated and his indigo eyes flicked frequently to hers. She, as usual, was withholding her judgment, enjoying listening to them pick over the details. Once they finished, she would weigh the points raised and tell them her decision.

Robin started to ask her opinion, but was interrupted by a knock on the door. At Sullyan's invitation to enter, a young lad appeared. She smiled warmly at the Manor's youngest Artesan Apprentice and said, "What is it, Tad?"

The tow-headed lad, now fourteen and full of new-found

confidence due to his status, snapped a very creditable salute.

"The King sends his compliments, Colonel, and asks that you receive his messenger."

She stood, drawing the two men with her. "Send her in, Cadet."

High King Elias Rovannon was known for his radical policies, policies not always fully supported by his counselors and court, and his latest innovation was the formation of a runner network set up to facilitate the speedy delivery of his personal messages. When mooted, the idea was welcomed until Elias revealed that the runners he intended to recruit would primarily be women.

His reasoning, that there were more women available since men filled most of the other posts, and that women were lighter than men, meaning they could ride faster and change horses less frequently, was forced upon his court, and so the messenger ushered in by Tad was a young woman in her twenties.

Sullyan knew that if Elias got his wish there would eventually be a far more efficient and secure messenger network covering the land. He understood how using trusted Artesans could transform the way the country was run, and not simply in the field of communications. His goal was to convince the people to trust Artesans, and his College was the first step toward its achievement. Until he succeeded, his runner system was the only means of guaranteeing speedy communications.

Sullyan greeted the runner respectfully. "Will you take refreshment?"

The woman, who introduced herself as Lyanda, gratefully accepted the mug of steaming fellan Bull held out to her. She sank into a chair, weary from having ridden nonstop from the capital. Once she had taken a few sips, she reached into her jacket and handed a slim package to Sullyan.

Sullyan only briefly glanced at the unbroken seal. Runners

were trusted and loyal, and also well trained in the defense of their duty, knowing how to use the light swords they bore. She spread the parchment on the table before her and Robin immediately leaned over her shoulder. Bull also moved around until he could read the King's script. Lyanda's face showed mild surprise at such openness, but Sullyan kept no secrets from either her life mate or her oldest friend. All three of them read the King's words.

My dear Brynne, the letter began, its informality typical of Elias when addressing his friends. *I trust this finds you in good health and that the arrangements for the inauguration of the new College are proceeding according to plan.*

I had it in mind that when I returned to Port Loxton after the ceremony I would bring back my new colt, Darius, as you indicated in your last letter that his training is all but complete. However, it has been brought to my attention that our annual fair and horse race, which will be held four days from when you receive this, would be an ideal venue for testing his mettle and quality.

Therefore, I am requesting that you bring him to court in time for the fair. You can return to the Manor with me when I come to conduct the inauguration ceremony at the end of next week.

I have dispatched a second message to Lord Blaine, asking him to release you from your duties, and I will expect you at court within the next few days.

The parchment was signed with Elias's usual illegible scrawl, but there was also an equally informal postscript.

Be sure you don't tire Darius on the way, Brynne. I intend to win the cross-country race on him!

Sullyan smiled. Every year during the fair, Elias held a special cross-country horse race in the castle grounds. Every year, he won it.

Bull snorted. "He wouldn't stand a chance if you entered on Drum."

Sullyan glanced at him, mischief in her eyes. The colt in question was only three and a half years old and not likely to be a match for her warhorse. At six years old, Drum was in his prime.

Her grin widened. "Now, there is a thought."

Robin looked scandalized. "You can't do that, Sullyan. Think how it would look if you beat the King in his own race!"

Sullyan glanced at Lyanda and the two women shared a smile. "King Elias may be passionate about racing, but I have heard he is also a good sport," the runner said.

"I have heard that too," said Sullyan, the light of challenge in her eyes. Robin, recognizing the look, shook his head in mock despair. "But that aside, gentlemen," she continued, "this means I will be unable to join your exercise. You will have to take my place, Bull, to stand for Robin and see that my orders are carried out."

Robin was about to protest the implied slight when he saw the teasing glitter in her eyes. He grinned before sobering. "But if Bull comes with me, who will go to Port Loxton with you?"

She gazed at him. Two years ago she might have rebuked him for implying she needed protection, but last year's events had changed things. It was an Artesan rule that they never went anywhere alone if they could avoid it, traveling in pairs to back each other up if necessary. If Elias's plans for the College materialized and the current tide of mistrust was turned, this precaution might become redundant. For now, though, it was neither politic nor safe to ignore the dangers.

"Who would you suggest, Robin?" she asked, knowing there was only one choice.

Robin knew it too. "Taran, of course. You know I trust him."

Robin was well aware of the deep feelings Taran harbored for Sullyan. But he also knew that Sullyan was totally committed to their marriage, and that Taran was too honorable to act on his feelings.

Sullyan smiled and reached for fresh parchment to pen a reply to the King's command.

✣ ✣ ✣ ✣ ✣

The runner had gone, carrying Sullyan's reply back to the King. Bull and Robin had also left, to finalize their arrangements for the military exercises in Andaryon. Having made sure there was fresh fellan brewing in the apartment she now shared with Robin, Sullyan sent young Tad in search of Taran. She left the apartment door open so he would know to come through when he found the adjoining office empty.

He didn't keep her waiting, and entered in response to her call. He looked around, probably thinking that despite Robin's occupation the apartment was not much altered from the very first time he had seen it. Early summer sunlight slanted in through the open windows and the breeze carried the sounds of men drilling outside. The familiarity of the room and the sounds were both fitting and comforting.

He gave Sullyan a warm smile as she handed him the inevitable cup of fellan. Sinking into a chair opposite her, he raised his brows as he sipped the drink.

She handed him the King's message. "Read this, will you?"

He did so, grinning as he took in the postscript. Handing the letter back he said, "I take it you want me to look after something for you while you're away?"

"Yes, Taran," she replied, holding his gaze. "Me."

As she had expected, he was confused. "Robin and Bull are committed to conducting this joint exercise in Andaryon over the coming week," she explained. "As you know, I had intended to go with them, but this... request from the King takes precedence. Especially as he has already obtained my release from the General. Therefore, I need someone to stand for me while I am away. So, my friend, do you fancy a trip to Port Loxton?"

Taran's eyes widened. A curious expression came over his face, half pleasure and half apprehension. His tone was wary as he asked, "What does Robin say to this?"

Sullyan sighed. Taran's regrettable lack of self-confidence, coupled with his highly developed sense of honor, left him vulnerable to feelings of insecurity where Robin was concerned. Not only was Robin a Master Artesan, two full levels above Taran, but the Adept was also aware that Robin knew of his love for Sullyan. He was painfully over careful not to offend Robin's sensibilities where she was concerned.

She tried to reassure him, but knew of someone who could do it better. "Robin trusts you, Taran, as do I. You should be confident of that by now. Do I take it you are willing then? We might even get the opportunity for some training on the way, although this is really a pleasure trip."

She had slyly dangled the one inducement guaranteed to persuade Taran had he been reluctant, which he wasn't. Recognizing her ploy, he grinned. "I am at your command, Colonel, as well you know. When do we leave?"

"First thing tomorrow," she said, the warmth in her eyes making Taran flush. "Be sure to pack something suitable for court, and remember that we are going to attend a fair. There will be festivities and, I am sure, plenty of unattached young ladies."

He pursed his lips. He was aware that she hoped he would find someone else to lavish his attentions on, but he resisted whenever the subject arose. The simple truth was that he didn't want to. He had accepted the fact that she couldn't return his feelings, but he was also aware that she was deeply fond of him. She had even told him as much when she had asked him to stay at the Manor, in a desire to be completely honest. She would continue to wish that he would find someone to share his life and experience the love he had to give, but if he didn't care to she could hardly force him. He seemed content to accept and treasure her friendship, supporting both her and Robin as best he could.

Sighing, she sent him to instruct the stablemaster to have their mounts ready for the following morning.

✠ ✠ ✠ ✠ ✠

After delivering Sullyan's orders to the stablemaster, Taran made his way back up to the Manor, enjoying the warmth of the sun. He passed a small group of men returning from guard duty, most of whom greeted him with smiles. Their captain, however, did not.

Taran nodded civilly as Parren stalked past. His greeting was ignored, as he knew it would be, but he refused to let the scarred man's animosity bother him. Parren had no personal reason to dislike Taran, aside from the fact that he was friendly with Sullyan and Robin. Taran saw no need to antagonize the other man if he could help it.

He was still pondering the reasons for Parren's hatred when he saw Robin and Bull approaching. They fell into step beside him and Robin threw a companionable arm about Taran's shoulders.

"I hear you'll be standing in for me over the next few days," he said.

Through the physical contact Taran felt Robin's ease, and he suddenly knew that the younger man had deliberately sought him out. "I'll do my best to look after her," he said.

The Major's indigo eyes twinkled. "I know you will, Taran. There's no one I'd rather trust her with, except Bulldog, of course. Shame the old goat's past it."

His teasing earned him a punch on the arm and a growl from Bull. "Impudent pup!"

Once again, Taran was impressed by the depth of maturity marriage had given Robin. The impetuousness of fifteen months ago was slowly being replaced by a growing sense of responsibility, but he still retained his youthfulness and easy good humor.

Robin had gone through all kinds of perdition over the last four years, starting with the terminal illness and subsequent death of his beloved sister, Jessy. His profound love for Sullyan and his sacrifices during a traumatic period in their lives had found their ultimate reward in her acceptance of him as life mate. This culminated in a stunning ceremony nine months ago, when the Hierarch of Andaryon had presided over a triple wedding at the stone circle just to the north of the Andaryan Citadel, Caer Vellet. Duke Marik and the Princess Idrimar, Robin and Sullyan, and Cal Tyler and Rienne Arlen had all made their pledges to each other under Pharikian's benevolent gaze. Remembering the lavish celebrations that followed and the happiness of the three couples still brought pleasure swelling into Taran's heart.

He smiled. A year ago he wouldn't have traded places with Robin for the world, but the intensity of his experiences had molded and changed Robin for the better. He was now one of the most respected officers at the Manor, something not even General

Blaine could dispute. Taran was proud to be associated with him.

Robin plainly sensed these thoughts, for he laughed. "Easy, Taran! You're embarrassing me."

Taran grinned back, unrepentant and now totally at ease with his assigned duty, just as Sullyan had no doubt intended.

✤ ✤ ✤ ✤ ✤

Brynne Sullyan had another visitor late that afternoon. Rienne Arlen, Sullyan's personal healer, knocked on the door just as her friend was finishing off her packing. She had managed to catch Sullyan before she headed for the senior officers' hall and her evening meal.

Following Sullyan's gesture to enter, the dark haired healer came and sat on the bed. Rienne also exhibited the glowing contentment brought by a happy marriage, and both she and Cal had settled comfortably into life at the Manor. However, it wasn't her personal life that was the current focus of Rienne's attention. She had something else on her mind and scrutinized Sullyan as she moved about the room.

Having carefully folded the final garment, Sullyan sat down. Rienne studied her face. "How are you feeling now, Brynne?"

Rienne was the only one of Sullyan's friends who felt truly comfortable using her given name. Both Robin and Bull had known her as Sullyan for too long to change easily, although Robin did use her first name in moments of passion. When Bull wanted to be informal he merely shortened her last name to Sully as he had always done. But Rienne liked the sound of the unusual first name and used it unselfconsciously.

Sullyan considered her question before replying. "I feel fine, Rienne, honestly. I have had no more dizziness or sickness. In fact, I have given it no thought for days now."

Despite her best efforts, Sullyan had not long been able to hide

14

her recent indisposition from her healer friend. Intermittent sickness had been plaguing her, mainly at meal times, and Sullyan was never a hearty eater, and it hadn't taken Rienne long to notice. Sullyan had fobbed her off for a while, but her most recent bout of dizziness, worse than all the rest, had alarmed her. She had been forced to confess it to Rienne, and was quite prepared to let the healer check her over. She didn't want to be unwell during this trip to Loxton.

Rienne examined her carefully before holding out her hand in a way that brooked no refusal. Sullyan sighed but took the hand as she allowed the empathic healer access to her psyche. Rienne's own vision lost focus as she concentrated on the aura of Sullyan's mind. Finally satisfied, she released her hand.

"Yes, you're right. You're in very good health, as always. Whatever it was must have passed."

Sullyan accepted Rienne's findings philosophically. Artesans were never ill in the normal sense. Being able to control their own life force, they were rarely subject to the diseases suffered by the ungifted. Apart from the terrible consequences of Rykan's brutal rape, the only time Sullyan ailed was when wounded in battle. Her ordeal at Rykan's hands was well in the past now and her body had fully recovered. Yet this recent sickness concerned Rienne, despite Sullyan's apparent good health. Had Rykan's abuse left an unknown legacy, one neither the healer nor Sullyan could detect?

Rienne stood to leave. "Take care of yourself in Port Loxton, won't you? And be sure to let me know if these bouts of sickness return."

Sullyan smiled at her friend, and Rienne knew she had dismissed the sickness from her mind. The healer left, only remembering when she reached the infirmary that she hadn't told Sullyan of the decision she and Cal had recently made.

Chapter Three

Sullyan and Robin woke well before reveille, as they usually did when out of their normal routine. Sullyan stirred as her life mate took her into his arms and brushed his lips against the back of her neck. She responded sleepily, turning and wrapping her legs around his slim hips. Sharing his mounting passion for the first time in some days, she allowed herself to be swept away by his love.

The depth and intensity of her feelings caught her by surprise, as they often did. Their delight in each other hadn't faded one bit since their wedding, even though Sullyan's recent bouts of sickness, which she had hidden from Robin if not from Rienne, sometimes affected her desire for physical intimacy. Linking herself to Robin body, psyche, and soul, she allowed her emotions free rein.

As they rested close together afterward, Robin gazed into her eyes. "You will take care of yourself, won't you, love? I know this is a pleasure trip, but we still haven't discovered who created that weapon of Rykan's. And you know there are people at court who bear us no love."

She snuggled closer. "I will be on my guard, Robin. This trip will give me the chance to ask Elias about his own investigations. He is reluctant to commit his thoughts to parchment, and it is a wise precaution if there is a renegade Artesan out there somewhere. Taran and I will keep our eyes and ears open while we are in Loxton. You know what fairs are like. People love to gossip and we might hear something interesting. I also want to keep a close eye on Elias's advisors, to see if any of them appear uncomfortable while Artesans are among them."

She gave her life mate a kiss and slid from the bed, throwing on one of Robin's spare shirts which she often used as a nightshirt. As she freed the tumbled masses of her hair, she sensed the pang of concern that rose in Robin's breast. They had not been apart since their marriage nine months ago, and although last year's terrors were well behind them, she knew he couldn't quite forget the sick, hopeless fear of losing her.

She smiled over her shoulder. "It had to happen sometime, Robin. You have your own responsibilities now, and I have mine. We had to expect this when we accepted promotion. We are fortunate still to be at the same garrison now we are wed, let alone in the same company. It was hard work getting Elias to agree to that, and we must not give him reason to regret it.

"Do not fret, love, I will be quite safe. I am fit and healthy, and Taran is very nearly as skilled with the sword as you are."

Since joining the Manor officially, both Taran and Cal trained regularly with Falkerk, the Manor's weaponsmaster. Falkerk had been trained by Elias's legendary swordmaster, Master Ardoch, who was reputedly the best in the land. Taran had become a very capable swordsman and Cal, who had found out almost by accident that he was skilled with a crossbow, was now deemed second only to Robin. Not even Falkerk could out-shoot the Major.

Thoughts of Cal prompted Sullyan to ask, "Is Cal going to Andaryon with you?"

"I could hardly leave him behind," said Robin. "He's become a valued member of the company. Dexter is very impressed with him, and he's doing so well that I think we might put him forward for promotion soon. He'd make a good captain one day."

"That should please him. Rienne would be very proud."

Sullyan knew how much soul-searching Cal had done before deciding to take the King's Oath. Rienne had been unsure about it, but Sullyan appreciated Cal's motive. The need to belong was a desire she understood.

Robin nodded and arose. He and Bull were leaving after breakfast. As he moved about the room, Sullyan admired his slim and muscular form. Sometimes, she still found it hard to believe she was married to this remarkably handsome young man.

Once they finished dressing, they collected their packs and made their way to the senior officers' hall. Bull, Cal, Rienne, and Taran were already there, along with General Blaine and Colonel Vassa. Sullyan and Robin murmured greetings as they accepted fellan from Bull and food from Tad. Although no longer a kitchen boy, Tad still served them. He did whatever he could to be close to Robin.

With breakfast over, the four of them took their leave. They made their way to the horse lines, where Solet and his lads had their mounts ready. Sullyan's company was assembled and waiting, needing only Robin to lead them.

He and Bull fastened their packs and mounted. Robin leaned down from Torka's back to clasp hands with Sullyan before leading his troop on their way. Taran mounted his own stallion, a look of surprise crossing his face when Sullyan vaulted into young Darius's saddle instead of mounting Drum. She secured Drum's reins to the pommel of his own saddle and the huge black stud followed as she led the way out of the horse lines.

They skirted the side of the Manor house and rode along the gravel drive. As they approached the main gate, they saw it was open. The sentry saluted Sullyan smartly and grinned at Taran as they passed.

"Take care, Colonel. Look after yourself, Taran."

"Thanks, Wil," called Taran, giving the sentry a wave as he

followed Sullyan at a canter down the road.

The morning grew warmer by the hour, the sun unchallenged in a vivid blue sky. As they rode farther from the Manor, Taran began to look about with interest. Sullyan knew he had never been to Albia's capital city, nor traveled much through the north of Loxton Province. He had wandered the southern parts frequently with his father, but had hardly ever been north of Hyecombe before coming to the Manor.

Sullyan kept a northwesterly heading through open, gently rolling terrain. They skirted villages and towns, Sullyan telling Taran their names as they passed each one. The sun was high overhead and they were both ready to rest by the time they came to the ford of a wide stream. After splashing across, Sullyan guided them off the road before drawing rein on a grassy bank beside a dark, swirling pool.

She slid from Darius's back, hooking the reins loosely over the pommel. Drum, who had followed closely behind them with no command from Sullyan, shouldered the mahogany colt aside and waded into the stream to drink. Darius laid back his ears but made no other protest. Taran's mount, the biddable Thunder, waited patiently until both horses had drunk their fill before coming forward to slake his own thirst.

Sullyan took the pack of supplies from Taran's saddle and sat cross-legged on the grass. "Just loop the reins over the pommel, Taran," she said, seeing that he wasn't sure how far to trust his horse. "Thunder will not stray."

He did so and left the horses to please themselves. He and Sullyan relaxed on the short grass, eating a little cheese and fruit which they washed down with clear stream water.

✣ ✣ ✣ ✣ ✣

Taran lounged on one elbow, covertly watching Sullyan. As this was a pleasure trip, she bore no rank insignia and had left her tawny hair partially loose. Her shirt was open at the neck, showing the sparkling fire opal at her throat, and her sleeves were rolled up, allowing the sun to tan her arms. The long scar down her left forearm, inflicted by the Andaryan Commander Vanyr, had faded to a pale line, but the skin of her left hand, damaged in the Firefield during her duel with Rykan, was much darker than the right. It was a constant reminder of how close she had come to death.

All this went through Taran's mind as he watched her finish an apple. She tossed the core casually to Drum, who picked it up with velvety lips. The warmth of the sun and the contented munching of the horses were soporific, and Sullyan leaned against the grassy bank, her hands behind her head. Looking totally at ease, she closed her glorious eyes.

Now Taran was free to study her openly. He tried hard not to let his feelings get the better of him, but the sight of her slim form on the grass, tawny hair spilling out around her, had its usual intense effect. He took in the serene expression on her beautiful face, the fire opal sparking with each beat of her heart, and the gentle swell where the soft shirt covered her breasts. His body responded, his imagination creating forbidden images. He was unable to control them and they played through his mind as he sat lost in a dangerously delicious reverie.

A tiny movement brought him back. With a guilty start, he realized she was watching him.

"Taran Elijah," she reproved softly, "behave yourself!"

Betrayed by his body, he blushed bright crimson and turned his head away. He heard her sigh as she pushed herself upright, but couldn't meet her gaze. He was struggling for control and failing dismally. He had gone too far in his fantasy, and now not even acute embarrassment could cool the heat of his loins.

She spoke gently. "Why do you do this to yourself, Taran?

You really need to learn some control, my friend, or your passions will drive you mad." Tears came to his eyes, and she reached out toward him. "Ah, Taran, Taran, what shall we do with you?"

She didn't complete the gesture, realizing in time what a mistake it would be. He could not bear her touch without pain, and he was too close to the edge right now.

Irritable with embarrassment, he said, "I know, I know! I'm sorry." He forced himself to meet her eyes, but the love and sympathy he saw there, when what he really deserved was censure, only added to his plight. Deeply shamed, he looked down.

In a light tone, she said, "What you need is distraction. Discipline and control can be applied to other things besides metaforce. While learning to master your powers, you also learn to master your emotions."

His head snapped up, incredulous. "Are you suggesting we do some training now? How can I concentrate in this state?"

Unmoved, she smiled. "But, Taran, you are in just the right state to practice the influence of Fire."

He frowned. As she settled comfortably into her usual cross-legged pose, she said, "Think, my friend. The four elements exist within each of us, some of them stronger than others. This is why some Artesans are better at influencing one element above the others. Do you recall, after your confirmation as Adept, that I said you had the capacity to become a Master?"

Taran nodded, although his inexperience and frustration at that time had not allowed him to believe her.

"I said that because even then the depth of your passion was clear to me."

He colored again. He hadn't known she had guessed the strength of his feelings so early in their relationship.

"Do you not see, Taran? We carry each raw element within us, and passion, or spirit, or desire, call it what you will, is just another form of Fire. You have that element very strongly within you, especially just now"—she laughed as his face flamed again—"so you will not have to reach very far to find it. You really must learn to accept your emotions. Accept them and use them. They are a fundamental part of you, and if you keep trying to suppress them you will never be able to grow.

"Come, let me show you. Lay out your pattern."

He was reluctant to open his mind to her, guilty at the images there, but his hunger to learn tempered the ache of physical need. He could never refuse her teaching or the confidence of her mind's touch upon his, so he did as she asked.

Reaching within, touching the secret depths of his psyche, he projected his intimate pattern onto the substrate. Sullyan did the same, her pupils dilating, and the two structures shimmered and sparkled side by side.

Taran stared at the immense complexity of Sullyan's pattern, so different to his. She must have caught his thought for she said, "Different, yes, but look here. What do you see?"

He looked and was amazed. One portion of her pattern corresponded almost exactly with his. He frowned, perplexed.

"That part of my pattern represents my mastery over Water," she explained. "And this," she indicated another area, "is the part representing mastery over Earth. See how similar they are to yours?"

He was astounded, never having noticed how closely these two areas matched. "But your psyche is so much deeper and more complex than mine," he said. "How will I ever be able to master the other two elements?"

There was no censure in her tone as she said, "Ah, you still do not understand. I am a Senior Master, and my pattern reflects that, but it was not always as complex as it is now. The structure grows as your powers grow, not the other way round. This is why practice is so important. The stronger you become and the surer your handling of the elements you do control, the sooner you will be able to master those you do not.

"Now, let us link together and I will try to show you how to influence Fire."

He sensed her power, warm as love, amber as honey, flowing toward him, surrounding his psyche. As he accepted the contact, he felt a familiar awe at the depth of her strength. His embarrassment faded as he lost himself in the process of harnessing his metaforce.

Once they were linked, he followed her lead as she showed him how to recognize and isolate the element of Fire within his psyche. Then she taught him what Fire looked like in its raw state, when it was quiescent within the substrate. She told him she couldn't help him shape or call it, he had to learn that for himself, but once he had memorized its unique signature, he watched as she reached through the substrate, calling Fire to her will. He saw how her vast strength latched on to it, bringing a dancing flame forth to shimmer on her hand, and he marveled once more at the power at her command. Not one glimmer of Fire escaped her control.

She released it and invited him to try. But this level of expertise was beyond him, and Fire was so very strong, stronger by far than Water. He struggled and he knew she could tell that instead of controlling he was actually stoking the fire within him, fanning the heat of his desire rather than taming.

The heat of his passion was rising, but she mercifully broke their link by touching him lightly on the arm. Tears came to his eyes, fueled by his anger at his failure to control either the raw element or his body's reaction.

Sighing, she took pity on him.

"Do not torture yourself, Taran. You have not failed, you merely need to practice and improve your strength. In the meantime, I have a suggestion that might help with your current...

ah… problem."

He glanced wretchedly at her and she stood, gesturing with her hand. He rose obediently and followed her to where the stream tumbled frothing into the pool. "Sit where it is cool. Look into the water."

He did so, leaning forward to stare into the rippling depths. Sullyan stood at his back, hands resting lightly on his shoulders. This gentle contact did nothing to calm his inner turmoil, although the water's cool mist did soothe his overheated face.

"Look deep into the water," she murmured, and he did so, waiting for her contact in his mind.

Her sudden shove sent him plunging into the cold pool. It was a complete shock. Had he been less absorbed in his shame he might have suspected what was coming, but he hadn't. He surfaced, spitting water and spluttering with outrage. Turning, he could see her almost helpless with laughter on the bank. He cursed expressively and lunged from the pool, grabbing at her, but even breathless she was too quick for him. Standing well out of reach, she turned, regarding him with merry eyes.

"Is your blood a bit cooler now?"

He glared at her, his clothes sodden, hair dripping. Her infectious good humor gradually overcame his irritation and he broke into a grin. "You witch! Look at me, I'm soaked through."

She cocked her head. "You brought a change of clothes, though, surely?"

He colored yet again, realizing he would have to change in front of her unless he wanted to ride in sopping wet leather. He didn't have her carefree attitude to nudity, had never been able to emulate her ease around members of the opposite sex.

Sullyan guessed his thoughts and casually waved her hand. "Oh, have no fear. I will turn my back."

She did just that, busying herself with the horses while Taran, muttering curses, shed his wet clothes and put on dry ones. She approached him when he was done and he was surprised to see diffidence in her eyes.

"Am I forgiven?"

He could hardly believe she was serious. "For what? I was at fault, not you."

Amazing him again, she dropped her gaze. "Not entirely."

His eyes widened as she admitted, "Never think that I am immune to desire. You are a very attractive man, and under different circumstances I think there would have been something between us. Maybe I should not tell you this. You know my heart belongs to Robin and I could never betray his love. But I would not see you take sole responsibility for these feelings. It is not healthy and it will prevent you from growing as you should.

"So hear me well. I do love you, Taran, although I have controlled my feelings, shaped them into a deep and abiding friendship. You must do the same, for upon that basis we can share our love without endangering our other commitments. You know that Robin is aware of your feelings, but he is secure in the knowledge of my fidelity, and that is how it should be. I treasure his trust and love and will never do anything to damage them. That would destroy him, and what harms him would injure me also.

"Am I making myself clear to you?"

Taran stared into her golden eyes. He was astounded. She had never spoken so frankly about her personal feelings before. He knew she valued him as a friend and fellow Artesan, but he had not known she bore him the kind of love he so desperately desired. If only her heart wasn't already pledged! He too was unsure whether knowing she loved him would help or hinder, but it was her way to be honest with her friends and he wasn't surprised she had chosen to tell him. He only hoped he could justify her trust and learn to do what she had done; see their relationship as a merging of close friends who could completely rely on each other, both for power and support.

"Yes, Brynne, you are," he said, his uncommon use of her given name conveying his sincerity. "I'll try to do the same. I have no intention of letting either you or Robin down. I value your friendship too highly for that." He took a deep breath. "Now, hadn't we better move on?"

Smiling, she approved his change of subject. "It is not too much farther now to the tavern where we will spend the night." She mounted Darius once more. "And if fortune favors us this evening, we may meet an old friend of mine. Someone I have not seen for far too long."

She refused to elaborate, and Taran was forced to curb his curiosity as they rode into the heat of the afternoon, Drum trailing obediently as before.

Chapter Four

Taran had long forgiven Sullyan by the time she next drew rein. The land had been rising steadily for some two hours and the sun, although still shining strongly, was beginning to dip to their left. There was even a faint breeze, and they enjoyed its cooling caress as they let the horses breathe.

Gazing over the land spread out below him, Taran caught a glimpse of steel gray far away to his left. "Is that the sea?" He had never been to the coast and was looking forward to his first sight of the ocean and the bustling city of Port Loxton.

Sullyan nodded. "What you see are the Western Reaches. If you look carefully, just above that dark smudge of forest, you can see the spire of Loxton's Minster."

He stared hard, not entirely sure that he could, but Sullyan had already turned Darius's head back to the road. Tearing his eyes away, Taran followed her.

It was late afternoon when they finally drew up outside a double story stone building nestled in a copse of trees. Propped beside the door was a wooden sign with the name Hazel Tree carved into it. Looking around, Taran could indeed see coppiced hazels among the press of trees surrounding the inn.

The place appeared to be closed. Sullyan dismounted and thumped on the door with the butt of her knife. After a few moments, it opened to reveal a stocky, bald man. His brown and weathered face broke into a smile when he saw who his visitor was.

"Sullyan!" he exclaimed, holding his arms wide and coming forward to embrace her. "It must be two years, at least."

"Two and a half, Jed," she replied, returning his hug. "Do you have rooms for the night?"

"Always for Kingsmen, and especially for you." He eyed Taran appraisingly. "One room is it?"

She grinned and shook her head. "Two, if you please."

The innkeeper raised his brows. "I thought you were wed now?"

"I am, but Robin is away on exercise at the moment. This is Taran Elijah, a friend and fellow Artesan."

Jed shook Taran's hand. "Any friend of Sullyan is welcome here. Come in, if you please. I'll get the boys to see to your bags and horses."

They left their mounts hitched to the railing and followed Jed inside. He yelled, "Zane, Devis!" and a pair of young boys came clattering down the stairs. Both had Jed's brown, round face, although the older lad had green eyes and auburn hair instead of his father's brown.

As he passed her, Sullyan caught the older lad by the arm. "Be especially careful with the youngster, Zane," she said, pressing a small silver coin into his hand. "He belongs to the King and deserves your very best treatment."

Zane gasped in delight. "All your horses will get the best treatment, Lady."

She grinned and gave him a gentle push on his way.

Jed ushered his guests into the smallest of two snugs and bade them sit. He disappeared behind the bar, returning a few minutes later with a tankard of ale for Taran and a glass of fruit cordial for Sullyan.

They nodded their thanks and drank deeply, relaxing into the comfortable atmosphere. Taran was impressed by the quality of the ale, which was nutty and full of flavor, far superior to anything he had tasted before. He complimented Jed and was rewarded with a wide smile.

Jed settled himself into a chair and regarded Sullyan knowingly. "So, Colonel, what brings you here after all this time?"

"We are on our way to Port Loxton, delivering the King's new colt in time for the horse fair," she replied. Her face wore an innocent expression, and Taran watched the by-play with bemusement.

Jed grinned and wagged his finger. "There are more direct routes to Loxton than this, and I know you are not attracted by the quality of my ale. So?"

She gave up the game. "All right, Jed! Will he be in tonight?"

The innkeeper's eyes twinkled. "He usually is this time of year. He was here last week and, strangely enough, he was asking about you. I think he misses you."

She sobered. "How was he?"

"Oh, you know." Jed rocked one hand in a gesture of doubt.

"As bad as that?" The sadness in her tone made Taran frown, but she didn't explain and he didn't like to ask.

Eager for the latest news from the Manor, Jed changed the subject. He had heard something of Sullyan's experiences in Andaryon from other Kingsmen who had visited the inn, but he wanted details only she could give. Sullyan satisfied his curiosity without giving too much personal detail, and Taran took note, determined not to let slip things she might want kept private.

The inn was beginning to fill and soon Jed had to leave them to serve behind the bar. His youngest son, Devis, brought their food, and even Sullyan did justice to the delicious meat, gravy, and vegetables. The taproom was becoming crowded and Taran was not surprised. With ale and food of this quality, Jed's inn must be very popular.

After finishing their meal, Taran and Sullyan left the snug and joined Jed's other guests. The sun had set and the lamps were lit, giving the taproom a welcoming, cozy glow. The tavern door opened once more and the buzz of conversation died. As Taran turned to see why, his breath caught in his throat. The most beautiful young man he had ever seen was standing by the door.

All heads turned to watch as the newcomer moved gracefully to the bar. Jed handed him a glass of what appeared to be plain water, and the silence stretched on while he slowly drank. To Taran, it felt like a silence of profound respect that no one wanted to break.

He studied the striking young man, who was perhaps an inch or two shorter than the six-foot Taran. He was slim and lithe, his graceful movements suggesting the deportment of a trained dancer. He had slender fingers and long, flowing hair, which was the startling color of creamy new milk. But it was his face that so affected Taran's breathing, and the Adept reflected that had he been of that persuasion, he would have wanted this breathtaking stranger in his bed.

The man's face was smooth, the skin pale and clear. His nose was straight, the mouth well shaped, and the cheekbones high and fine. His eyes, however, were his most arresting feature. Almond-shaped under curling lashes and graceful brows, they were dark, liquid, and full, like the eyes of a deer.

The gaze of those eyes swept across Taran's face and his heart stopped within his chest.

It was fitting that Sullyan should be the one to break the silence, as her lilting voice was no intrusion into the absence of sound. Holding the stranger's fey gaze, she inclined her head.

"My Lord Fiann."

The beautiful man set down his glass and crossed the room, his eyes never leaving hers. His features betrayed no expression, he seemed totally serene. When he reached Sullyan, he took her left hand and sank to one knee. To Taran's surprise, he then made the brow-lips-heart salute of an Artesan to his Master.

Sullyan lifted his hand to her lips. "There is no need of that between us, my Lord," she murmured. "It is good to see you again. Are you well?"

"I am well, Sullyan, as you see."

Fiann's voice was another shock. Taran had expected it to be light and youthful, but it was one of the deepest voices he had ever heard. It was perfectly modulated, yet carried unfamiliar overtones.

Fiann rose fluidly and took the free chair at their table. Jed immediately bustled over with more drinks, giving plain water to the newcomer as before. "I have heard tales of you recently," Fiann continued, his eyes still fixed on Sullyan's.

She replied lightly. "There are many tales about me. Not all of them are true."

"These were true," he said. "Yet you are here, and so I conclude that you triumphed."

She dropped her gaze. "I did, my friend. But not without cost."

He laid a hand on her arm. "We gain nothing without cost."

"Let us talk of other things. Fiann, this is Taran Elijah, an Artesan Adept and a very good friend of mine. Taran, this is the Lord Fiann, the finest bard in all the realms. I have known him since I was a little girl. He taught me everything I know of music."

Fiann accepted Taran's proffered hand, and the Adept was startled to sense a featherlike touch on his mind. He also caught echoes of what seemed to be great age and a powerful yearning.

The bard glanced at Sullyan. "He is unaware?"

"He has not been with us long. With your permission, my Lord?"

Fiann inclined his head, and Sullyan turned to Taran.

"Fiann is a bard, as I have said, but he is not quite as he

appears. He is also a lord and was a great chieftain among his people before being outcast from his lands. Now he is a wanderer who has no home.

"Fiann is a Sinnian from the Second Realm, and he is a hundred and thirty years old."

Taran's mouth dropped open, but he hastily closed it when he realized they were waiting for a response.

"A Sinnian?"

Sullyan nodded. Taran had only ever traveled to the Fifth Realm and knew very little about the other three. "Why was he outcast?" he asked.

Fiann's dark eyes flickered and Sullyan said, "That is too personal a question for so brief an acquaintance, Taran."

The Adept felt himself blush. "Sorry." Fiann's face remained impassive, yet Taran felt he had taken no offence. He tried a safer topic. "How did the two of you meet?"

Sullyan smiled. "It was on the Downs, near the village where I was raised. Fiann was doing his customary rounds of the area and we happened to meet one day. Discovering that I had a love for music, Fiann began to teach me. We would often play together when he visited us."

She said no more, but Taran had the feeling that there was much more to the story.

Fiann was watching her with his dark, liquid eyes. "But then you went away," he said, a note of deep sadness in his voice.

She looked at her hands. "My life took a different turn, my friend. As did yours."

They fell silent. Taran was about to ask another question when Jed came over, inclining his head respectfully. "They're ready for you now, my Lord."

Taran looked round in query. As if he had been expecting the summons, Fiann stood, but he didn't immediately follow Jed.

Instead, he held out his hand to Sullyan. She stared at him in surprise.

"I will not play alone while you are here," he said.

Taran saw shy pleasure steal across Sullyan's face. Taking the Sinnian's hand, she rose, and together they walked through the press of locals. The inn was full to bursting now. Taran hadn't realized how many people had come in while the three of them were talking.

The reverential hush that had greeted the Sinnian's first appearance now descended again. Jed had placed two chairs by the unused fireplace, and Taran saw that a selection of musical instruments was standing behind them. Most prominent among these was a harp. There was also a guitar, a fiddle, and a flute.

The inn's patrons settled themselves, still in silence, and Taran moved to the side of the room to get a better view. Fiann took up the fiddle, bow poised over strings. Gesturing for Sullyan to take the guitar, he murmured, "'Larksong,'" and she nodded. With the guitar under her arm, she closed her eyes and began to play a simple country melody. The instrument had a soft and mellow tone, and Taran soon recognized the tune. Once she had played it all the way through, Fiann touched bow to strings, and thus began the most magical evening of Taran's life.

He had heard Sullyan play and sing many times and loved the sound of her voice. She had a great range and could render a song in anything from a throbbing contralto to a soaring soprano. He considered her a gifted musician, and indeed she was. But Fiann was a bard of many years' experience, a virtuoso of his art, and he far outshone Sullyan in the mastery of his musical talent. His fiddle became the trilling song of the lark, rising high on summer breezes fragrant with meadow flowers. His audience listened in rapt silence to the rise and fall of the bird's flight, poignantly rendered over the background of Sullyan's melody.

They changed tempo, now playing of tumbling streams alive with fish, and the still, sacrosanct places of the forest. Sometimes the notes were playful, like fox cubs sparring outside their den. Sometimes they were somber, invoking the slow majesty of the earth. Some of the tunes invited their listeners to clap their hands or stamp their feet in joyful abandon. Yet others caused them to fall silent in deep and reverent awe. But all the melodies were stirring, affecting everyone who heard.

At last the medley ended, and Fiann set the fiddle aside. As Sullyan placed the guitar in its stand, the bard moved to sit behind the harp. Laying his beautiful hands on the strings, he glanced up at her. "'Meadowsweet,'" he said, and she nodded, once more closing her eyes.

The song, a lively country melody about a swordsman returning from war to his sweetheart, was unfamiliar to Taran, but he heard one or two people in the audience humming the tune. Sullyan's voice was a perfect accompaniment to the harp and she followed its pitch faultlessly. Taran noticed that many of the inn's patrons also had their eyes closed.

That song over, Fiann stood, gesturing for Sullyan to take his place. Judging by some of the expressions Taran could see, this was either very rare or completely unheard of. Even Sullyan seemed a little overawed as she seated herself behind the instrument and spread her hands on the strings.

Fiann said a word that Taran didn't understand, but he saw Sullyan's start of surprise. When she brought the harp to life, Taran knew why. It was the tune she had played for Lord Rykan in Marik's mansion, and Fiann sang the words in the Andaryan High Language. Halfway through, he gestured minutely with one hand and Sullyan blended her voice with his in perfect harmony. The gentle beauty of it brought tears to Taran's eyes, and he wasn't the only one affected.

When the final strains of the outland song died away and the throbbing harp finally stilled, Fiann brought Sullyan to her feet. Taran thought the entertainment must be over, that they intended to accept the acclaim of their audience; listeners who had not once broken the evening's magic with applause. Instead, he turned to face Sullyan and they stood together, their hands clasped and their eyes closed.

An expectant hush came over the crowd.

They began to sing simultaneously, a haunting melody the like of which Taran had never heard. Fiann's deeply resonant voice was the perfect foil for Sullyan's lighter tones, and his range was astonishing. Then, suddenly, as though his very bones were coming alive, Taran could hear other voices, other harmonies, although the audience was rapt and no one else was singing.

Realization shivered down his spine. Somehow, Sullyan and Fiann were singing through the substrate, although he had never known it was possible. The subliminal blend of voices flowed through his soul, thrilling his blood, and judging by the looks of delight and astonishment around him, most of the audience could feel it too.

The song swelled to an almost unbearably poignant crescendo and the tears in Taran's eyes were mirrored in many others. Finally, the song quivered away to silence and the two singers broke apart. The innkeeper, recognizing a finale when he heard one, led the audience in a rapturous burst of applause that went on and on. Coins, both silver and gold, rained into mugs placed on the tables, and slowly the inn's privileged patrons began to file out into the warm summer darkness.

When they were gone, Jed approached the pair by the fireplace. Onto a table he poured a stream of coinage, which Fiann split into three piles. Jed gathered up one portion and the Sinnian slid another across to Sullyan.

She stayed his hand. "No, Fiann, I have no need of it. You keep it, or share it with Jed as you will. The King provides for all my needs."

The bard held her gaze for a moment before passing a few more coins to Jed. The rest he kept for himself. The innkeeper took his share and, after enquiring what time they required their mounts the next day, bade them all goodnight. Taran also made a move toward the stairs, but halted when he realized Sullyan hadn't left the table.

She was gazing into the Sinnian's eyes, the bard's face showing the first sign of expression Taran had seen. It was a look of pain, and it caused Sullyan to reach out, taking up one of his hands.

"Is it so bad, my Lord?" she murmured.

He sighed. "It is becoming so."

"Is there anything I can do?"

A slight shake of the head was her answer. Then he said, "But I do have something to ask of you."

Her gaze sharpened. "Name it, my friend."

He sat down again, a sudden weariness evident in his body. Sullyan sat too, concern in her golden eyes.

"It will not be long now," said Fiann, his voice so low that Taran could hardly hear him. "When the time comes, will you perform the rite for me?"

She bowed her head, but not before Taran had caught the glitter of tears in her eyes. "You know I will, my Lord. You have no need to ask."

She brushed his face gently with her hand and the bard smiled at her. Taran's breath caught in his throat. Seeing such an expression of trusting love on that beautiful face nearly stopped his heart.

"Then I am content."

The bard stood, gathering the night's earnings into a pouch at his belt. He drained the last of his water and wrapped his instruments in their respective leather covers, leaving them standing by the hearth. Sullyan watched him in silence. He passed behind her on his way to the door, trailing one hand lightly across her shoulders. She didn't turn her head but continued to sit, unmoving.

Once the tavern door had closed and she still showed no sign of rising, Taran came back to her. "Isn't he staying at the inn?"

She raised her head and Taran saw the unshed tears. "No, Taran. Sinnians will not sleep within stone walls. Jed takes care of his horses and instruments, but Fiann will sleep under the stars. He will be gone before dawn."

Despite the undercurrent of deep grief in her voice, Taran simply had to know. "What exactly was he asking of you?"

She sighed. "Fiann is very old, even for a Sinnian, and they live much longer than Albians. Since becoming an outcast, he has spent more time than is good for him away from his own realm. He returns when he can, but the strain of outland living is now taking its toll on his health. He knows he will not live much longer.

"He spends much of his time in Albia, so it is more than likely he will die here. If he does, he will be far from the customs of his people and will be denied the rites his faith requires. These are vitally important to him, both as a Sinnian and as a bard. I am familiar with those rites and, as I am now the nearest Fiann has to a family, he was asking me to conduct those rites at his death."

Taran nodded in understanding. "But how will you know when and where it happens?"

Despite her somber mood, Sullyan smiled faintly. "Did your father teach you nothing about Sinnians?" The Adept shook his head. "Sinnians are natural Artesans, able to control their metaforce from birth. Their natural rank is Adept, and although some are capable of raising themselves to Adept-elite, most see no reason to bother. They also set great store by family. In their culture, their family is their life. Sinnians are bonded to their loved ones in a way we can hardly conceive. For them, banishment is a death sentence, for it severs those ties. In a small way, Lord Fiann and I share a similar bond. Believe me, I will know when his time comes."

For a moment, Taran was silent. Then he asked, "Can you tell me why he was outcast?"

She raised unseeing eyes to the door through which he had passed. "Fiann made a bad marriage, a forbidden marriage. You see, not only is Fiann a gifted bard, he was also the leader of his clan. As chieftain, it was his duty to wed the daughter of another clan chief in order to cement an alliance. But while on his traditional rounds one summer he fell in love, lost his heart so deeply that it could never be taken back. This brought disgrace and ridicule on his people, and the other clan attacked. They survived the war, but Fiann was blamed for bringing death and destruction instead of protection. For this he was outcast, and even though his wife is now dead, he can never return to his clan."

"He married an enemy's daughter, then?"

"No," she said, her eyes full of pain. "He married an Albian."

Chapter Five

The next morning, just as he finished dressing, Taran felt Sullyan's gentle touch on his mind. Shrugging into his combat jacket as a precaution against the rain that threatened to fall, he opened the door. Sullyan was standing in the passageway, pack in hand. She too was wearing her jacket, gold rank insignia and battle honors showing proudly against the dark leather.

Even in the gloomy passage, he could see that her face was pale. "Are you all right, Sullyan?"

She waved the question away. "I am well enough, Taran, I thank you. Are you ready?"

Unwilling to question her further, he snatched up his own pack and followed her down to the snug, where Jed was laying out breakfast.

While they were eating, Jed's two boys sauntered in and announced that their mounts were ready. Once Taran had eaten his fill and Sullyan had drunk her fellan, they went outside and she made a show of inspecting the horses. The lads watched her, affecting unconcern. When she pronounced herself satisfied, they grinned and scampered off.

Jed reappeared and handed Sullyan a replenished pack of supplies. He also carried two small stone jars of ale, which he presented to Taran with a smile. "Something to remember the Hazel Tree by."

Taran accepted, deeply touched by the gesture.

Having thanked the innkeeper for his hospitality, Sullyan mounted Drum, leaving the King's colt free.

Taran hesitated. "I haven't settled my account yet," he said.

She regarded him from Drum's tall back, her face still pale but her manner serene. "The King has already paid, Taran. You owe nothing."

"But not my share, surely?" He had not expected this.

She nudged the stallion forward, giving Jed a farewell wave. Taran vaulted onto his mount and moved off after her.

"Elias pays a network of innkeepers to hold rooms available for those traveling on King's business. It saves us from having to search out suitable lodging in busy times. It also ensures good quality service."

"But I'm not a member of the King's forces," protested Taran. "I'm quite willing to pay my way."

She glanced at him, her face still showing a measure of discomfort, which Taran attributed to Fiann's somber request the evening before. Her expression warmed as she acknowledged his desire not to take advantage of his position.

"Oh, but you are, my friend. You may not have taken a formal Oath, but let me assure you, the King considers you very much a part of his forces. Did he not award you battle honors for your part in repelling Rykan's invasion last year?"

"Well, yes, but—"

"And will you not be a member of the King's College of Artesans?"

"I... yes—"

"Make no mistake, Taran Elijah, you are as much a part of the Manor as I am."

Unable to argue, Taran rode on in silence.

They made good time without pressing the horses, and Darius

trailed them faithfully, just as Drum had done. Taran was surprised that the young colt would follow them with no direction from rider or lead-rein, and remarked on it.

"Horses are herd creatures," said Sullyan. "They like their own kind around them. Darius will not willingly leave his herd companions, and that includes you and me. I have reinforced his instincts with training, and he is an agile learner. All Mandias's progeny are quick to learn. Darius will not disappoint the King."

They stopped only briefly for a light noon meal and to rest the horses. There were a few other travelers on the road, some of whom were obviously also heading for Port Loxton. Everyone they met accorded them respectful nods, mindful of their rank badges and weapons. Taran wore his sword by his side and Sullyan bore hers at her back, an ostentatious statement of their abilities.

Around the middle of the afternoon, as they were approaching the outskirts of a small village, Taran caught sight of a low hill surmounted by an ancient stone circle. It reminded him of the tor at Caer Vellet where Sullyan and Robin were wed nine months ago. It clearly awakened memories for her too, for she left the road and sent Drum up the hill, right to the edge of the ring, where she halted. She sat silently, staring into the open space enclosed by the stones, her eyes unfocused.

Taran followed her and sat by her side for some time. He recalled that the same tor at Caer Vellet had also been the site of Commander Vanyr's funeral pyre, and wondered which memory held more power for her. To ease her from her reverie, he eventually said, "I've often wondered what these places were for, who built them, and why."

Sullyan turned her head slowly and regarded him with an odd look.

"What?" he said.

She gave a small sigh. "Taran Elijah, are you telling me that

41

you have never raised the power of Earth within a stone circle?"

He frowned and shook his head, embarrassed by her surprise. He had obviously handed her yet another example of how flawed his early training had been, and he cursed himself for speaking his thought aloud.

Sullyan either ignored or was unaware of his chagrin. She slid gracefully down Drum's shoulder, letting the reins fall. The huge stud immediately dropped his head to crop the grass. Taran also dismounted and she beckoned to him. "Come with me." He followed her, leaving the horses to graze.

Together, they walked into the space encompassed by the stones, an area roughly fifteen feet in diameter. The stones themselves were spaced about five feet apart, although two of them had fallen over the centuries. Rough-hewn and spotted with lichen, they still exuded an atmosphere of mystery and age. The closer Taran came to the circle's center, the more he felt their majesty.

Sullyan halted in the very center. In hushed tones, so as not to disturb the peace of the place, she said, "Look about you, Taran. What do you see?"

Thinking he was missing something obvious, Taran studied the circle. There were eight monoliths, all set deeply into the earth, except for the two that had fallen, one outward, the other sideways, still with its base partially buried. Apart from the lichen and the weathering of the years, there were no markings that Taran could see. The space they enclosed was smooth and grassy, sloping slightly toward a depression in the center. To one side of this hollow was a much smaller block of stone, lying on its side, half-buried in the turf.

Something about this area tugged at Taran's memory. Sullyan smiled encouragingly and suddenly he had it. The space within the stones and the depression in the turf had exactly the same feeling as the cellar in his old house at Hyecombe. The place where he had first learned to influence the element of Earth.

Seeing his understanding, Sullyan's smile broadened.

"Is that why they were built?" asked Taran. "As natural containers for the element of Earth?"

"Well, if not, there was a very powerful coincidence at work," she replied. "These stones are granite, which invokes a very powerful form of Earth element. It is also an effective Earth barrier. The soil beneath the stones prevents leakage, and the depression in the center captures and shapes the energy, as does the circle itself.

"Each monolith is surrounded by its own sphere of power, so the gaps between do not matter. As you know, once called and activated, Earth element runs to itself, so as the power is raised it creates its own impenetrable boundary."

Taran caught the undercurrent of excitement in her voice as she added, "Come, Taran. This is one experience you must not miss."

She guided him to the small stone at the edge of the depression and bade him sit. Then she stepped back. "Just reach out and raise power. Place no restrictions on it. Do not seek to form a portway. Just let the raw power accumulate and watch what happens. Draw power from each stone in turn."

To aid his concentration, Taran closed his eyes. He still envied Sullyan and Robin their more casual grasp of power. Neither of them needed such preparation, but his essential lack of self-confidence and the knowledge of his own shortcomings worked against him, and often he had to enter a sort of trance before accessing his metaforce.

Breathing deeply to calm his mind, he attuned his psyche to the element of Earth. Then he reached out to the nearest monolith and called on the power it contained.

Nothing happened.

Thinking he was perhaps not focused enough, Taran drew and held a breath. Then he tried again.

Still nothing.

Confused, he reached for the next stone. Although he could clearly sense the forces it contained, a blank wall met his efforts. Not a flicker of power could he raise.

He drew back in puzzled embarrassment. Opening his eyes, he turned to Sullyan.

"Oh, Taran," she sighed, shaking her head, "if ever I doubted how patchy and incomplete your early training was, you have just convinced me of it."

He flushed crimson. It seemed he had once again made a fool of himself without even understanding how. He cursed under his breath and tried to turn away from her, but a strong grip on his forearms prevented him.

He gazed down at the hands that gripped him, amazed as always by her physical strength, honed by years of discipline and training.

"What happened just now was not your fault," she said. "Strength and talent are useless without the correct guidance, and that you have not had. Blame for this lies mainly with your father, but some of it, I am ashamed to say, lies with me."

"You?" he objected. "How can you be to blame?"

"You are very quick to protest my innocence, but far too swift to deny your own. I should have gone over your early training once you decided to stay at the Manor, but I did not. Now I have caused you pain and shame, when this should have been one of the most glorious of Artesan experiences. I will never forgive myself for that."

He stared into her dilated eyes, sensing the love and pride she felt for him. But she was also berating herself, and he couldn't bear that. He was ashamed for having distressed her.

Her temper snapped abruptly. "Taran, stop that! Oh, if only your father were here now. I would make him pay dearly for your lack of self-esteem."

He was startled by her anger, which evaporated quickly. He was used to her mercurial moods, and thankful they weren't often directed at him. He lived in dread of the day she really had a grievance with him.

Giving herself a shake, she said, "Your pardon, Taran, but I cannot abide self-pity. Now"—she took up his hand once more, drawing him firmly back to the low stone—"sit. Look around and tell me, literally, what you see."

Although apprehensive of making a fool of himself yet again, he did as she asked. "A stone circle."

"Exactly. The key word being 'circle.' Now think of the element of Earth in connection with a circle. What does that tell you?"

With another hot rush of shame, Taran understood. Every Artesan learned that the elements were tied to one of the four cardinal points of the earth's magnetism. The element of Earth was linked to the western cardinal, and Taran knew, with a certainty which should by now have been instinctive, that had he begun with the monolith standing due west, the power would have flooded out.

He closed his eyes, despairing.

He heard Sullyan move to stand behind him and felt the gentle touch of her hands on his shoulders. She murmured, "Link with me, Taran," and he opened his mind.

The depth and vastness of her power engulfed him, taking his breath away. It was a warm amber glow suffusing the deepest parts of his soul, and it soothed his shame like a balm. It was impossible to hide from her when she caught him up like this. He felt her cast a shielding blanket over his self-doubt, covering it with approval, love, and pride.

Too much humility will stunt your growth and prevent healing. Now come with me and I will show you what you have missed.

He was drawn with her as their shared power reached out to the western cardinal stone. The raw forces of Earth sprang from it immediately, running sunwise around the other stones as she called on each in turn, creating a shimmering ring of power. Taran was pleasurably reminded of the confirmation ceremony she had performed for him when he had achieved the rank of Adept.

Draw power into the bowl, Taran.

He dutifully called the power to him. It rushed inward, flooding into the center of the circle, lapping them both in coruscating sparks. Calling to the element within their bones, it suffused their bodies with power and surged singing through their souls. Linked in a more fundamental way than ever before, they became one with the world and with each other. Feeling its untamed and mystical power, sensing lines of energy crossing the land, seeing twisting columns of elemental force rising over the terrain for miles around.

See how they all link together?

Sullyan's lilting mental tone was saturated with the exultation of rushing forces. Taran knew he could not have contained such might if not for her controlling touch on his shoulder.

All the ancient mystical sites where the raw forces of Earth naturally occur are connected. From here, we could speak across the entire world—across the Veils, as far as we wished to reach! The power here is almost infinite, its use limited only by the ability of the wielder. Do you feel it?

The question was rhetorical. He knew she could sense what he felt, and she shared his wonder and delight at such unfathomable potential. Yet she was strong enough to contain it where he was not, and she subtly tempered his reactions, guarding against the temptations of ultimate power. In undisciplined hands, such quantities of raw element could be immeasurably destructive.

Linked in this way, they seemed to flow over the land, buoyed by the substrate through which the power moved. The landscape appeared to be fluid, its summer colors muted to shades of shimmering pearly-gray. Here and there were pockets of disturbance; peaks and spikes caused by the thoughts and emotions of people in villages and homesteads. Softer mounds and swirls showed where animals grazed. And through it all, majestic and puissant, soared the columns of natural Earth force.

Taran was dazzled, overcome. Never had he seen such sights before. Sensing the gradual overwhelming of his spirit, Sullyan brought them gently down from the ecstatic heights to which they had climbed. She slowly released her hold on Earth, letting the monoliths reabsorb their power. This, Taran knew, was as important as controlling his responses, as any leakage of such forces could devastate a huge area.

When the power had fully dissipated, she came round to face him, and he saw the echo of his own joy in her eyes.

He hardly knew what to say. Breathless, unable to articulate the true effect of the experience, he whispered, "Such strong feelings."

She nodded. "A powerful Artesan would be well-nigh omnipotent within such a circle."

For an instant her eyes narrowed, but then she smiled.

Taran shakily took her hand, his recent almost orgasmic experience too strong, too fundamentally thrilling, to shrug off lightly. "Thank you," he said, unable to convey what he truly felt.

She gazed at him. "Taran, I want you to promise me something."

Her tone was serious and it made him wary. "What?"

"I want you to promise me that if ever I show signs of becoming arrogant or overbearing where my skills are concerned, you will instantly remind me of this afternoon." He began to protest but she growled, "Promise me!"

Shaking his head, he agreed.

✤ ✤ ✤ ✤ ✤

By the time they approached the inn where they would stay that night, the cloud cover had increased and the first splashes of rain were falling. The temperature hadn't dropped, however, and Taran eyed the clouds, looking for signs of a storm.

It didn't materialize, and their clothes were only slightly damp when they drew rein behind the inn. It was a much larger establishment than Jed's and, judging by the noise, it was already nearly full.

Leaving their horses in the care of stable lads, Sullyan and Taran entered the inn. The landlord took their packs before showing them to the last vacant table in the taproom, where they sat studying the inn's many customers while waiting for their food.

"Did you expect it to be so full?" asked Taran, surprised by the noisy throng.

Sullyan nodded. She was keeping a wary eye on the crowd, some of whom were showing signs of drunkenness.

"Most of these will be heading for the fair," she replied, reaching for her cordial. Taran had already consumed one tankard of ale, although its brown sweetness was nothing like Jed's malty brew. "There will be rich pickings for Loxton's footpads over the next few days," she added, nodding to the bulging coin pouches many of the revelers wore openly at their belts.

"Isn't the capital safe, then?" asked Taran. "What with the King's Guard and, I presume, a city constabulary, I'd have thought thieves would have a very hard time there."

"Loxton is a large and busy port city. It is a major center for trade. People come and go all the time, and not even the King's

Guard can keep track of them all. We will need to keep our wits about us during our stay."

The evening passed with no trouble from the crowd other than rowdiness. As Taran and Sullyan stood to make their way to their rooms, she gave the drunks a look of deep distaste.

Heavy and incessant rain rattled the roof as they climbed the stairs, audible even above the noise from the taproom. Taran didn't allow it to disrupt a good night's sleep.

Chapter Six

It was still raining heavily the next morning, the clouds dark and low. Odors of wet wool, wet leather, and wet horse assailed Taran's nostrils as he and Sullyan set off from the inn two hours after dawn. They rode with their hoods and cloaks wrapped tightly around them, blankets protecting the horses' backs. Sullyan was riding Darius again, Drum following biddably behind.

After a few miles, Taran saw a deeper darkness ahead. This gradually resolved into a tight mass of trees, and he guessed it must be the forest Sullyan had pointed out two days ago. From what he could see through the gloomy rain their road ran straight through it. He frowned. It would be as dark as night in there unless the rain let up.

"Do we have to ride through that?" he asked.

She nodded. "That is Loxton Forest, and it extends right up to the city walls. From this direction it is the only way into Port Loxton. To ride around it would take too long. Be warned, though, it is a notorious haunt of footpads and highwaymen. Ready your sword and keep your eyes open. I doubt we will be troubled, armed as we are, but you never know."

Taran had already noticed that Sullyan's sword was at her hip, not strapped across her back as usual. Now he knew why. He made sure his cloak was not fouling his sword hilt as he followed her toward the forest.

They rode beneath dripping boughs. The road was wide and well-traveled, but the press of trees along its edge was dense, the undergrowth of tangling bramble. Taran thought there would be many places to stage a good ambush, if one had a mind to.

Riding in silence, they remained alert, their hands never far from their weapons. It was still early, but footpads did not keep regular hours. After half an hour or so, a sound from behind made them turn. An expensive-looking coach drawn by four matched chestnuts was approaching at a good clip. The coachman, well wrapped against the weather, showed no signs of livery. Next to him on the box was a large man who held a drawn sword across his knees.

This man examined Taran and Sullyan as they drew aside to let the coach pass. Taran glimpsed two cloaked and hooded figures inside as it rumbled by. The smell of wet harness-leather and crushed leaves washed over him.

From the corner of his eye he saw Sullyan make a curious hand gesture. The guard on the box turned to stare, and Taran was even more amazed when he made the gesture in return. Once the coach was well ahead, he commented on this.

"He was one of us," said Sullyan. "King's Guard. There are times when it is politic for us to travel inconspicuously, such as when guarding nobility, as I imagine he is doing, but there are still methods by which we can identify ourselves."

"How did you know he was King's Guard?"

From within her hood, she smiled. "His bearing was unmistakable. It is quite common for members of Elias's court to have an escort of Kingsmen when they travel the Forest. As you have seen, it is an ideal hideout for brigands, and any footpad worth his salt would know that a coach of that quality could only be carrying gentry. It would be too tempting a target to miss."

As they rode on the rain gradually eased. The air began to soften and, very slowly, the temperature increased. Steam rose from wet leafmold whenever the cloud cover broke enough to let the sun through.

Suddenly, Sullyan stiffened. She hissed Taran's name and he drew rein beside her, straining his ears. She raised her hand for silence, but the gesture was unnecessary. They both heard it quite clearly. The sound of men shouting, and a woman's shrill scream.

Sullyan threw him a dark glance and drew her sword. Taran did the same. Nudging the horses, they rode on at a cautious trot. They halted just before a blind bend in the road, hearing the clash of steel and the occasional high-pitched scream. The screaming seemed to hold more outrage than pain, but fear was also evident. Sullyan's face was grim. Taran knew that her brutal experience at Rykan's hands had given her an intense hatred of men who abused women.

"Slowly, Taran," she cautioned, and they edged carefully around the bend.

In the clearing before them was the coach they had seen earlier. The horses were loose and wandering, having been cut free of the traces. The coachman was lying on the ground, but the Kingsman was fighting for his life. Two men had engaged him and a third had herded the coach's occupants out onto the grass, where he stood menacing them with his sword. They were both women and they clung together for support, fearfully watching the desperate fight before them.

Before Taran and Sullyan could act, the Kingsman was cut down, collapsing lifeless to the ground. He had sold his life dearly but to no avail. One of the women started screaming hysterically while the other stared fearfully but defiantly at her tormentor.

"Taran," hissed Sullyan, "you take the one by the coach. Make sure he has no time to use the women as a shield. I will take the other two. Ready?"

Swallowing, Taran nodded. Swords in hand, they sidled out of the trees, trying to move as quietly as possible. Fortunately, the brigands were intent on their prize and didn't immediately see the approaching pair. Easing forward, Taran and Sullyan picked their targets, choosing lines of attack. When one of the men finally saw them and barked a warning, the battle-trained stallions leaped into a flat-out gallop, sending the brigands scurrying to defend themselves.

Taran aimed straight for the man by the coach, who retreated, putting his back to the vehicle. As his horse rushed between the brigand and the women, Taran yelled at them. "Get behind the coach!" He wheeled Thunder round, slashing at the man on the ground.

At first the women seemed too terrified to move, but then one grabbed the other's hand, yanking her behind the coach. Panicked shrieks sounded and Taran heard a woman's voice snap, "Shut up, Lily!" Then his opponent's sword was slashing at Thunder's legs, and he needed all his concentration to keep them both alive.

✢ ✢ ✢ ✢ ✢

Sullyan registered the women's dive for cover as she closed with her targets. They separated and she smiled grimly. One would engage her left side, the other would attack her undefended right.

It was exactly what she wanted them to do.

A split second before reaching them, she barked, "Drum, right!" The huge warhorse, following hard on Darius's tail, surged out from behind her and charged the man to her right, snaking his head and baring his teeth. The attack was so unexpected and Drum's charge so viciously focused that it forced the brigand to leap violently aside. He swung his sword wildly, trying to hamstring the horse. Squealing with battle fury, Drum pursued him.

Sullyan knew that the big black would harry his quarry without getting close enough to be cut. His tactics would keep the man occupied until she could deal with him, although if the brigand tripped and fell beneath Drum's hooves there would be nothing left to deal with. Turning her full attention to the swordsman on her left, she prayed that Darius's training would prove sufficient to protect them both.

✤ ✤ ✤ ✤ ✤

Taran was finding his man a difficult opponent. The villain obviously had some experience fighting a mounted swordsman. He slashed at Thunder's legs and underbelly whenever he had the chance. Fortunately, the bay was an experienced warhorse and danced aside.

Taran got in a few telling blows as Thunder carried him past. The stallion pivoted on his haunches and closed in again, the Adept seeing the beginnings of fear on his adversary's face. The brigands had obviously planned a simple ambush against one armed guard and two women. Now they were facing two expert fighters and three dangerous horses. An easy morning's work with the promise of rich rewards was fast becoming too costly.

When Taran next closed in, his opponent aimed a well-timed thrust which pierced the flesh of Taran's upper arm just as the Adept leaned into his swing. But the move had left the man's chest vulnerable and Taran's stroke caught him across the ribs. While not life threatening, it was enough to dissuade him. With no help forthcoming from either of his fellows, the brigand turned and fled. Taran decided against pursuing him and looked to see if Sullyan needed help.

He needn't have worried.

✤ ✤ ✤ ✤ ✤

She had already accounted for her first man, although it was a stumble by Darius that gave her the opening. Seeing her horse unbalanced, her opponent made the mistake of thinking she would be too. He was wrong. As he came on, Sullyan used Darius's awkward forward momentum to run the man through. His shocked expression as he died might have been funny under other circumstances.

She engaged the last man, but his comrade's fate had sapped his confidence and he was showing signs of desperation. She yelled at him to surrender but he refused. She was about to attempt to disarm him when a dark shape loomed behind him. Drum's iron-shod forefeet came down on his head, ending his battle.

Once the noise had died away, Sullyan glanced at Taran, who asked, "Do you want me to go after the other one?"

She shook her head. "He will give us no more trouble."

Dismounting from Darius, she gave the colt's nose an approving rub. She was pleased with his behavior. After all, stumbling over a prominent tree root was one of the risks you ran when fighting in a forest.

She stooped over the man Drum had killed and sliced off a portion of his cloak. As she walked round the side of the coach, where pitiful sobs could still be heard, she used the cloth to clean her blade. "It is safe now, ladies," she called. "The brigands are dead."

One of the women looked up and caught sight of Sullyan's bloody sword. She screamed, shrinking away with a horrified look as she pressed herself against the coach.

"Oh, stop it, Lily," snapped the other woman. "If I'm not mistaken, we've just been rescued by the famed Colonel Sullyan. You're certainly safe now."

She turned to Sullyan, holding out a dainty hand. The hood of her cloak had fallen back, revealing the face of a young woman aged around twenty. She had small oval features, pale green eyes, and shoulder-length blonde hair. Beneath her fine quality wool cloak she wore an expensive-looking ruby velvet gown. Gold rings adorned her fingers and more gold glittered around her neck.

Sullyan briefly took her hand.

"My sincere thanks for coming to our rescue, Colonel. I am the Lady Jinella, and this is my maid, Lily. She's very nervous, as you see, but a good maid for all that."

"I am pleased we were able to assist you, my Lady," replied Sullyan. "I take it you are both unhurt?"

Lady Jinella nodded. "Yes, thank you. We are only shocked and frightened. My uncle will be most grateful to you, although I think the safe return of his coach and gold will please him better than our good health!"

"Indeed?" said Sullyan tartly. "Then he is a fool."

"No, Colonel," smiled Jinella. "Just a miser."

These disrespectful words brought a shocked gasp from the maid, Lily, and the younger woman snapped at her again.

"Gently, my Lady," reproved Sullyan. "She has had a nasty shock. I dread to think what would have happened had we not been close enough to aid you. Give her time to recover her wits. Now, if you would help us round up the carriage horses, we will escort you into the city."

Lady Jinella obviously wanted to protest being given such a menial task, but she couldn't very well refuse. Leaving her maid clinging nervously to the door of the coach, she gingerly approached the nearest chestnut. It raised its head, allowing her to catch hold of the bridle.

Taran went to help her and she smiled gratefully. She let her eyes rove over his face, clearly liking what she saw.

"We haven't been introduced," she said, holding out her hand.

Taran took it, raising it gallantly to his lips as he told her his name. She blushed prettily, and then her gaze dropped to the blood staining the sleeve of his jacket. "Colonel," she squealed, "your companion has been hurt!"

"It's only a scratch," protested Taran as Sullyan straightened from examining the dead guard. She came forward to inspect the wound. Taran had already used metaforce to stem the flow of blood, but the cut still stung and ached. Mercifully, the brigand's sword had only pierced the muscle without slicing right through.

Ignoring his protests, Sullyan ordered him to strip off cloak, jacket, and shirt. Jinella openly admired his well-formed naked torso while Sullyan expended power to heal the wound further.

"Are you both Artesans, then?" Jinella asked, watching Sullyan work. The Colonel merely nodded, leaving Taran to dress once more. She went to check on the coachman while Taran and a speculative Jinella collected the other horses.

The coachman wasn't dead, only stunned. The brigands had caught him a blow to the head with the flat of a blade and left him unconscious. Grateful that they had not been completely heartless, Sullyan attempted to revive the man. She had no desire to drive the coach herself as she feared other brigands might take advantage of their situation. Despite her ministrations and his own powers, Taran was not fully fit. If she could rouse the coachman, he would be very useful.

Once he had regained consciousness, Sullyan guided him back to the coach. Taran had located the spare harness leather that every prudent coachman carried and was re-hitching the team, watched with open admiration by the Lady Jinella. Noting the young woman's interest, Sullyan regarded her through narrowed eyes, a small smile on her lips.

"Will you ride with the coachman, Taran?" she asked. "That arm needs rest and you can keep an eye on him at the same time. I will ride point." She turned to Jinella. "My Lady, I am afraid that you and your maid will have company inside the coach."

Jinella frowned. "Oh? Who?"

Sullyan indicated the dead guard and Jinella's face fell.

Sullyan crossed to the dead Kingsman. She wrapped him in his bloodied cloak and laid his sword on his chest. With Taran taking his shoulders and she his feet, they managed to bundle him into the coach. Taran's wounded arm ached when the job was done.

The coachman had managed to reach the box and his hands were on the reins, but his eyes were wide and glazed. Taran climbed up beside him and spoke softly to him, trying to help him get over the shock. Jinella and Lily entered the coach. Lily, who was older than her mistress, closed her eyes and gave a small squeal when her foot touched the dead man. Jinella ignored him completely.

Sullyan mounted Darius, leaving the other two stallions loose. Taran nodded to the coachman and the team started forward at a stately pace, continuing its journey to Port Loxton.

Sullyan rode beside the coach, alert for trouble. After a while, the Lady Jinella pushed down the carriage window.

"Have you come for the fair, Colonel, or do you have business with the King?"

"Both, my Lady," said Sullyan. "I am delivering this horse to the King. Elias intends to show him off at the fair tomorrow."

Jinella clearly had no interest in horses, as her next question showed. "And will your companion, who so bravely defended us today, be attending the fair too?"

Sullyan wasn't fooled, although she replied artlessly, avoiding the younger woman's eyes. "I imagine so, my Lady, although it may be a little tedious for him if I am occupied with the King."

There was a brief silence before Jinella said, "Does he have no one to escort? Surely someone so handsome has a sweetheart?"

Sullyan smiled privately. "Actually, no, my Lady. Captain Elijah is unattached."

Jinella's green eyes sparkled. "Unattached? How fortuitous! Well then, Colonel, do you think he might be persuaded to act as my escort? For I too am unattached and I must confess that today's events have left me feeling rather nervous. I really don't fancy walking through a crowded fair with only Lily beside me. How do you think he would feel if I asked him to be my protector?"

"I would not presume to speculate about Taran's feelings, my Lady. I can only tell you that he is honest and gallant, and that he has a very well defined sense of honor. I think that if you put your request to him as eloquently as you have put it to me, Taran would find it hard to refuse."

"Really?" murmured Jinella, her eyes narrowing. "Would he now?"

✦ ✦ ✦ ✦ ✦

The little party finally came in sight of Loxton's walls. Taran could smell brine in the air and hear the raucous cries of seabirds. He was excited at the prospect of seeing the sea and a working port, something he had never experienced before.

The guards stationed at the Forest Gate acknowledged them, saluting Sullyan's insignia and bowing to Lady Jinella as the coach rumbled into the city. Taran glanced over his shoulder to see the two loose warhorses still following closely behind.

The streets were thronging with people and the buildings were bedecked in festive bunting, slightly bedraggled after the heavy rain. The city's outer precincts were mainly residential, with half-timbered, black and white houses overhanging the narrow streets. As the party neared the city center, houses gave way to craftsmen's workshops, potters' and tanners' outlets, and shops selling all manner of foodstuffs. There was a curious mingling of odors that was not altogether pleasant, as brine coming in off the sea competed with the smells of cloth, leather, and food. Fascinating as it was, Taran was glad to leave this area as their party moved onto the main avenue leading to the castle.

The crowds faded away, as few people were heading for the castle. Apart from their party, the road contained only one or two members of the King's Guard and a few noblemen out riding with their ladies. All took note of Jinella's coach, but no one addressed them.

Taran knew that Port Loxton had grown up around Loxton Bay, a deep crescent cut into Albia's western coastline below towering chalk cliffs. The wharves of the port marked the western boundary of the city proper, and Loxton Castle stood in its own park-like grounds to the east of the wharves. As the coach rolled up to the heavy castle gates, he could see the fortified structure itself at the end of a long, straight avenue bordered by trees. The city crowded close to the park's stone walls to the east and south, but within the walls it was tranquil except for the area being readied for the fair. All manner of tents, booths, marquees, and stalls were being set up, and workmen and craftsmen were milling around, unloading their wares and claiming pitches, hoping for the best place to display their stock.

There was a contingent of guards at the castle gates. As the coach came to a halt, their Commander stepped onto the road. Sullyan nudged Darius toward him, her cloak thrown back to reveal her rank badges and battle honors.

The young officer, whose own insignia proclaimed him a Lieutenant-Major, came forward to speak with her. He was grinning broadly.

"Welcome to Port Loxton, Colonel Sullyan."

He had a pleasant, good-natured face, dark brown eyes, a laughing mouth, and a mop of curly brown hair. He held out his hand and Sullyan, smiling warmly, leaned down to clasp it.

"Denny. It is good to see you again."

"And you, Sullyan. The King told us to expect you, but he didn't say you were riding escort. Where's Hallian? I thought he was guarding this coach?"

"Captain Hallian met more trouble than he could handle," she replied, sliding down Darius's shoulder. "He is inside. I regret that we were too late to save him. The coachman was also injured and will need some attention. The ladies are safe, though. We were able to make sure of that."

Denny peered in through the window. "So I see. I'm sure the Baron will be very pleased to have his precious… property… returned safe and sound."

After nodding politely to Jinella, he said, "We'll take over now, Colonel. One of my men will take charge of the coach and deliver the ladies safely to the castle. Fergus!"

As a second man approached, Taran climbed down from his perch. Lady Jinella leaned out of her window and called to him.

"Captain Elijah, please allow me to extend my warmest thanks for your brave and timely rescue today." She gazed into Taran's eyes, making him blush. "Especially as you were wounded in our service. I know that my uncle, the Baron, will want to recompense you. He will reward you handsomely for your trouble, I have no doubt of that."

"Oh… er… there's no need, my Lady," stammered Taran. "The Colonel and I were happy to be of service."

"Gallantly said, Captain," she murmured.

Taran, who was unaccustomed to being addressed by his honorary rank, ducked his head. Jinella, however, wasn't finished.

"This may be a little forward of me, but I have another favor to ask you."

"Name it, my Lady," he said, his chivalry causing a pretty

flush to rise in her cheeks.

Her eyes demurely downcast, Jinella continued. "I must first speak with my uncle and gain his permission, but then, if I may, I will seek you out with my request."

"I am at your service, my Lady," replied Taran, puzzled.

Fergus, who had already climbed up beside the pale-faced coachman, clicked his tongue at the horses to start them up the avenue toward the castle. Jinella cast a backward glance out of the window and Taran stared after her before collecting his horse's reins.

Sullyan didn't miss Jinella's self-satisfied smirk, or the brief wave she gave her before turning away.

Chapter Seven

The Lieutenant-Major had obviously found the exchange between Taran and Jinella highly amusing, as he was still grinning when he said, "You should seek out the Chamberlain. Lord Kinsey is expecting you. The garrison stablemaster will see to your horses."

He put his hand to Darius's nose and the young stallion snuffled it curiously. "So, this handsome fellow is the King's new colt, eh? I hope you've trained him well, Colonel. Elias has great hopes for him in the race tomorrow."

Sullyan swung onto the colt's back. "The horse will not disappoint the King, Denny, but I might."

His eyes widened. "Are you entering Drum? Gods, don't put it about too widely just yet. Let me get good odds on you first!"

Sullyan was still laughing as she and Taran made their way up to the castle. They veered aside before reaching its walled courtyard. Riding around the western side of the wall, they came to the barracks. One of the men who were busy about the compound called for the stablemaster as Sullyan and Taran rode in. As they were loosening girths and removing their packs, he came up to them.

"So," he said, according Sullyan a smart salute even as he was admiring Darius, "this is the King's new colt?"

Sullyan had removed Darius's light saddle and the stallion's back wasn't even damp. The stablemaster, an amiable young man who was clearly nothing like the Manor's irascible Solet, ran his hands over the horse's legs and picked up a front hoof.

"He's a fine beast, Colonel. More bone than most of ours, more substance without the weight and, unless I'm much mistaken, more intelligence."

"Indeed, Josh," she said. "He should be a valuable addition to the King's breeding herd. He needs a good rub down and a light feed. He saw combat this morning, which I did not intend, although he acquitted himself well. He took no hurt, but some cold water on those legs would not go amiss if Elias still intends to race him tomorrow."

"Try to stop him," said Josh, grinning as he took Darius's bridle.

"Do the same for Drum, if you please," she added, rubbing Darius's nose in farewell. She turned to Taran. "What about you, Captain? Will you be entering the race?"

Surprised to be asked and puzzled by her use of his honorary rank, Taran shook his head.

"A pity," she said. "I believe you would have at least one supporter cheering you on."

He stared at her in silence and she turned back to Josh. "We will not need the bay again until we leave for the Manor with the King."

Grooms ran over to take Drum and Thunder. Sullyan gathered up her pack, gesturing for Taran to do the same. "Come, Captain, I will show you the bathhouse. We both need to wash after this morning's exertions. I want to check on that wound, and then we need to see about replacing your jacket and cloak."

"There's no need, Colonel," he protested, following her example as far as her title was concerned. "I'm perfectly capable of mending these. They're not that badly ripped."

She turned, giving him a warm look. He flushed, as he often

did under her direct gaze. "Captain," she reproved gently, "no one under my command goes about in mended clothing, and certainly not under the King's roof! Besides," she smiled, "we need not burden Elias with the cost. It is my intention to exact the price from Lady Jinella's uncle. Surely a Baron would not begrudge the savior of his niece's honor, not to mention her life, replacements for clothing damaged in that service. Do you not agree?"

Taran could hardly refuse, but he was relieved that the King wouldn't be paying for two such costly items of apparel.

He accompanied Sullyan toward the bathhouse. Before they got there, she was hailed by the young officer who had met them at the gates. He strode up to them, grinning widely.

"You look pleased, Denny," said Sullyan. "You must have been given good odds."

His grin broadened. "Fifty-to-one!" he crowed, rubbing his hands together. "Mainly because the booksman I chose has never heard of you or Drum. Hah! Just wait 'til that gets out. You won't be able to get evens then."

"What are the odds on the King?" asked Taran.

The young officer laughed. "Are you mad, man? No one bets on the King. The Queen doesn't like it, she thinks it's disrespectful. She doesn't like him riding in races either, but so far he's managed to hold on to that pleasure."

Sullyan glanced sharply at him and he made a face. "Don't look at me like that, Colonel. You know it's true. And anyway, I don't say that sort of thing in public." He turned back to Taran, an irrepressible glint in his eyes. "No, my friend, you can get a price on any of the runners save Elias."

Sullyan snorted. "I hope the King places a bet on me, then."

Denny stared at her before roaring with laughter. "Oh, Sullyan, I've missed you!" Then he sobered. "My lads all want to hear your account of the duel with that demon lord, you know. Is it true you lost? And that he nearly killed you?"

She gave him a straight look. "Yes to both."

He shook his head. "I never thought I'd hear you admit to losing a fight. The Master won't like it."

Taran frowned at the censure in the officer's tone. "There was more to it than just swordplay," he objected.

Sullyan shot him an irritated look and he flushed, wishing he had held his tongue. But it was too late. Denny pounced on him.

"Were you there?"

"Er... sort of."

"You're an Artesan too?" At Taran's nod, Denny said, "Well, I'd watch your step, both of you. The King might favor you, but few others here do."

Sullyan caught his arm. "What have you heard?"

He flashed an impudent grin. "I'll trade you. Once you've freshened up, you tell me and the lads the tale of that duel, and then I'll tell you what I've heard."

Taran glanced at Sullyan, expecting her to be annoyed, but she agreed easily enough. "Very well, that sounds like a fair trade to me. Once we have bathed and seen to Taran's injury, we will meet you by the barracks."

✧ ✧ ✧ ✧ ✧

Taran was relieved when the garrison bathhouse turned out to be much more civilized than the Manor's. Instead of just one large room with lots of tubs and no privacy, the garrison bathhouse had numerous small cubicles and tubs behind screens, as well as a larger room with a small communal pool.

There were also women here, runners from the King's messenger service, Taran supposed, and Sullyan left him for their company once she had tended his injury. Two sessions of healing from a Senior Master, plus Taran's own attentions while riding on the coach, had brought it along nicely. Once he had bathed and washed away the dried blood, he was left with an angry red scar and a dull ache. The muscle would need a bit longer to recover fully, but otherwise he was fit.

Damp, clean, and dressed in fresh clothing, he met Sullyan outside the bathhouse. Her tawny hair was loose down her back, framing her face with its shimmering masses. Taran tried not to stare.

"We had better go and speak with the Chamberlain, find out what arrangements have been made before we get sidetracked by Denny's men," she said, and led the way toward the arch giving onto the castle courtyard.

There were more people about now, and most of them nodded pleasantly as Taran and Sullyan passed. Just before they reached the steps to the castle's great double doors, they heard a hail. Turning, Taran saw a small, swarthy-skinned man walking toward them, trailed by a page. The man wore a long-suffering look with the air of someone who would much rather be somewhere else. Sullyan's eyes narrowed as she watched his approach.

He was conservatively dressed in black breeches, dark blue linen shirt, and black tunic. He wore no ornament, which was unusual in a society where men as well as women wore lavish jewelry at court. Taran recognized him immediately, but it took Sullyan a moment longer. Little wonder, thought Taran, for they had never formally been introduced, and she had been in no state to notice him on his last visit to the Manor.

Halting in front of her, he executed a barely courteous bow. His page announced him and Taran saw comprehension in Sullyan's eyes.

"Baron Reen," she said, inclining her head in imitation of his grudging bow. "To what do we owe this pleasure?"

The man's gray eyes shifted between her and Taran, and the

Adept had the distinct impression that his presence wasn't welcome. Sullyan waited him out. At last he said, stiffly polite, "I gather I owe you a debt of thanks, Colonel."

Taran wasn't surprised when Sullyan chose to be difficult.

"Do you, my Lord?"

The Baron's lips thinned, but he tried to hide his irritation. "My niece, Lady Jinella, informs me that you rescued her from forest brigands this morning. She wishes me to offer you recompense."

Taran didn't miss the inference that he personally had no wish to reward them. He was acting under duress and wanted them to know it.

Sullyan didn't miss it either, and her gaze turned topaz-hard. "We only did our duty, my Lord, as anyone would under such circumstances. I thank you for your offer of recompense, but I assure you it is not necessary."

Reen's expression lightened. He thought he was going to escape with both honor and purse intact. Sullyan's next words, however, disabused him of that notion. Continuing as if struck by a sudden thought, she said, "However, my Captain here was wounded in your service and a considerable amount of expensive clothing was damaged. His cloak, combat jacket, and shirt were all ruined by the brigands' steel, and he will be severely out of pocket if he has to replace them."

Embarrassed, Taran betrayed an involuntary start. In his mind he heard her sharp warning—*Be still*—and subsided.

On hearing the list of damaged items, the Baron turned pale. The shirt would not be too costly, but the jacket and cloak, if they were to be of suitable quality, would require a significant outlay. If he skimped and purchased inferior material, however, his ingratitude would undoubtedly get back to the King.

He was trapped and he knew it.

Trying to put the best face possible on the situation, he stiffly said, "Colonel, I would not dream of allowing your Captain to bear the cost of these items. If you will let me have the damaged clothing for size, I will replace them immediately. It is the least I can do."

Sullyan nodded. "We left them with the garrison quartermaster, my Lord. I trust your niece is none the worse for her adventure?"

Reen replied brusquely, no doubt keen to end the interview. "She is well, Colonel, thank you for your concern." He turned to Taran. "Captain Elijah, my niece wishes to speak with you after the evening meal. I trust this is convenient?"

Taran glanced briefly at Sullyan, who ignored him. "Oh, of course, my Lord. Please tell her I look forward to it."

The words were scarcely out of his mouth before the Baron sketched a hasty bow. As he stalked away they heard him instructing the page to fetch Taran's damaged clothing.

"What an odious little man!"

Taran was amazed. He had rarely heard Sullyan pass judgment or make derogatory comments behind anyone's back. She was normally politeness itself.

As they resumed their walk to the castle steps, he raised his brows at her.

"Taran, what do you remember of the Baron when he accompanied the King to the Manor last year? I had other things on my mind at the time and do not recall much about him."

Taran wasn't surprised. "I don't think he spent much time talking to anyone," he said slowly. "He seemed to want to keep out of the way. But I do recall he looked very uncomfortable during the Hierarch's confirmation ceremony. He must have eaten something that disagreed with him, because Tad told Robin that he'd seen the Baron being physically sick behind the pavilion after you left with the King and the Hierarch. It stuck in my mind because Tad was terribly amused to see someone so proud and aloof kneeling on the grass spilling their guts. He took great delight in describing just what the Baron looked and sounded like."

She smiled. "Did he? That is very interesting. Perhaps I should have a little talk with our youngest cadet when we return. Did you, by any chance, sense anything from the Baron while we were speaking just now?"

"Apart from the fact that he didn't want to be there? No," he admitted. "I wasn't paying him much attention."

She halted, and he saw in her expression just how seriously she was taking this. "From now on, Captain, you must be more aware. Indeed, we must both be constantly alert. We are fortunate to have the support of the King and I am hoping to have a private word with him before the fair begins. He may have some news for us, but until then, stay vigilant. We still need to find the creator of Rykan's Staff, and a good first step would be to discover who at court has no love for our kind. We might possibly glean some useful information from Denny later, but we must be wary of everyone until we have more knowledge. So keep your shield up and be on your guard. Watch for anyone who seems uncomfortable around us, anyone who is reluctant to talk. Listen to gossip—eavesdrop if you must! This is a deadly serious business, and our lives may depend on our success.

"Now, let us find the Chamberlain, and then I have an appointment to keep with the garrison."

They found Lord Kinsey, chamberlain and secretary to the King, in his office. He was a thickly built man with blond hair and washed-out blue eyes. He greeted them cordially, informing them that the King had ordered rooms made ready for them in the castle's private apartments.

"It was my intention to quarter with the garrison, Lord

Chamberlain," Sullyan protested.

Kinsey was aghast. "With the garrison, Colonel? Certainly not! That would hardly be appropriate."

"What could be more appropriate than a colonel of the King's forces quartering with the King's Guard, my Lord?"

He turned disapproving eyes on her. "But you are not just a colonel, are you, my dear?"

Realizing the futility of argument, she backed down. "Very well. Since the King has ordered the arrangement, we will not offend him by refusing."

Kinsey huffed. "I should think not! I'll have a servant take your things up to your rooms. The King sends his apologies for not being here to greet you, but he received an urgent message earlier that demanded his attention. He will speak with you in the morning."

"I thank you, my Lord. We will await his summons."

Returning to the sunny courtyard, they walked back under the heavy stone arch separating the castle from the garrison. The military buildings were all very functional, built of the same sandy-colored stone as the castle itself. Some were obviously as old as the main structure, which had been constructed generations ago by Elias's ancestors, while others had been added later.

As he and Sullyan strolled toward the training ground, Taran could see that a practice session was in progress. Fourteen or fifteen men, Denny among them, were also hanging around outside the arena, watching those within. As he drew closer, Taran could see five pairs of fighters sparring under their swordmaster's eye.

The man drilling the fighters was a tough-looking grizzle-haired individual who appeared to be in his early sixties. He was pacing round his students, studying their movements and making acid comments whenever they failed to impress. Taran wondered if he was the King's legendary swordmaster, Master Ardoch.

71

Sparing the occupants of the arena only the briefest glance, Sullyan approached the men by the rails. "Heads up, lads, here she is," called Denny, drawing his companions' attention away from the arena.

The men greeted Sullyan, crowding eagerly around her. Taran was amazed to find that she knew most of them by name, and wondered how that could be when she had only been here twice before.

Denny saw his puzzlement and guessed its cause.

"Most of us who are stationed at the castle have also spent time at the Manor," he said, fondly watching his men. "Many of these lads were in Sullyan's cadet group."

He grinned indulgently at all the good natured banter going on. Once it had died down a bit, he called, "Sullyan, is our old friend Glinn Parren still at the Manor? Is he still carrying a torch for you?"

Taran was shocked. So that's why Parren was so hostile toward Robin!

Sullyan's eyes turned hard and she flicked Taran a glance. "I put that out for him a long time ago, as well you know, Owyn Denny. I did not come here to talk about Glinn Parren. Do you want to hear this tale or not?"

Effectively sidetracked, Denny dropped the subject as he and his men concentrated on Sullyan's words. She leaned back against the wall of the building bordering the arena, hands resting on her sword belt as she spoke, leaving out as much painful personal detail as possible.

Taran, who had heard it all before, turned to lean his elbows on the railing, watching the swordplay. He could immediately see that the old weaponsmaster knew what he was doing. The exercises he had set his students were complex, and he instantly pulled them up on anything they executed with less than complete precision. Time and again he corrected them, even going so far as to show them himself until they got it right. His acid tongue and barbed comments lashed anyone foolish enough not to pay attention. Now and again, his eyes strayed to the group by the wall.

Once Sullyan had gone through her tale and the men began asking questions, Denny came to Taran's side. "That must have been some duel," he said casually, his eyes on the swordplay. "You said you were there. Did you see it?"

"Most of it." Taran was cautious, not wanting to reveal his experiences on that fateful day. "She was very skilful."

"She had an excellent teacher, as we all did." Denny nodded at the old swordmaster. "But I don't think the Master will agree with you. She lost the fight, after all."

Denny's words stung Taran. "She was hardly fit to fight at all!" he retorted. "Rykan was taller, heavier, had a longer reach, and was in very robust health. And he'd also—" He broke off, furious with himself for nearly revealing a very personal piece of information.

Denny grinned. "It's all right, I won't pry. I know what Sullyan's like about not giving things away. She's always been the same. It's none of my business anyway. But the Master won't be impressed if she uses ill health and a stronger opponent as an excuse."

"Excuse!" blurted Taran. "She did defeat him, after all!"

The man's smile widened in a knowing way, and Taran frowned, fearing that this lively-minded officer was making assumptions he shouldn't. "Easy, man," Denny said. "I'm baiting you."

Taran grimaced. "Sorry. That wasn't a good time for any of us."

"No, I suppose not." Denny turned his head. "Whoops, look out!"

Following his line of sight, Taran saw that the training session was over. Master Ardoch had dismissed his students, many of whom were massaging bruised muscles, and was approaching the group by the wall. He ducked under the railing and came to stand before Sullyan, his hands on his hips, his eyes on her face.

Nudging Taran sharply, Denny hissed, "This should be good."

Sullyan had fallen silent and was watching the swordmaster with a neutral expression. The men around her pulled away but didn't go far. There was a peculiar tension in the air that made Taran nervous.

Sullyan broke the silence. "Master Ardoch." Her greeting was soft, toneless.

He inclined his head and answered in the same way. "Colonel Sullyan."

As he looked her over, his gaze came to rest on the hilt of her sword. The man's eyes narrowed.

"Is that blade of demon forging?" Ardoch's voice had a strong burr that originated in the Torlands of Albia's eastern mountains.

"It is."

He held out his hand and she unsheathed the sword, offering it hilt first. Master Ardoch inspected the weapon, testing the flexibility of the steel, its weight and balance. Finally, he nodded and handed it back to her.

"A good blade. Is it the one ye used against the demon laird?"

"Yes, Master."

"Then why did ye lose?"

Arrested in the act of sheathing the sword, she turned her golden gaze on him. "Because he was too strong."

Taran heard gasps from the men.

Master Ardoch frowned, unimpressed, as Denny had predicted. "That's no excuse. Most men are stronger than ye are. Did I not teach ye how to overcome a more powerful opponent?

Have ye forgotten my lessons, lassie?"

Taran was shocked by his belligerent tone and glanced at Sullyan, fearing her temper.

She remained unruffled. "Never, Master. I used your training to good effect, believe me. But some battles are best won by means other than the sword, and this was one of them. I could have done no more."

He held her gaze before drawing his own sword. "It's been a few years since ye had any decent instruction. Ye'll be out of touch with the latest moves. Let's see if ye remember what I taught ye. Unless ye're too busy, of course?" He glanced around the assembled men, most of whom wouldn't meet his gaze.

Taran didn't miss the anticipatory gleam in Denny's eye as Sullyan shrugged. There was concern in her tone as she said, "I am happy to oblige you, Master, but are you sure this is a good time? I would not want to tire you. After all, you have just finished a training session."

Another audible gasp ran round the men, and Taran gathered it wasn't a good idea to talk back to Master Ardoch.

"Don't cheek me, girl!" he barked, waving Sullyan into the arena as she swiftly braided her hair.

The men crowded the rail to watch, Denny again leaning next to Taran. He was grinning. "Now the old bugger will get a run for his money." Taran raised his brows. "Sullyan was always the Master's star pupil," Denny explained. "She amazed everyone when Blaine relented and let her start weapons training. She was only thirteen! But what no one knew was that she'd been watching our lessons for months, practicing alone with some old sword she'd found. The beauty of it was that ancient sword was twice as heavy as someone her size should have been using, so when the Master gave her one the correct weight, she was already far stronger than he thought. And no one had ever told Sullyan that most people used only their right hand. She'd been practicing with both hands and the first time she switched, the Master was so surprised she nearly disarmed him! No one's ever done that, and he's never forgotten it. Now he holds her up to the rest of us as some sort of paragon, but you won't hear him praise her to her face. Some say she's his equal now, but you'll never get him to admit that either. Watch and learn, my friend. Watch and learn and judge for yourself."

Taran did. He had seen Sullyan fight and fence many times, both with inferior opponents and those more worthy of her. Master Ardoch, however, was something else. Age had not slowed him; he was as supple as a man in his thirties. His sinewy arms were strong, his grip sure. He was as graceful and agile as Sullyan, and the similarity of their styles was immediately apparent to Taran. He watched in fascination as they tried all manner of tricks and maneuvers to get the better of each other, but they were too evenly matched. Many a stroke was loudly appreciated by their audience, and they seemed to be enjoying themselves immensely.

"Ach, ye're too slow, girl," Taran heard Ardoch accuse her. She had just neatly sidestepped a vicious swing which would have sheared off an arm had she not been so quick.

"Quiet, old man," she replied, driving him relentlessly backward until he was forced to disengage and slide away. "You talk too much."

They circled each other a while longer, testing out various moves, until a bell sounded in the distance. "Evening meal," explained Denny when Taran turned enquiringly. The two combatants ceased their bout and raised their swords in the traditional salute before strolling back to the accompaniment of loud applause. They were scarcely out of breath.

Master Ardoch had his arm about Sullyan's shoulders. "Ye need to watch what ye eat, girl. Ye're getting fat."

She grinned. "And you are getting old, Master."

This drew another gasp from the men, and even Denny looked shocked. Taran gathered that the subject of the Master's age was taboo.

The swordmaster narrowed his eyes. "Witch!"

She merely smiled, according him a mocking courtly bow. "I thank you for the compliment, kind sir."

He roared with laughter and walked off in the direction of the barracks. "See ye at the fair, lass. Don't ye lose me my money!"

Chapter Eight

The large hall where the senior officers dined and relaxed was deserted except for the serving lads. Sullyan chose a table by the wall, away from the open window and far enough from the door so they would not be overheard. They waited, exchanging small talk until their food was served. Taran and Sullyan had missed their noon meal due to the fight with the brigands, but until the appetizing smells hit him, Taran hadn't realized how hungry he was.

They dealt quickly with the food, and then settled back with fellan. Taran followed Denny's example in adding a glass of amber brandy, but Sullyan, as usual, refused.

"So, Owyn," she began, "tell me what you have heard at court."

The young officer regarded her as he sipped his brandy. "There isn't much," he admitted, "and I've not heard anything specific. I do have a strong suspicion, although I wouldn't mention it to anyone but you."

He hesitated, glancing apologetically at Taran. "I don't mean to insult you, Captain, but I need to be sure. Sullyan, how far do you trust him?"

Her eyes widened. "Taran? I trust him with my life, and have done on several occasions." Taran colored at the vehemence of her tone. "Whatever you say, you can be sure that none of it will ever be broadcast from Taran's lips."

Denny nodded. "That's good enough for me."

He was silent a moment, considering his words. Sullyan held her peace, waiting him out. Eventually, he raised his eyes.

"There's one man here at court who makes no secret of his hatred for Artesans, and that hatred includes outlanders—all outlanders. He's not alone in his opinions, I'll grant you, but this man is more outspoken and influential than any of the others. He says what he likes with no fear of censure, and he's doing his best to persuade the other nobles to his point of view. He's gaining supporters and even has the backing of the clerics. He's a prominent lay speaker at the Matria Church here in Loxton, and you must know that many Churchmen consider Artesans to be practitioners of witchcraft."

Sullyan nodded. "You speak of Baron Reen."

"Yes," said Denny, "I thought you might already know about him. But what you might not know"—he leaned forward, lowering his voice—"is where he gets his power from, and why he's immune to Elias's anger. Reen is the Queen's man through and through, and it's widely accepted that his opinions are also hers. We call him the Queen's Kitten, although not to his face, of course! He's her countryman and was her personal advisor when she lived at her father's court. Word is she refused to be parted from him, and so he came here with her retinue when she wed Elias four years ago."

"Owyn, are you suggesting that the Queen is actively opposed to Artesans? How can that be, when Elias so openly supports us?"

Denny shrugged. "She would never publicly speak against him, of course, but her mouthpiece can. And Elias can't touch Reen without implicating her. That's how the Baron gets away with voicing his opinions, and it's why he follows Elias everywhere. He'll be among your party when you return to the Manor, mark my words. He's the Queen's spy, and he makes sure she knows everything Elias does or says.

"Elias hates him, of course, but he has to tolerate him. The Queen relies on Reen for everything, and he never leaves her side, except to accompany the King. Elias has learned to accept it. After all, it's much better to know the spy in your camp than to be wary of everyone."

Sullyan clearly didn't like what she was hearing. "We had already guessed some of this. The Baron was extremely uncomfortable when he attended the Hierarch's confirmation ceremony with the King last year. I believe he even had to sit with some of the Andaryan nobles at dinner that night. Given his hatred of outlanders, it is no wonder his stomach rebelled. It would have been interesting to see his face."

Denny snorted. "I'd be amazed if he managed to eat anything at all. The man's so prejudiced he wouldn't accept water from an outlander if he was dying of thirst. But weren't you at that dinner? I thought you dined regularly with royalty these days?"

Sullyan's face hardened at his lighthearted reference to that painful time, but she carried it off well enough. "The food was a little rich for me that night, Owyn. Does the Baron have many supporters among Elias's counselors?"

"There are those who share his views, though they don't voice them openly. He doesn't really need supporters as long as he has the Queen. Sofira thinks so highly of him that she even permits him his own guardsmen." The young officer grimaced and sipped his brandy. "He doesn't flaunt them under the King's nose, though. They're quartered at his mansion just outside the city."

He leaned forward to whisper once more. "The Queen is not widely liked at court, you know. Even Elias doesn't seek her company. It was a political alliance, a marriage of convenience. There's no love there, believe me."

"But they have children, don't they?" asked Taran. "Surely they can't hate each other that much."

Denny rolled his eyes. "Yes, of course they have children! A girl of three and a boy born last year. But what does that have to do with anything? If Elias didn't do his duty and give her children, her father wouldn't think it much of an alliance, would he? And Elias has to have an heir. Anyway, you don't need to like someone to lie with them and get children."

"No," murmured Sullyan, her face pale. "You do not."

"Are you all right?" asked Denny, noticing her sudden pallor. Taran sympathized, wondering if she would ever get over what Rykan did to her.

She shook herself. "Yes, I thank you. Your words have given me much to think on. I hesitate to ask this, but would you keep your eyes and ears open for us at court? Any information you might pick up could be very useful."

"Of course I will, you don't need to ask. You helped me often enough when I needed it. I'm happy to return the favor."

Leaving Denny to his brandy, Taran and Sullyan strolled back to the castle in the dusky light. The sunset's pink glow promised a fine day for the fair. Mounting the castle steps, Taran turned to Sullyan and asked about Denny's reference to needing her help.

Sullyan smiled at a private memory. "Owyn Denny has done well for himself since transferring to the castle, but he was not a natural soldier. He was among my cadet group, and his good nature often made him the butt of practical jokes. Denny is a master of such tricks himself, so they did not trouble him, but he did fear he might not pass the training course if some of his more serious rivals sabotaged his efforts in the final tests. I helped him where I could and ensured that those who plotted his failure did not achieve it."

Something in her manner, coupled with Denny's remarks at the training ground, gave rise to a suspicion in Taran's mind. "Was one of his rivals a cadet named Glinn Parren?"

Sullyan's eyes hardened as they always did on hearing that name. She treated Taran to a penetrating look that advised him to pry no further. "Yes," was all she said.

They entered the castle, nodding to the sentries. The wide entrance hall was warmly lit by fragrant lamps, its stone walls hung with tapestries, its flagged floors covered with colorful rugs. Sullyan hailed a servant, requesting directions to their rooms. The man offered to take them but before they could accept, Taran heard his name called. Having forgotten the Baron's message, he didn't immediately recognize Lady Jinella gliding toward him, followed by Lily, her maid.

The young noblewoman had bathed and changed her gown. Her hair was artfully arranged, with tendrils of blonde curls framing her face and coiling about her neck. Her gown was of dark green satin trimmed with gold, and her hands glittered with rings. She had applied a soft blush to her cheeks and her shining green eyes were darkly outlined.

The effect was dazzling and Taran held his breath. He waited for her to approach and took her outstretched hand, bowing courteously over it. "My Lady," he murmured.

Jinella cast down her eyes. Sullyan moved a little way off out of courtesy, and Taran shot her a pleading glance. She ignored him.

"Captain Elijah," said Jinella, "did my uncle find you earlier today?"

"Yes, my Lady, and I must thank you for your insistence of recompense for our rescue. I assure you, it was totally unnecessary." Taran tried to release her hand, but she tightened her fingers and he was too much the gentleman to insist.

"Oh, no," she said warmly, "it was the least I could do. You were so gallant and brave. I hate to think what might have happened had you not come along when you did. Lily and I owe you our lives, and we will never forget your heroism."

Taran blushed furiously, especially as she was pointedly ignoring Sullyan's part.

Jinella smiled at his discomfort. "Captain, I would never presume on your good nature, but I wonder... would you consider doing me another favor?"

Trapped by her eyes and her hand, Taran had nowhere to go. "Of course, my Lady. Please name it."

She lowered her gaze again. Speaking hesitantly, she said, "I am a recent arrival here at court, Captain, and I am alone apart from my uncle. I would dearly love to attend the fair tomorrow, but that dreadful experience in the forest has left me more than a little nervous. As my uncle will be attending the Queen, I have no escort. I fear to go abroad in the crowds all alone, attended only by my maid."

She turned her head away, as if shamed by her admission. "Oh, you must think me a very faint-hearted creature." She raised her eyes so suddenly that she caught Taran with the full force of her gaze. But he was already cornered, and Jinella was simply making sure he was firmly on the hook before reeling him in.

Taran tried a last, desperate struggle.

"Not at all, my Lady, anyone would feel nervous after such a terrible ordeal. I would deem it an honor to escort you, but I may not be free. My duty is to attend the Colonel."

He turned in appeal to Sullyan, who was fighting to compose herself. Jinella also turned to her, a glitter in her soft green eyes. "Colonel," she wheedled, "surely you do not expect the Captain to attend you the entire day tomorrow?"

Sullyan ignored Taran's pointed look. "No indeed, my Lady. Taran Elijah is off duty tomorrow, as I have already told him. Had you forgotten it, Captain?"

He gave her a flat stare.

Turning back to Jinella, she continued, "As this is his first time in the capital, I am sure he would welcome such agreeable company on his day off. And you will find him a most attentive and interesting escort. Now, if you will both excuse me, I intend to retire. I wish you both a good night's rest."

She turned away, gesturing the servant onward.

Irritated by her refusal to help him, Taran gave up. "Where and when shall I call on you, my Lady?"

She smiled. "Any of the servants will show you to my rooms, Captain. I will be ready by mid-morning. I bid you good night."

He made a small bow as she left him and Lily threw him a sly smile as she followed her mistress.

✤ ✤ ✤ ✤ ✤

The morning of the fair dawned misty with the promise of a fine day. The seabirds were up early, their raucous cries echoing about the rooftops. Taran rose and dressed himself with care, not knowing whether to feel anticipation or trepidation. It wasn't that he disliked Jinella, truly, he had no feelings for her one way or the other, but he had been looking forward to another day in Sullyan's company. He was now denied that pleasure, and he hoped Jinella wouldn't spend too much time browsing the craftsmen's stalls. Taran had no intention of missing the horse race, which was scheduled for mid-afternoon.

Sullyan's rooms were next to his but there was no response to his polite tap on her door. He wasn't surprised. She would have been up at dawn, as usual, probably checking on Drum. Ensuring he had sufficient coinage tucked away inside his jerkin, he made his way toward the aroma of breakfast.

He entered the rather grand dining hall, a little intimidated when all eyes turned on him. There were a surprising number of people in the hall, all dressed in their fair finery. Taran's own clothes, although perfectly presentable, were plain by comparison. He tried to ignore the stares and helped himself to meat and bread.

He was just finishing a delicious selection of exotic fruit when he realized that the darkly dressed man coming toward him was Baron Reen. Taran hurriedly stood and made the Baron a bow. The swarthy man halted in front of him, regarding him with unfriendly eyes.

"Captain Elijah, I trust these will be satisfactory?"

The servant who followed him handed Taran a wrapped bundle. The Adept laid it on the table and uncovered a sumptuous dark green cloak of thick wool, an expensive-looking leather jacket, and a soft linen shirt. Stunned by the quality of the material, he stammered his thanks. Reen ignored him and stalked away. Taran just stood there fingering the jacket, which was silk-lined and would fit him very snugly. He was so engrossed that he didn't sense or hear anyone coming up behind him, and jumped when Sullyan touched a fold of the cloak.

"This is top quality, Taran," she said, glancing up at him. "Better even than King's issue."

The Adept was shocked by her appearance. Her eyes were wide and feverish, her pallid cheeks sunken.

"Sullyan, you don't look at all well. What's happened?"

She shook her head. "I am well enough, Taran. I am a little tired, that is all. Maybe I ate something yesterday that did not agree with me."

Taran stared at her, unconvinced. "Do you think you ought to ride in the race today?"

A hint of color came to her cheeks and she grinned at him. "Of course I shall ride! I cannot let Owyn and Master Ardoch lose their money, can I? Now, is there any fellan?"

⁜ ⁜ ⁜ ⁜ ⁜

The Lady Jinella was also in two minds about the day. Her uncle had visited her before she retired the night before, and what he had told her threatened to color her enjoyment of the occasion. She went over it in her mind while Lily brushed out her hair and dressed it for the day.

Jinella was the daughter of Baron Reen's older brother. He had married a Loxton woman and took her to live on the family estate in Bordenn. The province was in the southwest of Albia and was ruled by client king Lerric. Albia's provinces had been governed by client kings for generations, and when Elias succeeded his father as High King, he did nothing to change the arrangement. It worked very well and relieved the Crown of the burden of governing each separate province. Provided each client king embraced his policies and obeyed his dictates, Elias was content.

Jinella's father died of the winter flux when she was fourteen, and her mother immediately left the estate and took her young daughter back to Loxton Province, to live with her own relatives. Although wealthy enough, she lacked connections and Jinella's prospects looked slim. But then Elias married Lerric's daughter, Princess Sofira, and Jinella's uncle, the Princess's confidante, became an influential figure at court. The eighteen-year-old Jinella was fast learning the intricacies of society, and she had quickly decided she was not going to marry some minor noble's useless third or fourth son: not when her uncle was the High Queen's chief advisor. She knew that if she could persuade him to champion her, her looks and intelligence would attract a much better class of suitor.

Since attaining her majority a year ago, Jinella had badgered her mother to write to Reen and beg him to introduce her at court. Jinella's mother had never trusted Reen and was loath to approach him. Jinella refused to give up and finally, out of frustration, her mother gave in and sent a letter to court. Reen was none too eager to champion the girl at first as he had never approved of his northern sister-by-marriage, and considered his niece to be thoroughly spoiled.

However, when he finally met the adult Jinella, he revised his opinion. She was intelligent and pretty and, as she had hoped, he realized that securing a good match for her would reflect well on him. Position, money, and power were vitally important to Reen. To Jinella's delight, he secured the Queen's blessing, arranged rooms for Jinella within the castle, and brought her to court.

Since her arrival three weeks ago, she had been the model of decorum. Her uncle had reluctantly loaned her his coach two days ago so she could collect some gowns from her mother's house, and had arranged for Captain Hallian to guard her. He was furious when she told him of the incident in the forest, but it seemed he was less angry over the attack on her person, or even his valuable coach, than he was at hearing that her saviors were Artesans. When she told him that one of them was the famed Colonel Sullyan, he was horrified and very nearly physically sick.

She went on to blithely announce that not only did she expect him to reward her rescuers, but she also intended to spend the day of the fair with one of them. She simply couldn't understand why her uncle's revulsion nearly overwhelmed him.

She didn't have time to puzzle over the reason, however, for he visited her chamber later that evening and told her that he would give his permission for Captain Elijah to escort her on one condition. She was to get as much information out of the man as possible.

Not having a devious nature, she refused point-blank. She was genuinely drawn to the handsome Captain and, although he was not what she had in mind for a future husband, he would certainly do as an escort. Looks and a gallant disposition were acceptable enough when the alternative was not having an escort at all.

The resulting argument was fierce.

Her uncle made it quite clear that he would not tolerate her forming more than a passing acquaintance with anyone who practiced "unnatural acts." He told her bluntly that her inheritance, which he had control of, was forfeit if she took her interest in this man any further. He had no objection to her amusing herself briefly with him provided she obtained as much information from him as she could. As far as Reen was concerned, she would obey him or risk everything. He left her seething with indignation.

Now, mulling over this outrageously patronizing interview, Jinella allowed the rhythmic movements of Lily's brush to soothe her. How dare her uncle try to manipulate her! She had no intention of doing what he wanted; at least no further than her own curiosity warranted. She would decide what, if anything, she passed on to him, and she knew she could dissemble well enough to convince him he was getting all she knew. She refused to be controlled by him and considered his using her fortune against her a very base act.

Having decided to go her own way, she glanced in the mirror and approved Lily's work. She chose her gown with care, seeing no reason why it should not both flatter her figure and impress her escort.

She heard the light tap on her door around the middle of the morning. The maid showed the Captain in and invited him to wait in the luxurious small drawing room while her lady completed her preparations.

Jinella observed her visitor from behind the partially closed door, exchanging whispered comments with Lily about his looks and person. Lily was apt to giggle, so Jinella kept some of her more intimate observations private. She was unwilling to admit, even to herself, just how attractive she found him.

She was thoroughly looking forward to having him to herself for the day, and was determined to break through his polite but formal manner just as soon as she could. After all, she was attractive, witty, and good company. He had no reason not to fall for her charms. Who knew where it might lead? She had not yet experienced a physical relationship with a man, but was perfectly willing to be persuaded that she should. Her uncle's completely unreasonable veto only served to heighten her curiosity.

With pleasurable anticipation, she drew back from the door, took one last look in her mirror, cautioned Lily not to get in the way of her fun, and swept regally into the drawing room.

Taran stood and made a small bow. "Lady Jinella," he said politely.

Jinella was pleased to see that he noticed her careful preparations. She had elected to wear her bronze satin gown with its low-cut bodice and short ruffled sleeves. Lily was carrying the matching fringed parasol, which Jinella would definitely need once the sun reached its height. About her neck she had fastened an expensive gold necklace with flat polished links that would catch and reflect the sun, drawing attention to her creamy skin. Her only other adornment, apart from her rings, was a pair of diamond earrings.

Taran was appraising her much as she had evaluated him, and she was sure he could appreciate her appeal when compared to Colonel Sullyan's more delicate features. Jinella was taller than the Colonel and, she had to admit, more robustly built, although she would have fainted with outrage had anyone used the word "robust" in her hearing. Jinella was perfectly proportioned and possessed all the appropriate curves. How could her escort resist?

She held out a slender hand and he gallantly took it, raising it briefly to his lips. Jinella's heart fluttered. "I hope you have plenty of energy today after your heroism in the forest, Captain. There are many fascinating stalls and displays to enjoy at the fair, and as I have never attended one here before, I want to see it all."

He inclined his head. "Then we have something in common, my Lady, for I have never attended such an occasion either. My village held a fete with its neighbors once a year, but that was on a very small scale."

She smiled winningly and touched his arm. "As we are to be companions for the day, I think we might be a little less formal, don't you? My name is Jinella, or Jinny if you prefer. And you are Taran. Is that right?"

"Yes, my ... Jinella," he amended, flushing.

Oh, he was so sweet! This was going to be a very good day. Her smile widened. "That's better. Now we can behave like friends, as I hope we are. For I owe you a debt, Taran, and if I can repay you even a little with my friendship, that will make me happy. Shall we go?"

She linked arms with him and left the suite, Lily trotting behind.

Chapter Nine

Sullyan had not risen early that morning as Taran had thought. She had not answered his light tap at the door because she was in no state to do so.

Waking at her customary hour, she had lain still in her bed, trying to control the violent nausea roiling in her stomach. Uncharacteristically losing the battle, she succumbed to the wracking spasm in the suite's small privy. White and shaking, with a numbing lassitude spreading through her bones, she returned to bed to let it pass.

The incident frightened her. It was not the first time over the last few months she had woken feeling unwell, but it was the first time she had been unable to control it. As an Artesan, she was never ill, and so was ill equipped to deal with it. The poison of Rykan's seed had caused her similar symptoms. Although she had long since purged his poison, she still feared the damage it had wrought. Rykan's physical presence had caused the symptoms to worsen, and her vast Artesan powers had been useless against the pain. So it was now, and she had no idea why.

A couple of cups of bitter fellan and a brief talk with Taran at breakfast improved things. She had an appointment with King Elias that morning and could do without the distraction of ill health. After dressing simply in a light cotton shirt and dark breeches, she waited in the anteroom to Elias's private audience chamber, thankful that the affliction seemed to have passed.

The anteroom was not as luxurious as she might have

expected, but it did have comfortable chairs, rugs on the floor, and a vast stone fireplace where giant logs would blaze in wintertime. There were four large windows with thick leaded glass, through which she could see the gaily colored tents of the fair. Even at this distance the sound of crowds gathering was unmistakable. Sullyan sat and watched the far-off figures moving about the fairground.

A small, furtive sound suddenly caught her ear. Glancing at the metal-studded door, which was slightly ajar, she caught a flash of movement behind it. It seemed that someone was lurking outside. She sat still and silent, waiting for whoever it was to show themselves.

Another sound reached her ears. Was it a murmur of protest or a low moan? She heard receding footsteps and wondered if the person had left. Then the door began to move, slowly opening further into the room. She still couldn't see who was there; they must be standing by the wall and pushing the door with a hand or foot. She waited.

Eventually, the door was wide open. She could see right down the hallway leading to the private apartments, where she and the other guests were housed. Still the mystery person did not appear. She briefly considered rising and going to the door, but then decided against it. She waited. She could hear the soft shuffling of feet by the wall, as if whoever stood there was unsure of their welcome.

On impulse, she said softly, "Enter, if you will. I do not bite."

There was the hint of a giggle, a childish sound. She knew it could not be the King's little daughter, as she had seen both his children taken to the fair by their nursemaids. As far as she knew, there were no other children in the castle. Perhaps it was some servant child encouraged by the holiday atmosphere to try for a forbidden look at the King's private rooms.

"Would you like to come and sit with me?" she said, keeping

her voice soft.

There was another brief shuffle and then a head appeared abruptly round the door. She was startled.

Her visitor was not a child, but a youth. His age was not immediately apparent. He had a bright shock of wild red hair, but this was not what caught her attention. It was his face. His light skin was freckled all over, but his eyes were wrong. They were mismatched; one was dark blue and the other honey-brown. They were also unevenly set, one higher than the other. And he had a squint. But the smile on his face was engaging and she returned it.

"Hello," she said.

His grin broadened, showing uneven teeth. "'Lo," he slurred, his voice thick and immature. He sidled awkwardly round the doorframe, never taking his eyes off her as if he thought she might pounce on him. She felt surprise when his body was revealed.

He had a crooked back, his right shoulder deformed into a hump which caused his body to slouch. He also had a club left foot, which accounted for the shuffling. He was older than she had first thought too, probably in his mid-twenties. He was clearly nervous and approached her shyly. She schooled her expression to interested pleasure.

"What are you called?" she asked.

He frowned. His tongue came out of the side of his mouth and a thin trickle of saliva ran down his chin. Then his odd eyes cleared and took on a sly expression.

"You tell first!"

"Very well," she agreed, "but promise to tell me your name after."

He took a great leap toward her. "Promise!" he cried. He landed awkwardly and caught up her left hand. His grip was unnaturally strong and he squeezed her hand painfully, completely oblivious to her discomfort. Not wanting to upset him by protesting, she used metaforce to dampen the pain.

He frowned as her eyes dilated with the expenditure of power. "Name!" he demanded, giving her hand another squeeze.

"My name is Brynne," she said.

He dropped her hand as if it burned him. "Brynne?" He crouched down in front of her, bringing his uneven face level with hers. "Brynne?"

"Yes," she said, "Brynne. Now, what is yours?"

A latch clicked as the door opposite the hallway opened. A loud voice thundered "HUW!" and the red-headed lad leaped to his feet, shrieking in fear. He stumbled backward into the door.

King Elias strode into the room. "What are you doing here, Huw?"

The boy cringed against the door as if he feared Elias would strike him. He began to cry. Sullyan rose and moved closer, frowning at the scene.

"We were just making each other's acquaintance, your Majesty," she said, coming close to the trembling Huw and putting out her hand. Huw grabbed it and clutched it to his chest. She could feel the panicked beat of his heart.

Elias looked down at her. "I'm sorry about this, Brynne. I hope he's not being a nuisance. I'm afraid Huw doesn't really know what he's doing. The city constabulary found him running wild a couple of years ago and didn't know what to do with him. He seemed to have no family. Someone brought him to the Queen's attention and she took pity on him. I think she hoped one of her physicians might be able to help him, but it looks like he's a hopeless case. They all say he was born deformed, and that his brain is damaged. He behaves like a four-year-old child. He's harmless enough and my daughter seems to like him, so Sofira keeps him around to amuse her. I don't know how he got up here, though. Normally he's confined to the nursery wing.

"You know you're not supposed to be in here, Huw, don't you?" he said, raising his voice as if the boy was deaf.

Huw seemed to have forgotten his fright. He dropped Sullyan's hand, made a rude face at Elias, and sidled round the door. "Pretty," he slurred. "Pretty Brynne."

"Yes, Huw, I know she is. Now, you run along to the fair. I expect Seline and Eadan are wondering where you are."

The names of the King's children had an electric effect on the lad, and his face transformed with delight. Stumbling into the hallway, he broke into a shambling run.

Elias turned back to Sullyan, sympathy on his face. "Poor lad. He dotes on my children, and especially my son. I don't think there's any harm in him, but he doesn't seem to understand how strong he is. The nursemaids daren't let him get too close in case he hurts Eadan. They're a bit frightened of him, I think. Did he hurt you?"

"No, your Majesty, of course not." She glanced down the hallway, but the lad had disappeared. "He seemed very lonely, somehow."

Elias sighed. "Yes, I suppose he must be. He has no real friends, only people who tolerate him. I keep telling Sofira to find him somewhere more suitable, but she's determined to keep him. I think she hopes that adult company will work some miracle on his simple mind."

As Elias turned from the doorway and ushered Sullyan into the audience chamber, she asked, "Has an Artesan ever tried to help him?"

The King glanced at her. "Do you think you could?"

"I have no idea, your Majesty. I could try."

Elias dropped into an easy chair and gestured for Sullyan to take another. "You can drop the formality now, Brynne, we're both off duty." He gave her a mock-stern stare. "Only an hour ago I learned that you've had the temerity to enter my horse race as a rival. I think we can deal with each other on equal terms, don't you?"

She gave him an impish look. "As you wish, Elias. Have you by any chance placed a bet on me? You should, although I doubt you will get such good odds as Owyn Denny."

He stared at her in astonishment for a moment before roaring with laughter.

✤ ✤ ✤ ✤ ✤

Taran quickly discovered what good company Jinella could be, and he enjoyed escorting her round the fair more than he thought he would. Lily stayed a few paces behind her mistress, and Taran gradually forgot about her. As neither he nor Jinny knew anyone at court, they were unmolested as they strolled around the booths and trade stands, admiring the wares for sale. They watched the displays and entertainments, and soon discovered that there were also arms competitions taking place. Jinella tried very hard to persuade Taran to enter one, but he steadfastly refused. He used his scarcely healed injury and his desire to relax and enjoy her company as his reasons. While flattered by the latter, as he intended, she was nevertheless piqued that she would not have the pleasure of basking in the reflected glory of his undoubted success. She appealed to his pride in his skill as a means of persuasion, but he was unshakeable.

"Do you really want to see me lose because my sword arm isn't up to full strength?" he asked. Pouting, she let it drop.

One thing she did not let drop was his hand. She had clasped it very early on in the day, saying the crowds made her nervous. Taran, resigned, allowed her to guide him about like a puppy on a leash. She chattered incessantly and seemed to have an insatiable curiosity. He answered her many questions as best he could. He had already exhausted his early life and background, and then she started on his talents.

As they stood side by side watching a display of horsemanship by some of the King's Guard, she asked him, "How long have you been an Artesan, Taran?"

His eyes on the prancing horses, he replied, "All my life, really. We're born with it, although it's not always apparent."

She took a sharp breath. "It's not something anyone can learn, then?"

He flicked a glance at her. "No, Jinny. You either have the talent or you don't. It's not like riding or shooting. You can't just learn it."

"How do you know if you've got it, then?"

Taran turned to face her, sensing genuine interest. "It usually manifests itself by the time you reach twelve or thirteen. Some people discover it much younger, and some when they're much older. Sullyan, I believe, discovered her talent at a very early age."

Jinella's lips thinned. He noticed she did this every time Sullyan's name cropped up. "You really do admire her, don't you?" she said.

Her tone was a touch acidic, but Taran ignored it. "How could you not? She's extremely skilled, highly talented, powerful, and very beautiful. She's also the most unassuming person I've ever met, which is quite remarkable when you consider her merits. There's no one else remotely like her, Jinny."

"Well, thank—" Jinella changed her mind mid-sentence. "What's your relationship with her?"

"She's my teacher, my friend, and my superior officer."

"Oh! So, you're not in love with her, then?"

Taran frowned. "She's already wed to a man who's also a very good friend of mine."

Jinella stared at him and he felt his color rising. Had she noticed he hadn't actually denied it?

She abruptly changed tack. "How did you discover your... talent? Can you read people's minds, like they say? Can you read mine?"

He was thankful for the change. "Of course not. It doesn't work like that. People who are not Artesans have a very effective natural barrier that can't be breached by force. I couldn't use my powers to make you do anything you didn't want to. I can read your emotions, and I could do things that would affect you through my mastery over the elements, but apart from that, you're quite safe from me."

Jinella stared intently. In a small voice, she asked. "But could you kill me? I've heard it said that Artesans can kill with their powers. Have you ever killed anyone that way?"

He was horrified. "No, of course I haven't! That's the sort of thing ignorant people say. It's a gift, what we have. It's something precious and wonderful, and I don't know anyone who would use it to kill. We're not like that."

A fleeting memory crossed his mind; Robin's voice describing how Sullyan had drained Rykan of his essential self before striking off his head. That was different, he thought, but he couldn't explain it to Jinny. She wouldn't understand.

His vehemence had made Jinny nervous. Maybe she was worried she had upset him. Maybe his voice had been too loud; perhaps he had allowed his indignation at her ignorance to show. He didn't want to frighten her, and sought to get back to their earlier easy companionship.

"Should we find something to eat, Jinny? I don't want to miss seeing Sullyan win that horse race. I also want to place a bet before the odds get too short. Are you coming?"

Jinella allowed him to lead her toward the food stalls, her lips thinning at yet another mention of Sullyan's name. As she walked by his side, her eyes were clouded and thoughtful.

✤ ✤ ✤ ✤ ✤

Sullyan's meeting with the King was short, as Elias could tell her nothing new. Neither of them had made any progress toward finding the person responsible for making Rykan's Staff. There had been no further attacks against Artesans since she had destroyed it, and Elias was of the opinion that the threat was over. Sullyan remained unconvinced.

The Hierarch of Andaryon had agreed to question Rykan's former nobles, if any of them could be found, although they all knew that the unlamented Lord Sonten was probably the only one who could have given any real information. As he had perished in the siege of Taran's village, that knowledge was lost. Sullyan would pay Pharikian a private visit after the inauguration of the College to inquire after his progress in the investigation.

Acknowledging the futility of speculation, Sullyan and Elias abandoned the subject. The King wanted to know how the Artesan College's first outside student was progressing. Aged just twenty-one, the olive-skinned Lord Ozella hailed from Beraxia, a hot and dusty country far across the southern seas. He was on secondment from his government and had come to Loxton mainly to learn the workings of a diplomat, and also more about the Artesan craft. Ozella had the beginnings of power, but the Beraxian masses had little in the way of education and superstition was rife. Any peasant child showing signs of emerging power was immediately killed, and only those born to privileged families had any chance of reaching maturity. Even then, they were rarely taught to control their gifts.

Ozella's father was a more enlightened individual who had traveled widely in his role as ambassador. He recognized the advantages available to the trained Artesan and had asked the Beraxian Chief Minister to send Ozella, his second son, to Elias for diplomatic and Artesan training. Elias, in turn, had sent Ozella to

Sullyan.

Sullyan described the young man's development—or lack of it—as they left Elias's private rooms and made their way to the stables, where they would collect their mounts for the race. Elias was troubled as he listened to her account of Ozella's many failures, and she sensed it. When she was done, she asked him why he was so concerned.

"I received an urgent message yesterday from Ozella's father," he said, his blue eyes clouded. "He's quite distraught because his two daughters have vanished."

"Vanished? How?"

"The girls had been staying with friends in South Fells Province and were making their way home. They never arrived. Their carriage was eventually found, well away from the proper route, and the coachman and guard were found dead some days later. But of the two girls there was no sign."

"When was this?"

Elias sighed. "Last week. I'm amazed we received the news so quickly, especially when you consider the message had to reach Beraxia first. My network of runners is proving very fast and efficient. Anyway, Ozella's father is awaiting a ransom demand, as that's the only reason he can think of for their disappearance. So far, he has heard nothing. He begged me not to tell his son. He fears Ozella might be captured as well if he tries to find them."

"How old are the girls?"

"Sixteen and nineteen, I believe."

Sullyan shook her head. "If you tell him, he will want to return home immediately. If you do not and something... permanent happens to them, he will be distraught that you denied him the opportunity to help."

Elias shrugged. "I know, but I can't go against his father's wishes. I can't take responsibility for his safety if I do."

"I will say nothing, then. But he will be sorely vexed if he finds out we withheld this knowledge."

"I'll just have to take that risk."

When they reached the stables, they found both Drum and Darius waiting for them. The horses' hides were gleaming, their tails glossy from the brush. Sullyan moved around Drum, checking his legs and hooves, while Elias made friends with the colt. So far the King had not had the leisure to spend any time with him. Darius nuzzled his hand and gently accepted the half apple Elias had brought him. The King walked admiringly round his new acquisition, comparing the colt to Drum's powerful and faultless physique.

"If he performs for me as well as this black brute does for you, I shall be well pleased," he said, slapping Drum's neck.

Sullyan grinned. "We shall soon see."

She vaulted effortlessly onto Drum. Elias more decorously used the mounting block, as befitted his station. Neither horse bore a saddle, as was the rule of the race, but each would be fitted with a weighted cloth once all the entrants had weighed in, in order to handicap lighter jockeys such as Sullyan.

The King, simply dressed in a white shirt and dark red breeches, moved gracefully on the young stallion's back as they jogged out of the stables and down to the course. It was set in the vast parklands surrounding the castle and incorporated natural jumps such as fallen trees, the stream running down to Loxton Bay, fences and gates, and even a short tunnel below a folly which had been built by Elias's father. The whole race would last about fifteen minutes with the runners negotiating the entire course twice.

Sullyan and Elias joined the other riders who were gathering. There were eleven runners in all, and Sullyan studied them. Most she dismissed instantly as being no match for the Manor-bred horses. Two were lean and long-limbed and looked like they had a fine turn of speed, but she thought they were probably too highly strung to cope with the more testing obstacles. Only one, a raw-boned chestnut with a rather ugly head, was an obvious rival. He was strong and powerful and was looking about with interest, much as Drum and Darius were doing. His rider was a slim young man in russet red. Sullyan saw him studying the two Manor horses, probably identifying their threat.

Hearing her name called, she turned to see Denny, Ardoch, and some of the King's Guard approaching. They clustered around her and Elias, giving them advice and information about the runners. While speaking with them she caught sight of Taran by the rail, and smiled to see the firm clasp Jinella had on his arm. She spared him a wave, and he waved back.

The riders weighed in and received their weighted cloths, which were placed on the horses' backs and fastened with a surcingle. Anyone whose cloth fell away during the race would be disqualified. Then the horn sounded to summon them to the starting line, and they formed up side by side behind a red ribbon held by two stewards. At a signal from the starter, the ribbon would drop and they could race.

Sullyan nudged Drum closer to Elias. "That large chestnut is our only serious rival," she whispered. "We should easily outrun the others. I think we should hang back and let the field thin out. Then the three of us can race properly on the second lap."

Elias raised his brows. "Do you never stop thinking about tactics, Brynne?"

She grinned. "It is what you pay me to do, your Majesty."

He grinned back. "Well said! All right, I like your plan. Why exhaust ourselves and risk our horses' legs when these also-rans will drop out on their own?"

"Exactly," she said.

✦ ✦ ✦ ✦ ✦

Taran leaned on the rail and studied the horses. He couldn't see many that looked like they might give Sullyan or the King any trouble. He returned Sullyan's wave and touched Jinella's arm, drawing her attention to the beginning of the race.

Jinella, however, wasn't paying him any heed. She was watching someone in the crowd, craning her neck to get a better view. Taran scanned the press of people that had gathered to watch the race, but couldn't make out who she was looking at. Suddenly, Lily gave a small squeal and Jinella stiffened. She turned to Taran, an expression of disgust on her face.

"Oh, Taran, look! Here comes that dreadful simple boy who lives in the nursery. I want to move farther down."

Taran glanced at the redheaded lad, who was rocking his body forward and back on the railing while he watched the riders prepare. "Why? He looks harmless enough. I think he likes the horses."

"It's the way he looks at you," she hissed behind her hand. "He's an adult, with an adult's feelings, but he has the mind and manners of a horrid little boy. And he dribbles! He frightens me, Taran. He's strange and I don't like him. Please let's move farther down."

Taran was irritated but couldn't ignore Jinella's distress. They moved farther along the rail, which meant he didn't have such a good view of the start.

"They're lining up," he said, straining forward for a better view. Jinella didn't seem interested in the slightest and hadn't once glanced at the horses. But neither did she want to relinquish his arm, so she had to endure his distraction. After all, the race would only take fifteen minutes.

Chapter Ten

There was one fair-goer who also had his mind on other things besides horse racing. Baron Reen strolled about the fair attended by two servants; one to carry his dark blue sunshade and one to carry his purchases. Not given to unnecessary spending, he had nevertheless made one very expensive purchase, intended as a gift for his niece. He had observed her more than once during the day, and smiled to see her hanging on the arm of her despised Artesan escort. They were talking, so she was hopefully learning much in the way of useful information. The Baron anticipated an interesting trawl of news. His gift would be both reward for her obedience and an ease to his conscience; not that he felt particularly guilty over his manipulation. After all, hadn't she done the same in begging him to bring her to court? Since she was here, she might as well prove useful.

Reen approached the race course with time to spare. He selected a shady spot near the finishing line, opposite the exit to the folly tunnel, and leaned against a tree. He had no need to stand at the railing like a commoner. His servants would keep his view of the race course clear. Satisfied, he glanced around.

His lip curled in distaste when he saw the shock-haired simple lad, the youth's eyes glued to the milling horses, a line of saliva drooling down his chin. Reen turned away, disgusted. He had nothing but contempt for the boy. The Baron despised anyone not fully in command of themselves, and couldn't understand why his Queen had ever seen fit to take the boy in. Her children found him amusing, he supposed, and it wasn't his place to question his lady's motives. Ignoring the crowd's rising excitement, he relaxed in the shade and permitted his manservant to prepare him slices of cool fruit.

✤ ✤ ✤ ✤ ✤

The horses wheeled and curveted, catching their riders' excitement. Foam dripped from their mouths as they impatiently tossed their heads. The booksmen were still calling the odds, but word was out and there were no more long odds to be had on Sullyan. Those who had given them at first were trying to think up ways to avoid paying out should she win.

The horses finally stilled long enough for the starter to flourish his flag. The ribbon dropped to the ground, shredded instantly by churning hooves as the eleven riders urged their mounts forward. Sullyan and Elias didn't surge ahead with the others but stayed at the back of the field as the horses careered toward the first obstacle: a line of post and rail fencing.

Two of the leading riders were unseated as their mounts, overexcited by the roar of the crowd and the press of horses, got too close and pitched over the top rail. They landed in a heap to great cries from the watching crowd, and those coming behind were forced to leap awkwardly over them. Both horses surged upright and galloped off. Their riders had been thrown clear. One limped badly when he struggled to his feet.

Sullyan and Elias were far enough back to see and avoid the mêlée. Their mounts leaped the fence cleanly farther down. Glancing over her shoulder, Sullyan could see the rider of the chestnut emulating their tactics and easing back on his horse's mouth. She grinned at him and saw his answering smile.

The field thundered toward a stand of trees growing along the banks of the Lox, a swift-flowing stream running down to Loxton Bay. It wasn't very wide, but it was deep and its bed was rocky.

The banks were steep and friable and would need careful handling to jump well. A few of the other horses had taken hold of their bits and wouldn't answer their riders' commands. One, a long-legged bay, took off far too soon with a mighty leap, and landed half in the water. The bank was so steep that he was unable to struggle out and his rider, half-unseated by the huge jump, only just stayed on. He had to pull his horse back into the stream and wade along until he could find a shallower bank to scramble up. He would be far behind when he finally managed to get out.

Another horse tried to refuse and, forced to jump by its rider, took off too late. The crumbling bank disappeared under its hooves. They made it across, but the horse pulled up lame, probably having strained a tendon. The field was down to seven already. Drum, Darius, and the chestnut were running together at the rear. Their riders eyed each other, trying to gauge their staying power. Sullyan was confident that Drum could outlast either of them in a flat race, but the obstacles in his path would tax his strength as much as theirs.

Toward the end of the first lap, another runner dropped out when his weight-cloth fell away over a huge fallen tree. That left six horses. Two of these were blowing hard and Sullyan didn't think they would last the course. Drum and Darius were not even sweating, and the chestnut didn't show signs of distress either. The last horse was an iron gray, one of the lean types she had first picked out as a possible rival. It was still running well and its rider was clinging expertly to its back. These four, then, were the contenders in the second lap.

In single file, they barreled through the tunnel under the folly and crossed the starting line again, flashing past the watching crowds. Sullyan vaguely heard voices yelling her name. Denny, Master Ardoch, Taran, and the other men were all urging her on, and she wondered how Elias would feel at his Guardsmen changing their allegiance. Feeling the time was right, she asked Drum to lengthen his stride.

He did so at once, and she knew that the huge stud was thoroughly enjoying himself. Bred for combat, power, and speed, he possessed a lively intelligence. She had nurtured this by involving him in as much challenging activity as possible to keep his brain sharp. He would recognize the race for what it was and give his strength and heart to his rider.

Noting her increase in speed, Elias asked the same of the colt. Darius was quite happy to keep up with his herd-mate and lengthened his stride obediently. He flattened his ears at the strange chestnut on his right, who was matching his pace and coming too close. The iron gray, pushed hard by its rider since leading though the tunnel, now began to fall back.

They flew the post and rails and approached the river again. One or two of the riderless horses were still milling about the course. Steered toward a clear section, Drum and Darius leaped the stream together, black beast and mahogany in perfect stride. The chestnut was only a second behind.

Sullyan smiled. She loved fast riding and was enjoying the race immensely. Elias glanced over at her and she began to laugh. This was her only failing; the speed of wild riding often made her laugh and she could lose concentration. Elias grinned to hear her, and all thoughts of the race disappeared from her mind in the wild exhilaration of her powerful mount, the wind of speed past her face, and the sheer joy of such rushing freedom. This was how she often felt when using her Artesan powers.

The chestnut was at last falling behind, unable to match the Manor horses for stamina. Emerging from the trees by the stream, Drum and Darius thundered round the top of the course, scarcely a nose between them. There were only three obstacles left: a huge fallen oak with a downward slope on the landing side, another post and rails, and the tunnel. The tunnel was the final and most difficult obstacle. Twenty yards long, dark and dank inside, it was only just wide enough for one horse at a time. Whoever reached it first was almost bound to win.

Fully stretched out now, both stallions laid their ears flat. Sullyan and Elias lay along necks sweaty from exertion. Nostrils red and extended, powerful hindquarters bunching and flexing, the two horses pelted headlong for the fallen tree.

Sullyan took a gentle feel on Drum's light bridle, bringing him instantly under control. Thoroughly obedient even when his blood was up, he marginally shortened his stride and flew the tree faultlessly. Elias, not knowing his mount so well, took more of a pull and Drum eased a nose in front.

But Darius was young and fit and he soon raked back Drum's lead. Sullyan could hear the crowds yelling encouragement and both mounts responded as their riders asked for yet more speed. Racing breakneck for the post and rails, Sullyan decided not to take a pull this time but trust to Drum's balance and fitness. She sat still and allowed him to measure his own stride. He flew the fence with ease and she laughed for sheer joy.

She heard Elias urging his younger horse on. Throwing caution away, he touched Darius with his heels just before the fence, and the colt made a mighty leap. He landed just ahead of his herd-mate and the King pushed him harder, stretching his lead as much as he could. Sullyan laughed breathlessly just behind him. It seemed Elias would make the tunnel entrance first, and there was nothing she could do about it.

✣ ✣ ✣ ✣ ✣

Seeing the horses approaching the tunnel, Baron Reen straightened. He eyed the tree growing a few yards beyond the tunnel mouth and nodded in satisfaction. Throwing away the rind of his fruit, he concentrated on the charging horses.

It was the most closely contested race anyone could remember. Darius flew into the tunnel, Drum hot on his haunches. The tunnel was dark after the bright afternoon sun and the going was slippery. Knowing the prize was surely his, Elias allowed Darius to slacken his pace, not wanting him to slip on the tunnel's treacherous floor. As the colt hurtled out into the brightness once more, the King laid himself along Darius's powerful neck. Blinded by the sun, Elias neither saw Reen's intense stare nor heard his quietly spoken word.

✤ ✤ ✤ ✤ ✤

Sullyan followed the mahogany colt as closely as she dared without Drum treading on his heels. She would use her mount's superior strength to draw abreast of Darius in the last few yards, for she had no intention of losing the race to Elias. They would cross the finish line nose and nose.

She was about to press heels to Drum's heaving sides when she felt a sudden, shocking surge through the substrate. With no knowledge of its origin or purpose, she had no chance of negating its effects. Horrified, she saw the ground in front of her suddenly buckle violently, heaving directly into the speeding horses' path. The sudden shifting of the ground beneath their feet caused the racing stallions to squeal in fear. There was a dreadful tearing sound, and then a deep *whump* as a tree toppled right across the course. Drum, slightly farther from the center of the disturbance, managed to keep his feet, but his wrenching swerve and valiant leap nearly unseated Sullyan.

She heard a great gasp from the crowd and not a few screams. Her heart stopped as Darius, closer to the toppled tree, was caught by the falling branches and sent flailing to the ground. Sliding, snorting, and squealing, he threw his rider in a wild tangle of arms and legs. Elias's body skidded along the earth and fetched up hard against the railings. With a sickening thump, he lay still.

Chapter Eleven

It was mid-afternoon, and Bulldog and Robin were relaxing under a warm summer sun. The morning's exercises had gone well and the leader of the Andaryan forces, Commander Barrin, was lounging on the ground beside them. They were drinking Bull's evilly strong fellan and listening to the soft strains of Cal's longwhistle, coming from where the dark-skinned young man was sitting, his eyes closed, lost in his music.

The rest of the men, both Albian and Andaryan, were gathered in groups, talking amongst themselves while waiting for the final exercise to begin. This last maneuver would take place within the forests to the east of the Citadel, and afterward there would be feasting. The Albians would return to their own realm the following day.

Each side had taken turns as the aggressor in the planned maneuvers, and it was now the Albians who would attempt the capture of a fictitious Andaryan-controlled strongpoint. Several of the junior officers had already been assigned temporary commands, and it was Robin's intention to give Cal command in this final phase. He had become increasingly impressed by the young man's grasp of tactics and the easy but confident manner with which he both gave and took orders. It reinforced Robin's decision to recommend Cal for promotion when the King came to inaugurate the new College. He had not yet mentioned this to Cal, but he did have Bull's full support as well as that of Cal's captain,

Dexter, both of whom shared Robin's opinion.

Although these were merely training exercises, both Robin and Barrin had posted scouts and sentries. There might be nothing for them to report on, but it was good practice for the men. So they were all surprised when they heard the sound of galloping hoof beats. Robin stood, trying to identify the rider. It turned out to be one of Barrin's scouts, and the Andaryan Commander frowned as he rose to meet the man.

The scout made straight for him, his horse scattering dirt as it slithered to a halt. Robin's puzzlement deepened as he registered the scout's distress. He couldn't hear precisely what the man was saying, but he did catch the words "under attack." He immediately barked commands at his own men, all of whom leaped for their mounts, weapons ready. He didn't know what Barrin was up to, but he wasn't going to let the Andaryan put one over on him by springing a surprise attack.

Barrin's expression was ominous as he left the scout and marched stiffly over to Robin. "I don't know what you think you're doing, Major, but you won't catch us out like that!" He abruptly grabbed the reins of his stallion.

Robin raised his brows. "Whatever it is, Commander, it has nothing to do with us."

Barrin snorted and prepared to mount. "You seriously expect me to believe that when there's an armed force of Albians heading straight for us? You've kept units in reserve, Major, it's obvious. Don't make the mistake of thinking me stupid!"

Robin shook his head. "Commander, I give you my word I know nothing about this. If there is an armed force from Albia anywhere near here, then let me assure you, it's not from the Manor. Neither is it under my command."

Barrin froze. "Then what the Void's going on? If it's not part of the exercise, we could be under attack for real!"

"We'd better go and see," said Robin. "We can't afford to let them approach the Citadel, whoever they are. You have command, Barrin. We'll back you up."

Barrin swore and sprang into his saddle. He approached the scout, who was panting after his hard ride. The man answered his Commander's new set of questions as best he could. Barrin swore again, barked orders to his lieutenants, and called tersely to Robin.

"They are about sixty strong, approaching from the northwest. Smoke was seen rising from two villages, so if this really isn't your doing those people are in deep trouble. I don't know what the raiders' objectives are, but we have to stop them. If you really want to help, cover the right flank."

Robin nodded. He and Bull formed their own men into units, with Dexter and Cal each at the head of about eighty men. Bull glanced at Robin as they took up their positions on the right of Barrin's forces.

"Sixty?" he murmured. "That's a sizeable force for casual raiders. What's going on? They can't really be Albians, can they? We haven't done that sort of thing for scores of years."

Robin shrugged. "I don't know, but I can't see why the scout would lie. Barrin's rattled, so it has to be real. We'd better be careful, Bull. I suggest we hang back a bit until we see how the land lies." He gave the big man a hard stare. "And if it comes to fighting, you're to keep out of it, do you hear?"

Bull returned the look and didn't reply.

They rode at a fast canter, following the scout's lead. The woodlands to the west and north of the Citadel weren't as dense as the forest to the southeast, and soon they saw the smoke that had alerted the scout. The man pointed, drawing Barrin's attention, and before they had gone much farther they all heard the shouts, screams, and unmistakable sounds of fighting. Barrin barked orders and surged ahead to repel the raiders.

Robin held his men back, allowing Barrin to engage first. But it was quickly obvious that this was no exercise, and also that their adversaries were unarguably human. Robin had no choice but to commit.

"Bull," he yelled, "take charge of Cal's unit, will you? Keep an eye on him for me."

The big man reluctantly drew rein, growling, "Yes, sir."

Robin felt a pang of sympathy for him. He was mindful of the instinctive reaction to fight that had ingrained itself in Bull over many years. He appreciated how hard it was to ignore once the blood was up. However, he also knew Bull's weakened heart couldn't take the strain, and he knew how vicious Sullyan's temper would be if any harm came to the big man. Bull knew it too. He wasn't happy to be ordered out of the fighting, but he obeyed Robin's command and told Cal to lead his men farther out on the flank to catch any stragglers.

And then there was no more time for thought. They were among the raiders and fighting through the trees. Steel met steel with deadly intent.

The battle was intense but short. Barrin and Robin fielded by far the superior force and the raiders' leader soon realized this. Once he saw the size of the company ranged against him, he turned and fled. They all heard his hornsman sound a retreat.

Robin's three units had become scattered through the trees. He and his own men were to the west, Dexter was off to the east, and Bull was behind them. The big man was still nursemaiding Cal, although his terse reports to Robin through the substrate indicated that Cal was doing very well.

Robin became aware that the raiders he was pursuing had vanished. One minute they could be glimpsed through the trees about eight hundred yards ahead; the next, they were gone. Suspecting an ambush, Robin slowed his men and wheeled about, searching for the raiders. There was no sign.

Bull, do you still have sight of the enemy?

No, came Bull's terse reply, *they've disappeared.*

Bring the men over here, will you?

Robin contacted Barrin through the substrate and received the same response. Puzzled, they regrouped, none of them with any explanations.

Riding back the way they had come, Robin dismounted by a group of dead raiders sprawled on the ground. Bull and Barrin followed suit. Crouching down, they examined the bodies. They were human, right enough, yet they bore no distinguishing marks of any kind. They wore a motley assortment of clothing, and their weapons were the sort anyone with a reasonable amount of coinage could obtain. Bull and Robin exchanged worried glances.

Barrin wasn't worried. He was furious. "How do you explain this, Major?" he demanded.

Robin stood and faced him. "I can't, Commander. They're human, that much is obvious, but as to who's behind this, I can't say. Someone must have given them access through the Veils, but none of these was an Artesan. Perhaps their leader was, although I didn't sense anyone working. Did anyone else?" The Artesans in the group shook their heads. "We'll have to make reports to the Hierarch and King Elias," continued Robin. "I assure you, Commander, we'll do our best to sort this out."

Barrin wasn't impressed. "And who's going to compensate the people of these villages? Their homes and livelihoods have been destroyed."

Robin bridled. "Who compensated our people when yours were raiding wholesale through the Albian countryside a few years ago?"

He felt Bull's restraining hand on his arm. "Let's not have the wake before the bloody funeral, gentlemen. The damage has been done. Let's see what we can do to help these poor people before we make our report."

Muttering under his breath, Barrin marshaled his men, checking that those with wounds were able to ride. Robin did the same. Once formed up, they approached the burning village. It was completely destroyed, and dead bodies lay in the street, including many women and children. Peasants and farmers all, they had been completely unprepared for such a vicious attack.

The few survivors gathered in the street once Barrin convinced them to come out of hiding. They regarded the Albians with fear. Disturbed, Robin signaled a withdrawal, leaving Barrin to reassure the villagers and tell them to make their way to the Citadel, where they would be cared for. The Commander's expression was grim when he finally left the ruined village and made for the second pall of smoke that was still rising into the sky.

When they reached it, the story was much the same. Robin again held his men back so as not to alarm the already terrified villagers, but it took Barrin some time to convince them that the Major's forces weren't there to finish what the raiders had started. He wasn't helped by the fact that one farmer had seen the raiders and overheard their leader telling his band that the King's man would reward them well for their work.

Robin felt sick when he heard this, and Bull's florid complexion reddened further. "But that's nonsense!" he blurted.

The farmer, who was clutching his pitchfork as if it was the only thing keeping him alive, stared belligerently up at Bull.

"You calling me a liar, human?" His slit-pupiled eyes blazed with anger. "I may only be a simple farmer, but I know what I damn well heard! Look what they've done to my home. Our village is burned to the ground. Can't deny that, can you? Getting greedy, your king, is he? Thinks he can take our land from us? Well, just let him try! You'll see we're not so frightened of you on your big horses when we band together. You'll not drive us from our homes."

He advanced on Bull, brandishing the pitchfork. Bull's stallion snorted and sidestepped, anticipating a charge. Robin, Dexter, and Cal all closed ranks around the big man to protect him should the need arise, but the farmer stopped short of attacking him. Instead, he spat forcefully on the ground at the horses' feet and glared at Bull in disgust.

Barrin turned to Robin. "I think you'd better leave. Let me deal with this. Go back to the Citadel. I'll follow on when I've made some arrangements for these poor people."

He turned dismissively, leaving Robin no option but to take his advice.

✤ ✤ ✤ ✤ ✤

It was evening, and Robin was facing a furious Lord General Anjer. The planned feast had been canceled; the food would be distributed among the surviving villagers when they arrived at the Hierarch's gates the next day.

"I honestly can't tell you any more, Lord General," said Robin as he finished his report. "The raiders were human, but I can assure you they didn't come from King Elias."

"But the farmer definitely heard one of the raiders say that the King would reward them?" put in the Hierarch, throwing a calming glance at Anjer who was bristling with righteous rage, his black eyes blazing. Anjer wanted Barrin's report, but the Commander had not yet returned. He had wrung every possible detail from Robin and now wanted to go over it all again. The young man felt like an overridden horse; exhausted and lame.

"Yes, Majesty," he replied, as patiently as he could. "But as I've already said, King Elias has no reason to order raids into Andaryon. Even if he did, he wouldn't send common brigands. He would order his forces out, and then we at the Manor would know about it. I beg you, Majesty, be reasonable. My Lord General, surely you realize that if King Elias had a grievance serious enough to warrant punitive action, his first move would be to send Colonel Sullyan here as his Envoy?"

He appealed to the two powerful men, his hands spread before him. At the mention of Sullyan's name, Anjer's temper cooled. Aside for his admiration for her, she was directly responsible for the fact that he now had a baby daughter, and he had even named her after Sullyan, calling her Brianne.

Pharikian nodded wearily. "He's right, Anjer. She'd have been here long ago if there was any kind of problem."

"Very well, Major," said Anjer curtly, "I'll accept what you say. But you understand my anger. Two villages destroyed and all those people killed or made homeless! This has come with no warning, and just when relations between our races were improving. It's a very serious development and we need to find out who's behind it."

"I agree, sir, and I'll be reporting to both General Blaine and Colonel Sullyan tonight. It may be that they know something about this, although I think I would have been told if they did.

"Majesty, my Lord, please rest assured that we'll do everything we can to sort this out. I know that neither the King nor General Blaine would do anything to jeopardize relations with Andaryon. I can state that with no fear of contradiction."

Chapter Twelve

Sullyan was closest to the fallen Elias. She wheeled Drum around, leaping from his back before he completed the move, and sprinted for the body of the King. As she reached him, many of the bystanders came rushing toward them, including Baron Reen, who was brushing leaves and twigs from his clothes and roaring loudly for help.

Sullyan flung herself down beside the unconscious Elias and laid a hand on his brow. Before she could reach into him to begin healing, rough hands seized her shoulders and thrust her violently away. She stared up into the furious face of Baron Reen.

"Get away from him, you treacherous witch! You've done enough damage. I'm not going to let you finish what you started."

Shocked by the accusation, she made no response as others clustered around the prone body of the King, feeling for a pulse and loosening the collar of his shirt. She stood and backed off, Reen still staring savagely at her, his hand on the hilt of his sword.

"What the Void happened, Sullyan? Is the King all right?"

She turned to see Taran looking down at Elias with a horrified expression. Jinella and her maid were right behind him, tears in Lily's eyes.

"Is he dead?" shrilled Jinella, her hand at her mouth. "Has she killed him?"

Taran frowned at her. "What are you talking about? No one's killed him. It was an accident, that's all." He swung back to face Sullyan and froze when he saw her expression. "Wasn't it?"

She made a negative gesture and he fell silent. When she felt his tentative contact, she slammed down her shield. Taran gasped with the abrupt pain of it and gave her an injured look, not understanding her caution. But that brief moment of sensing some unknown Artesan manipulating Earth had alarmed and frightened Sullyan, and she wasn't taking any chances. Explanations would have to wait. Ignoring Taran's puzzled hurt, she turned back to Elias.

His physician was now in attendance, having been close by at the Queen's insistence. The King was showing signs of regaining consciousness, and there were sighs of relief all round. The physician helped him to sit, although he still looked badly shaken. He looked around in groggy alarm.

"Brynne?" he croaked.

Brushing aside Reen's threat—he still had his hand on his sword—she shouldered past him to kneel by Elias's side. Looking deeply into his fogged blue eyes, she felt disturbed by what she saw.

"Just stay still, your Majesty," she soothed, "all will be well. Will you permit?"

Before the Baron could stop her, she sent her senses into Elias. There was bruising to his skull where his head had hit the railing and she reduced it, calming the resultant swelling before it could affect the King's brain. She could hear Reen protesting all the while. He was proclaiming loudly that the accident had been her doing, and telling the crowd that he had heard her give some command or other just before the tree toppled. They all knew Artesans could do things like that, didn't they? Was he the only one to hear her laughing before the tree fell?

He wasn't, of course. Others had heard her laughter and the people started to mutter. Taran regarded the crowd with concern, frowning as their murmurs grew louder. Sullyan ignored them. She was concentrating on Elias, who was returning to himself. His physician watched her carefully and with suspicion, but as the King had called for her, he couldn't force her away.

Elias felt his head gingerly and raised his eyes. "Thank you, Brynne," he breathed. "I feel better now."

The physician helped him stand and Sullyan looked round for their mounts. A Kingsman had already caught Drum's bridle and was leading him over, but Darius, who had struggled shakily to his feet after his crashing fall, was snorting and backing away. Sullyan soon saw why. With hands outstretched and tears pouring down his face, the deformed youth Huw was hobbling toward the colt.

"Get that imbecile away from here!" shouted Reen, a mixture of fear and disgust on his face. Huw was sobbing, mumbling about the "poor horse," obviously distressed to think the colt might be hurt. The young stallion, still trembling from his dreadful fall, tossed his head and sidled away, alarmed by the youth's jerky movements. The Baron made a lunge for Huw's arm, but the lad shrieked and dodged him awkwardly, terror in his mismatched eyes.

Sullyan moved to intercept him. "Gently, Huw," she soothed, and reached instinctively for his mind to pacify him. She encountered a void, a blank wall, which was unexpected and gave her pause. But the King's condition was her main concern and she couldn't afford to be distracted. She had to calm the boy in order to reach Darius, and they had to get Elias back to the castle.

"The horse has taken no hurt," she murmured. "He is only frightened. And the King will be well too, although he will have a sore head for a while."

Huw clutched her hand. "Hurt head? Horse not hurt?"

"Not hurt, Huw, they will both be well. Come, see for yourself, but gently."

Pulling him by the hand, she led him toward Darius, using her soft, trilling whistle to calm the anxious beast. The horse allowed her approach and she laid her hand on his nose. She heard Huw perfectly imitating her characteristic whistle, and was amazed. Darius responded by snuffling the boy's hair, making him giggle. It calmed him and he smiled, showing uneven teeth.

"Horse not hurt. Pretty Brynne."

"There, Huw. Now we must lead the horse to the King. You can walk with us. I think he likes you." She disengaged her hand and took Darius's bridle. Huw just stood where he was, staring with wide eyes as she led the colt toward Elias.

Before she reached him, Baron Reen stepped into her path, his hand still on his sword. Darius snorted and threw up his head. Drum whinnied loudly.

"Stay back, you treacherous witch," snarled Reen, drawing his sword and pointing it at her breast. Unarmed, she halted, unable to counter his threat. Out of the corner of her eye she saw Ardoch come forward, about to draw his own weapon. She signaled him and he subsided.

Elias, however, had heard Reen's words. "Baron," he rasped, "that's enough! This was an accident. It was no one's fault. If I hear you accusing Colonel Sullyan again, you'll have me to deal with, do you hear?"

"But I heard her!" protested Reen, falling silent when he saw the King's furious expression.

"I said enough!" Elias raised his voice to the crowd. "And that goes for the rest of you. This was a simple accident, there was no intent to injure and no one is to blame. Was anyone else hurt?"

No one came forward, and Elias glared hard at those around him. "I don't want to hear any wild rumors circulating the city. Do I make myself plain?"

The crowd muttered as he turned a pale face to Sullyan. "Brynne, will you accompany me back to the castle? I think we both need some quiet and cool refreshment." She inclined her head and he raised his voice again. "The rest of you, go back to the fair and enjoy what is left of the day. To those of you with bets, I pledge that all wagers will be honored once the placings have been agreed." He waved the crowd away and they began to disperse, still muttering among themselves.

Sullyan beckoned to Taran, who came to her side at once. Someone helped the King to mount and he started slowly back toward the castle, waving off his physician's plea to wait for a carriage. Sullyan and Taran walked behind him, the Colonel leading Drum. Baron Reen stalked at the rear.

Lady Jinella, abandoned by Taran without a second thought, could only stand and watch them go.

Queen Sofira was at the castle steps to meet her lord. She stood imperiously on the top step; perfectly straight, slim, and tall, her honey-blonde hair piled on her head in elaborate coils. There was disdain in her pale and angular face. Even her eyes were stony gray, no hint of softness anywhere. Her cheeks were sunken and her lean body showed no sign of having borne two children.

She stood looking down on the little group approaching the steps, no concern in her flat expression. Her eyes flicked from Sullyan to Reen before she turned her attention to Elias.

"So, it finally happened. Haven't I warned you not to ride in these silly races, my Lord?" Her voice was brittle. "When will you stop taking these ridiculous risks?"

Sullyan noticed Elias closing his eyes briefly, but whether from the effects of his fall or as protection from the Queen's spite, she could not say.

"Bring him inside," Sofira ordered. "Not you!" she snapped as Sullyan and Taran made to follow.

Elias raised his head as he mounted the steps and he stared hard at his Queen. "They are here at my request, Madam." His voice was low and neutral, but it was made of iron.

She shot him one look and backed down. "Whatever my Lord desires," she said, stalking before them into the castle. Sullyan exchanged a look with Taran.

They helped Elias into his private suite, and he sank into an easy chair with a great sigh of relief. The inevitable bruises and stiffness from his fall were making themselves felt, and Sullyan wondered if she would be permitted to help him. Yet she made no offer. Taking into account all that had happened and what she was beginning to suspect, she didn't feel like pushing herself forward right now.

The Queen sent a servant scurrying for refreshment before crossing to the window and seating herself in a straight-backed chair. The light from the afternoon sun obscured her features from those in the room. It was a blatant act, and Sullyan wondered at it. Baron Reen followed them in and moved to stand behind Sofira's chair, where he could observe everyone.

"Well, my Lord?" the Queen said. "Are you going to tell me what happened?"

Elias sighed. "A tree fell. My horse stumbled and threw me, Madam. That's all."

Sullyan studied his face. He was still very pale and she hoped he would let himself rest soon.

"With respect, your Majesty," said Reen in a voice entirely devoid of respect, "that isn't precisely what happened, is it?"

Elias sat straighter in his chair. "What exactly was it you thought you saw, Baron?"

Reen was unfazed by Elias's tone. He had the protection of the Queen's presence. She smiled up at him. An unhealthy smile, and the first real emotion Sullyan had seen her display.

"Yes, my Lord Baron," she said, "would you be so kind as to tell us what you saw?"

Reen moved to the center of the room. "Madam, I happened to be standing near the finishing line and so had an uninterrupted view of the race course."

How convenient, thought Sullyan.

"I saw the riders come toward the folly tunnel. Colonel Sullyan was slightly behind his Majesty at that point. It was obvious to me that she was desperate to get past him and win the race."

He stared at Sullyan as he said this and met her agate glare. He continued, unperturbed by the hostility in her gaze.

"She was pushing her horse hard and causing his Majesty to ride faster than was prudent. I could hear her laughing as he was forced into such recklessness."

Taran made a tiny movement, as if he would protest. He knew why Sullyan had been laughing. She motioned urgently with her hand and he stilled.

Reen did not notice and continued his fabrication.

"As the horses came out of the tunnel, it was clear his Majesty would win the race. Just then, the Colonel noticed me. She saw her chance. She knows I disapprove of her kind, and she saw an opportunity to remove me. I heard her say something that sounded like a word of command, and suddenly the earth heaved, causing a tree beside the course to fall toward me. As it came down, it caught the King's horse, causing it to stumble and throw the King onto the rails. The Colonel's mount, of course, was able to avoid the disturbance because she guided it round where she knew the earth would buckle."

He turned, appealing directly to the Queen. "I was in considerable danger, Your Highness, and barely escaped serious injury. Yet my safety is not my prime concern. The Colonel's hatred of me nearly cost the King his life. She must be tried and dismissed from his service."

Queen Sofira rose from her seat, anger pinching her hard face. "How do you answer these charges, Colonel Sullyan?"

Before Sullyan could respond, Elias came to his feet.

"Peace, Madam! There are no charges to be answered here, only vicious and unsubstantiated accusations from one who has an unreasoning dislike of the Colonel's kind."

Queen Sofira opened her mouth to argue, but Elias stared her down. "I would bid you remember that the Colonel is a member of my forces, Madam, a valued and respected one at that. If any charges were to be brought against her, they would have to be approved by me. Since I was personally involved and would be the aggrieved party if these ridiculous allegations had any shred of truth to them, I say there is no case to answer.

"That will be the end of the affair, Madam. Do I make myself clear?"

At this reprimand before witnesses, the Queen's face turned paler still. She turned from her husband's anger, presenting her unbending back to them all. Reen, however, was still staring venomously at Sullyan.

"Baron!" said the King.

Reen flicked him a glance, realizing he could go no further. "As your Majesty commands," he said, barely inclining his head.

Elias wasn't satisfied. "I believe you owe my Colonel an apology, Baron."

Sullyan wished he would let the matter drop. Forcing Reen to apologize would only stoke his resentment. With stiff grace, Reen grated, "You have my apologies, Colonel."

She inclined her head politely, not trusting herself to answer. Turning instead to Elias, she said, "Your Majesty, I ask your permission to withdraw. You have had a very nasty shock and ought to rest. If you have further need of my services, I am at your command."

She knew Elias could not speak frankly to her in the presence of either his Queen or the Baron, and since he could not order Sofira to go and she would not part with Reen, any discussions would have to wait. Elias gave his permission and the two Artesans bowed themselves out.

Sullyan and Taran walked slowly back to the race course, intent on examining the area of Earth-shift. As they walked, she told Taran what she had sensed at the time of the incident and asked him if he remembered who had been standing near the railing when the tree fell.

He thought carefully.

"Well, there was Jinny and me, of course, Denny, Master Ardoch, and a few of the King's Guard. I also saw the Baron—oh, and that simple lad, Huw. I didn't see anyone else I knew."

Sullyan considered his words. "Except for you, none of those you mentioned has any Artesan skills. Of course, the person responsible need not have been close. They would only need to know which tree, and be signaled at the precise time." She eyed Taran. "What really bothers me is the determination of whoever was behind this afternoon's attack. Clearly, they were perfectly willing to see both me and Elias injured, or even killed. And that throws up another question. Who exactly was the intended target?"

Taran's eyes widened at this new speculation. Sullyan carried on. "It puts me uncomfortably in mind of Rykan's challenge on the Hierarch, and causes me to question our theories as to the real motives driving our man, whoever he is. The gracious Baron openly protests against our kind and would clearly delight in our downfall, but now I wonder whether he would also support a conspiracy to remove Elias, a king who makes no secret of his support for Artesans."

She frowned at her own musings. "Yet if that is the case, then surely the Baron risks showing his hand by casting such vehement accusations? Or was it that he merely saw an opportunity to discredit me? Because of his revulsion for our kind, indeed, for anyone who is not Albian, I find it hard to believe that he is more deeply involved. Surely he would not be able to control his repugnance or demean himself so far as to deal with our mysterious Artesan? But if he can, might he also have had dealings with Rykan?

"And there is still the question of whether the Artesan behind these attacks is cooperating willingly or being coerced."

She shook her head. Such thoughts were disturbing. "From what we have learned about Queen Sofira and the Baron, I doubt either would stoop so low as to deal with an Artesan or outlander. If either of them is involved, they must be using an intermediary. If they were Rykan's backers, they must have been planning to silence him somehow once he had overthrown the Hierarch. For how could they trust him once he had gained such power? I seriously doubt Rykan would have been permitted to keep the Staff had his challenge succeeded. I believe it would have been the instrument of his death, as was intended for so many others. I fervently hope it was the only one of its kind. At least the incident today bore none of the hallmarks of such a weapon."

She glanced at Taran, her eyes clouded. "My friend, I am talking in circles when what we need are facts. We must sift the substrate and see if we can glean any clues that might lead us to our adversary."

They arrived at the spot of the Earth-shift, where already servants were beginning to clear away the fallen tree. As they stood there, preparing to cast their senses through the substrate, Denny and Master Ardoch approached them, demanding to know what had happened and how the King fared. Sullyan briefly gave them the details and asked them to watch while she worked. There were still fair-goers about, and some were glancing curiously at them, no doubt recognizing her from the earlier incident. Sullyan was keen to know if anyone would show undue interest or concern in what they were doing. The two men readily agreed.

Once she had instructed Taran in what she required, they both used their metasenses to trawl through the substrate, searching for a signature or any clue to their adversary's pattern.

One pass later and they exchanged glances.

"Nothing?" asked Sullyan. Taran shook his head. "Then link with me, please," she said. He obediently meshed his pattern with hers and they used their pooled resources to do another sweep.

Still nothing.

Puzzled now, as it was virtually impossible to influence one of the elements without leaving a single trace, Sullyan suggested a Powersink. Taran smiled. He had not experienced one for many months. Sensing his excitement she asked, "Will you be able to cope?"

"I'll do my best," he said.

A warm clasp of the hand was his reward, and he laid out his pattern. Sullyan overlaid it with hers, and as the two imprints merged, blended, and strengthened, a soul-thrilling Powersink flashed into being. Their respective powers intensified, amplified by this method, and Taran reeled from the enormity of it. Once more, he received her steadying touch on his arm and was aware of her gaze as she gave him time to accustom himself.

"Are you stable, Taran?" she asked, no urgency in her tone.

He took a deep breath and let it out again, slowly. "I am now."

"Well done," she murmured, sensing his warm rush of pride.

Drawing on the vastly expanded well of power, they each did a separate pass through the substrate. Sullyan's frustration at their lack of success was evident from her expression, and also from the profanity she uttered as they broke their link.

"I cannot understand it, Taran," she said, surfacing from the

Powersink's glory. "There should have been some trace of him! The working I felt was very sure, very confident, and few indeed would be able to cause such a surge through Earth without leaving a sign. We are dealing with a very powerful Artesan here, my friend. We must be very careful." She deliberately captured his gaze. "That care must be applied also to our communications with each other. If the Artesan behind these events is as skilled as I suspect, he may be able to eavesdrop without our knowledge."

Taran was alarmed. "Is that possible?"

She shrugged, unwilling to commit. "I need to speak with Pharikian. Until then, act on the assumption that it is."

Denny and Ardoch reported on the unremarkable behavior of the fair-goers. "What will you do now?" asked Denny.

Sullyan considered this, her eyes unfocused. "Two facts are known. One: Baron Reen was conveniently on hand today and was quick to accuse me and voice his disapproval. Two: he had the unquestioning support of the Queen. In light of this, and in the absence of any other suspects, I suggest we concentrate on Reen for the moment. Owyn, you say he is bound to accompany the King when we return to the Manor?"

"Without a doubt. He's Elias's despised but inescapable shadow."

"Then I propose we use the Baron's prejudice against him. On the journey, I will take every opportunity to anger and unsettle him. Taran, you will observe him as closely as you can while his attention is on me. Try to remember everything he says and does. We will try to force a slip, make him say something he should not, and maybe that way we can further our investigations."

Master Ardoch nodded his approval. "I think I'll come with ye when the King rides out tomorrow," he mused. "This could be interesting, and it's been a while since I visited the Manor. The exercise will do me good."

Sullyan raised her brows and he smiled back, showing his teeth. "I have no love for yon Baron, lassie. I'll back ye up, and together we'll see if we can't force something out of him. Now, ye both need a drink and I know just where to get one."

✤ ✤ ✤ ✤ ✤

Baron Reen and Queen Sofira sat alone in the Queen's solar. The Queen sat straight-backed in a plain wooden chair, her hands folded in her lap. The Baron sat across from her, twirling a crystal goblet in his hand and watching the play of light through the ruby wine it contained.

Queen Sofira sniffed. "So that was the famed Colonel Sullyan? I can't see why Elias gets so excited about her. She's very small and no great beauty, in my opinion."

The Baron set down his goblet. "That may be so, Madam, but we shouldn't make the mistake of underestimating her. The King's forces think well of her and despite the impropriety of her position, she wouldn't have won the approval of so many military men merely with her looks. Whatever our thoughts on the matter, we mustn't forget that she has a reputation for shrewdness as well as great skill with the sword." He shivered. "Not to mention her… arcane talents."

Sofira's sharp face showed her disgust. "It's so unnatural! But you're right, Hezra, of course. She's managed to survive very well, despite our many attempts to remove her. Damn that outlander Rykan for being such a greedy fool! He should have killed her, like he was told to, when he had the chance."

"He should have taken better care of that weapon you drained the Treasury to finance!" growled Reen. "Had he not been so inattentive and allowed it to be stolen, he would not have had trouble with her in the first place. With him on the Andaryon throne and beholden to you for it, we would have had access to all the spellsilver we desired. Not only did his arrogant carelessness result in his death and the destruction of the Staff, it also caused us considerable inconvenience. Now we will to have to resort to our second plan in order to accumulate enough silver. And that means more traffic with those damned Andaryan outlanders. The sooner we put a stop to such blasphemy, the better."

Reen felt his face grow hotter as he spoke. His intense feelings and deeply held beliefs concerning outlanders consumed him, as usual. He struggled for calm.

The Queen, well used to his rants, nevertheless regarded him with concern. "I know you believe our action against this demon ruler is justified, Hezra, and you know I support your plan, but I'm still not happy about our side of it. Is it truly necessary?" There was a faint hint of pleading in her voice, and she glanced down at her hands, which twisted together in her lap.

Having composed himself, Reen hastened to reassure her. "We have been through this before, Madam. In order to convince both rulers of the gravity of the situation, my plan may be needed *in its entirety*. But you have no need for concern. Izack and I have things well in hand. No harm will befall him, you have my sworn word on that."

The Queen nodded reluctantly and sighed. "What is our next step?"

"My men are even now in the Fifth Realm, carrying out my orders. I should hear from them soon." Reen smiled unpleasantly. "And I intend to pay a visit to my niece. She spent the day with that captain who came with Colonel Sullyan. She seemed quite taken with him, silly girl, no doubt due to her rescue in the forest. You know what simpletons young women are. One gallant gesture and their hearts melt. But I told her to get as much information out of him as possible, and perhaps she learned something I can use."

"Will she do as you bid her, if she's that enamored of him?"

"Oh yes, Madam, she knows what's good for her. But even if

she fails me, we still have our contact at the Manor. I have great hopes for him. He hates and fears Colonel Sullyan as much as we do. And when I tell him of our other little plan, he will have access to their internal dealings as well. Imagine that, Madam, a spy in the middle of their camp! He should prove most effective."

He raised his goblet to the Queen and she returned the gesture, smiling coyly over the rim of her priceless glass.

Chapter Thirteen

Before retiring for the night, Sullyan prepared for her scheduled report to General Blaine. She knew he would be as disturbed as she by the events of the day. Settling herself on the edge of the bed, she quested for contact.

She raised him at once, but the General gave her no time to report her news. She listened in alarm as he tersely described the raids in Andaryon.

Were there any casualties, Mathias?

Only flesh wounds. The men are all safe and returning home. The Hierarch is greatly upset and the Lord General is furious.

Yes, she said, imagining the huge man's snapping black eyes and bristling mustache. *I expect he is. He has every right to be. Did Robin find any clues as to who they were or who sent them?*

Nothing conclusive. None of the dead wore livery or bore markings. You'd better tell Elias about this before you set out tomorrow. We can't have him finding out from someone else.

This alarming news underscored the seriousness of her own, and she quickly told Blaine about the day's events. When she reluctantly admitted that she could not rule out the possibility that it was actually an attempt on the King's life or hers, the General was shocked and horrified.

Make sure he brings a large and trusted escort with him tomorrow, Brynne. I'd rather he didn't come if what you suspect is true, but knowing Elias, you won't be able to dissuade him.

Sullyan assured him that Elias's honor guard would consist of the best men. Trusting her to keep the King safe, he broke their contact. Sullyan then reached for Taran's mind. She wanted to tell him of the Andaryan raids before he heard the news from Cal. He responded sleepily and it was clear he was preparing for bed, but when she reminded him of the possibility of an Artesan eavesdropper, he immediately agreed to come to her room.

✤ ✤ ✤ ✤ ✤

Frightened as she was by the King's accident that afternoon, Jinella's overriding emotion was outrage at Taran's casual abandonment of her at the snap of the Colonel's fingers. He had made her no excuses and hadn't even troubled to bid her farewell. Seething and slighted, she was forced to make her own way back to the castle, totally unprotected, through the press of shocked fair-goers. She fumed and cursed under her breath as she went, thinking that even if he had mentioned Sullyan's name far too often for her liking, he had behaved gallantly toward her up until then. She had expected better of him.

By the time she reached the castle, her anger and self-pity had risen to overwhelming levels. She stormed up to her suite and swept into her bedchamber, slamming the door in Lily's face. Throwing herself onto the bed, she indulged in a fit of bitter tears. It lasted some time. Finally, having purged herself of the worst of her pique, she emerged and allowed Lily to repair her tear-stained face. Outwardly she was calm, but jealousy made her sullen company for the rest of the day.

Two or three medicinal glasses of wine and some sympathetic words from Lily eventually calmed Jinella's wounded pride. Having taken time to reflect, she realized the awful significance of the day's events. Someone had actually tried to kill the King, and even a man as honorable as Taran could surely be excused a lapse of manners under such dreadful circumstances. The safety of their monarch took precedence over all other concerns, and Taran was a captain of the King's forces after all.

Following this reasoning, Jinella became convinced she should forgive him. She decided that a late evening call to his room, with herself in a state of vulnerable distress, seeking comfort and reassurance, might generate some interesting consequences. She told Lily she was retiring to bed with a headache brought on by the worry of the day. The presence of her maid at her side would not do at all, and she gave Lily strict instructions not to disturb her.

Alone in her bedchamber, she changed into a simple white velvet dress. It could almost be a nightgown and was intended to make her appear young and virginal. As indeed she was. She smiled at her reflection in the mirror. After an appropriate length of time, she slipped from her suite and silently paced the darkening halls.

She had barely rounded the final corner when she saw the door to Taran's room open. He stepped outside. She was about to call his name, but stopped. He was wearing only his breeches, and had his back to her. She watched him appreciatively, admiring his naked torso. She found it easy to imagine her hands on that smooth flesh, and how it would feel to have his strong arms around her. Wondering where he was going so late and in such a state of undress, she waited where she was.

Then she saw him open the door to Sullyan's rooms. The Colonel must be expecting him because he didn't knock, and she heard the Artesan woman's soft greeting as he entered and closed the door. Jinella felt her heart clench. Pale and shaking, her eyes wide and her expression grim with shock, she concealed herself behind the long drapes at one of the windows. There she waited.

It seemed like an eternity before her worst fears were realized.

Taran reappeared, running his hands through tousled hair. Sullyan stood behind him, wearing only a man's green shirt, which left very little to the imagination. Jinella could scarcely believe her eyes. "Shameless hussy!" she hissed, her teeth tightly clenched to still their tremor. She saw Sullyan place intimate fingers on Taran's arm, and saw the man's warm answering smile as he clasped her hand. He bid her goodnight. They didn't kiss, but that familiar touch said it all. Then he went to his own door, and closed it behind him.

Trembling with renewed rage, hot tears of jealousy and betrayal running down her cheeks, Jinella collapsed against the wall.

Eventually, worry that some castle servant might find her in this state roused her. She stumbled blindly back to her suite, throwing the door open when she reached it. Unable to hold back the tears any longer, she sank to the floor, sobbing loudly.

Her cries woke her maid, who ran out into the antechamber. Thinking her mistress had been safely abed, Lily had no idea what to do. She stood over Jinella, wringing her hands.

"Whatever is it, my Lady? Are you ill? Shall I call the physician?"

Jinella couldn't speak, couldn't tell Lily how heartbroken she was. She stopped her maid when Lily moved to call for the physician, but she refused to be comforted. Her hysteria mounted and Lily panicked, breaking away from Jinella's grasp. "If you won't have the physician, my Lady, I'll have to send for your uncle. Maybe he can calm you."

Lily rang for a servant and sent the woman scurrying for Baron Reen.

✥ ✥ ✥ ✥ ✥

Reen had decided to question his niece in the morning, before he left for the Manor with the King. Jinella was not an early riser, and her uncle intended to rouse her before her usual time; a ploy intended to unsettle her and encourage her to divulge what she had learned. After leaving the Queen's solar, he spoke with his personal Commander, Izack, and learned of the progress of his plans in Andaryon. Satisfied, he retired to his private chambers and was enjoying a leisurely brandy when the worried servant rapped on his chamber door.

Reen was irritated at being disturbed so late, especially when he learned that the cause was a childish fit of female vapors. Unmarried and childless, Reen had little patience with children. Jinella might be a grown woman, but he still thought of her as the spoiled child she had been before coming to court. When he arrived at her door and found her still indulging in hysterics, he was in no mood to be gentle.

"For Perdition's sake, girl, be quiet! You'll wake the whole castle. Are you determined to humiliate me? Control yourself. Tell me what's wrong and why I've been dragged here in the middle of the night. I warn you, there'd better be a damned good reason or you'll regret it!"

His imperious manner was just what Jinella needed. She allowed Lily to dry her tears and took several sobbing gulps of air. Lily guided her to a chair and she collapsed into it. Reen loomed over her like a thunderhead.

"Now, you silly goose, tell me what has upset you."

Jinella tried to compose herself, but a desperate light came into her eyes. Her voice sounded strangled, painful.

"He betrayed me, Uncle!" she cried. "Oh, he hurt me so much."

Reen's blood froze. "What?" he roared, heedless now of waking the whole castle. He gripped Jinella's upper arms tightly. "The bastard forced himself on you? Good gods, I'll carve out his liver!"

Jinella gasped, realizing what he thought. "No, nothing like that, Uncle! I didn't mean.... It's just that he assured me he was unattached—*she* assured me he was unattached—and all the time they've been seeing each other! I knew there was something between them, but he denied it. And now, tonight, I saw it with my own eyes. Oh, how could they do that to me, Uncle? How could they be so cruel?"

An unholy glee kindled in Reen's breast and he released his niece's arms. Seating himself in a chair across from her, he studied her pale face, her red-rimmed eyes, and her wronged expression. Privately, he smiled.

"Calm yourself, my dear. Lily, get your mistress a glass of wine. Get me one, too."

Lily curtseyed and obeyed. Jinella sipped at the strong ruby vintage, her distress gradually fading. Eyeing her over his own glass, Reen was pleased to see her more composed.

"Now, start from the beginning, my dear, and tell me everything. Tell me how he seemed, what he did, and how he behaved toward you. Tell me all the little signs you saw that told you they were enamored of each other. And then tell me what you saw this evening that finally convinced you."

Tears coming to her eyes again, Jinella obliged. She struggled to stay calm as she related her memories, and all the subtle signs she had seen without fully realizing their import. In a choked voice, she told him everything.

Her uncle sat quietly, his hands clasped around his wine glass, occasionally sipping but always attentive, ready with a sympathetic look or a click of the tongue at the many slights she had suffered. When she came to the events of the past hour and he heard what she had seen, his face took on an expression of righteous outrage.

"Well," he said when she was done, careful to conceal his glee, "you have had a very lucky escape, my dear. I will forbear to say that I warned you against associating with his kind, but I think you have done exceptionally well and carried yourself with admirable dignity in the face of this terrible shock. I have a little something in my rooms which might serve to console you. I will give it to you in the morning. But for now, my dear, you need to rest and recover from this dreadful ordeal.

"Never fear, Jinella, your inheritance is safe. I think you richly deserve what your father left you. I will personally see to it that these people pay for the injury they have caused you, you have my word on that. And I have no doubt whatsoever that we will find you an eminently suitable match here at court, and you will have the life and security you were born to.

"I am very pleased with you, niece. Very pleased indeed."

By the time he left her, Jinella was feeling soothed and vindicated. Reen, though, was chuckling inwardly at this rare and unlooked-for opportunity. It must be a sign from his God, he thought. Why else should Jinella have needed rescuing in the forest? Why else would it be those two who answered that need? He knew he would never have discovered their sordid little deception by himself, but his niece had been ideally situated to sniff it out. He hugged his delight to his chest. Trust a woman to uncover another woman's secrets!

His gorge rose when he thought of those two unnatural beings behaving so wantonly in the King's very castle, but he knew what a powerful weapon this was. Not only was it one he could hand to his disaffected young contact at the Manor, it was also something he could work on now, through his influence over the King's Guard. All it would take was a small gold coin placed in the hand of Jinella's maid, along with instructions as to what rumors to spread. How easy it would be to discredit and wound his enemies, proving beyond doubt that oaths, even those of marriage, meant less than nothing to these Artesans; a fact he had long suspected.

The presence of such a young and attractive woman as the Colonel among the lusty males of the King's fighting forces was as unhealthy as it was provocative, and he could use this incident as yet another lever with which to pry at Elias's misguided policies. What a gift it was!

Almost laughing aloud, he made for the Queen's apartments. He knew she would be alone at this hour for she and Elias only ever tolerated each other at best and avoided too much contact, and she would be as pleased as he with this latest turn of events.

✤ ✤ ✤ ✤ ✤

They were due to leave Port Loxton around mid-morning. Sullyan was thankful it wasn't earlier, as it gave her the chance to recover from yet another serious bout of nausea. She couldn't even bring herself to drink fellan that morning as the mere thought made her stomach heave, and she regretted permitting Denny to pour her that wine last night. She really ought to know better. Instead, she forced herself to eat some dry bread and, finally, she began to feel better.

King Elias readily granted her the private interview she asked for. His steward showed her into the King's presence, and she didn't miss the disdainful look the man gave her. She knew how many people had heard Reen's accusation the day before, and she wasn't surprised at some of the odd looks she received from the servants that morning.

Elias welcomed her into his private sitting room and looked narrowly at her. "Are you quite well, Brynne? You look a little pale this morning."

"I will be well, Elias, I thank you. I should know by now not to drink red wine in the evening."

"Shouldn't we all?" He smiled as he sat down. "I'm glad you asked to see me. I wanted to talk to you about yesterday. Was that 'accident' what I suspect it was?"

"I fear so, Elias. It had to be the work of an Artesan. And no," she forestalled his question with a raised hand, "I have no idea who was responsible. Taran and I made a thorough study of the substrate yesterday. Whoever it was left no trace that we could discover."

"Is that unusual?" The King leaned back in his chair, stretching out his long legs. Elias was dressed in leather breeches, long boots, linen shirt, and overtunic. He was deliberately wearing dull clothing, as was his habit when traveling through Albia. It was prudent to be unobtrusive, thought Sullyan, her fears uppermost in her mind, although a full contingent of King's Guard would soon be noticed in the countryside.

She met his gaze. She was dressed in her normal combat leathers and bore her sword by her side as she was now on duty. It was a measure of the King's respect and trust that she was permitted to go armed and alone into his presence. Only his most loyal officers gained that privilege.

"Yes, it is most unusual. Whoever was responsible for that Earth-shift was remarkably skilled and powerful."

"Could you have done it?" he asked. "Left no discernable trace, I mean."

She hesitated. "Probably. If I really needed to."

Seeing his puzzlement, she explained. "When an Artesan reaches for the power of Earth, or any of the elements, he has to use the portion of his psyche that most closely corresponds to the signature of that element. This leaves an echo, an imprint, if you will, in the substrate, as does the element itself when it responds. These imprints fade over time, but the stronger the wielder's power, the longer the image takes to fade. That Earth-shift must have been exquisitely controlled, otherwise it would have left no one in the vicinity standing. This indicates someone with very strong powers: a Master-elite at the very least.

"But to leave no imprint behind takes determination and very fine control, and also the ability to hide one's pattern within the element itself. Obviously, it can be done, but it is not a skill we foster as we generally have no need to conceal our working. Were I to take a few days to practice, I could hone the strength necessary to accomplish the feat. But it would take considerable effort and would tire me unnecessarily. It is not something I would do unless I saw a definite need.

"To possess the level of control necessary to do what was done yesterday, the Artesan concerned would have to be a Senior Master. And to my knowledge, there are only two of us in existence."

The King listened intently. She knew that the Artesan craft had always fascinated him, and that something within him yearned toward controlling the elements through his own life force. He told her once that he felt he would instinctively know how to do it, if only he had been born with the talent. For now, however, her words alarmed him.

"But if he can hide his working so well, surely he can also hide his existence? Isn't it likely to be some Andaryon lord with a grudge who's trying to foment trouble between our realms? After all, Rykan was going to use that Staff to overthrow Pharikian. I know Timar believes that the weapon was made elsewhere, but doesn't Rykan's rebellion suggest that the plot itself originated in Andaryon?"

Sullyan shook her head, her expression thoughtful. "Not necessarily. You must remember that Artesans are welcomed and encouraged in Andaryon, their talents nurtured and trained. They have no need of concealment. No, your Majesty, I am certain that whoever is behind this is not Andaryan. Both Timar and I believe he could very well be human. I also fear he is being coerced."

Elias sat straighter. "How on earth could you coerce such a powerful Artesan? How would someone like me, for example, succeed in controlling and manipulating you?"

Sullyan turned the full force of her gaze on him and saw him shiver. She knew he could almost sense the unimaginable energies she commanded, seething just below the surface, ready to flood out at her bidding. Seeing his discomfort, she lowered her eyes.

"You would have to have an unshakable hold over me."

She felt his sudden eagerness, feeling they were close to some kind of understanding. "Such as?"

She flicked him a glance. "Let us say, for instance, if you were holding and threatening someone very dear to me."

"Yes," he mused, his eagerness growing, "something or someone you were too frightened to risk. Someone too precious to endanger."

They stared at each other, their feelings shared. Sullyan was thinking of Robin, or even Bulldog, Taran, or Rienne. She could not imagine allowing harm to come to any of her dear friends, although whether threatening them could force her into attempting Elias's life, she could not say. She prayed she would never find out.

Elias, she knew, was thinking of his children; the only consequence of his alliance with Sofira he cared anything for.

Sullyan then told Elias about the raids into Andaryon by unknown Albians. He reacted as angrily and indignantly as she expected. He was on surer ground here, and determined to root out the perpetrators of this breach of his sworn word. He was proud of the alliance with Pharikian, something no Albian monarch had ever managed before, and the flow of trade goods had only just begun. Anything jeopardizing this arrangement struck at the heart of Elias's policies, and he wouldn't tolerate it. His scheduled visit to the Manor would give him the opportunity to discuss the problem with his General.

"Come then, Colonel," he said, throwing an arm about

Sullyan's shoulders. "We will raise this serious business with Lord Blaine. I take it your young Major will have returned from Andaryon by the time we arrive?"

"Indeed, your Majesty. I confess I am eager to see him."

"I'm sure you are," chuckled Elias, refusing to allow her disturbing report to rattle his good humor. He had been looking forward to the inauguration of his College for some time now and nothing was going to spoil the occasion. A trip away from Port Loxton also meant a respite from the Queen's disapproving presence, and that was always to be treasured, even if he did have to endure the company of her pet weasel, Reen.

They left the royal suite together. As they made their way to where Elias's escort was waiting in the garrison courtyard, Sullyan couldn't help noticing the stares, sniggers, and behind-hand whispers of the castle servants.

Lieutenant-Major Owyn Denny was in command of the forty-strong contingent of King's Guard waiting in the courtyard. Sullyan returned his respectful salute, which was marred by the knowing grin he made no attempt to hide. She ignored it.

Elias acknowledged the massed homage of his guard and raised his brows when he spotted Master Ardoch among the riders. The old swordmaster brushed aside the King's tacit query. He had trained Elias's father as well as Elias himself, and the two men knew each other well. Their relationship was much more complex than sovereign to subject, and the Master held a unique place at court. His decisions were his own to make. Elias accepted his presence with a shrug.

"Just let me know if the pace becomes too much for you, old man," he said. They all laughed at Ardoch's growled retort.

Sullyan swung up onto Drum. Taran, who had joined the group earlier and was already mounted, gave her a sharp glance. Sullyan had control of the nausea now and was giving it no further thought, but the Adept had something else on his mind and rode close to speak with her privately.

"Have you noticed the attitude of the servants this morning, Colonel? I've been getting some very queer looks. Even some of the Guard have been acting strangely."

Sullyan glanced at him, and then at the faces of the men around her. None of them met her gaze. She paused before shrugging. "I imagine that yesterday's events have left everyone feeling uncomfortable, Taran. Nervousness in the servants is to be expected; an assassination attempt always leaves fear behind. As for the men, they know they must be more alert than usual and are probably releasing tension as best they can. They will settle once we move out."

There was a delay while they waited for the last member of their group, and Elias quickly grew irritable. He was on the verge of sending a page to ferret out the tardy Baron when the man suddenly appeared, his niece walking beside him. Taran colored when he saw Jinella.

The Lady Jinella was resplendent in a gown of russet silk. Her sunlit blonde hair cascaded around her face and an expensive-looking diamond necklace sparkled at her throat. She spared Taran never a glance as she bid her uncle a fond farewell, but the look she aimed at Sullyan was venomous.

The Baron, dressed in flamboyant riding gear with a long cape flowing from his shoulders, mounted the chestnut pacer held for him by a groom. As soon as he was settled, the King gave the order to move out. He rode his roan charger at their head, accompanied by Denny. Taran and Sullyan rode just behind him, together with Master Ardoch. Drum put back his ears and snaked his head at the Torlander's gray stallion and received an admonitory swat on the neck from his rider.

"It's about time ye trained that unruly beast of yours," said

Ardoch. Sullyan replied with a pithy soldier's insult which drew an audible chuckle from Denny. She frowned at his back.

"You should have lost all your stake money yesterday, Owyn!"

"Ah, but I didn't, my Colonel," crowed the young officer over his shoulder. "Our generous monarch here declared the race a draw, with that chestnut coming in third. All wagers were honored and I made a killing!"

"You were very nearly not the only one," said the Baron loudly.

Sullyan turned to stare at him before pushing Drum up beside the King. "Your Majesty," she said deliberately, "might I ask why the Baron has been included on this trip? What useful function does he serve?"

Elias kept his expression neutral, although anyone who knew him well could see his irritation. "I suggest you ask him, Colonel."

Sullyan stared once more at the colorfully dressed Baron. "Very well," she said. "My Lord Baron, why have you come on this journey?"

Reen sat taller on his sedate pacer and spoke stiffly. "I am here to serve the interests of my Queen." No one could miss the lack of respect in his tone.

"And those are?" pressed Sullyan, riding closer. She shot Taran a pointed look, reminding him of her plan to unsettle the Baron, and his own task of watching the man's reactions. She hoped he wasn't dwelling on his ungallant treatment of Jinella. He had more important things to concentrate on.

Reen answered coolly. "The welfare of her subjects and their moral well-being."

"And are those not the King's interests as well?" Sullyan retorted.

"Well said, Colonel," added the Master loudly. Denny

grinned.

Shifting uncomfortably in his saddle, aware of the glances and flapping ears of the King's escort, Reen tried to retain his dignity. "Queen Sofira cannot travel about the realm as easily as his Majesty. Her responsibilities are to her children. As her trusted advisor, she has instructed me to stand in her stead and act as she would when occasion demands."

"Are you saying the Queen does not trust his Majesty to act when occasion demands?"

Sullyan knew she had the Baron on the run. He grew abruptly irritated by the grins of the men around him, and also by the stiff and unyielding back of the King, riding just ahead. It was too much for him to bear, and he snapped.

"There is no authority that requires me to discuss the Queen's personal business with you, Colonel! I am in her service and I follow her orders. Even you should be able to understand that."

Giving him a hard and knowing smile, Sullyan let the matter drop. She had noted his reference to following the Queen's orders and bleakly wondered just how far those orders might go. Without another word she pushed Drum ahead again, nearer the King, her choice of position sending an unmistakable message to the Baron.

She was pleased to see that Taran was watching the Baron covertly as the noble chewed his lip in angry frustration.

Chapter Fourteen

The rest of the day passed without incident and they made good time, riding at a comfortable canter. They would be spending the night at the country residence of one of Elias's nobles. They reached the sprawling manor house by dusk.

A feast was set out for them and they made short work of it, having been in the saddle for many hours. Sullyan conferred with Taran before they went to their rest, but although she and Master Ardoch had needled the Baron often during the ride and at the feast, none of them had noticed anything other than the anger their nagging comments deserved.

During the evening Sullyan contacted General Blaine, then relayed his words to Elias. Those involved in the military exercises in Andaryon had all returned safely, and Pharikian wanted to meet either with Elias or his representative to discuss the shocking raid on the two villages. The sandy-haired monarch was not surprised.

Despite the manor house's adequate security, Denny posted guards and set watches. Sullyan and Taran took their places within the Lieutenant-Major's arrangements. Sullyan was feeling uncharacteristically weary and wondered if her affliction would return in the morning. She had been very careful about what she ate during the day and had drunk nothing but water, so she was hopeful of feeling well when roused for her dawn watch-duty.

When the time came, she was pleased and surprised that the nausea had not returned. Even so, she couldn't face her usual morning fellan. The strong and bitter smell actually threatened to make her stomach heave when normally it called her compellingly. She also caught herself absently rubbing the bones of her left wrist, as she had done often while they were healing from the injury inflicted by Rykan in the arena. They had long since regained their strength, but today they seemed to ache and quiver. Irritated by the strange sensation, she forced herself to eat some bread, finding that its bland taste seemed to comfort her stomach. Thankful that something helped, she put some in her saddle pack.

The weather that morning was unsettled. There was a humid feel to the air and large patches of dark gray cumulus discolored the eastern horizon. The ground outside was damp, although she hadn't heard it rain during the night. There was a loamy smell to the air as the company mounted.

✤ ✤ ✤ ✤ ✤

Taran was glad of his new leather jacket, which kept out the wind blowing damply off the massing clouds to the east. Grimacing at the threatening sky, he made sure his cloak was close to hand. He saw that most of the men had done the same, as had Sullyan. He also noticed that the Baron, appearing late and last as before, was wearing even more elaborate clothing than the previous day. He was vividly resplendent in a green satin tunic over russet breeches, and his fine cloak was bright green trimmed with yellow. He stood out in stark contrast to the conservatively dressed Elias.

Denny's men formed up as usual around the King. Elias led them off and picked up the pace, and soon they left the manor house behind. Their route took them through the countryside, avoiding populated areas where possible. They were taking a shorter route than Taran and Sullyan had on the way out, and should reach the Manor by nightfall.

Around midday they emerged from a wooded valley and rode up onto the Downs, the trail affording a good view of the surrounding farmland. Taran, who had been looking about with his normal curiosity, spotted something in the distance. He nudged his stallion up beside Sullyan where she flanked the King, and touched her arm lightly to gain her attention. He pointed eastward.

"Colonel, isn't that Fiann over there?"

Sullyan looked where he indicated, a pleased smile lighting her face. The Sinnian bard was some way off, riding his small gray pony over the downlands. He was leading a pack animal laden with his instruments, and had not noticed their party.

"Yes, Taran, I believe it is."

At Elias's questioning look, she explained who the traveler was. The King was intrigued. "He is reputed to be a bard of exceptional talent," he said. "Do you think he could be persuaded to entertain us tonight, Brynne?"

"I will ask him if you wish it, your Majesty, although I warn you, he will expect rich payment."

Elias grinned. "If he's as good as they say he is, I'll happily pay him his worth."

"Be careful, your Majesty," she cautioned. "It is my opinion that no one, not even you, could pay Lord Fiann his worth."

"As good as that?" marveled the King. "This, I must hear."

"He has no equal," she said, "but if I can persuade him to accompany us, you shall judge for yourself. With your permission?"

Elias waved his hand and she touched heels to Drum. The big black leaped into a gallop and soon covered the distance between her and the Sinnian. Taran watched as the two of them greeted each other, only just catching the sneer of repugnance on the Baron's face. They were too far away for Taran to hear their words, but he could see that the Sinnian didn't immediately agree. Eventually, however, he inclined his head and turned his pony to follow Sullyan.

Elias studied the outlander with interest as his Guard parted to allow the bard's approach. Taran could see this didn't meet with the Baron's approval.

Elias inclined his head, greeting the bard gravely. "My Lord Fiann."

Fiann's eyes widened at this show of respect, although his strangely beautiful face betrayed no other expression.

"Your Majesty," he responded, his deeply resonant voice clearly surprising Elias, just as it had Taran.

"My Lord, would you do us the very great honor of playing for us at the Manor tonight?" asked the King. "Brynne Sullyan has been telling us of your prowess and we are keen to hear for ourselves."

Fiann was silent a moment but then said, "It would give me great pleasure to be able to do so, your Majesty."

Taran frowned, struck by the man's unusual choice of phrase. Sullyan seemed puzzled too, but Elias didn't notice. "Then if it pleases you, my Lord, ride with us to the Manor, where you will be provided with refreshment."

"I will ride with you gladly, King Elias," replied the bard, pulling his small mount and pack pony alongside the King's roan charger. Sullyan placed herself on his right side.

They rode on past midday, Sullyan and Elias deep in conversation with the milk-haired Sinnian. Master Ardoch occasionally joined in, and Taran alternated between listening to the bard's mellifluous voice and watching Reen's grim expression. He was concentrating so hard that he didn't hear Denny bringing his horse up close.

"Better put your cloak on, friend," the young officer advised. "We're about to get very wet."

He nodded behind him and Taran turned to see the sky a mass of purple-black clouds, their flattened tops towering high above. He thought he saw a flicker of lightning, although they were too far away yet to hear thunder. Not appreciating the thought of a soaking, he quickly unrolled his cloak and slung it over his shoulders.

Others were doing the same, and he gave the seething clouds another glance, trying to assess when the storm might hit. He could see it advancing across the countryside and frowned at the dense curtain of rain racing purposefully toward them. It came faster than he would have thought possible, totally obscuring his vision of the land behind.

His heart lurched. Something about the cloud mass and that wall of rushing water offended his senses. Concentrating hard, he brought his slowly strengthening powers to bear. He gasped. This was no natural summer storm. He pushed his stallion past Reen, who was also staring at the sky.

Sullyan was deep in conversation with Fiann and the King, and Taran suddenly remembered her warning about communicating through the substrate. Instead of questing for her pattern, he rode up beside her and touched her arm.

She turned. "What is it, Captain?"

He indicated the approaching storm, pitching his voice low. "There's something wrong there." He watched her pupils dilate as she employed her metasenses to scan the clouds.

Her eyes widened in alarm. "Well done, my friend," she breathed. "You are right. That is no natural storm." She turned in the saddle. "Your Majesty, there is something very wrong with this cloud mass behind us. We must be doubly on our guard. Whoever has raised this storm means us no good."

Elias glanced up and was about to respond when the advancing wall of water hit them, rushing over them with unexpected force. Wind came howling out of the clouds and sheets of stinging rain battered their faces, half-blinding them. Those who had not donned their cloaks in time found themselves struggling with folds of wind-torn wool. They were unable to react as swiftly as they should when Denny's loud shout shocked them.

"We're under attack! Form up! Defend the King!"

The guardsmen drew their weapons and closed raggedly into prearranged positions around the King. Glancing wildly about in the blinding rain and whipping wind, Taran saw what Denny had seen: a group of about fifty armed and mounted men bearing down on them from behind the concealing wall of rain. The King's Guard swung round to meet the threat, forced to face right into the teeth of the storm.

Lightning tore the sky in two and thunder blared.

"Taran!" yelled Sullyan as she used Drum to shepherd Fiann's pony alongside Elias. "Do what you can with that storm. I must protect the King."

Taran nodded and took himself to the back of the group, trying to keep out of the guardsmen's way. It wasn't possible to concentrate on fighting and use his metaforce at the same time. This unnatural storm was also part of the attack and needed an Artesan to counter it, so it was up to Taran to divert or disperse it. He gathered his will and tried to concentrate. Then the wave of attackers hit them, and the shock of the ambush doubled.

They were Andaryan.

The raiders attacked; yelling, hacking, and screaming; but Elias's Guard were the best trained fighting men in the country and they were defending their King. Led courageously by Denny, they repulsed the first assault and threw the raiders back, allowing themselves room to regroup. Sullyan and the Master fought side by side, flanking the King, allowing no enemy even close to Elias. Fiann and the Baron were to the rear of the King, also protected by this defense. The Baron's green and yellow cloak was almost luminous in the pouring rain.

Taran managed to shut out the noise and confusion around

him, but even so he was struggling. He had mastery over Water, but the elements of Fire and Air were also raging within the storm. Rain poured down in torrents and the wind howled directly into the Albians' faces, stinging and blinding their eyes. Taran strove his utmost to ease the conditions.

The Andaryans regrouped and came again, a spearhead of fighters making straight for Elias. Denny rallied his men, barking commands that were barely audible over the tumultuous roar of the storm. Once again the attackers were repulsed. Sullyan and Master Ardoch worked in a perfect harmony of strokes to provide deadly and effective cover for their sovereign. Elias was no mean swordsman himself and had his own weapon ready, but none of the enemy had yet breached the cordon to trouble him. Fiann sat his nervous pony behind the King, a strange expression on his unhuman face.

The Andaryans surged forward again and lightning forked the skies. The storm seemed to lash all the heavier just as the raiders' might was thrown against the King's Guard. Taran desperately pitted his strength against the elements but he was getting nowhere and tiring fast. Just when he thought he would have to admit defeat and pull out, he became aware of Sullyan's presence in his mind.

Taran, link with me! I am making my power available to you. Her mental tone was tight with split concentration. *Use it to push that storm away. Concentrate on Water. Use your mastery and my strength together. You can do it!*

Her presence vanished as she engaged another of their attackers, driving the man relentlessly away from his target.

Stunned by the gift of her fathomless power, Taran rallied. He tried to forget the weight of trust she had placed in him, and instead merged his pattern with hers. He was hit by a force every bit as strong as the gale-driven torrent and had to take a deep breath to steady himself. His blood singing with power, he hurled his vastly augmented strength against the element of Water. Finally, he could make some headway! He thrust down the thrill of controlling Sullyan's power and schooled himself to concentrate on the storm, bringing his will to bear on the rain, lessening its effects and slowly abating the downpour.

✤ ✤ ✤ ✤ ✤

From his position of shelter behind the King, Baron Reen sat his fidgeting pacer. He jerked irritably on the reins to stop the beast trying to turn its head away from the rain, and his struggle to control it concealed his satisfaction. This was just as well, for he knew it was essential to appear suitably afraid. He was angry with Taran for noticing the storm's unnatural nature before the raid began, but his ire was tempered by an unforeseen opportunity to be rid of yet another undesirable outlander. Completely unheard in the welter of sound around him, Reen muttered under his breath.

✤ ✤ ✤ ✤ ✤

Sullyan was panting hard. Another pulling back, another chance to regroup. A few of Elias's Guard were injured, although none fatally. Four of the raiders were dead and a few more were out of action due to serious wounds. Denny yelled encouragement to his men and they braced themselves for the next assault.

When it came, it concentrated wholly on Elias. Heedless of loss or injury, the Andaryans threw themselves against the King's defenders. Many were cut down as the Guards closed about them, trapping them in a noose of warriors. Sullyan and Ardoch were hard-pressed in the center of the mêlée as the Andaryans fought madly to reach Elias. The King now had to help defend himself.

Denny fought toward them with ten or so of his men, and the attackers fell back once more. But now the Guards were losing more of their own. Sullyan heard a warning shout and twisted in her saddle. A small group of Andaryans were winning through to

Elias from behind. She dealt swiftly with her current opponent and wheeled Drum to engage another.

Two of the raiders urged their mounts forward, lunging straight at the Baron. He screamed as a blade whistled past his head. Another came slashing at his mount's legs. The pacer, not trained for combat, shied violently to the left, dumping the Baron out of the saddle. He crashed to the ground and curled into a ball, his screams rising higher in pitch.

Sullyan had no time for the Baron, as his attackers were now heading for the King. Pressing Drum onward, she moved to block them. As one engaged her sword arm, the other dodged past her, his weapon aimed straight at Elias's back.

"Ardoch!" she screamed, but he was already occupied.

Too many things then happened simultaneously.

Taran, having caught his breath after pushing the storm far enough for the rain to ease, threw himself into the fight. He reached Denny's side where the young officer, beset by more opponents than he could handle, was overpowered. Taran dealt with one of Denny's assailants and Master Ardoch another, but they were too late to stop the blow which shattered Denny's sword arm and pierced his side. Taran heard Sullyan's gasp as Denny gave a great cry of pain, fell from his horse, and lay still.

The Andaryan who had dodged Sullyan's attack drove straight for Elias's unprotected back. Only the Sinnian bard stood in his way. The King, unaware and fully occupied with a frontal assault, had no hope of defending himself. Sullyan dispatched her attacker and screamed a warning, but swung far too late to reach the raider whose sword was about to pierce the King's back.

✠ ✠ ✠ ✠ ✠

The fighting had moved past where the Baron lay protectively curled-up, and he straightened with care. Bruised muscles and shattered dignity did nothing to suppress his triumphant grin as he watched the most heroic act of the battle. He could not have planned it better himself. Seeing the King's imminent danger, but unable to engage the raider because he was unarmed, the Sinnian bard suddenly kicked his pony so hard that it reared up. Fiann threw his body into the path of Elias's attacker, and received the raider's blade through his breast. He slumped with a moan and fell to the ground. Sullyan was on the raider in an instant, but too late to save the bard.

With their covering storm retreating and many of their number killed or severely wounded, the raiders broke off the attack. Less than twenty galloped off, unpursued by Denny's men as they swung round to check that their sovereign was unharmed.

Where before there had been shouting, the clash of steel, howling wind, and booming thunder, there was now a deathly silence, almost more shocking than the previous welter of sound. Then, the agonized gasps and moans of the injured made themselves heard.

Sullyan flung herself from Drum and fell to her knees, cradling the fallen Sinnian's head in her arms. Tears slipped down her cheeks and her eyes were vast and black as she put out all her power to try to reverse the inevitable. Bloody froth flecked his lips, his dark and liquid eyes gazing blindly. His hand tightened briefly on her arm as he whispered, "Remember."

Then his head fell back and he lay still. She bowed her head in grief.

✣ ✣ ✣ ✣ ✣

Taran dismounted and ran to where Denny lay gasping on the soaked and bloody ground. The young officer's face was gray and pinched, his lips blue. His right arm looked badly shattered, and the sword's tip had pierced his ribs. Working swiftly, Taran wadded up the bulk of Denny's cloak and packed it tight against his side to staunch the blood. The man groaned, barely conscious.

Taran glanced up as Master Ardoch knelt beside him.

"How bad is it?" the Torlander asked, wiping sweat from his face.

"Bad enough," said Taran, "but maybe not life threatening if we can get him some attention."

Ardoch grunted and rose. He approached Elias, who was talking to the men, praising them for their valiant defense. Before the Master could speak, however, everyone's attention was drawn to the sound of Baron Reen's voice raised in anger.

Reen was berating Sullyan. She had gently laid Fiann down and was staring at his body, anguish plain on her face.

"What on earth do you think you're doing, Colonel?" ranted the Baron. "You have duties to attend to, yet you spend valuable time sorrowing over a dead outlander! What are you thinking of? Your King could have been killed today, and if you hadn't brought that... creature... among us, the attack might never have happened. This is what you get for befriending those who have no right in our lands!"

Stung out of her grief, Sullyan turned on him, golden eyes blazing with anger. "Strange, is it not, Baron, that of all of us you come through this untouched and unscathed? We had no need to defend you, did we? Why is that, I wonder?"

"Just what do you mean?" he spluttered. "I was in as much danger as anyone! Didn't you see those raiders attack me? I fell from my horse! Had they turned back just then.... Well, let's just say I was fortunate to escape with severely bruised ribs."

"Fortunate indeed, my Lord, not to have to lift a finger in your own defense," she snapped. "I do not recall you raising a blade against your attackers! Had it not been for the swift reactions and self-sacrifice of this 'creature'"—she spat the word in Reen's face—"your sovereign lord would even now be lying dead upon the field. I very much doubt whether you would have tendered his

Majesty such selfless service!"

Reen's face turned purple and his eyes bulged. He had his hand on his sword hilt, the blade half-drawn. Sullyan made no move toward her own weapon, but her attitude suggested imminent violence. Taran knew the Baron would stand no chance if she attacked him.

Elias's strident voice cut across them. "Baron, Colonel, that's enough! There will be time for recriminations later, if you must. For now, we have more important concerns."

Sullyan visibly controlled her fury. "My apologies, your Majesty." She turned away from Reen, fortunately not seeing him spit on the Sinnian's body. White-faced, she approached Elias. "Are you well, your Majesty? Did you take any hurt?"

"I'm fine, Colonel," he said bluntly. "Others, however, are not." He indicated the stricken Denny. The young officer had by far the worst injury of those left alive.

Sullyan immediately crossed to Taran, who was still supporting the wounded man. Kneeling down, she assessed Denny's injuries.

"These are serious wounds, your Majesty, and require urgent attention."

Reen stalked up beside Elias and looked down coldly. "There's no time, your Majesty. It's far too dangerous to remain here in the open. How do we know those brigands won't return?"

Elias swung round on him, hard-faced. "Then what do you suggest, Baron? That we leave him here to die, or be finished off by raiders?"

Reen shrugged. "Let one of his men stay by him, or the Colonel, if she wishes. We can send a wagon back when we have gained the safety of the Manor. Your security must come first, your Majesty. It is what the Queen would wish."

Elias glared at him, his expression clearly saying he doubted the Baron's last words. "And what if it was you, Reen, lying there wounded and helpless? Would your advice be the same? Leave you behind to be picked up, or picked off, later?"

Unfazed, Reen stared at his sovereign. "But it isn't me, is it, your Majesty? So the question doesn't arise." He turned and stalked away.

Elias stared at his retreating back before kneeling down beside Sullyan and Taran. He kept his voice low. "Should we ever find ourselves in a similar situation, Colonel, you have my express permission to run that slimy bastard through while my back's turned. In fact, I would take it as a personal favor." Then he shook his head and indicated Denny. "Can you do anything for him?"

She looked grave. "I can try, your Majesty."

"Do your best," he said curtly. "If you can render him able to ride, even pillion, I'll be well pleased. I really don't want to leave him behind, but we have no way of making a litter. Let me know what you decide."

He stood up and moved away, assessing the other wounded. Master Ardoch accompanied him, sword drawn.

Sullyan turned to Taran, who was still supporting Denny's upper body, pressing the wad of cloth over the injured officer's side. She smiled faintly at him while running her hands over the mess of Denny's arm. "You did very well to disperse that storm, Taran. I was very proud of you."

He colored. "I couldn't have done it without your strength."

She regarded him narrowly. "Whoever raised that storm was very powerful indeed. Did you get a glimpse of the pattern behind it?"

He shook his head. "Yours was the only other pattern I saw. But I wasn't really looking." He felt shamed, wishing he had paid more attention. But there was no censure in Sullyan's eyes.

"This is becoming deadly serious, my friend," she murmured,

staring at him over Denny's body. "This latest attack was most definitely an attempt on the King's life, and it very nearly succeeded. Had it not been for Fiann," her voice choked, "Elias would not have survived." She shook herself. "But we must concentrate on Denny. Much as I hate to admit it, the Baron is right. We are too exposed here, and we must get Elias to the safety of the Manor before nightfall."

Asking Taran to link with her once more, she placed both hands on Denny's temples and looked hard into his half-closed eyes. Calling his name, she elicited a groaned response.

"Listen to me, Owyn," she urged gently. "We can numb your pain and get you fit enough to ride, but we need your help. Do you understand me?"

Denny groaned again and stirred.

"Easy, man," she cautioned, "just lie still. I only need you to look at me and be willing to accept what I tell you. Can you do that?"

He bit his lip and nodded fractionally. She sighed with relief. "Then open your eyes, Owyn. Open your eyes and look at me."

His unfocused, bloodshot gaze settled on her. "Taran, concentrate on his ribs. Numb the pain but do not send him to sleep. We do not want to have to tie him on his horse. Use my power again."

Taran reached for the healing amber essence of her metaforce and felt it flood toward him. He could sense Denny's lambent psyche and directed the flow of energy over the angry hurt deep in Denny's side. He heard the man gasp as some of his pain eased.

"Very good, Taran," approved Sullyan. "Now hold it there while I deal with this arm."

Concentrating hard, desperate not to miss anything, Taran watched Sullyan take hold of Denny's own life force and use it to blunt the pain receptors in his brain. The nerves carrying pain messages from his shattered arm went numb and Denny gasped again. His whole body had been trembling with the effort of not crying out, but he went limp as Sullyan's work relieved his agony. He passed out and she sat back, drawing a hand over her face.

She smiled wearily up at Taran. "He will recover shortly. His capacity to bear the pain was overloaded and only needs time to restore itself. We should bind his arm and chest while he is unconscious."

Chapter Fifteen

They made makeshift bandages and a sling from spare shirts and whatever material they could find. Then they propped Denny against a boulder and left him with one of his men watching over him. Sullyan looked for the King and spotted him standing by the fallen bard. Fiann's cloak was covering his body, and his pony and packhorse were standing near. Elias contemplated the covered form in silence, glancing up as Sullyan approached. He frowned, his gaze directed at her hands, and she realized she was rubbing the inside of her left forearm again. She stopped, but still he stared at her.

"Are you all right, Brynne? You're very pale and you look a little… strange. You weren't injured, were you?"

"No, your Majesty." She hesitated. "I have done what I can for the Lieutenant-Major, and he should now be able to complete the journey to the Manor. We are only about four hours away, so I will contact General Blaine and ask him to send a company to meet us, in case there are more raiders in the area."

She paused again, looking down at her hands. Elias's frown deepened. "What is it, Colonel?"

She raised her eyes, knowing her unshed tears betrayed her distress. "Your Majesty, I have lost a true and loyal friend today." She ignored the snort given by the Baron, who stood nearby, openly listening. "The last time I saw him, the Lord Fiann asked a boon of me, and it was not something I could refuse." Elias raised his brows in query and she took a breath. "I realize this is not the best of times, but still I ask your leave to fulfill that promise. As he saved your life at the expense of his own, I am sure you would want to see him honored."

"What exactly are you asking for, Colonel?" he said. Reen stirred, but Elias silenced him with a look.

"Lord Fiann asked me to conduct the rite of his passing, your Majesty. Will you permit me the time to fulfill that task?"

Reen spluttered a protest before the King could respond. "Oh, really, your Majesty! You can't even consider granting such a ridiculous request. He was only an outlander. It's not as if he was human! Does she really expect you, or any of us, to sit around while she conducts some meaningless rite? We're open and vulnerable here, we should ride on."

The shocking attacks on the King, the physical exertions of battle, her own recent less-than-perfect health, and the distracting tingling sensation she was experiencing in her left arm—not to mention Reen's vile and insulting comments—overthrew Sullyan's self-control. Unable to stop herself, she exploded. She advanced menacingly on the Baron, who recoiled and threw up his hands.

"Only an outlander?" she raged. "Meaningless rite? Just because the Lord Fiann was not born in these lands does not make him any less a man, my Lord! His beliefs and customs were as meaningful to him as yours are to you. I would venture to say more so! He showed more courage and humanity today than you could even recognize. He was a friend, my Lord Baron, and a true one. I doubt you even know the meaning of the word! He saved the High King's life and paid for that courage with his own. He deserves respect for that alone, not that you would understand. He would even have done the same for you, save that I would have prevented him!"

Her eyes shot sparks and her tone dripped venom. Pale-faced, holding his ribs, Reen retreated before her. Even Denny's men regarded her with surprise and fear. Taran stood by, his face showing concern, and Master Ardoch was also watching her carefully, his body poised for action. Had the Baron truly understood what she was capable of, he would already be running.

Elias rose to his feet and approached the two of them. Sullyan still held Reen's fearful gaze with her own, pinning him like a rabbit before a snake.

"I see no good reason for your continuing existence upon this earth, my Lord Baron," she spat, her voice low and threatening, "and I wish the Queen much pleasure of your joyless company! Bide here or ride on; it makes less than no difference to me."

She swung away abruptly and his sudden release from her stare caused Reen to stagger. Sullyan came face to face with Elias and halted, the intensity of her anger making her pant.

Elias regarded them both, and the Baron opened his mouth. Elias held up a hand and he subsided. "First, Baron," stated Elias, "the Colonel"—he stressed her rank as Reen had not accorded her the courtesy—"fought loyally and bravely to defend us today. I have yet to hear your thanks given to her or any of the men for their efforts in preserving your misbegotten hide."

He turned to Sullyan, who was mastering herself with difficulty, shamed by her outburst. "And second, Colonel, you did not need to remind me of Lord Fiann's sacrifice. It was a deed worthy of much honor and is something I will never forget."

He knelt down by the body, gently moving aside the folds of cloak from Fiann's lifeless but still beautiful face. Placing his hand on the dead man's brow, Elias murmured something under his breath. Then he stood. Facing Sullyan, he said, "Colonel, you have my leave to conduct your rite and honor the passing of a brave man. We will rest here until you are done." He glared pointedly at the Baron, who wisely chose to hold his peace. "The men will appreciate time to refresh themselves. Will you require any assistance?"

Sullyan inclined her head, her anger back under control. "I thank you, your Majesty. Taran and I will manage. Lord Fiann would also thank you for this courtesy, were he able."

Elias waved a hand and moved away, giving instructions for food and drink to be distributed among the men and arrangements to be made for the dead. Reen stayed where he was, glaring at Sullyan, one hand massaging his ribs, his lips thin and disapproving.

Sullyan ignored him. "Taran, help me, will you?"

Master Ardoch came forward too, and she flashed the old swordmaster a grateful smile. Together, he and Taran lifted the Sinnian, who was no great weight, and carried him farther from the makeshift camp. There was a clear patch of grass between some nearby boulders, and there she instructed them to lay the body down. She wrapped the Sinnian's cloak closely about him and then led over his packhorse. Releasing the bindings on the various musical instruments, she removed their covers. Tears glistened in her eyes as she placed the instruments carefully around the body.

Fiann's harp, that wonderfully crafted instrument which had so recently held Taran and an inn full of people enraptured, she placed upright at his head. The guitar she laid on one side of him, and the fiddle she set at his feet. His flute, after holding it lovingly for a few moments, she laid on his breast. Then she knelt by his side and placed her left hand on his brow beneath the covering cloak. She murmured the Sinnian words Fiann had once taught her. Her tears flowed freely now and she made no attempt to stop them.

Taran and the Master stood silently by while Sullyan bade an emotional farewell to one of her best-loved friends. Then she stood and motioned for the two men to step away. She stayed close to Fiann's side and slowly raised her arms. As she tilted back her head, she reached through the substrate, calling the element of

Fire. It responded to her command and blossomed in the air above the body of the bard. Then she began to sing.

Her lilting voice soared effortlessly into a sky clear of storm clouds. The men, sitting or standing as they were, ceased their talk to listen, and not one of them broke the silence into which her song ascended.

As the notes swelled, their tone subtly changed. The song became an anthem of hope, of friendship and renewal. As it did so, lifting their spirits with it, Sullyan called Air, and the wind of her calling blew gently through the strings of the harp. A melodious thrumming joined her song as she brought Fire down upon the body of her friend.

It was intense yet so exquisitely controlled that the instant it made contact, all wood, cloth, metal, flesh, and bone charred instantly to ash. There was no smell, no charnel odor, only the clean crackle and snap of elemental forces doing their work. Sullyan's song ended on a pure sustained note, and as its last strains faded, so she extinguished her Fire, using Air to swirl away all trace of the world's greatest known bard.

Taran watched as she lowered her arms and stood there, head bowed and shoulders trembling, emotion coursing through her. He wondered if he should go to her, but it was Ardoch who made the move.

"That was beautiful, lass," he murmured, enfolding Sullyan in his arms. "Ye did him proud."

Taran came away, leaving her to the Master's comfort. He crossed to where Denny, now awake, was accepting a drink from one of his men. The young officer's face was ashen, his lips gray.

"How are you feeling?" Taran crouched down next to Denny and accepted the hunk of bread and cheese held out to him by a Kingsman. He nodded his thanks. He hadn't realized how hungry he was.

Denny gave a pale smile. "I've been better."

Taran snorted, pleased to hear this spark of humor. "You were nearly very much worse!"

He had expected a weak retort, but Denny's attention was elsewhere. Following his gaze, Taran was surprised to see Sullyan once more approaching the King. She was composed, more like her usual self, but still pale. Taran could tell she had something else on her mind, and it was obviously troubling her. Elias watched her from his seat on a granite boulder and regarded her levelly as she kneeled before him.

"Your Majesty," she said, "I fear must seek your pardon."

Elias frowned, as did Taran. Clearly, this had nothing to do with Fiann's funeral rite. "What for, Colonel?" the King asked.

"For failing in my duty. General Blaine trusted me with your safety following the events at Port Loxton and, clearly, I have failed."

Taran saw Reen give a nasty smile.

Elias pursed his lips. "What do you mean, Colonel? You couldn't have known about the raiders."

She raised clear eyes to his. "No. But I was not quick enough to recognize the threat within the storm. It was Captain Elijah who alerted me to its unnatural nature, and it was he who dispelled it, enabling us to defeat the raiders."

Taran jumped to his feet. "That's not strictly true, your Majesty. Yes, I noticed the nature of the storm, but I was powerless to do anything about it until the Colonel lent me her strength."

"No, Taran," she said, a trace of impatience in her voice. "Most of what you did today was your own work. You used far less of my power than you think, my friend." She held up a hand to forestall his protest. "All I did was give you some confidence. The power you used to deflect the storm was your own. Do I not keep telling you to have more faith in your own abilities? Your Majesty, without Captain Elijah's invaluable assistance today, the battle might have had a very different outcome."

The King gave Taran an appraising look. "Is that so, Colonel? Well, I will bear it in mind. You have our heartfelt thanks, Captain."

Taran colored at the King's praise and stepped back, embarrassed.

Sullyan continued. "I have just spoken with General Blaine, and he has dispatched a company to meet us. Since they will be on fresh horses, they should be with us in about an hour and a half."

Watching her, taking in her pale face and the slight tremor of her body, Elias said, "You have had no refreshment, Colonel. We don't want you passing out from fatigue on the way. Take a moment to eat before we leave."

Taran noted how the mention of food turned her face even paler. "I thank you, your Majesty, but I have something in my pack. We really should leave now. By your gracious consent, I have already delayed us too long."

Reen muttered a comment which Elias ignored. "Very well. Mount up, men, and we will continue our journey. Someone help the Lieutenant-Major onto his horse."

The effort of mounting his horse wrung a groan from the injured man's lips, and fresh blood stained the bandages about his ribs. Sullyan nudged Drum alongside him once she was in the saddle. She touched him on the arm, looking into his pain-glazed eyes.

"Owyn, do you hear me?"

He nodded. "I'll be all right," he said through gritted teeth. "Let's get on with it."

"Taran, stay by him, will you?" The Adept nodded, and

Sullyan once more touched Denny's arm. "Owyn, Taran can lend you strength and numb some of the pain. You only have to let him."

Denny managed a grin. "Oh, go ahead, my friend. I don't enjoy pain so much that I'd want to stop you."

The party moved out once more, sadly depleted, wet, and demoralized.

✤ ✤ ✤ ✤ ✤

Rienne was deeply relieved when Cal returned unharmed from the exercise in Andaryon. She couldn't help fretting. It was silly, really. She had wholeheartedly backed his decision to take the King's Oath and was proud of both his desire to do so and his emerging skills as a leader. Yet pride didn't stop her fearing for him every time he went out. He had been badly injured during Sonten's siege of Hyecombe, and once he had fully recovered Rienne wanted to keep him that way. Besides, she was now as sure as she could be that her hopes had come to pass, and she needed him safe now more than ever.

On learning that Sullyan and Taran were due back that evening, Rienne left the infirmary earlier than normal. She wanted to be in the apartment she shared with Cal when he returned from his duties. Cal was rather surprised to see her when he entered, and raised his brows in query as he accepted the glass of amber liquid she held out to him.

Smiling up into his velvety brown eyes, framed by outrageously long eyelashes, Rienne reflected on how much he meant to her. They had grown even closer since their marriage, both finding meaning and purpose in the new life they had embraced. Now their lives would change yet again, and Rienne needed to know she had Cal's full support. They had both agreed the time was right to try for a family, and Rienne had spoken with Sullyan before broaching the subject with Cal, as she didn't want to jeopardize their position at the Manor.

Many of the fighting men stationed there were married, but the women all lived in nearby villages. There were no families or young children at the Manor. Goran, the cook, permitted some of the older children to help in the kitchens, but not until they were at least ten years old. Rienne didn't intend to give up her work as a healer, and needed to know she would not be asked to leave if she and Cal had children. Sullyan had assured her this would not happen, so Cal and Rienne went ahead with their plans.

Rienne now believed she was expecting their first child. She would ask Sullyan to confirm it for her, as Cal was not yet skilled enough to attempt the probe. Rienne didn't really need the confirmation, but she couldn't resist asking for her friend's reassurance. Besides, it would be a great way to tell her. But first she had to tell Cal.

He was smiling at her, drinking her in after their time apart. "Come and sit down, love," she said, indicating a chair. His smile turned to a small frown, but he sat down and sipped his drink.

Rienne gazed into his dark eyes. "I have something to tell you." His frown deepened and she smiled. "It's good news, Cal. Don't look so worried!" Deliberately teasing him, she said, "Cal Tyler, I have to tell you that your efforts have been rewarded."

He was perplexed. "What? What efforts?"

She smiled wider and giggled. "Oh, Cal, we're going to be parents!"

His expression caused her to laugh lightheadedly. As her words sank in his shock gave way to a huge and foolish grin, and she saw tears start in his eyes. They mirrored her own. He rose slowly, placing his empty glass blindly on a low table. It teetered and tipped over the edge, but he didn't notice. He crossed to her and kneeled by her side, taking up her hands. "Oh, gods, Rienne! How long have you known?"

"Only a couple of days. I want Brynne to confirm it for me, but I needed to tell you first. Cal, we're having a baby!"

He enfolded her joyfully in his arms, his happiness overflowing.

Eventually, they disengaged. "What's Taran going to say?" murmured Cal.

Rienne dried her eyes. "He'll be as proud as you are, I'm sure. It's Brynne I'm worried about. I know she says she's come to terms with being barren, but I don't believe her. She and Robin would make such good parents, and I know that having a family would make up for what she's lost. She still grieves for her own parents, you know. A baby would help her put all that sorrow to rest. I want to involve her as much as I can in our children, my love, and maybe that way I can help her. You won't mind, will you?"

"Of course not, sweeting. You'll need a friend and someone to help you get lots of rest. Involve her as much as you like! But I want to play my part too, you know." A sudden thought struck him. "Do you think he'll be an Artesan?"

She cocked her head. "He?"

"Or she." Cal smiled. "I really don't mind either way, you know. I was just wondering…."

"I'll ask Brynne," said Rienne, not having considered this. "She's bound to know. But I don't want you to tell anyone else until I've spoken to her, do you hear? And don't go around with that silly big grin on your face or everyone will guess. Especially don't tell Bulldog! Much as I love him, he couldn't keep a secret like this to save his mother."

Cal chuckled. "He'll make a wonderful uncle!"

She returned his grin.

✤ ✤ ✤ ✤ ✤

Taran passed the rest of the journey to the Manor in a state of growing apprehension. He lent Denny as much strength as the man needed to cope with his pain and the rigors of the ride, and it drained him. He slipped into a semi-trance, turning the events of the last six days over in his mind.

A dreadful thought suddenly hit him. Would Sullyan tell Robin of his shameful lapse that first day by the stream? Taran knew she would never use the incident against him, but he also knew she kept no secrets from her life mate. His stomach churned, and he was deeply fearful of what Robin would think. The young Major had trusted Taran with Sullyan's safety, and Taran knew he had betrayed that trust by overstepping his bounds. The fact that he would never have acted on his desire did nothing to excuse the fact that he had wanted to, and no matter how often Robin assured him that he accepted how Taran felt, Taran always felt guilty and awkward over the depth of his passion. Now he had even more cause to feel ashamed.

✣ ✣ ✣ ✣ ✣

Denny, riding by Taran's side, was in a considerable amount of pain despite Taran's flow of supportive metaforce. Trying to take his mind off it, the young officer studied Taran. The man's eyes were fixed on Sullyan and he appeared to be brooding over something. Denny thought he knew what it was. After all, Taran's feelings sat naked on his face. He was completely unaware of Denny's scrutiny, and the injured officer gave a knowing smile.

He had heard and observed Taran's many defenses of Sullyan at Port Loxton and had quickly formed his own conclusions. The juicy piece of castle gossip he had heard the servants passing round before they had left only served to cement those conclusions. It was obvious anyway. Protest how he might, Taran was clearly a man in love. Denny was looking forward to spending some time at the Manor and observing the results of this byplay. It just might, he thought, help alleviate the boredom of what was bound to be a long recovery.

He had always liked and respected Sullyan, not least for her help when they were cadets together. Yet she made it plain very early on in their friendship that she would never entertain any thoughts of a relationship with him. He eventually accepted this decision, unlike some, and bore her no ill will. But he had always wondered when scandal would strike her, as it was inevitable when one attractive female was surrounded by so many virile young males. He was interested to see how she coped with it. He eyed Taran speculatively, wondering how the good-looking Adept compared to the man Sullyan had married.

He was soon to find out.

✠ ✠ ✠ ✠ ✠

Taran came out of his reverie to see Sullyan riding ahead of their party. He understood why when his ears registered the sounds of approaching horses. It was their expected escort. He berated himself for his sinking heart when he realized Robin was leading them. He watched Sullyan and Robin exchange a brief but intense clasp of hands. They broke apart quickly, and Sullyan led Robin back to the King.

As they reached him, she said, "You have command, Major. Your Majesty, with your leave I will ride on ahead. The General will expect a full report on recent events and I must see him before I can rest. You are in safe hands now."

Taran saw Elias's puzzlement as he waved assent, and even Robin raised his brows at her phrasing. Before they could respond, she turned Drum's head and urged him forward, the big black surging into a ground-eating gallop. Soon, she was out of sight.

Robin deployed his men and rode round the remnants of Denny's command before coming over to Taran. The Adept turned crimson as Robin approached, failing to hide the awkward embarrassment he felt. Denny smiled faintly as he acknowledged

Robin's polite nod.

Robin took no obvious notice of Taran's discomfiture and greeted him warmly. "What was all that about?" he asked, referring to Sullyan's abrupt departure.

Taran struggled for composure. "She feels she failed the King today, but Elias doesn't see it that way."

Pulling Torka closer to Taran's horse, Robin pitched his voice low. "How was she while you were away?"

Taran shrugged. "Not always at her best. But she fought as well as ever today. She has nothing to blame herself for."

Robin smiled. "Well, you know what she's like." He placed a friendly hand on Taran's shoulder and looked the Adept in the eye. "Thank you for looking after her for me." Taran felt himself blushing furiously. Robin took this as a reaction to his praise and his smile deepened. "You know how much I appreciate it," he added, compounding Taran's misery. He nodded to Denny and pushed Torka forward to take up his position at the head of the party. Taran knew the Major had no idea of the real reason for his flaming face, and he couldn't guess how Robin would react if he found out.

Taran became aware of a low chuckling and turned to see Denny sporting a smug expression. "What?" he demanded.

Denny shook his head. "Oh, but you're a dark horse, my friend."

"What do you mean by that?"

The injured officer indicated Robin with a nod of his head. "I take it that's who I think it is?"

"That's Major Tamsen, yes," said Taran.

"And he's married to Sullyan?"

"You know he is. Why do you ask?"

Denny's lip curled. "Why do I ask? Captain, that is one of the handsomest men I've seen in a long while! You're a captain, he's a major, you're in love with his wife, and yet he thanks you for 'looking after' her?" He snorted. "I'd say you're treading a very dangerous path, my friend."

Taran's face flamed yet again, and he knew there was no use denying Denny's assumption. It would only make matters worse. Instead, he tried another tack. "He knows all about it."

Denny's eyes bulged. "He knows? I find that hard to believe! Why does he put up with it?"

"He's known from the start," snapped Taran, hating having to defend himself before the young officer. "It was before they were wed. And anyway, we're all friends. He knows I'd never do anything to jeopardize that."

Denny huffed, incredulous. "Well! I thought I was liberal, but I've never heard the like. This is going to be a very interesting few days."

He fell silent, exhausted by the exchange, and Taran stared sullenly at his saddle. His worst fears would come to pass if Denny didn't keep this quiet. Taran could hardly beg him to keep his mouth shut. It would only provoke the man. And he knew that soldiers were at their most talkative when bored and inactive through injury. Denny was likely to spread his gossip throughout the Manor, and there wasn't a thing Taran could do about it. He would just have to hope that the rest of the men treated it as old news.

He completed the ride in disgruntled silence.

Chapter Sixteen

Sullyan reached the Manor about an hour ahead of the King. She went straight to Blaine's office and remained closeted with him for the rest of the evening. When the royal party arrived, Elias and the Baron were entertained by Vassa, as Blaine had sent his apologies, still deep in discussions with Sullyan.

Bulldog was summoned to attend Blaine in order to provide Sullyan with firsthand details of the raids in Andaryon. Robin was still on duty, and the whole Manor was on extra alert after the shocking events of the past few days.

Messages were constantly being passed between the Manor and Port Loxton, especially now, so no one remarked on the runner who left shortly after the King's arrival. She carried an urgent and personal message for the Queen, although she had no idea of its contents. Runners were trusted implicitly not to break the seals on the messages they carried, and this one bore the King's crest. Even if it fell into the wrong hands, its contents would arouse no suspicion nor direct any unauthorized reader to suspect it was not from the King. Its author, Baron Reen, had taken great pains to ensure that, while reflecting that the King's invention of a secure runner system was well-conceived indeed.

✣ ✣ ✣ ✣ ✣

Along with the other wounded, Lieutenant-Major Denny was settled into the infirmary by Rienne and her team of healers. She gave him a powerful sleeping draft before treating his injuries. His badly broken arm reminded her of Cal's at the siege of Hyecombe, and she could only hope that Denny would recover as well as Cal had. He was too young to be crippled, and it would not be for lack of her care if he was.

She was busy with her patient until late and was not there when Taran returned to their shared rooms. By the time Rienne arrived, he had already gone to his rest. Rienne was pleased. She didn't want anything spoiling her surprise.

✣ ✣ ✣ ✣ ✣

Baron Reen endured the meal in Elias's and Vassa's company with self-satisfied calm. Despite his aching ribs, he was feeling a certain amount of pleasurable anticipation after discovering the note concealed under his pillow earlier. Its contents had lifted his disgruntled mood considerably.

Dinner over, he sat alone in his room in a large, velvet-upholstered wing chair, pleasantly full of roast goose and sipping at a very acceptable brandy while awaiting his visitor. In his right hand he toyed with two gold rings which chimed faintly while he appreciated the play of lamplight through the dark liquid and cut crystal in his left.

The room contained only one other chair, not as comfortable as the one supporting Reen's weight, and the vast four-poster bed. The bed's heavy drapes were tied back, as the weather was currently warm, but the matching drapes at the closed windows were drawn shut. Reen would have preferred some fresh air, but he dared not open the windows until his visitor had gone. The King had retired for the night and the Manor was quiet, but he could not discount the possibility of someone overhearing.

When the tap at his door finally came, Reen was in a mellow mood. As he admitted the sallow-faced young man he couldn't resist a theatrical glance up and down the corridor and a hissed, "Are you sure you weren't seen?"

Captain Parren slipped inside, closing the door soundlessly behind him. He regarded the Baron with scorn. "I'm an officer of the King's forces, Baron, and a damned good one! Give me some credit for intelligence."

Reen smiled faintly. "Is that why you're still a captain when everyone else has been promoted over you?"

Parren snarled. "I already told you the reasons for that!"

Reen held up a hand. He had Parren right where he wanted him, but he just couldn't resist reminding the young man why he was there and what he stood to gain—or lose.

"Come and sit," he invited smoothly. "Have some of this excellent brandy." Parren hesitated. "Oh, come on, man!" snapped Reen. "We're on the same side. Now do as I ask and leave your prejudice aside for the moment. I have news for you."

Parren took the indicated chair and accepted the glass the Baron handed him. He managed to utter ungracious thanks, causing Reen to smile again.

"That's better," he said once the young man had taken a few sips and relaxed his stiff frame. "Now, the first thing I have to tell you is that our benefactress is pleased with your progress so far."

"But I haven't done anything."

The Baron waved his hand. "We're about to change that. But before I tell you our plan, our lady wanted me to say that she recognizes the risks you are running and appreciates the danger you have embraced in her service. She will reward you richly once we have achieved our goal, but in the meantime she wishes you to have something on account."

From inside his doublet, the Baron withdrew a small leather pouch. It rang faintly as he passed it to Parren. The young man took it, his eyes widening as he emptied a small heap of gold coins into the palm of his hand. He stared up at the Baron. "But this is too much!"

Reen tutted. "Would you refuse our lady's generosity? That is only a small part of what she believes you are worth, and she gives it now to show you how highly she esteems your service. I assure you, there'll be much more if all goes as we plan."

Parren shrugged and slipped the coins back into the pouch. He tucked it away inside his jacket. "Just tell me what I can do," he said, his acerbic manner tempered by his desire to prove worthy of his pay.

Reen gave another inward smile of satisfaction. Surely his god had guided his steps on the day he met this admirable young man! "You have heard of the two recent attacks on the King's life?" he asked.

Parren nodded. "A pity they didn't succeed in their objective."

The Baron sucked in a breath. "Be careful what you say!" he hissed. "That was treason you just uttered and it could get you killed. Where would we be then?"

Parren flushed, the scar down his right cheek standing out starkly. Seeing his discomfort, the Baron calmed. "And anyway, they succeeded very well. Yes, we would not have complained had they brought about the demise of our chief opposer. But their main objective was to test my... ah... control over our other associate."

Parren nodded in understanding, but Reen knew he understood only as much as Reen intended. Parren was not privy to the details of the plan.

"And who is this... associate?" the Captain asked. "I assume you've allied yourselves with a demon witch. Is it one of that renegade Rykan's men?"

This was more than Reen was willing to divulge, and he waved Parren's curiosity aside. "The less you know about such matters, the better. No," he added as the younger man scowled, "it's not a matter of trust. We both know how powerful these people are, but we don't know exactly what they're capable of.

You might have no defenses against them stealing secrets from your mind. Believe me, Captain, it's your welfare we're thinking of. Leave the details to us. You're running enough risks already."

Parren was only partially mollified. No doubt he was questioning how they could fight the likes of Sullyan and the other Artesans at the Manor when they commanded the kind of power Parren could only dream of.

"We have put a little plan in motion," Reen confided. "One guaranteed to give us access to their secrets and private dealings."

At the young man's disbelieving look, the Baron held out the two rings he had been toying with earlier. Parren took them and frowned up at the Baron. "And these are?"

Reen smiled nastily. "Tools of control, Captain! You recall that Elias sent a young man here, a Beraxian, to be a member of this new so-called College of his?"

Parren nodded. "Lord Ozella, yes. He's useless, as far as I can see. Hasn't found life here easy, or fitted in at all well."

Reen chuckled. "What a shame! Well, he's going to find life a whole lot tougher from now on." He sobered and leaned forward. "We plan well ahead, my lady and I. You see, those rings belong to Ozella's two young sisters, both of whom were cruelly and mysteriously abducted nearly two weeks ago. Their father has been instructed to await a ransom demand and to inform the King of their disappearance. Ozella knows nothing as yet. You will have the pleasure of telling him, and you will also let him know that the girls are being held as surety for his cooperation and good behavior. Do you see how far we trust you, Captain? You will be the one to control him and you will pass on to me, via the King's very efficient and discreet runner service, any useful information you obtain."

Seeing the beginnings of nasty pleasure dawn in Parren's eyes, the Baron leaned back. "Think of it! Eyes and ears within their very ranks. Information available only to you, to use as you see fit. You will be acting on your own initiative, Captain. We give you free rein. All we ask is that you keep us informed of any developments." He smiled. "It is fitting, is it not, that we use one of their own, someone they would never suspect, to effect their downfall?"

He and Parren laughed together and toasted their success with more brandy. Parren was clearly delighted with this turn of events, but there was one other thing on his mind.

"And what of Sullyan and Tamsen, my Lord Baron?" he asked, more respectful now in the light of the Baron's trust. "They are so powerful and protected here. What can I do to damage them?"

Reen settled smugly back in his chair. He regarded the young man before him, well aware that this was Parren's real goal. What he was about to hand him would be honed and sharpened into a very effective killing tool. Of that, he was sure.

"What do you do to someone you are unable to hurt physically?" he mused, as if to himself. "How do you damage them without implicating or risking yourself?"

"Well?" demanded Parren, eagerness overcoming manners.

"Don't be so impatient, young man. You will learn, in time, that careful planning and prudent management can allow you to exert influence where it is least expected. Over members of the King's forces, for example. Even over people such as those you despise."

Parren's face showed doubt. "What? You can exert influence over Sullyan and Tamsen? What kind of influence? How?"

The Baron shook his head and smiled. "Never you mind! You want to know how to hurt these people?" He held out his hand before Parren's face and slowly clenched his fingers into a fist. "You take and destroy something they value. You strip them of something precious!"

Satisfaction swelled his heart as he saw Parren's answering smile.

✣ ✣ ✣ ✣ ✣

Robin woke languidly the next morning, a little later than usual. Reveille was never sounded when the Manor had royal guests. The men were all roused by their sergeants, and senior officers were supposed to be disciplined enough not to need rousing, although their valets could always be relied upon when necessary. But Robin had been on duty until late the previous night and had no intention of being woken too early.

A slight sound disturbed him and he rolled over in the bed he shared with Sullyan. She had been soundly asleep when he came in, looking worn by her recent experiences as well as the aftermath of a long debriefing with General Blaine. She hadn't even stirred as Robin settled to sleep against her. He reached out an arm for her now, but she wasn't there.

Opening his eyes, he saw that she was fully dressed and the faint sound he had heard was made as she buckled her sword belt. Watching her appreciatively and feeling the warm stirrings of passion—he had missed her while they were apart—he raised himself on one elbow and smiled. But the warmth in his eyes faded as he took in her pallor and worried expression.

Without thinking, he asked, "What's wrong, love?"

"What is wrong?" Her voice was sharp with rare irritation, making him frown. "You ask me that? Two serious incidents, both of which could have cost the King his life in as many days. *Two!* Both could only have been executed by a powerful Artesan. Both were nearly successful, and both were carried out right under my nose! How can you ask me what is wrong?"

She swung away from him. "Someone is laughing at us, Robin. Playing with us. I do not like it. Add to that the fact that I lost one of my oldest and dearest friends yesterday under circumstances I should have prevented, and I think you might understand my mood today."

He slid from the bed and came to hold her, alarmed by her manner. Her temper was mercurial, it was true, but it was rarely turned on him. It was also unlike her to be so rattled by events, although he appreciated the gravity of the situation.

She wouldn't allow him to comfort her. "I must attend the King and the General again this morning," she said, "and I suggest you prepare to do the same. There will be a diplomatic mission to the Hierarch very shortly. We have to understand what is happening before more life is lost."

She left abruptly, leaving Robin puzzled and more than a little hurt by her tone. In truth, he was becoming concerned. This wasn't the first time she had spoken coldly to him or rejected his loving advances. On quite a few mornings over the past weeks, maybe even months, if he thought about it, she had been less than enthusiastic when he wanted to share his love. He was even starting to wonder if she was cooling toward him. Yet at other times she was very passionate, and he was confused as to what was causing such strange moods.

For the moment, he pushed his concerns to the back of his mind, although the small worm of doubt refused to vanish completely.

✤ ✤ ✤ ✤ ✤

Humming tunelessly in a rare good humor, Captain Parren strolled toward the stables in the morning sunshine. He was rolling the two gold rings over and over in one hand, and now and then he glanced down and smiled thoughtfully. Today promised to be a good day and, he hoped, the start of many more.

He was casually stalking the olive-skinned young man who had walked here a few minutes earlier. He knew his quarry would return this way, it was the only track leading back to the College. Satisfied, he leaned on the rails of an empty paddock and put the rings back in his pocket. After ten minutes or so he drew his sword, making a show of inspecting the blade. He suppressed a smile as he heard the other man returning.

From the corner of his eye, Parren watched the young man come down the track. Ozella had seen him, of course, but was taking no notice. As he approached Parren, he gave the lean officer a slight nod and made to walk on past. He was brought up short as Parren whipped his sword across his path, blocking his progress.

Ozella started in surprise. "What did you do that for?"

Parren grinned and sheathed the weapon. He had Ozella's attention now. He beckoned and Ozella came closer, indignant but still curious. Parren reached into his jacket pocket and withdrew the rings. He held them out on the palm of his hand.

Ozella frowned, and then his almond eyes widened. He went pale. "Where did you get those?" He grabbed for the two rings, but Parren was too quick and snatched his hand away.

"Not so fast, my foreign friend. You recognize them, then?"

"Of course I recognize them. They belong to my sisters! What are you doing with them?"

Parren was silent a moment, giving Ozella's annoyance and apprehension time to build. He dropped the rings back into his pocket.

"Well, now," he said smoothly, "let's just say I'm holding them for safe-keeping."

Ozella turned even paler. His skin took on an unhealthy hue and his dark eyes grew larger. "What do you mean? Why would they need safe-keeping?"

Parren turned lazily and leant his weight on the rail. "Well, you wouldn't want them stolen now, would you? And the men holding your sisters are most unscrupulous where gold is concerned. And not only gold, of course." He turned to gaze at Ozella, a chilling expression on his face.

The young man swallowed, looking suddenly nauseous. He turned trapped eyes to Parren's. "But why are you holding them? What do you want from me?"

Parren showed his teeth. "Very good, my friend, you catch on fast. It's a shame you're not so quick to learn your lessons here, isn't it?"

"What are you talking about?" Ozella was plainly confused by the change of subject. "What have lessons got to do with my sisters? Why have they been taken? Where are they? You bastard, you'd better not have harmed them!"

Anger suddenly overcoming fear, Ozella grabbed at Parren's shoulder. The Captain was ready for him and had the point of his sword resting against Ozella's sternum before the younger man realized he had moved. Staring mutely down the length of steel and then up into Parren's intense glare, Ozella saw death and a lack of choices. He sagged.

"Please, just tell me they're all right," he begged, his voice sounding knotted and painful. "I love my sisters. They're so young…."

Parren weighed his capitulation and found it satisfactory. He sheathed his sword. Ozella would come to rue his lack of application to swordplay as much as he would his other failings, Parren was sure. He turned his back on Ozella to show how little he feared him. The younger man made no move.

"So far," said Parren, his tone nonchalant, "they are unharmed. Their continuing health and well-being, however, depends on you."

Parren could almost hear the defeat in Ozella before he spoke. "What is it you want?"

Parren turned his head. "Nothing too onerous, I assure you."

His kept his tone mildly friendly, hoping to unsettle Ozella further. "Information, my friend, that's what I want. The use of your eyes and ears. And the assurance of your loyal, and silent, compliance."

"Information about what?"

Ozella asked the question automatically. He was trapped and he clearly knew it. All he needed now was the means to keep his sisters safe. As soon as he realized what was happening, Parren was sure he would do whatever he was asked to guarantee their release.

Parren grinned broadly. He was experiencing a raw and heady sense of power. He would repay them all for passing him over! He was a good soldier and an even better officer. He should easily have been a major by now. Twice, his promotion had been blocked by Robin Tamsen, and he nurtured festering grievances with Sullyan that went back years. They came surging to the surface as he reviewed them, and an almost orgasmic pleasure swamped him as he anticipated his just revenge.

Wrenching himself from these gratifying thoughts, he proceeded to tell Ozella precisely how to ensure his sisters' safety.

Chapter Seventeen

It was Inauguration Day for the new College, but the morning was taken up by a hastily convened meeting between General Blaine, King Elias, and Colonel Sullyan. Sullyan had already told the General of the suspicions she had formed in Port Loxton, and also of her fear that substrate communications might not be as secure as they thought. She needed to discuss these fears with Elias so the three of them took breakfast in Blaine's private apartments, something not even Sullyan had ever done before.

Blaine's suite was on the third floor of the Manor, along with Vassa's rooms and the senior officers' hall. It consisted of a functional but comfortable sleeping room, a small privy and washroom, a cooking area which Sullyan thought was hardly ever used as she prepared fellan there, and a large living room furnished with comfortable chairs and couches. Blaine's valet, Hyram, was stationed outside the door with strict instructions to admit only those expressly summoned, and the thick stone walls and sheer three-story drop outside would ensure there was no danger of their being overheard. In addition to these precautions, both Blaine and Sullyan had their shields down tight.

Sullyan was thankful that her stomach was behaving itself as she was in desperate need of fellan. She only felt fatigued, although she was still plagued by the tingling sensation in her left forearm which, inexplicably, had now begun to affect her right. Some of her temper with Robin that morning had its roots in this strange discomfort.

She brought a tray of cups through to the living area and placed it on a low oak table. She served Elias and Blaine before taking her own drink, and then seated herself on a wooden chair facing her monarch and commanding officer. They both thanked her, and an uneasy silence fell as they sat sipping the scalding fellan.

As was often the case, Sullyan spoke first. "With your permission, your Majesty, General?" The two men nodded. She laid aside her cup and faced Elias. "Taking all the known evidence into account, and especially following the incident at the horse race and yesterday's attack, I think we must now accept that the perpetrator of these events and the person responsible for creating the Staff and backing Lord Rykan are either the same person or part of the same group."

Elias regarded her sourly. She ignored his displeasure. "We all agreed last year that there had to be almost limitless funds behind this plot, and it is now also clear that this is not merely someone with a grudge against Artesans or their supporters. The two attempts on your life prove it is far more serious than that."

Blaine cleared his throat. "In the light of what Colonel Sullyan has told me, Elias, I cannot but agree with her conclusions. If not for your patronage, Artesans would stand no chance of overcoming the people's prejudice. You are our only champion. Removing you would seriously jeopardize the few advancements we have made, and if an Artesan was implicated in your death I doubt any of us would survive the reprisals."

The King sat in silence. His eyes strayed to Sullyan and she held his gaze as she spoke again.

"Both these attempts, your Majesty, were undeniably the work of a skilled and powerful Artesan. The fact that on neither occasion could I detect any traces of the controlling psyche is a source of great concern to me."

Blaine was clearly troubled by this too, but Elias had no knowledge of the history of Artesans and scant understanding of the craft.

"There's no need to be so formal, Brynne," he said absently, unsettled by what he had heard. "This isn't an official state meeting. Why does being unable to detect the Artesan concern you so?"

"Maybe it should be an official state meeting, your Majesty," she responded. That drew a sharp look from Elias. She turned to Blaine without answering the King's question. "General, might I suggest we mount an immediate diplomatic mission to the Hierarch of Andaryon? First, to offer our sympathy for the recent destruction caused by Albian raiders—your Majesty, some sort of recompense from the Treasury might be politic and would be much appreciated, I am sure—and second, to officially enlist his aid in finding whoever was responsible for the attacks. Someone gave the Albian raiders metaphysical access to his realm, and as our attackers yesterday were undeniably Andaryan, Pharikian has to take some measure of responsibility."

General Blaine nodded and she turned back to Elias.

"Forgive me, your Majesty, but before I voice my suspicions concerning our enemy, I would like to confer with Timar. Due to his great age and the fact that Andaryon has always encouraged the Artesan craft, he knows much more of our history than I do. He might be able to throw some light on a matter which has been puzzling me. I would also like to ask whether he has been able to locate any of Rykan's former nobles, as they may possess valuable information. And a visit to Lord Marik might be advisable, to see if he discovered any clues in Rykan's records as to his accomplices."

"You're convinced he wasn't acting alone, then?" asked Elias, curiosity overriding unease. He leaned back in his chair, stretching long legs in russet-red breeches. In a simple cream shirt with his sandy-blond hair falling in his eyes, he appeared much younger than his thirty-one years.

"He plainly was not, your Majesty," she pointed out. "Otherwise these recent attacks would not have occurred. No, there is someone more than powerful behind all this, someone not only with a high-ranking Artesan's power at his command, but also that of State."

"State?" Elias sat up abruptly. "Why do you say that?"

"I say it because of the amount of gold I believe changed hands over the creation of the Staff. And also because of the attempts on your life."

"Explain," snapped the King, disturbed.

Sullyan lowered her gaze. This would not be easy. The dreadful suspicion planted in her mind by Denny would not go away and needed airing, if only to eliminate it. But it would not be well received. She raised her eyes to the King, determined to face his ire as best she could. She had volunteered for this. She already felt she had failed Elias, so she was the obvious choice to broach such a painful line of enquiry. Even so, she couldn't just blurt it out.

"Your Majesty, what would have happened had either of the attacks succeeded in taking your life?"

The King's gaze sharpened. Blaine remained silent, having agreed the night before to let Sullyan take the brunt of Elias's anger. "My Queen would become Regent for Eadan until he was old enough to rule," he said shortly.

Sullyan nodded. "As you know, it has recently become apparent that Baron Reen is foremost among those who oppose the legitimization of the Artesan craft."

191

She paused and Elias gave a curt nod, unsure where she was headed. She took a breath.

"We also know that Baron Reen is Queen Sofira's confidante and liegeman. On the first day of our journey here he made reference to following her orders, and she insists he accompanies you wherever you go."

The King's countenance darkened and Sullyan glanced down at her hands. Still, it had to be said.

"Your Majesty, how far do you trust the Queen?"

Elias's expression hardened. "Are you suggesting the Queen is trying to have me killed? Do you know what you're saying, Colonel? You are accusing her of High Treason, an offence which carries the death penalty."

"It is only a suspicion, your Majesty," Blaine said. "We've had precious little to go on so far, barring Reen's flaunted dislike. Even that might just be the posturing of a small-minded and prejudiced man, or it might be a ploy to deflect us from our real adversary. Who knows? But we can't discount any possibility, however far-fetched."

There was silence before Elias gave a deep sigh. "All right, I can understand how your suspicions arose. I can't pretend that the Queen and I enjoy a completely... harmonious marital relationship. She made that obvious after the horse race. I suppose I can't complain. I wed her for political reasons, to keep her father in line, not for love. I had hoped affection would come in time, but it hasn't. However, she's never opposed my policies and I do not believe she would try to have the father of her children murdered. Reen, now... well, he's another matter."

Sullyan could feel Elias watching her as he spoke, but she didn't raise her head or react in any way. He frowned, finally noticing just how tired she looked.

"Brynne," he said gently. She looked up and met his gaze,

although her discomfort was plain. He pursed his lips. "There's no need to be so downcast. I have every confidence you'll find the one responsible for all of this. I trust your loyalty and judgment."

She lowered her eyes once more and murmured, "You can trust my loyalty implicitly, your Majesty, but my judgment failed you yesterday."

Elias glared at her. "Aha! So that's what this is about. That's what all this formality is for. Brynne, how can you think you failed me when you fought the way you did in my defense? What more could you have done? Do you think you should have been killed instead of Lord Fiann?"

His rather blunt words brought tears to her eyes. "I deeply regret he was forced to that act, yes, your Majesty. Had I realized sooner what the manipulation of that storm meant, I might have prevented much injury and loss of life."

"And had you been prescient, you might have averted the whole damned thing!"

Sullyan flinched at Elias's tone. Seeing this, he rose abruptly and crossed to her, holding out his hand. Unable to refuse, she took it. He raised her and looked down into her misted eyes. His own had softened considerably in the face of her distress. He placed his hands on her shoulders.

"Brynne Sullyan, you are truly a remarkable person. I don't know anyone who could have endured what you did at the hands of that brute Rykan and still go on to beat him in single combat. Oh, it doesn't matter what weapons you used," he snapped, cutting across her protest. "You must know that I consider you the finest member of my forces, with the exception of Mathias here, of course, and I acknowledge and appreciate the depth of your loyalty.

"But you're still human, Brynne, and we humans are not perfect. Not even you. So stop blaming yourself for what you couldn't prevent. Forget it! I need you to carry on telling me the things I don't want to hear, and that's a royal command. It's what I pay you for. Do you hear me, Brynne?"

She was overwhelmed by his praise. "Yes, your Majesty," she managed.

He muttered a pithy oath and thoroughly startled her by enfolding her in a huge hug. "Enough 'your Majesties'!" he growled.

"By your command," she weakly replied.

He grinned and released her. "That's better. Now, we've wasted enough time." He retreated to the couch and seated himself. "Your suggestion of a meeting with Pharikian is a good one. I imagine he's not best pleased at the latest turn of events. You are to assure him the raids were nothing to do with us. I hope he knows I would never resort to such tactics. And I agree to your proposal of recompense, although I won't accept any blame. Offer him what compensation you think reasonable, to show my goodwill. Just don't bankrupt me! Let me know the outcome of your meeting and we'll take it from there.

"Now, enough of these suspicions. I'm not going to let some misguided and murderous bigot deflect me from what I know is right. I've been looking forward to this day for too long. What's the schedule for the inauguration? I hope you're going to give me a tour of the College before the ceremony!"

✣ ✣ ✣ ✣ ✣

Rienne spent the morning in the infirmary. She was still full of her news, and the effort of keeping it to herself was beginning to tell. She supposed she was likely to be irrational and to suffer odd moods during the first few months of her pregnancy, and she mustn't overdo things in this delicate first stage. But she was desperate to tell Sullyan so everyone else could know.

She nearly told Taran at breakfast that morning, but the Adept seemed preoccupied. She managed to resist the impulse and stick to her resolve that Sullyan should be the first to know. Yet Sullyan remained closeted with Blaine and the King all morning, and the inauguration ceremony was scheduled for mid-afternoon, so there was no chance for Rienne to get her alone.

Although not a practicing Artesan, Rienne's strong empathic link with Sullyan guaranteed her a place in the College. She held no rank, as she had no influence over the elements, but she understood on a deep and emotional level how Artesans thought and what they felt. This made her the obvious choice as their dedicated Healer. As such, she would be present at the inauguration. It would be attended mainly by Artesans, although some of the Manor's non-gifted residents also had permission to watch.

Once the ceremony was over, there would be an all-company assembly on the parade ground by order of the King. Elias had decided it would be politic to address his forces and announce how he intended to deal with the current situation. By now, courtesy of the men who had escorted the King from Port Loxton, everyone had heard the story of the horse race, and also of the battle in the storm. Unfortunately, these were not the only stories the men from Port Loxton circulated.

Rienne had heard the odd snippet of gossip, but she was far too busy to take much notice. Besides, rumors concerning Sullyan often circulated the Manor, although never as prolifically as right now. Rienne was used to ignoring them, as was Sullyan. Today, however, she couldn't seem to avoid them.

The wound in Denny's side was narrow but deep and needed frequent draining. His badly broken arm had been set and only needed time to heal, but the puncture wound had become infected. Rienne was flushing it for the second time that morning when she noticed Denny watching her closely. Eventually she put down her soiled cloth and stared him in the eye.

"What?"

He smiled charmingly. "Healer Arlen, I believe you're very friendly with Colonel Sullyan, is that right?"

Rienne's eyes narrowed. "Yes. What of it?"

"And with Captain Elijah?"

She sighed. "Yes, Lieutenant, we're all friends here." She bent once more to his side, reapplying the hot cloth to the angry soreness of his wound. "My life mate Cal, Taran, and I lived together before we came here."

Denny raised his brows even as he winced at the pressure of her cloth. "Well, I must say I never realized you Artesans were so liberal."

She straightened. "And just what do you mean by that?"

"It's only that I'm a little surprised someone like Major Tamsen puts up with competition from someone like Captain Elijah, that's all. From what I remember of Sullyan when we were training together, I'm amazed she's encouraged such scandal."

"Scandal?" Rienne frowned. "I don't know what you're talking about. There's no scandal. There's no competition, either. Brynne's in love with Robin, not Taran. I don't know where you got these nasty ideas from, Lieutenant, but I'll warn you against repeating them. There's not a grain of truth in what you're insinuating, and you ought to think twice before spreading such lies. If Robin Tamsen heard what you just said, you'd find yourself in more trouble than you could handle. And I'll tell you something else. If I hear any more of that kind of talk in my infirmary, you'll be out the door so fast you won't know what's hit you—infection or no infection. Do I make myself plain, Lieutenant?"

"Yes, ma'am!" grinned Denny, sounding completely unrepentant. Rienne finished her attentions with rather less than her usual care.

Taran came into the infirmary some time later, looking for her.

The inauguration ceremony was about to start. Blaine had taken the King through the College, and Elias declared himself satisfied with the completed building. All those invited to be present at the inauguration were now assembling.

Rienne observed Taran as they strolled toward the College. She thought he appeared strained and care-worn, although had she not heard Denny's distasteful gossip she might have put it down to shock at someone trying to kill the King. Now, however, Denny's words caused her to wonder.

"Taran," she asked, placing a hand on his arm, "are you all right?"

He gave a guilty start, as if coming out of a shameful reverie. She frowned.

"I'm fine, Rienne."

His hasty reply convinced her otherwise. "Have you heard the rumors going around?" she asked, trying to keep her tone casual. Out of the corner of her eye she saw him flush. A dreadful suspicion crept into her mind.

"What rumors, Rienne? You know what soldiers are like. Any juicy bit of gossip soon becomes fact when different companies get together." He didn't meet her eyes as he spoke.

"Stop it, Taran, I'm not a fool!" she said harshly. He stopped in his tracks, alarmed. "Tell me straight," she demanded, swinging round to face him, "have you done anything lately to be ashamed of?"

His flaming face and hurriedly averted eyes confirmed the worst. Her own eyes widened in shock and disbelief. "Oh, Taran, I don't believe it! How could you?"

He had the grace to look thoroughly miserable. "I didn't mean to, Rienne, I just got carried away! But she was so good about it, you know how she is. And as if that wasn't bad enough, there was all that business with Lady Jinella. I know I treated her badly, but events were moving so fast I just didn't have the time to apologize. She would have to be Reen's niece. That only made it worse! And then I couldn't stop worrying that Sullyan would tell Robin how I'd let my feelings get the better of me, and I just felt more and more ashamed of myself. Now I can't even look at him without remembering what an idiot I was, although Sullyan was very calm about the whole thing, she knows how I feel, after all, and only laughed at me once she'd dunked me in the water—"

"Dunked you?" Rienne stared at him, perplexed. She grabbed his arm. "Taran, I need you to tell me the plain truth. Did you, or did you not, make love to Brynne?"

"What?" His voice was harsh and he turned pale. "Is that what they're saying? No, of course I didn't! I lost control of my emotions, that's all. How could you even think that of me? You know how much I respect her and Robin. I'd never let either of them down like that! I'm surprised at you, Rienne. I thought you of all people would understand."

He wrenched his arm away and turned from her, pain and shock in his eyes. He clearly hadn't realized the length to which the rumors had gone, and Rienne had no idea what misconception the gossip had sprung from. What would he do when Robin heard it?

Hearing the truth in his voice, Rienne regretted her words and was thoroughly ashamed for doubting him. She knew him very well, as well as she knew her own life mate, and was aware he could be trusted to a fine degree. She had allowed Denny to put ideas into her head which normally she would have laughed at. Perhaps her condition had rendered her vulnerable to such doubt, but that didn't absolve her of blame. She shook her head, a tear appearing in the corner of her eye.

"Oh, Taran, I'm so sorry." She took his arm again and turned him, seeing distress and misery plain on his face. "Of course you'd never do anything so dreadful. But you were acting so guilty, and I misunderstood… I don't know what came over me. I only hope you can forgive me.

"But, Taran, the men from Port Loxton obviously misunderstood too. They have been spreading some very credible-sounding stories about you and Brynne. Some of our own men have been heard repeating them, so it's only a matter of time before Brynne and Robin hear them too. It would be better if you took Robin aside and told him the truth of it yourself, no matter how awkward you feel. It'll save unpleasantness later."

Taran sighed. "Yes, I know." Some of the pain left his face, but it was replaced by more embarrassment. Rienne guessed he was seeing himself explaining his shameful conduct to the Major. "I'll try to do it after the assembly, but I don't know what the King's plans are. If he sends Robin's company out again, I might not get the chance to speak to him before he leaves."

"I'm sure you can catch him for a few minutes, Taran. But just in case you can't, I'll mention it to Brynne. I need to speak to her anyway, so I'll make sure she knows what's going on. Although she might have heard already. Not much escapes her."

"You're right there," agreed Taran sadly.

Rienne took his arm in a friendly way and they walked to the College together.

Chapter Eighteen

Ozella watched as the Manor's inhabitants filed into the Refectory, the largest room in the College. Elias and Blaine were talking quietly to Bull and Sullyan. Vassa stood close by, and Master Ardoch had also come to watch. Cal was next to Robin, with young Tad hovering at the Major's side as usual. Captain Dexter was also there, along with most of Sullyan's company.

Ozella hadn't wanted to attend the ceremony, yet to stay away would have drawn unwanted attention, and he already had more of that than he could cope with. He was sick with worry and heartily wished he were elsewhere. He just couldn't take his mind off his sisters and was frantic for their safety. Parren's smug, scarred face kept appearing before his eyes. He couldn't stop his mind constantly replaying the chilling eagerness in the man's voice as he told Ozella what he must do.

Ozella would do his best, which wasn't saying much, but he was already torturing himself by wondering whether his sisters were really still alive. He had no way of knowing, and Parren had told him that if he tried to get a message to his father, he would be responsible for the unspeakable acts of violation the girls would suffer. He trembled as he recalled Parren's vivid description of that violation, sure the captain was feeding his own disgusting desires.

Ozella was not only terrified for his sisters. He doubted his own ability to hide his fear from his fellow Artesans and was petrified they would find him out. Parren had assured him he only had to keep his mind closed and his mouth shut to be safe, and Ozella never questioned how the giftless Parren knew this. Ozella had no choice. All he could do was act as normally as possible and await his first instructions.

Taran and Rienne were the last to arrive, and on seeing them take their places the King called the gathering to order. He stood at the far end of the long Refectory, the sunlight from its windows slanting in to stripe the floor with gold. The seats and tables had all been moved to the sides of the room and everyone stood facing Elias. The King looked round at their expectant faces and smiled.

"First, my friends, let me thank you all for coming and welcome you to the King's College of Artesans. You're here to witness the inauguration of what I hope will be the first of many institutions of its kind. Not only will it serve to nurture and train those just starting out in their craft, but it will also encourage those who are currently unsure or afraid of their innate gifts. In this way, I hope to improve relations between Artesans and those who fear and oppose them.

"I hope you will all find the atmosphere of the College and the support of your peers valuable as you study, and that it will enable you to develop and grow both as human beings and as Artesans. I must admit, I find the frankness and closeness with which Artesans deal with one another very refreshing, and it is something I wish to foster among all the men of the fighting companies.

"So, my friends, those are my aims and reasons for establishing this College. All that remains is for me to wish success to every one of its members, and to declare that from this moment, the first King's College of Artesans is officially open!"

There was applause from those assembled and a murmuring arose, many commenting on the King's words and speculating on what the future might hold now that there was a legitimate and supportive center of learning. Ozella noticed that Taran had tears in his eyes, and he wasn't the only one. The Beraxian wondered if Taran was thinking of his late father, whom he had heard used to be Taran's mentor. How proud would he have been to see his son a part of this?

Elias then turned and nodded to Sullyan, who produced a package that had lain unnoticed on the table behind her. Elias smiled his thanks. He cleared his throat and a respectful silence fell.

"This is a very special occasion and you are all quite remarkable people." The King smiled, clearly enjoying himself. "I want it to be widely known that I support the Artesan craft, and so I conferred at great length with General Blaine and Colonel Sullyan as to how we could encourage Albia's people to recognize and follow my example. It was suggested that we adopt the same system as the one identifying members of my forces, namely insignia dedicated to those who are Artesans. Such a system will show our people that Artesans have my full backing and authority. I hope you will wear these symbols with pride.

"Lord Ozella, will you step forward, please?"

Ozella nearly fainted with fright. He had kept out of the way at the back of the room, intending to slip away as soon as he could. Hearing his name called so unexpectedly sent a shockwave through his system, and he was suddenly convinced he had been discovered. As they all turned to look at him and he saw the pleased expression on Elias's face, he realized his mistake. He would have to keep a tighter rein on his reactions from now on, he thought, or he would give himself away. Shakily, he approached his monarch.

"Lord Ozella," said Elias, "Colonel Sullyan informs me that your rank is Artesan-Apprentice. It gives me great pleasure to give you this first of the new emblems, and to declare you a member of the King's College of Artesans."

Elias pinned a gold rank-badge to Ozella's shirt, and the embarrassed young man stammered awkward thanks as he stepped hastily back. Those around him peered curiously at the badge, which was a narrow bar of gold bisecting the underlying symbol of Elias's House, the Rovannon sun-circled crown.

Young Tad was called next, and he received the same badge as Ozella. But then he compounded Ozella's confusion by not only pledging his loyalty to the College, his King, and his fellow Artesans, but also by according Sullyan, as the highest-ranking Artesan present, the brow-lips-heart salute due her seniority and power. Sullyan, smiling in approval, returned the young lad's homage, and the assembled men applauded Tad's achievement and sense of ceremony. Ozella's face went scarlet with shame.

As Apprentice-elite, Cal was next. His badge consisted of two bars over the royal symbol. As he returned to Taran and Rienne, having followed Tad's example and been similarly applauded, Ozella heard him murmur, "A straight bar denotes Earth, then."

There were currently no Journeymen, and so Taran, as Adept, was next. His rank-badge consisted of two golden bars in parallel undulating lines, representing his mastery over Water. Like the others, they also overlaid the Rovannon crown. As he fingered his own emblem, Ozella could see how well made and designed the badges were. Taran's feelings of pride and privilege were plain on his face as he gave Sullyan her due. Ozella saw answering emotion in her and Robin's eyes, yet Taran seemed to avoid the Major's gaze.

Then it was Bull's turn. The big man's rank-badge, representing an Adept-elite's ability to influence Fire, was a straight bar of gold with stylized flames along its upper edge. Robin followed him, his insignia of two flame bars reflecting his mastery over Fire. Mathias Blaine received the same badge. All three men honored the King as well as their Senior Artesan.

There being no Master-elite, the only Artesan left was Sullyan herself. Her badge was markedly different to the rest. In order to acknowledge and reflect her mastery of all four of the fundamental elements, her badge contained all the characteristics of the others, to which was added the straight bar carrying curls of stylized Air. They were arranged one above the other over the Rovannon sun and crown. Cleverly incorporated around the disc of the sun at the cardinal points, each element was represented by its corresponding precious stone or jewel. Diamond for Earth, the iridescent jade-pearl for Water, a fire opal for Fire, and the rare and treasured zephyrite for Air.

Zephyrite was a stone found only on the highest of mountains where the constant abrasion of the wind sometimes exposed veins of this curious gem. Due to its porous and crystalline nature, zephyrite emitted a strange and eerie keening when the wind blew through it. Usually greenish in color, it emitted a blue glow once the sun was down.

Ozella was impressed with the quality of the workmanship. The badges had been made by the King's personal goldsmith. Where Elias had obtained the zephyrite from, he couldn't imagine, and the fire opal could only have come from Andaryon. Sullyan stood admiring her badge for a few moments before lifting her eyes to the King. Like the others, she pledged him her loyalty, but as she turned from doing so, her badge proudly gleaming above her left breast, Ozella was amazed to see every Artesan go down on one knee before her. Caught out, he hastened to do the same. In perfect unison, they accorded her once again the brow-lips-heart salute due a Senior Master. Even Blaine was doing so. Tears standing in her eyes, Sullyan returned their homage.

Elias stood grinning behind her.

✣ ✣ ✣ ✣ ✣

Immediately after the ceremony, the inhabitants of the Manor not on guard duty assembled on the parade ground to hear the King's address. Baron Reen, having deliberately boycotted the opening ceremony of the blasphemous College, was now shadowing Elias as usual. As he did so, he watched carefully for signs that Parren had managed to speak to Ozella.

He flanked Elias as the King, along with Blaine and Sullyan, faced the assembled throng from the platform below the pavilion. An expectant hush fell over them as Elias raised his voice.

"Men, you have doubtless heard by now that relations between Albia and Andaryon have once again been threatened by hostile action. This took the form of an attempt on my life, which occurred during our journey here yesterday."

Angry muttering rose from the assembled companies. Elias held up a hand and it died away.

"The other incident you may have heard of occurred during a horse race at Port Loxton. This is not necessarily connected to yesterday's events, and until it has been thoroughly investigated, I want no wild speculations as to who might be responsible. This is a royal command and I expect it to be obeyed."

As one, the men saluted their sovereign, indicating their obedience to his will. Unseen behind the King, Reen smiled faintly. He knew the damage was already done. Enough people had heard his condemnation of Sullyan, and that, coupled with the steps he had taken before they left Port Loxton, would ensure the spread of rumor. Not even a royal decree could stop it now.

Elias continued. "What some of you will not have heard is that there have also been raids into Andaryon by Albians. At least two villages in that realm were wantonly destroyed. This displeases me greatly, as it is a flagrant and deliberate flaunting of my express orders. I am determined to identify and bring the perpetrators to justice, and I assure you, their punishment will be swift and decisive. I charge each of you with searching for those responsible.

The Albians who were killed in the Fifth Realm were unmarked, and there were no clues to their commander or the reasons behind their actions. We do not yet know whether yesterday's attempt on my life was in retaliation for the villages' destruction, or for some other, unknown reason.

"In order to assure Andaryon's ruler of my continuing goodwill and utter condemnation of any hostile action between our realms, I have instructed Colonel Sullyan to mount an immediate ambassadorial mission to Caer Vellet. I have also authorized her to offer recompense for the destruction of the villages as a gesture of our good faith."

Reen narrowed his eyes and his mood soured. He would have to inform the Queen of this new drain on the Treasury. They were fortunate that Elias had not so far noticed the absence of the gold Sofira had cunningly liberated in order to purchase the raw materials necessary to manufacture the Staff. This was solely due to the fact that the Queen was effectively Albia's Treasurer. Her control of the royal coffers, and the clerks who kept the accounts, would be sorely tested if this sort of charity was to be doled out with any kind of frequency. It was a development he had not foreseen.

He tugged himself out of his thoughts, for Elias was still speaking.

"I have also authorized the Colonel to investigate the raids into Andaryon, as well as those into our realm. While she is away, General Blaine will organize the rest of you to watch for and counter any further raids into our land or threats to our person. I need not remind you that the capture of any such raiders is preferable to their deaths, as information about the identity of their commanders is paramount.

"We intend to send a clear and unequivocal message to whoever is behind this flagrant breaking of the treaty that we will not tolerate their actions, and we will certainly not allow such base tactics to endanger our trade alliance. I have every confidence that you will do what you can to support my will in this."

A few of the men raised a cheer, which quickly spread. Elias acknowledged the cheers before dismissing the men, pleased by their show of support. Reen stood behind him, a small smile on his face. The King's last statement about not allowing recent events to sour relations with his outlander friends would be tested to breaking point when Reen implemented the next stage of his plan.

His gaze fell on the pale features of young Lord Ozella, whose unease was clear to see. It then transferred thoughtfully to the smug face of Captain Parren. Reen knew he would have to contrive to speak privately with his associate before Colonel Sullyan set out for Andaryon. He now had a very important message to pass on.

✣ ✣ ✣ ✣ ✣

Before Sullyan spoke to those who would accompany her to Andaryon, she had another matter to address. Once Blaine and the King had excused her, she sought out Tad. She found him where she expected to; at the horse lines, seeing to Robin's mount. The tow-headed youngster had attached himself firmly to Robin and often performed duties more befitting a squire than a cadet. It was an unprecedented situation and not entirely appropriate, but Robin didn't have the heart to refuse his service.

The boy was grooming Robin's horse, but he stopped and stood to attention when he saw Sullyan approaching. She was aware that she always overawed him, and the fact that she was married to his hero gave her an added aura of mystery in his adoring eyes. He snapped a slightly shaky salute, which she nonchalantly returned. He stayed at attention until she released him.

"Stand easy, Cadet. I have come to ask you a question, if I may."

Tad's wide eyes betrayed his disbelief that she was asking his permission.

"Come walk with me, if you will," she said, glancing meaningfully at the stable lads nearby.

Tad looked their way, noting their curious stares. Laying aside his brush, he fell into step beside her, his bearing indicating how important he felt.

They walked out of the stable yard and along the track leading to the breeding pastures. Until they reached the open fields, Sullyan held her peace. Tad did likewise. It was only when they were well out into the pasturelands that she turned to him and spoke.

"Tad, I would like you to tell me what you can recall of Baron Reen's behavior when he accompanied the King on his last visit here. The day Major Tamsen achieved his Mastery."

Tad glanced at her, hesitant. "I was honored to be chosen to serve at the King's table that day, Colonel," he said. "The Hierarch's page, Norkis, told me what to do. He served the King and the Hierarch, while I served the others. I really liked Norkis, Colonel. Why is it that some people dislike demons, I mean, Andaryans, so much? They're really not that different to us."

Sullyan agreed and smiled at Tad's innocent confusion. "There are some in Albia who believe that outlanders should not be classed as people at all, Tad," she said. "There are even those who still refuse to believe that the other realms exist, incredible though that is. And prejudiced people will latch on to any difference in order to justify their hatred: color of skin, tone of voice, the shape of one's eyes, to name only some. They feel threatened by anyone who does not conform to their idea of normality, and try to deny them their place in life. Take the current distrust of Artesans as a case in point. But carry on, Tad, if you will."

"Well," said the youngster slowly, "the King and the Hierarch and General Blaine talked during dinner. Mostly about the differences between our realms, and what we might be able to learn from each other. But Baron Reen hardly said a word the whole time. I noticed that he kept watching the Hierarch through half-closed eyes, and he had a very strange look on his face. You know, Colonel, he reminded me of the way the stable cats watch a rat before they pounce."

Sullyan grinned. She could just imagine the predatory look on the Baron's swarthy face.

Tad continued. "Anyway, after dinner Baron Reen moved as far from the Hierarch as he could, but he also seemed to want to stay very close to the King. It was almost as if he thought the Hierarch might pull a knife on the King, and he didn't trust him an inch. But King Elias wouldn't have invited him or dined with him had he feared the Hierarch, would he, Colonel?"

"Indeed not, Tad," agreed Sullyan, pleased with Tad's quick and enquiring mind. He was developing observational skills that would stand him in good stead both as an Artesan and as a soldier.

"After they all went into the pavilion," said Tad, "I went out to the parade ground to be ready to hold the Major's horse when the honors were given out." His eyes shone at the memory. "I was so surprised when he was promoted, Colonel. Almost as much as he was, I think. Did you know they were going to do that? Had you asked the General—? Oh!" Tad's face turned crimson as he remembered her circumstances that day. "No, you couldn't have, could you? I'm sorry, Colonel."

"Never mind, lad," soothed Sullyan, laying a friendly hand on his shoulder. "I am pleased that your memories of the day are happier than mine. All turned out well in the end. I was as proud of Major Tamsen as you were, for both his achievements. Now, what else do you remember?"

Dragging himself back from embarrassment and hero worship, Tad said, "I was watching the Major trying to break the General's Firefield, but I do remember seeing the Baron's face once. He was staring hard at someone, but it wasn't the Major. I remember wondering who he was looking at, but I never did see who it was. And then the portway opened, and you appeared on the parade ground, and all I could see and hear were the men and their cheering.

"I moved nearer the pavilion to get a better view. I stayed watching while you completed your test, and while the Hierarch confirmed you as Senior Master. After you, the General, the King, and the Hierarch left the pavilion, I was just about to go back for the Major's horse when I heard a strange noise. I went round the back of the pavilion to see what it was. It was quite funny, really, although I didn't laugh at the time because it wasn't polite. But the noise was coming from Baron Reen. He was on his knees in the grass, puking his—oh, I beg your pardon, Colonel, I mean he was being very sick all over the ground."

"Was he indeed? And then what did he do?"

"He got to his feet very slowly and wiped his mouth. He looked awful, all pasty and greenish. I thought he couldn't have eaten something bad because no one else was sick, and Chief Cook Goran was very particular that day about who he let into the kitchens. But whatever it was didn't go away, because the Baron still looked ill and was very shaky on his feet. I wondered whether I ought to help him, but he didn't look like he wanted help. And I didn't like him, Colonel. There was something... not right about him. Do you know what I mean?"

She smiled. "I do indeed, Tad. You have been most helpful. Now, I have heard promising reports lately of your progress from both Major Tamsen and Captain Elijah. They are impressed with your diligence. If you carry on as you are, it will not be long before you are ready to be confirmed in the next rank."

The boy's eyes widened and he stammered his thanks.

"And how is your weapons training?" she asked, recalling a comment of Robin's that because Tad was a year younger than most of the other cadets he was having problems keeping up with his fellows.

The youngster's face fell. "Oh, not too bad, Colonel. I am trying."

"I am sure you are," she soothed. "Remember, you can ask any of us for extra tutoring if you feel you need it. We would not see you fall behind the other boys."

Tad's mouth gaped. "Any of you, Colonel?" He clearly found it impossible to believe that either of his idols would bother to instruct a mere cadet in the art of swordplay.

She grinned at his stunned expression. "You are an Artesan, Tad, not just a cadet. You are one of us now, and we look after our own. Never forget that! Now I must prepare for my meeting with the Hierarch. But, Tad," and she caught him by the shoulder, "keep your wits about you over the coming weeks. These are troubled times and everyone must stay alert. I do not for one minute think that raiders will attempt to attack the Manor, but we cannot be complacent. If you hear or see anything suspicious, mention it to someone more senior. You will not be rebuked or laughed at if you are wrong. It is often the little things that those of us with more weighty matters to consider often miss. Remember, you are part of a team, young Tad. We all have our part to play.

"Now, the Major might need his horse again soon, so you had better go finish your duties."

Tad snapped a smart salute and said, "Good luck, Colonel." She could feel him staring after her as she left to prepare for her mission.

Chapter Nineteen

The Baron accompanied the King back into the Manor, but Elias dismissed him firmly at the door to Blaine's private suite. He tried to protest this exclusion, citing the Queen's instructions, but Elias was having none of it. There was nothing Reen could do, and Hyram's presence outside Blaine's door put paid to any notion of eavesdropping.

He returned instead to his suite and wrote a hasty note to the Queen, then roamed the corridors trying to work out how to get Parren alone. Fortuitously, he saw the sullen Captain walking toward him. As Parren came closer, Reen hissed, "I need to speak with you urgently. Where can we go and not be disturbed?"

Parren raised his brows. He had clearly not expected Reen to speak with him again before the King left the Manor. After a moment's hesitation, he said, "There'll be no one in the commons at this hour, so it should be safe enough. I'm on an errand for Colonel Vassa right now, but I'll be free to meet you there in fifteen minutes. Do you know the way?"

The Baron nodded and moved on, not wanting to be seen talking to Parren. The less contact he had with the officer the better, but this matter couldn't wait. He strolled down to where the King's runners had their quarters and dispatched his message to the Queen. He was unsure of Elias's plans for returning to Port Loxton, but if Parren could accomplish what Reen required, stage two of his plan could get underway.

✣ ✣ ✣ ✣ ✣

On the way to her rooms, Sullyan called on both Taran and Bull to ask them to accompany her on this latest mission. Bull accepted the order easily, but Taran seemed reluctant. For a moment she even thought he might protest, but he held his peace and she didn't have time to question him. She put his reaction down to uncertainty in the light of the current situation, but it preyed on her mind as she hastily packed. When she heard the light tap at her door she half expected it to be Taran, but instead her visitor was Rienne.

Smiling a welcome, Sullyan resumed her packing while Rienne sat on the edge of the bed. Sullyan could sense that the healer had something on her mind but was content to allow her to speak in her own time. Rienne watched her friend with a slightly puzzled frown.

"Brynne, have you heard the latest rumors going round the men?"

Sullyan glanced up. "Which rumors? There must be half a dozen at least, by now."

Rienne shook her head. "I'm not talking about the attempts on the King's life. I'm talking about you and Taran."

That got Sullyan's attention and she immediately stopped what she was doing. "Tell me."

Rienne's expression was wary. "You won't like it."

"Would this have anything to do with why Taran was less than pleased to be told he is coming to Andaryon with me?"

Rienne lowered her eyes. "Probably. There's a nasty rumor going round that you and Taran have slept together."

Sharp anger stabbed at Sullyan. "What? Who has been saying that?"

Rienne stared at her, startled by her furious reaction. "It was started by the men from Port Loxton," she said slowly, "and

Lieutenant-Major Denny in particular. He seems to think he has proof."

Sullyan's emotions changed from furious to hurt to stony. "Does he indeed? And I suppose Taran has heard these malicious lies?"

"I'm afraid so. I don't know if Robin has, though. Taran was going to speak to him as soon as he got the chance, to tell him it's all nonsense, but he wasn't looking forward to it."

Calmer now, Sullyan said, "No, he would not be. But he is unlikely to get the chance before we leave, as Robin is on duty for the rest of the day."

She sighed in sudden irritation. "Oh, I am so tired of these constant rumors. They have followed me all my life. Where this particularly nasty one has come from, I cannot imagine. Denny is no stranger to gossip, and the juicier the better, but he has never spread outright lies before. Not concerning me, anyway." She eyed her dark haired friend. "Rienne, would you speak to Robin for me? He will not heed the rumors, of course, but I would not like him to hear them first from the men."

Rienne nodded. "If I can."

Sullyan watched her closely. Something in the healer's manner suggested she had something else on her mind. Their strong empathic link meant that nothing much escaped Sullyan's notice where Rienne was concerned. She came and sat next to her friend on the bed.

"There is something more. Tell me."

Rienne smiled, and Sullyan felt the healer's concern over Taran and the rumors evaporating, replaced by excitement. She raised her brows, her own heart clearing of annoyance. Rienne took up her hand.

"I have some very happy news to tell you," she said. "Cal and I decided a couple of months ago that the time was right to try for a family. I want you to confirm it for me, Brynne, but I'm pretty sure I'm pregnant."

There was a moment's frozen silence before Sullyan threw her arms around the healer and hugged her close. "Oh, Rienne," she exclaimed, "I'm so happy for you!"

Sullyan had been expecting this news for some time and had anticipated her own delight, but even she was a little surprised at the depths of her reaction. Mixed in with her joy was a surprising bitterness, and she almost regretted hearing Rienne's news when motherhood was something she could never hope to experience for herself.

She knew Rienne could sense her conflicting emotions, and was angry at herself for spoiling the moment. She suddenly realized that she was weeping. She calmed with an effort and pushed out of the healer's arms. "Ah, ignore me, Rienne. I do not know what is wrong with me lately. I seem to be weeping at a moment's notice. I am so very happy for you both. Cal must be very proud of you. And Taran, too."

"Cal is," agreed Rienne, "but we haven't told anyone else yet, not even Taran. I want you to confirm it for me first."

Sullyan smiled. "You know it is not necessary, but of course I will."

She placed her hand on her friend's still-flat belly. Her eyes dilated as she used her powers to gently probe Rienne's body, just touching the embryo consciousness nestling within. There was a faint but definite response. Her eyes misting over again at that touch of new life, Sullyan withdrew.

"Oh, yes, Rienne," she breathed, "you are most definitely pregnant."

Rienne began weeping too, and the two women laughed and hugged again. "Do you want to know what sex it is?" Sullyan asked.

"Can you tell already?"

She nodded. "But you may prefer to wait until it is born."

Rienne considered this. "Don't tell me just yet," she decided. "Let me talk to Cal. If he wants to know, you can tell us. If not, I'll wait with him. But, Brynne, one thing I did want to ask you. Can you tell if the baby will be an Artesan?"

Sullyan nodded emphatically. "It will be, yes. With an Artesan father and an empathic mother, it would have to be." Her voice dropped. "Just like my own parents."

Rienne gave a start. "When will his or her powers become apparent?" she asked, trying, Sullyan thought, to divert her friend's sudden melancholy mood.

"Impossible to tell. Some people are born with their powers emerging. Some see their powers surface at puberty, while others have to wait until they are adults. As an empath you should be able to link with your baby in the womb. Just keep directing your thoughts toward her—or him," she added hastily as Rienne smiled, "and eventually you will feel a response. Oh, Rienne, I can hardly believe it! This is such wonderful news."

She hugged the healer once more, and Rienne frowned at her renewed tears.

"Are you quite well, Brynne?" she asked, detaching herself from Sullyan's arms and looking intently into her eyes.

Not wanting to worry her at this delicate time, Sullyan said, "I am simply tired. I have not had much sleep lately, and I doubt I will get much over the next few days. These are very worrying times and we all need to be doubly vigilant."

"You've not been eating enough either, I'll bet," stated Rienne, eyeing Sullyan's slender form. "Have you had any more sickness?"

"That seems to have stopped now," Sullyan told her. "It happened twice while we were away, but on both occasions I had drunk a glass of red wine. I will not do so again. It seems to disagree with me."

The healer frowned. "There's no reason why it should. A small amount of red wine can be beneficial, especially for the blood."

"Perhaps, but I do not usually drink. Maybe I should stand by that decision from now on. I have had no more sickness since I stopped. And if only I could be rid of this strange sensation in my arm, I would be happier still."

At Rienne's insistence, Sullyan described the odd sensation she had experienced in her left forearm and once in her right. The healer seemed overly interested in these symptoms and there was an intense look in her eye when Sullyan finished.

"Any other unusual feelings?" she asked. "Any strange taste in the mouth? Have you gone off any foods lately?"

Sullyan shook her head, forgetting her sudden revulsion to the smell and taste of fellan three days ago.

Rienne sighed. "Well, I want you to promise you'll tell me if you experience any other odd sensations," she ordered.

Amused by her insistence, Sullyan promised. "Very well, although I assure you, I feel perfectly fine. But now you must excuse me. I have to leave soon. Timar is expecting us, and I know he will be very happy to hear your news. I will be sure to give him your regards. Please do try to talk to Robin for me? This is too delicate a matter for me to bespeak him though the substrate, especially as I have my suspicions that our communications are not as secure as they should be. When I return, though, I will have some stern words for Owyn Denny. Of that, you may be sure!"

✠ ✠ ✠ ✠ ✠

Having completed his errand for Colonel Vassa, Glinn Parren slipped unnoticed into the deserted common room. There was no sound from the kitchens. Goran and his lads were taking their afternoon break before preparing the evening meals.

He sat at a table near the door, absently toying with the two gold rings the Baron had given him. The sound of footsteps alerted him, and he rose as the door opened. Baron Reen strode into the room and shut the door firmly behind him.

"I will be brief, Captain. I presume you have spoken to Ozella and told him of our little... arrangement?" Parren nodded. "Good, because there is something he has to do. Tell him it is imperative that he accompanies Colonel Sullyan on her mission to Andaryon. We have to know what is said when she meets with the Hierarch."

Parren narrowed his eyes. "There isn't much time. What if she refuses to take him?"

The Baron thrust his face close. "He must make sure she doesn't! This will be the first test of your control. Convince him that his sisters' safety depends on his success. Hint at whatever consequences you please, I can ensure they are carried out if he fails. But he must accompany the Colonel. It is vital that I know what they say. Our lady has placed great faith in you, and it is not to your advantage to let her down. Now, you should hurry. The Colonel will be leaving soon."

Parren made for the door, a nasty gleam in his eyes. "I won't let you down, my Lord. You can rely on me."

The Baron showed his teeth as the young man left the room.

Parren was pleased Sullyan was going. She was likely to be out of the way for several days, and he intended to spend that time well. From what the Baron had told him, a visit to Lieutenant-Major Denny would be worth his while. But for now he concentrated on finding Ozella.

Parren thought hard as he stalked the Manor's corridors for his prey. He wasn't at all sure where he would find the Beraxian at this hour, not with the Manor's usual routine disrupted by the King's visit. Ozella could be anywhere.

He eventually ran him down where he should have looked first; at the horse lines. Fortunately for Parren, the stall housing Ozella's beast was some way from where Solet's lads were preparing the mounts for Sullyan's party. Making sure he was unobserved, the Captain slipped into an adjoining stall. Ozella started on seeing him.

"Stay quiet, man, this is important," warned Parren. "I have a task for you and it's one you can't afford to have fail if you want to see your sisters alive again."

"What is it?" Ozella had turned pale, and Parren knew he had been dreading this moment.

The young officer smiled. "You are to go with the Colonel when she leaves for Andaryon. We want to know what passes between her and the Hierarch. I suggest you speak to her right now. She's leaving soon, and you haven't much time."

"But how am I supposed to do that?" cried Ozella. "She'll never take me!"

"You'll have to convince her then, won't you?" snarled Parren. "And keep your voice down."

Ozella began to panic. "But what if I can't?"

"Don't fail me, Ozella," hissed Parren. "The men holding your sisters have already been restrained from acting on certain... ah... desires. I would hate to have to tell you I couldn't control them any longer." He stared hard at Ozella to make sure the young man took his meaning. He needn't have worried. The expression of desperation on Ozella's face was proof enough.

The young lord's shoulders slumped. "You really are a sick bastard, aren't you?" he whispered.

Parren grinned and waved a hand. "Your insults mean nothing to me, my friend. But you're wasting valuable time. Your sisters' safety is entirely in your hands. Just remember, we need to know every single detail of what is said in the Colonel's meetings.

Commit to memory everything you hear. If you can't be in the room, listen at the door or eavesdrop in that sneaky mind-reading way you Artesans have. Do you understand me? We want to hear every arrangement they discuss: times, places, people. Got that? Now go."

Ozella stared at him with loathing before sprinting for the stable door. Parren waited a few moments in case anyone had seen Ozella's hasty departure. Then he strolled casually away, well pleased.

✤ ✤ ✤ ✤ ✤

When Sullyan collected Bull from his rooms, she asked him whether he had heard the rumors Rienne had mentioned. He had, but she was gratified to hear that he had steadfastly ignored the nasty gossip, even going so far as to put a few of the men straight when he heard them repeating the story.

"No one in your company gives it any credence, Sully," he assured her as they walked together toward Taran's rooms. "It's mainly going round the men of the other companies, and even they aren't taking it seriously."

"I should hope not," she retorted. "There are enough stories circulating about me as it is. I could do without Denny stirring the pot."

"What I can't understand is why he seems so sure of himself," rumbled Bull. "Something must have set this rumor off, and it does seem to have spread very quickly."

Sullyan sighed. "All I can think is that the young woman who attached herself to Taran at Port Loxton had her nose put out of joint when he left her so abruptly. Perhaps she decided to repay his lack of manners by spreading malicious tales. She is Reen's niece, after all, so her nature is likely to be tainted by the same prejudices as his. But why Owyn Denny should be so convinced, I have no idea. He has no quarrel with me that I know of. In fact, he agreed to keep his eyes open for us back at the castle. That is, if his injuries do not prevent him from returning with the King."

"He'll be healed enough by then, surely?" said Bull as they approached Taran's door. "Elias is bound to stay here while this situation is unresolved. Blaine won't allow him to return to Loxton just yet."

Sullyan shrugged. "I have no idea what the King's plans are. He will certainly stay here until we return from Andaryon, but when last we spoke, he had not decided how much longer he would remain."

She rapped sharply on the door of the suite that Taran shared with Cal and Rienne. When the Adept opened it, he had his pack on his shoulder and his sword by his side, ready to accompany them. Even so, Sullyan saw the reluctance in his eyes.

"Taran," she said firmly, "you are to forget these malicious rumors. They are nothing more than the small-minded entertainment of bored soldiers. They will be dropped tomorrow unless they see we are affected by them. Bulldog has had the sense to dismiss them and you must do the same."

Her curt tone caused Taran to flush. "Has Robin?" he asked.

She sighed. "Rienne is going to speak with him for me. Stop worrying. We have more important matters to concern us than the petty revenge of one mean-spirited girl!"

She turned away, leaving Bull to reassure Taran with a friendly slap on the shoulder.

They were halfway to the horse lines when they heard the sound of running feet. Ozella panted up to them, halting in front of Sullyan.

She frowned at him. "What is it, Ozella? I am in a hurry."

The young man winced at her tone. Like Tad, he was rather in awe of her, although she had shown him nothing but kindness. Plucking up his courage, he said, "Colonel, I wanted to ask if I could accompany you on your mission to the Hierarch." Seeing her hardening expression, he plowed on before she could refuse. "I know I've not been much use so far, and I'm not very good at my lessons, but that's because I've not seen any reason to practice. My father wants me to be a diplomat when I return home, so maybe some real experience would motivate me. I'll not get in your way, I promise you. I'll see to the horses or just sit in the background. You'll never know I'm there. I've never had an opportunity like this before and I may not get another. Please, Colonel, let me come with you!"

Sullyan listened in silence, hands on hips. Ozella hopped from foot to foot in what could have been eagerness or desperation. He was shielded, so she couldn't tell which. She regarded him for a moment before turning enquiringly to Bull.

The big man shrugged. "It might just do him some good. He's right, he's had no practical experience of what being an Artesan means, so a trip like this should open his eyes. And I can look out for him if needs be."

Sullyan sighed. She was in no mood to discuss the merits of taking him. She just wanted to be gone.

"Very well, Ozella. Stay out of the way and learn what you can. But I warn you," and her tone brought a flash of fear to the young man's eyes, "we can spare no time for instruction. This is a serious business and we have to concentrate on the matter in hand. Bulldog may be prepared to look out for you, but I am not."

"I understand, Colonel. I won't get in the way or hold you up, I promise you. I'm already packed and even my horse is saddled."

Ozella was almost crying with relief. Sullyan regarded him a moment more, sensing his distress but not the reason behind it. She didn't have the time to question him so she walked on. Ozella fell in behind.

On reaching the horse lines, they found their mounts waiting.

Drum was fidgeting on his halter rope, having caught his rider's tension. Sullyan fastened her sword belt across her back and mounted Drum, with Bull and Taran following suit. Ozella mounted his own skittish beast and followed behind them. Sullyan lead the way out of the yard, past Captain Parren who was lounging against a stable wall, and rode down the track leading to the ridge where they would construct their tunnel, well away from the Manor's inhabitants.

✥ ✥ ✥ ✥ ✥

Robin was in an uncharacteristically morose mood. He was a bit hurt that Sullyan hadn't taken the time to say farewell. He appreciated the gravity of the situation and knew she was probably concentrating on what she and the Hierarch would discuss. Nevertheless, they always said a few words of farewell whenever one of them left the Manor.

Not today, though. Robin had hardly spoken with her since her return from Port Loxton. Even so, he hadn't failed to notice her distracted and irritable manner. This was so out of character that he couldn't get it out of his mind. His concern, plus a nagging uncertainty about the state of their relationship, had granted the vicious little rumor he had heard earlier more power than it should have had. And when he considered the embarrassed looks he'd seen on Taran's face and the furtive way the Adept had been avoiding him, Robin grew even more suspicious. So when Rienne approached him just before the evening meal and asked for a moment of his time, he was half expecting what she had to say.

She sat down across from him in the commons where Robin was taking a quick break from his duties. He only had a few minutes, as the current state of alert would afford him no more.

"What is it, Rienne?"

The healer raised her brows at his sharp tone. "I was talking to Brynne before she left—"

"Oh, she found time to speak to you, did she?" There was a bitter note in Robin's voice. "She didn't find any for me."

Rienne looked puzzled. "That's a little unfair, Robin. You know how busy the King's kept her. And I sought her out, not the other way around. Anyway, I know what's bothering you."

Robin glanced at her, regretting his harshness. He was very fond of Rienne. He laid a hand briefly over hers by way of apology. "Yes, I'm sure you've heard these vile stories too."

She nodded. "And that's all they are, Robin—stories! You know how deeply Brynne feels about you. I've seldom seen two people so in love and so committed. And you know very well that Taran would die before he'd do anything to hurt either of you, don't you?"

Robin didn't reply. Of course, she was right. He knew it on a deep and instinctive level. But *something* had happened while they were away, and there was no gale without wind.

"Robin?" Rienne deliberately caught his gaze, looking concerned by his silence. "Brynne asked me to tell you that she was paying no attention to the gossip. She wanted to make sure you weren't, either. Taran would have spoken with you too if he'd had time, but he didn't know Brynne was going to ask him to go to Andaryon."

A sly and completely unexpected voice in the dark places of Robin's mind whispered, *How convenient.*

"Don't you let this fester and contaminate what you have together," warned Rienne. "Nothing is worth that. Just remember how strong you are and what you both went through to get where you are now. You can't let anything jeopardize that. Promise me, Robin."

He looked at her, wondering why her insistence was stoking his apprehension rather than soothing it. He remembered the look in Taran's eyes when he met the King's party after the Andaryan attack, and the Adept's strange reaction when Robin thanked him for taking care of his life mate. He also recalled the absence of softness in Sullyan's eyes the morning after her return, and how her coldness had affected him even before he had heard these nasty rumors.

He wasn't sure where these feelings of insecurity were coming from, but he decided to find out more while she was away. Get to the bottom of the tale. Perhaps then he could lay it to rest and forget it, as Rienne was so firmly advising.

He smiled at her to stop her worrying, but there was no warmth behind it. He was far from easy in his mind.

Chapter Twenty

The Manor party emerged from the substrate tunnel onto the vast plain below the Citadel. A company of Velletian Guard came toward them from the south gate, Commander Barrin at its head. The Andaryan greeted Sullyan cordially, although there was a hint of stiffness in his manner. She introduced Ozella before falling in on the Commander's left, allowing him to escort her party to the Citadel.

Barrin's men left them at the gates, but the Commander rode with them up the Processional Way and into the palace courtyard. There they dismounted and gave their horses to the grooms. They saw General Ephan approaching them, the double-starred crown of his rank insignia gleaming on his breast. Sullyan greeted him gravely and accorded him the Andaryan military salute. Taran and Bull followed her example, with Ozella lagging behind.

Ephan regarded her gravely. "You are welcome here, Colonel. The Hierarch has asked me to inform you that you are invited to dine with him this evening in his private suite. He wishes to speak informally about the recent hostility between our realms. I trust this meets with your approval?"

"I am happy to accede to the Hierarch's wishes, General," Sullyan replied. "We will attend him at his convenience."

As they traversed corridors very familiar to Sullyan, she noticed Ozella staring about as he followed behind, trying to take in every detail of his surroundings.

✤ ✤ ✤ ✤ ✤

Since emerging from the trans-Veil tunnel, Ozella had been feeling very strange. He was experiencing an odd dichotomy of self, in that he almost felt he was two separate people. The Ozella part of him walked in a daze, no conscious thought guiding his steps; while the other part, the part that was using his eyes and ears, was fully alert, missing nothing. Half his mind was analyzing everything he heard and saw, but the other half was numb and unresponsive. On a deeply personal level, his psyche screamed in protest at this violation. On a practical level, there was absolutely nothing he could do about it. He didn't understand it. He trailed the others, who ignored him, seeing nothing odd in his gauche staring.

✤ ✤ ✤ ✤ ✤

They were shown to their rooms. Sullyan was allocated her usual suite while the three men shared an apartment farther down the corridor. They retired to rest, Sullyan making full use of the heated bathing pool her quarters boasted, thinking fondly of the many times she and Robin had used its warm luxury to indulge their love. She eventually emerged from the water and dressed in a simple dark green gown to await the Hierarch's summons.

It arrived via his page, Norkis. He still resembled the younger Tad, and gave Sullyan the cheeky grin she remembered so well. He called on the men, and they all followed him down the hall toward the Hierarch's private chambers.

They were not alone when they reached their destination. Pharikian had arranged a dinner party of sorts. Norkis bowed the Albians into the room and announced them. Sullyan was greeted with many smiles as first Pharikian, and then his daughter, Princess Idrimar, came to embrace her. They were followed by Lord General Anjer, his tiny wife Torien, the Master Healer Deshan, and finally Baron Gaslek, Pharikian's secretary. The Albians greeted their hosts warmly, all but Ozella, who seemed completely overawed.

The formalities over, they were shown to seats and offered drinks. Sullyan stuck to her resolve and accepted only cordial, despite Deshan's assurance that one small glass of wine would do her no harm.

While waiting for the food, Sullyan turned to Princess Idrimar. "I do not see your husband here, Highness. I had hoped to speak with him."

Idrimar, her former melancholy manner much improved since her marriage to Ty Marik, turned her naturally pale face to Sullyan and smiled. "Then I am sorry, Lady, for the Duke is not here. He is kept busy overseeing the construction of our new palace and I have not seen him for nearly a week now. He is working hard to get it finished."

Catching the undercurrent of excitement in Idrimar's voice, and also the expression of pride on her father's face, Sullyan studied the older woman. The Hierarch smiled as realization came to her, his elderly face seeming almost youthful.

Sullyan suppressed a startlingly intense pang of rue. It seemed as if everyone around her was suddenly breeding. "Oh, Highness," she exclaimed, "my sincerest congratulations."

Idrimar blushed. "Ty says it is twins!" She clasped her hands protectively over her belly.

Sullyan remembered that Idrimar was a twin herself, although her sister had died at birth. "He must be so proud of you," she murmured. Idrimar nodded and sighed contentedly.

Sullyan knew that the Hierarch was watching her. She had not broadcast the fact of her barrenness, but both Pharikian and his physician would be aware of this most grievous consequence of Rykan's abuse. The Hierarch was probably concerned as to how she would react.

As a distraction, she turned to him. "I do not see his Highness Prince Aeyron either, Majesty. Is he away from home again?"

"Only for a short while," replied Pharikian, his manner betraying a slight unease. "He is currently entertaining the sons of two of my senior nobles, the Lords Tikhal and Corbyn. They have come to participate in our discussions tomorrow. Our sons have gone on a hunting expedition, but they will return in a couple of days."

Seeing her raised brows, the Hierarch explained. "Lord Tikhal, as Lord of the North, controls the vast mountainous region of Morvaigne. Lord Corbyn holds Quarlock, a large tributary province on Morvaigne's eastern borders. Tikhal is senior landholder since Rykan's demise, and Corbyn is his highest ranking noble."

He paused and sighed. "I am sorry to have to tell you this, Brynne, but both Tikhal and Corbyn have experienced raiding by Albians over the past few weeks. Quarlock in particular has suffered quite badly. Lord Corbyn has a volatile nature and has been more than vocal in his displeasure. I invited both lords here to air their grievances before I learned of your visit, so I asked them both to wait, as this will afford us all an opportunity to discuss what may be done.

"It was Corbyn's suggestion that his son and Tikal's might enjoy a hunting trip. I confess I saw an advantage in agreeing to the plan. Tikhal is fiercely loyal to my House, and his son Rand shares his father's views. However, I am less sure of Corbyn and Kethro. Corbyn has always been troublesome, but we thought that if Aeyron could befriend his son and gain his trust, then the civil unrest that traditionally follows the passing of a Hierarch might be avoided. If Aeyron can persuade both Heirs to formally pledge their support, then many of the lesser lords will follow their lead. It might prevent the ugly and inevitable scramble for power when my son accedes to the Crown."

Despite her concern over the news of more raiding by Albians, Sullyan smiled. "Is that not a very radical change of policy, Majesty? The constant struggle for power seems to be at the very root of Andaryan society."

"That has certainly been true in the past," he conceded, returning her smile. "But your King Elias is not the only forward-thinker, Brynne, and if we are serious about cementing ties between our realms then it is in my interests to smooth the path if I can. Elias is likely to outlast me as a ruler by a good few years, and I would rest easier for knowing that he and Aeyron will share as profitable a relationship. Provided we can clear up this matter of raiding, of course."

Sullyan nodded. "I hope the Heir has taken a suitable guard with him on this hunting trip, Majesty."

Pharikian smiled. "We are not being formal this evening, child. You may use my name. And yes, he has taken a company of Velletian Guard with him, although they have only gone into the Haligan Forest."

✤ ✤ ✤ ✤ ✤

Ozella, still struggling with a mind that wasn't wholly his own, suddenly felt as if he had been released from a restraining hand. His body gave an involuntary jerk, and he nearly spilled his wine as he caught himself on the arm of his chair. All eyes turned to him and he felt his face redden with shame.

"What is it, lad?" asked Bull.

Seeing Sullyan's frown of annoyance, he swallowed hastily. "Sorry," he managed, his face burning, "I drank too fast...."

"Sip it slowly, lad," chuckled Bull. "This red wine's potent stuff!"

The incident was laughed off and Ozella was forgotten. The talk flowed on around him and he belatedly remembered Parren's instructions. He went cold when he realized he couldn't remember a word of what had been said, and fervently hoped he hadn't missed anything important. Parren would be waiting for the details when he returned, and if he didn't satisfy the young sadist, his sisters would suffer. Trying not to show his fear, Ozella concentrated harder, determined not to miss anything else.

✣ ✣ ✣ ✣ ✣

After the dishes were cleared away, they were about to retire to the Hierarch's solar when Lady Torien, who had been absent for a while, returned carrying a crooning bundle which she deposited in Sullyan's lap. She was smiling shyly.

"I thought you might like to meet your namesake, Lady."

Sullyan sat staring in confusion at the baby in her lap, unsure what to do. The baby gazed up at her with ice-blue eyes, and one tiny fist reached toward her face. A strange emotion came over Sullyan as she touched that fragile hand. The small and perfect fingers uncurled and clasped hers. She smiled down at the baby, who suddenly gave a bubbling chortle. Shaking her head in wonder, Sullyan gently gathered up the infant and gazed into her slit-pupiled eyes.

"Hello, Brianne," she murmured. The baby hiccupped, reached out her other hand, and fastened it around the chain at Sullyan's throat. "Oh no, little one, that is not a toy," she said, disentangling the prying fingers. "No doubt your father will give you finer jewels when you are old enough to wear them."

She cradled the baby upright on her lap and her huge eyes misted over as the little fingers fastened on her long, tawny hair. She looked up at Torien and Anjer, seeing their proud and indulgent expressions. "She is a very beautiful little girl," she breathed. "You are very lucky."

It was impossible to disguise the pain beneath her words. Sullyan held the baby up to her mother and Torien gathered little

Brianne into her arms, smiling as she released Sullyan's hair from the clutching fist. Deprived of her plaything, the baby began to cry.

"I'm sure you'll be having one of your own soon," said Torien. Hushing her daughter, she missed the expression of loss on Sullyan's face.

Pharikian stepped in and mercifully saved her. "It's time we retired to the solar," he announced, silently acknowledging Sullyan's grateful look. "Norkis is preparing fellan there. You must excuse us, Torien. We have much to discuss and it is already growing late."

He stood, and they all rose with him. Sullyan ran a gentle finger over the baby's downy cheek as Torien carried her past.

✣ ✣ ✣ ✣ ✣

Reen was growing anxious, and frustration was setting in. It was imperative that he return to Port Loxton immediately. Events were moving faster than he had expected, but this opportunity was far too good to miss. Although he was certain he could cope with organizing the Andaryan end from the Manor, the castle was where he would be needed most. He suffered a rush of frantic thought as he searched for a workable plan.

Despite his urgency, he couldn't suppress a glow of satisfaction. Sending Ozella with Sullyan was a masterly stroke. The Beraxian's brief stay at Port Loxton had given Reen's "associate" time to learn Ozella's psyche, and this was now paying off in a way Reen could never have foreseen. In order to capitalize on it he needed an excuse; something urgent enough to warrant his immediate return to the castle without involving the King. A message from the Queen was out of the question. Anything serious enough for her to demand Reen's return was bound to attract Elias's attention. He frowned. He needed something more personal.

Then he had it. His niece, of course. He could order her to

back up any story he might concoct, especially in the light of that very expensive necklace he had bought her. And if she decided to be difficult, he could always threaten her inheritance once more. Perfect!

He hurried to his rooms and brought out parchment and his copy of the Queen's seal which, together with the one bearing the King's crest, never left him. He paused for a moment, organizing his thoughts, and then began to write. He was no forger, although he had tried very hard to master the art, but he could disguise his own hand well enough.

He scanned what he had written and smiled. Good enough. He dripped wax onto the folded parchment and pressed the Queen's seal to it. Once it had set and cooled, he ripped it open. Then he bundled his clothes together, disarranged the bed covers, poured a large measure of brandy of which he gulped half, and quit the room.

He knew that Blaine and Elias had not retired. His room was next to the King's and he hadn't heard Elias come in. With any luck, Vassa would be with them. The more witnesses to his distress the better. Breaking the habit of a lifetime, he ran for the stairs leading to the upper floor.

Reen had never run more than two steps in his entire adult life. He wasn't built for running. When he reached the top of the stairs he was white and sweating, and his heart was racing unpleasantly. He actually felt ill, which was perfect. Stumbling and gasping, he made for Blaine's door and the figure of Hyram stationed outside.

"Quickly, man," he rasped, "I must speak with the King!"

Hyram was an eminently trustworthy valet and followed Blaine's orders to the letter. He was, however, unaware of the current suspicion surrounding the Baron and only saw one of the King's nobles in distress. He instantly knocked on the door and entered. Reen could hear him speaking in urgent tones.

He reappeared and ushered the barely recovered Baron inside. Blaine, Vassa, and Elias all turned to look at him. Blaine and Elias had frowns of suspicion, Vassa's face expressed concern.

"Good grief, man," said Vassa in his deep voice, "you look awful! What on earth's happened?"

Thank you, Vassa! thought Reen with an inward smile, outwardly schooling his expression to one of shock. He ignored the Colonel and turned instead to Elias, clutching his parchment in trembling fingers so the monarch could see the Queen's seal.

"It's my niece, your Majesty," he blurted. "The Queen has sent for me most urgently. Poor Jinella is grievously ill. I am advised to go to her at once."

Elias regarded Reen's pasty face. The Baron had frequently appeared before him in anger, but never so obviously in distress. "But you can't go now," he said, reasonably, "it's the middle of the night. And besides, it's not safe. There may still be raiders about."

Damn, thought Reen, *trust you to think of that.* Aloud, he said, "General Blaine, do you have a carriage I might use, and maybe two swordsmen to act as coachman and guard? That is all I would need. I simply must leave now. I may be too late otherwise."

"Is it that serious, my Lord?" asked Blaine. Elias's frown deepened.

"It seems so, General," replied Reen in a small voice, twisting the parchment between agitated fingers.

Blaine went to the door and Reen heard him giving Hyram instructions. He returned after a few moments. "There will be a carriage ready directly, my Lord. If you're sure you must go at once...?"

"Oh, I must, General Blaine. I could not rest otherwise. I would never forgive myself if... But I am most sorry for the inconvenience. And I do thank you. I will have your carriage returned immediately I arrive at the castle."

Blaine waved his thanks away. "Do you need assistance to pack, my Lord? Hyram can help you."

"Only to take my things down to the carriage, General. That would be most helpful."

Within twenty minutes Reen was on his way, leaning back at his ease in Blaine's comfortable closed carriage. There was a stone bottle of fellan at his side, thoughtfully provided by a sleepy Goran, liberally laced with brandy against the chill of the night. His heart pounded excitedly and a self-satisfied smirk sat on his lips. He took a pull of the beverage and listened to the coachman urging the team into the night.

✣ ✣ ✣ ✣ ✣

Those gathered in the Hierarch's private solar were also indulging in the comfort of strong fellan. Sullyan, having overcome the rush of emotion roused by Torien's baby daughter, was carefully considering her next words. Bull and Taran stayed close but silent, and Ozella had taken the farthest seat away from her. After that odd episode earlier he hadn't spoken again. He seemed distracted and weary and was certainly showing none of the eagerness he had displayed that morning.

Sullyan realized the Hierarch was waiting for her to speak and dismissed the Beraxian from her mind.

"Timar, King Elias wishes me to convey his deepest sympathies over the destruction of the two villages," she began, "and as a gesture of goodwill he has authorized me to offer you a measure of compensation for the relief of the displaced inhabitants. He was shocked to the core, we all were, to hear of Albians raiding your realm. He was most insistent that I assure you he had no foreknowledge whatsoever of these atrocities, and we are even now taking steps to discover who was responsible."

The elderly ruler waved a hand to indicate his understanding. "I appreciate Elias's offer and his sympathies, child, but you may tell him compensation is not required. I did not believe for one moment he was in any way connected with these raids, although there are those in my forces who do not share my confidence."

"Centuries of prejudice and mistrust are not put aside overnight, no matter what our rulers decree."

Pharikian inclined his head. "Indeed. But what concerns me more was the report that Elias himself has been the subject of hostile action."

Sullyan spent some time explaining what had happened both at Port Loxton and on the journey to the Manor. Pharikian listened gravely and was distressed to hear of the death of the Sinnian bard, Fiann.

"I knew Lord Fiann well," he said. "He was my welcome guest on many occasions. I regret I never heard the two of you sing together."

Taran spoke up, surprising Sullyan. "It was an unforgettable experience, Majesty."

Pharikian's slit pupils settled with penetrating perception on the Adept's face. "Yes," he said softly, "I imagine it was."

Taran shifted uncomfortably, looking as if he had unknowingly given something away. Just as he began to redden under the Hierarch's scrutiny, he was released as Pharikian's attention returned to Sullyan.

"Do you have any suspicions as to who was behind the attacks?" he asked.

She vaguely registered Ozella stirring in his chair. "We do," she replied. She laced her fingers around her cup and tucked her legs beneath her. "But our only real suspect cannot be solely responsible, for he has no Artesan talent. Whoever caused the Earth-shift beneath the King's horse and tampered with the storm before the attack has consummate and exquisite skills. He also has access to allies from Andaryon. Timar, do you know whether Ty

Marik found any records concerning the Staff when he destroyed Rykan's palace?"

From the corner of her eye she saw Ozella bring his hands to his head, as if it pained him. He had his eyes closed.

"I believe not. I asked him to look most carefully, and I am sure he did. You would have been informed had he discovered anything of interest."

"And what of Lord Sonten's holdings? Who has the lordship of Durkos? It may be that Sonten and his nephew were more involved with the Staff's creators than we supposed."

"Marik gave Sonten's lands to Nazir, with my blessing. Sonten's poor wife fled the place when she learned his fate, and no one knows what became of her. They had no children, as you know, which was why Sonten championed his nephew in the first place. So that trail is cold."

Sullyan frowned. "What of Rykan's lesser nobles? Has anyone questioned them? Sonten ranked the highest, but there were other vassals. I know for a fact that there were two Artesans in Sonten's party before he invaded Albia. One was Commander Heron, who perished with Sonten when the tunnel collapsed. But there was at least one other."

Pharikian shook his head again. "You would have to speak with Marik on that score. Rykan was a private and secretive man. He never discussed his affairs with me. He was always a rival even before he had any hope of gaining sufficient power to challenge me."

"He was a ready and willing co-conspirator then," she mused. "I wonder how he was recruited? Our suspect is a violently prejudiced bigot and I cannot imagine him entering into relations with an outlander, not even to foment unrest. This is our dilemma, Timar. Although the existence of the Staff gave us clues to the purpose behind Rykan's involvement, challenging your rule was clearly not our adversary's ultimate goal. If it was, the troubles would have ended with Rykan's death. We have no reason to suspect the existence of another Staff, which was my original fear, so its creation was also not the culmination of their plan. Rykan's death, or the Staff's destruction, must have been a grievous blow, but they obviously still have a goal in mind as these latest hostilities prove. What, then, do they ultimately hope to achieve?"

Deshan regarded her over his cup. "Can you not apprehend this suspect of yours and question him?"

Once again, Sullyan was distracted as Ozella shifted on his chair. She glanced at him. His face looked gray and his eyes were unfocused, as if he felt nauseous. She gave Bull a pointed look, and the big man nodded. He would keep an eye on Ozella. She could not have the young Beraxian disrupting these talks.

Irritated, she transferred her gaze to the physician. "The situation is... delicate, Deshan." Bull gave a snort, which earned him a sharp glance. "He has allies in high places, and we cannot afford to antagonize them. Also, as we know that he has at least one associate with Artesan powers, we cannot afford to alert them to our suspicions too soon. This brings me to a question I would ask you, Timar."

Pharikian cocked his head. Her unspoken hint about their enemy having backers in Elias's court had not passed him by, and he was frowning. Behind him, watched by Bull, Ozella shook his head as if trying to dispel an irritating buzz in his skull.

Sullyan continued. "You know much more of Artesan history than I do. Do you remember the last time there was a Supreme Master living?"

Pharikian appeared surprised, and Taran gave her a startled look. She knew that he had not known such a rank existed until recently.

Pharikian turned thoughtful and did not directly answer. "Do you suspect a renegade Supreme Master, Brynne?"

She shrugged. "In truth, I do not know what I suspect. All I do know is that on both the occasions when I sensed our adversary working, I could not find his pattern in the substrate. Taran and I did a thorough investigation after the Earth-shift, yet found no evidence of tampering. Admittedly, a good hour had passed before we conducted our search. But the storm that was used to cover the ambush was being manipulated right over our heads, and still we could sense nothing. Am I right that the ability to conceal one's signature is a characteristic of the Supreme Master?"

Pharikian nodded. "It is one characteristic, yes. There are others, of course. In answer to your earlier question, I was a very young lad when I last heard anyone speak of a Supreme Master, and he died a couple of hundred years before I was born. The knowledge of what the rank bestowed will be recorded in our archives, though. If you wish, I will ask Gaslek to search it out. He is a great scholar of our ancient records and knows what they contain better than anyone."

"That would be helpful, Timar. And there is something else. I have been concerned as to whether our substrate communications are still secure. Do you know whether a Supreme Master would be able to overhear Artesans speaking privately without their knowledge?"

The Hierarch frowned in alarm. "Do you suspect this has happened?"

She fixed her gaze on her cup. "I do not know. During the horse race, when the first attack occurred, there was no one nearby, and certainly no one in line of sight, with any Artesan powers, except for Taran and myself. Our chief suspect was there but, as I have already said, he has no talent. Yet that Earth-shift was placed precisely and timed to perfection, although whether its target was Elias or me remains unclear. I would swear no one was invading my thoughts at that time, but I was concentrating on the race.

"And then, on our journey to the Manor, the storm concealing our attackers came directly for us. Once again, the raid was exquisitely timed. Yet neither Taran nor I felt any kind of surge whatsoever. None of the raiders was an Artesan, yet someone afforded them passage through the Veils, both before and after the attack. The entire ambush was orchestrated as if our enemy was standing among us. I have the most horrible suspicion that we are being watched. Watched in a way we cannot detect."

An uncomfortable silence fell. Sullyan regarded the Hierarch while he considered her words. Deshan also studied him worriedly. Sullyan spared a glance for Ozella, whose face had changed from pale to flushed. He must surely be coming down with a fever. She was about to ask Bull to take him back to his room when she sensed Pharikian's aura of concern. She cocked her head. "What is it, Timar? What do you know?"

He gazed at her. "Nothing for certain. But if your suspicions are well-founded, what is to stop your... *our* adversary from listening to us now?"

Bull gasped and Taran turned pale. But Sullyan had already considered this. "Nothing. But if he is, he will give himself away sooner or later. Especially now we are alerted to the possibility."

She heard a small sound and turned to see Ozella slump down in his chair. Whatever fever was afflicting him, he had finally succumbed to it and fallen asleep. At least now he would disturb them no more.

Pharikian raised his brows at her and she shrugged. He ignored the Beraxian and answered her point. "You may be right, Brynne, and I will certainly ask Gaslek to search out details of the Supreme Master's abilities. But there is one other possibility which you might not be aware of. You might be dealing with a sport."

"A sport?" said Taran. "What on earth's that?"

"Lay-talent," murmured Sullyan, gazing at Pharikian. "A natural Artesan, one who has no need of training, who instinctively knows what to do and how to use his powers."

"Is there such a thing?" asked Taran. "I've never heard of it."

Sullyan turned to him. "Ah, but you have, although only recently. Do you not recall me telling you about Lord Fiann?"

Understanding flooded Taran's face. "Oh yes, you told me Sinnians are born able to control their own metaforce."

"Exactly, up to the level of Adept. They are a unique race in that they are all lay-talents, or 'sports,' as Timar puts it. But in other races the phenomenon is extremely rare."

"So, if the person behind these attacks is a sport, he must be a Sinnian, is that right?"

"No, that is not possible. No Sinnian has ever attained higher rank than Adept-elite, and our adversary is far stronger than that. Rare though it is, lay-talent could potentially occur in any of the races that produce Artesans, and I am more than convinced that our enemy, whoever he is, is Albian."

Pharikian stirred, drawing Sullyan's gaze once more.

"I might have a plausible explanation for how your chief suspect is managing these attacks." Her eyes glittered sharply. "You say he was present during both attacks?" She nodded. "And you are absolutely certain he has no Artesan talent?"

"None that has ever been trained, or even identified," she said. "I suppose it is just possible he could be a latent, although I have never felt as much as a glimmer of power from him. But he is so vehemently opposed to our kind that I am sure he is not."

Pharikian nodded. No Artesan, not even a Supreme Master, would be able to conceal himself from the determined scrutiny of a Senior Master without betraying trained shielding.

"There is another trait peculiar to some sports which I ought to make you aware of," Pharikian continued. "This is unconfirmed

241

until Gaslek can find the reference but I am fairly sure that they can sometimes hear the thoughts, and I mean directly from the person's mind without needing access to their metaforce, of anyone they know well. Even the ungifted."

There were gasps of incredulity and sudden understanding. Sullyan felt her face drain with shock. This was something she had never even considered. Her heart labored with despair as she fought to collect herself.

"It all fits." Her voice was full of hopelessness. "And if it is the case, then we are all in worse danger than I ever thought. We have no clue to the identity of our Artesan adversary, be he Supreme Master or sport, and now we might never find out. For if they can communicate in this way, then he need never show his face. He can completely conceal his pattern, so even if we were alert while they were communing, we would still not identify him.

"Without proof of conspiracy or wrong-doing, Elias cannot remove our suspect from either his court or his presence. If he did, it would alert the man's allies, and that would be disastrous. Elias would be irreparably discredited. We cannot afford that. He is the only monarch in Albia's history to be sympathetic to our kind. All we can do is to try to ensure that any plans or discussions are conducted out of our suspect's knowledge, and that will be nigh-on impossible."

Her voice broke on a note of despair. "Timar, I cannot see a way out of this. I cannot see how to stop them gaining their objective, whatever it is. They have already nearly succeeded in taking Elias's life, both times right under my nose, and that hurts, I can tell you, and they could strike anywhere, at any time, without alerting us to their presence. How can we proceed?"

Pharikian watched her with sympathy. She could not conceal her distress, both for her King, to whom she was fiercely loyal, and for her fellow Artesans, all of whom, including herself, were now in serious danger of their lives. And from an unknown enemy.

She knew how to handle the sort of danger she had faced from Rykan, both the poison and the duel. Direct actions, whether using the sword or her Artesan powers, were familiar and she knew how to employ her talents to best effect. But invisible strikes from an unknown enemy, one whose goal was clouded in mystery but was obviously on a world-changing level, was like fighting mist.

The elderly ruler reached out and took her hand. He clasped it warmly, trying to convey some comfort.

"It's getting late, child, and we're all tired. Deshan tells me you're not quite yourself at the moment. All this worry is wearing you down, I think."

Sullyan shot Deshan a less-than-friendly look, but the physician grinned back, unrepentant. He knew her too well, she reflected. Her part-demon blood gave him a greater insight into her state of health than even Rienne had.

"We all need some rest," Pharikian continued. "We have talked enough for one night. Your young companion might need some attention, I think. I will speak to Gaslek before retiring and get him started on those archives. Maybe he will turn up something useful. If anyone can do it, he can. Tomorrow we will meet with Tikhal and Corbyn and see what they have to say. But I have to warn you, Brynne," his eyes turned hard, "they will take no prisoners. Corbyn in particular is far from happy. Perhaps a good night's rest will refresh us and we can come at the problem with renewed vigor."

They parted then, Pharikian walking Sullyan to the door with a fatherly arm across her shoulders. Deshan gave her a small bottle as she left the room, instructing her to drink its contents before sleeping and informing her blandly that he would be able to tell if she did not. He ignored her intimidating stare.

Bull had to rouse the sleeping Ozella by poking him sharply in the ribs. He rolled his eyes at Taran as the Beraxian startled awake. "These young lads," he grumbled, "they've no stamina. Come on, Ozella. You wanted to know how to conduct a tricky diplomatic situation, but you've just missed the best example you're ever likely to see. You'll have to do better than this if you want to serve your country!"

✣ ✣ ✣ ✣ ✣

Confused and disoriented, Ozella stumbled after Bull. He shook his head, trying to clear it, wondering where the last hour had gone. All he could remember was a peculiar, nauseating buzzing in his mind. A cold sweat broke out on his skin as he realized he could recall almost nothing of the entire evening's conversation.

Trying to hold back tears as he imagined what Parren would say to his lack of information, and dreading to think what the consequences would be for his sisters, he hurried after the others.

Chapter Twenty-One

Sullyan woke an hour after dawn, having experienced her best night's sleep in weeks. Half afraid that Deshan's potion would prove too strong, she had nearly braved his and Pharikian's displeasure by not taking it. She had been feeling unusually tired and low, though, so had eventually taken the Master Physician's advice. Now, far from feeling heavy-headed as she had feared, she was enjoying an almost luxurious sense of wellbeing.

Unfortunately, it didn't last.

A sudden commotion in the corridor outside shocked her to full awareness. She heard running feet, slamming doors, shouts and screams. With a dreadful sense of foreboding she leaped from the bed, only just remembering to throw on a robe. Wrenching open the door, she stepped into the hallway.

There were people everywhere; servants running and yelling, guards barking conflicting commands. Thoroughly alarmed yet unable to get a sensible reply to her questions, Sullyan turned toward Pharikian's chambers. She was about to contact him via the substrate when she saw Norkis pelting toward her. He hadn't seen her, his eyes were wild and full of tears, and she had to catch his arm to stop him rushing past.

"Norkis," she snapped, "what has happened?"

He gulped, his throat too constricted for speech. Sullyan used her metaforce to calm his terror. Seeing some of the panic fade, she asked her question again.

He heaved a breath and gasped, "It's the Heir, Lady!"

"What about the Heir?"

"He was attacked," the young page blurted. "The whole party was attacked. One of the Velletian Guard managed to get away and has only just reached the Citadel. Oh, Lady, Prince Aeyron has disappeared. He's been abducted!"

Sullyan wasted no more time. Leaving the sobbing page, she dashed to her rooms and threw on her combat leathers, sending a sharp mental command to Taran and Bull. Fortunately, they had also heard the commotion and weren't far behind her. As they all emerged from their rooms, Sullyan saw Lord General Anjer and the Hierarch striding toward them. Pharikian's face was lined and gray. He looked older and frailer than she had ever seen him.

With a swift salute for Anjer, she asked, "Where did it happen, my Lord?"

"In the Haligan Forest," replied Anjer tersely. "We don't know the full story yet. The swordsman who made it back was weak from blood-loss and very nearly incoherent. Barrin has taken a company to investigate. We're following now."

"We will aid Barrin, Majesty." Sullyan barely waited for his nod before sprinting down the corridor. Bull and Taran fell in behind and Ozella, frightened and confused, trailed them.

She ran for the horse lines in the early gray light. Ephan had told her via the substrate that their horses were being saddled, but when she arrived Drum wore only his light bitless bridle. Pushing away the groom carrying her saddle, Sullyan leaped onto Drum and urged the big stud to a canter. She pounded toward the west gate, the three men following as best they could.

The gate stood open and the sentries snapped Sullyan a respectful salute as she flew past them. She was well known from the war against Rykan, and none of the Hierarch's troops would hinder her without a direct command from Anjer. Followed by the other three, she galloped for the Forest.

Tracking Barrin by the imprint of his psyche, she soon found the site of attack. Barrin threw her a sour look as she slid from Drum but gave her no further attention as his men continued to search the area. There was no sign of Prince Aeyron or the two lords' sons. There were signs of a great struggle, though, and about fifteen dead men, eleven of whom were Velletian Guard.

Bull and Taran pulled up and dismounted, and Bull knelt to examine one of the dead men. He glanced up at Sullyan. "This one's human, Colonel."

Barrin heard him. "Yes, Colonel," he spat, not bothering to disguise his fury, "so are these others! No markings on any of them, no clues as to who commanded them. Just like last time! But this time, they knew exactly what they were doing, didn't they? Only four of them dead, as opposed to eleven of ours, and the three highborns taken. That smacks of a well organized ambush, wouldn't you say? Attack just before dawn, when the sentries are at their weariest thinking their watch nearly over, and before the others are awake. Is that how you would have done it, Colonel?"

Barrin was referring to some of the tactics she had employed against Rykan. She paid no heed to Barrin's spleen, recognizing the man's feeling of failure. Thoughts of his predecessor, Torman Vanyr, flashed through her mind. She would have given much to have him here instead of Barrin.

Ignoring the furious Commander, she turned to Bull. "The swordsman who made it back only said that Aeyron had been abducted, not the two lords' sons. Use your tracking skills, Bull. Follow some of these hoof prints and see if you can locate them. I will do what I can to help you. Taran, with me!"

Without waiting for an answer, she leaped back onto Drum and turned his head toward the Citadel. Taran hastened to obey. He urged his galloping stallion up beside Drum, laying low over the horse's neck. A smaller party was just leaving the Citadel's west gate, the Hierarch's golden mare in their midst. Yet she didn't aim to intercept them, heading instead toward the northern side of the Citadel.

"Where are we going?" yelled the Adept over the wind of their speed.

"Just ride!" was her barked reply.

✤ ✤ ✤ ✤ ✤

Having just come off early watch duty, Parren collected his breakfast from the commons. There was a good chance Rienne Arlen would not have begun her rounds of the infirmary yet, so he should have a clear half-hour to do what he wanted. It didn't really matter if she came in before he was finished, but he would rather not have her there.

Taking a bite from a hunk of warm bread and following it with sweetened tea, Parren sauntered over to the infirmary. With a satisfied smirk he saw that Healer Arlen wasn't there. Spotting Lieutenant-Major Denny lying in the bed farthest from the door, he made his way over.

Denny was only just awake, judging by his bleary looks. He was stiffly bandaged to keep his arm immobile and the wound in his side was stitched, so he found it hard to move. When Parren put his half-eaten meal down on the table by his bed, the young officer grunted, "Here, man, do me a favor and help me sit up, will you?"

Parren awkwardly put his arm under Denny's shoulders to help him sit. Wincing at the pain, his face pale, Denny finally got himself comfortable.

Peevishly he said, "To what do I owe this honor, Captain?"

Parren turned away. "If you're going to be like that, Lieutenant, I'll leave you in peace. I thought you might like some company. I thought you'd be bored, shut up in here. Perhaps I was mistaken."

"All right, all right! I'm sorry."

Hiding a sly smile, the thin man turned back and perched on the edge of the bed. He picked up his bread and took another bite. "So... how are you feeling?"

Denny looked longingly at the bread. The infirmary had not received its morning meals yet. Seeing this, Parren tore off a chunk and handed it to him.

The young Lieutenant took it with surprise. "Thanks! They don't give you enough to keep a rat alive in here."

"I wouldn't know. I've never had to spend any time here, myself." Parren's tone managed to convey his contempt for those foolish or careless enough to get themselves injured.

Denny's eyes narrowed, clearly disliking the junior officer's implied criticism. "Then you've either been very lucky or you've kept out of the worst of the action!" he snapped.

"I'm definitely leaving," said Parren, "you're too prickly."

Denny closed his eyes and sighed. "I can't help it. I'm going mad with boredom. Why don't you tell me what's been happening lately? Give me some juicy gossip."

What Parren really wanted was for Denny to give him gossip, but he was happy to relate what he knew of recent events and how the Manor forces had dealt with them. His own version, of course.

Talk inevitably turned to Sullyan, as they had both trained with her at the Manor. Although Denny had heard Sullyan's tale of the duel with Rykan, he had not heard the full story of the battle to lift the siege at Hyecombe. Needing no encouragement, Parren told him, making much of his own part and managing to imply that Robin had blocked his promotion. Parren was so skilful that he soon had Denny's sympathy.

"Yes," mused the Lieutenant, "we heard a bit about that at the capital. But I never realized you had been intentionally blocked by the Major."

"No?" Parren tried to sound casual. "Well, he's always been jealous of me. It's not the first time he's tried to discredit me or have me dismissed."

"Really?" Denny's eyes were wide.

Parren told him of their illicit duel over a year ago, twisting the tale so thoroughly that Robin came out as the instigator, tipping Sullyan off in advance so she could catch Parren in the act.

Denny marveled. "You were lucky not to get hauled before a martial court for that."

Parren nodded. "Fortunately, Colonel Vassa saw through their spite. He knows what a good field officer I am, and he persuaded the General not to proceed with it. Sullyan was so angry that she did this." He indicated his face. "It was her own form of law, she said. She made sure I was unarmed first, though."

Denny whistled. "She really did that?"

"She also had my loyal Sergeant and Corporal transferred away. I don't know why you're so surprised, Lieutenant. She's been biding her time all these years, just waiting for a chance to pay me back for trying it on with her when we were in training. Although, if you remember, she encouraged me in the first place. It was a mean trick to play on a man, letting him think she wanted it and then turning on him."

Denny frowned. "That's not the way I heard it."

Parren shook his head. He would have to twist the facts yet again. He had never made a secret of how badly he wanted to lie with Sullyan, and had been mortified when Sullyan publicly refused to accept him. Now was his chance to pay her back for all the humiliation she had forced upon him.

"No," he agreed curtly, "I don't expect it was! She very cunningly put it about that I'd tried to force her. And, of course, everyone believed her. They had no reason to, it's not as if I'd ever done something like that before. I never had any trouble getting women into bed, so why should I have turned nasty on her? But her dammed lapdog, Hal Bullen, backed her up as usual, and Blaine believed them."

Parren spat on the floor, careless of the junior healers. They stared at him with dislike but didn't have the rank to rebuke him. Eyes gleaming with righteous indignation, he said, "She hasn't changed. You had a lucky escape when she turned you down. But there have been others, you know. This Taran Elijah isn't the first, and he won't be the last. You mark my words."

Denny gaped at him. "Are you sure about this? There have always been rumors and stories about her, but I always thought she was above all that." Parren snorted and Denny shook his head. "Why does her company follow her so loyally if there's been all this scandal? And why does the General put up with it? To hear the officers talk, especially Master Ardoch, you'd think she was some sort of goddess."

"Oh, don't get me wrong," said Parren hastily, realizing he might have gone too far, "there was never any scandal. Blaine would never have stood for that. No, no, she's far too clever. Only those of us who have eyes to see realized what was going on. As for her company, well, they're men, aren't they? If you were getting, what shall we say, privileges from your senior officer, would you broadcast it?"

Denny spluttered breadcrumbs. "What, all of them?"

Parren shrugged. "No, probably not. Who knows? It doesn't go on at the Manor, but out on patrol? That's a different story. Think about it. How many men are stationed here? And how many women? Only a handful, most of whom are ancient, barring one or two of the healers. And they're out of bounds." He saw Denny's disbelieving stare. "You doubt what I say? Then believe your own eyes. You saw through her and Taran quickly enough at Port Loxton, didn't you? They were only there a few days, yet they couldn't fool you."

Parren's flattery worked. Denny's ego needed boosting after his injury and the bored Lieutenant needed little further encouragement to tell what he had seen and guessed at Port Loxton. It was tenuous enough, as Parren quickly realized, but the fact that it was Baron Reen's niece who had caught them, and Taran himself who had as good as admitted that he and Sullyan were lovers—although Parren knew perfectly well what Taran had really meant—all added weight to the rumors.

When Denny fell silent, the Captain nodded sagely.

"You see how it is?" He allowed the senior officer to catch a flash of righteous anger. "We don't stand a chance. These Artesans stick together, and because they're so powerful, there's nothing we can do about it. They're slowly taking over. First Blaine, who is one of them, of course, although he didn't used to be so bad, and now the King. They've started at the top, I'll grant them that. Where it'll all end, I don't know. And if they succeed in removing the King, who knows what will happen to Albia?"

"What are you saying?" hissed Denny. "You can't seriously accuse Sullyan of trying to kill the King!"

"Why not? Who else could it be? We know it's someone with unnatural powers, don't we? And she was there, both times."

"Lower your voice, man." Denny gave a worried glance around the room. "I might accept what you say about her love affairs, but I'll never accept she tried to kill the King. She fought against the raiders! Killed a good few, too."

"Well, she wouldn't show her hand in front of witnesses, would she? She was hoping her outland allies would do the job for her. And what's a dead demon, more or less? She's very friendly with the demon ruler, you know. She's even supposed to be related to him in some perverted way."

He was silent a moment before urging, "Think about it,

Lieutenant. She came from nowhere, found by Blaine, as the story goes. No parents, no origins. And she's not like any of us, is she? She even talks oddly." He eyed Denny. "How well do any of us really know her, eh, Lieutenant? Where do her true loyalties lie? Tell me that."

Denny had no reply. His mouth was hanging open and he shut it hurriedly. He looked like a man with much to think about. Parren tried hard not to grin. "Here, I can trust you not to go spreading this about, can't I?" he said. "I'm in enough trouble already. I can't afford for my name to be associated with stuff like this. I only told you to help relieve the boredom."

"Oh, don't worry, Captain," said Denny, "I won't mention your name. My lips are sealed, believe me."

Rienne appeared then, bearing Denny's breakfast on a tray. She narrowed her eyes when she saw Parren, and the Captain rose, giving Denny a knowing look.

"Good morning, Healer Arlen," he said, nodding with exaggerated courtesy as he walked away from the bed.

"Captain Parren." Rienne spoke coldly, and Parren felt her eyes on his back as she watched him leave. Curious as to what she might say to Denny, Parren stopped just outside the door. After a few seconds, he risked peering back into the room.

Rienne had deposited the tray at Denny's side and stood staring down at the injured Lieutenant. "What did he want?" she said.

Denny gave a lopsided shrug. "He was keeping me company."

He yawned and Rienne frowned. "Don't go exerting yourself. You're still recovering, remember? And don't pay any attention to anything Parren says. He's a bitter young man with a vicious tongue. He only has himself to blame for his misfortunes, so don't waste pity on him."

Parren smiled as Denny watched Rienne move on to her other

patients. The healer's tone and strong words had brought a thoughtful look to the Lieutenant's eyes.

✢ ✢ ✢ ✢ ✢

Galloping flat-out, Taran followed Sullyan round the north wall of the Citadel. The Adept supposed they were heading for the stone circle where the wedding ceremonies had taken place nearly a year ago. The Citadel's sentries watched as they urged their mounts toward the hill. Sullyan halted Drum just outside the monoliths and slid from his back, letting the reins fall. She sprinted for the circle's center, Taran on her heels.

On reaching the center, she turned to him. "Raise the power of Earth as strongly as you can. Quickly, man!"

Setting his questions aside, Taran turned to the western cardinal stone and drew in his will, calling on the element of Earth. The ancient stones began to thrum as the sluggish forces rose, flowing sunwise, linking the monoliths together. When the circle closed, pulsing with power, he called the element to him. It came, surging across the grass. He gasped at its strength. This was very different from when Sullyan had shown him the technique. He turned to face her, wondering what she wanted.

Urgent as she was, still she smiled her praise. Taran flushed with pleasure.

"Continue to call the power, but give control to me."

He obediently opened his mind and felt her take him over, body and soul. Her amber force suffused him, his will subservient to hers. She never took total control, always leaving a private portion of his psyche untouched. He felt her throw out her own vast powers, augmented by the anchoring forces of Earth. She channeled the energies along the intricate swirls of her pattern until her psyche throbbed with force.

Eyes huge and black, she turned her attention to the Forest—to the site of ambush. Many patterns were visible here: the Hierarch's unmistakable psyche, Anjer's, Barrin's, Bull's. Taran, intimately linked to her, understood she was looking specifically for Aeyron's imprint. It was immediately apparent that there was no hope. The taint of spellsilver was evident, and Aeyron had suffered its deadening effects. Through Sullyan, Taran could sense the instant his pattern had vanished from the substrate.

Frustrated and angry, she cast farther afield. She was acquainted with neither of the two lords' sons, yet here she had more luck. About two miles east of the ambush site, she detected two muffled psyche imprints. Here, perhaps, were the two boys Aeyron had been entertaining. Although their patterns were also smothered in spellsilver, Sullyan could tell they were alive.

Bulldog.

Taran heard the big man respond. Sullyan reported what she had found and told him where to direct Barrin.

If he doubts you, go to Anjer. He will listen. But be careful, there may still be raiders in the area. Do not leave Timar unprotected.

Breaking her link with Bull, she urged Taran to call ever more strongly on the power of Earth. He was amazed when even deeper strength flowed out. Without her steadying influence, he felt sure he could not have contained it. It was a vast relief when she took the power and cast it out again, using the energy as a fine probe to examine the substrate in the vicinity of the attack.

Unwilling to distract her with questions, Taran concentrated on keeping a constant power flow. He watched her work, marveling at her control. Just when he was beginning to tire, he felt her stiffen, sensed her shock. Sharpening his attention, he detected nothing amiss. Then she curtly instructed him to release the power.

Mindful of the need to let the stones resorb their energies, it was a few moments before he was free to ask her what she had found. When he turned his head he was concerned to see her staring distractedly at the ground, arms hugged tightly about her chest, an expression of fear on her face.

He placed a gentle hand on her shoulder. "What is it, Sullyan? What did you see?"

She raised her head, her face pale and her eyes wide. He felt his stomach tighten. She took a trembling breath and opened her mind once more to his. Confused, he accepted the contact, concentrating on what she showed him.

"What do you see, Taran?"

He frowned. "Only... well, nothing."

Displeased, she shook her head. "That is not true, is it?" she snapped. "Tell me."

Alarmed, he looked again, but there was nothing amiss. "I don't understand," he protested. "There's nothing but my pattern and yours."

Tears started in her eyes and he took her hand. "Tell me what's wrong!" he said in a sharper tone than he had ever used with her before.

She flinched but did not rebuke him. Her voice was low with a touch of panic as she said, "I found a trace in the substrate where the ambush occurred."

He raised his brows. "Show me."

Distraught, she cried, "I already have!"

"But—"

"Taran," she snarled, "what is this?" She thrust an image of her own psyche against his inner eye. He told her. "And this?" She presented another pattern.

Puzzled, he compared the two. "Don't play games with me, Brynne," he pleaded. "I know I'm not as strong as you, I don't understand—"

She almost screamed in her distress, shocking him. "Taran, this is the trace I found in the substrate!"

He looked again. "But… that's your pattern… isn't it?"

She nodded slowly, her body trembling, tears welling in fearful eyes.

✤ ✤ ✤ ✤ ✤

Baron Reen was feeling nauseous. The jolting of the carriage, the earlier efforts of concentrating on a three-way conversation, and the heady triumph flooding his righteous soul all conspired to unbalance him. Taking a huge swallow of laced fellan and choking on the fiery liquor, he lay back against the velvet seat, sweat beading his swarthy face.

He had done it. He could scarcely believe it, but he had done it. It was sooner than he had anticipated, but that didn't matter. The arrangements had been in place for some time. Now, thanks to Blaine's comfortable carriage and indefatigable escort, he was only about two hours from Port Loxton and the Queen.

Grinning through his discomfort, he imagined Sofira's face. How delighted she would be at this news! And how interested to learn that their enemies were no nearer to discovering the truth, no matter their suspicions. He hoped he hadn't released Ozella too soon from his thrall, but he had been spooked by some of their suggestions and had feared discovery.

He smiled smugly. Let Captain Parren think that he alone controlled Ozella. Although, he mused, Parren had probably already outlived his usefulness, thanks to this latest success.

Let Colonel Sullyan try her vaunted diplomatic skills on this *one!* he thought, savagely. War was surely inevitable now. She would be kept fully occupied by her military and ambassadorial duties, and he would be free to fulfill his lifelong ambition: putting an end to the blasphemous traffic with outlanders.

Should Elias die fighting the war, that would work in Reen's favor too. With Sofira as Regent for Prince Eadan, he, Hezra Reen, would be more necessary than ever as her chief advisor. Lord

Levant, Elias's First Minster, supported far too many of the King's liberal ideas. Reen knew Levant would be powerless to resist should the Queen decide to pension him off, and they would ensure he got a sizeable fortune and a manor somewhere suitably obscure in recognition of his long and loyal service.

By now the brandy-laced fellan was doing its job and the Baron's unruly stomach calmed. He stared out of the carriage windows, realizing they were not far from Loxton Forest. It had been an uneventful journey, and he smiled at the memory of Elias's concern. As if he was in any danger! Those responsible for the attack on the King were being paid well to do his bidding. The fact that they were pagan outlanders troubled Reen's conscience not at all. He saw nothing remotely hypocritical in using the instruments of evil against evil itself. In fact, he considered it justified, highly appropriate, and profoundly satisfying.

Well pleased, anticipating a warm bath and a hearty, if late, breakfast, Reen allowed his eyes to close. The carriage continued on its journey, carrying him toward the admiration of his Queen.

Chapter Twenty-Two

Sullyan was quiet and withdrawn as Taran followed her back to Haligan Forest. She sat Drum easily, moving to the motion of his paces, her face closed and her eyes distant. Taran still didn't fully understand what had upset her so, but he didn't want to distress her by asking questions.

She held her peace until a stiffening of her spine and the dilation of her eyes told him she was communing with someone.

"Bulldog says they have found the two lords' sons," she reported once the link was broken. "Both are unconscious but otherwise unharmed."

"And Prince Aeyron?" he asked gently.

"There was no sign." She turned hard eyes on him. "Taran, I would appreciate it if you do not speak of what I told you on the tor."

He nodded. "Whatever you command, Colonel."

They rode on into the Forest, Sullyan using Bull's psyche as a beacon, and soon came upon the Hierarch's party returning to the Citadel with the two unconscious boys. Sullyan nodded to Bull and Ozella before falling in beside Pharikian. Taran thought the elderly ruler looked decidedly ill.

"Thank you for your assistance in recovering Rand and Kethro," he said, his voice rough with emotion. "Their fathers will be most grateful. Fortunately, neither has sustained serious harm and Deshan will help them revive."

"Perhaps they will have news of Prince Aeyron, Majesty," she replied, laying a hand on his arm.

"Perhaps."

Taran wasn't surprised to see tears in the old man's eyes, and felt a pang of sympathy. Sullyan glanced at Anjer, who rode like a brooding thundercloud on Pharikian's other side.

"Were there no clues as to where the Prince has been taken, my Lord?" she asked.

The massive man shook his head curtly.

The Hierarch spoke, hopelessness in his tone. "You found no trace of him in the substrate, Brynne? I felt you using the circle."

Sullyan ducked her head. "No, Majesty, only that he was also wearing spellsilver."

Pharikian nodded wearily, and Taran surmised he had done the same search with the same results. Only he obviously hadn't seen what Sullyan had.

They rode back to the Citadel in silence, flanked by Barrin and the Velletian Guard. The Commander kept casting hostile glances at the four Albians, and Taran grew increasingly uncomfortable. Barrin was plainly furious and would have sent the four of them packing had he been able.

On passing through the Citadel gates most of the Guard returned to their duties, and a reduced party rode up to the palace. The townspeople lined the streets to show their support. Taran heard ugly mutterings about human raiders and saw many an angry glance directed at him and his friends. Yet no one dared voice their anger before Pharikian. His people both loved and revered him and felt the same for his son. There was a deep sense of distress and sympathy about the crowd.

Once in the palace courtyard, two older men rushed up to the Guards carrying Rand and Kethro. The lords had been prevented from joining the search party in case raiders were still in the area. Frantic with relief, Tikhal and Corbyn now took charge of their respective sons.

Tikhal, the Lord of the North, was known to the Albians. Sullyan had met him when he had escorted Aeyron home after the war with Rykan. But none of them knew Lord Corbyn or the two sons, and Taran saw Sullyan watching Corbyn closely as he examined Kethro.

Corbyn was tall and wiry with sunken cheeks and pale blue eyes. His hair was jet black and fell in an unruly fashion into his eyes. He had a condescending manner and kept flashing the Albians mistrustful looks. Tikhal, however, seemed less judgmental and even gave Sullyan a wan smile as she moved toward him.

"The boys will be well, my Lords, once they have rested and the effects of the spellsilver have worn off," she said. "As soon as they have recovered we will see what they can tell us about Prince Aeyron."

"You can forget about speaking to my son," snapped Corbyn. "You're not coming anywhere near him!"

"Lord Corbyn, it was Colonel Sullyan who found your son," said Pharikian, dismounting wearily from his yellow mare, "so this anger is gravely misplaced. You owe her your thanks. The boys' imprints were muffled by spellsilver. Without her skill in reading the substrate, we might still be searching."

Far from being cowed by Pharikian's rebuke, Corbyn seemed angrier than ever. He came closer, and both Taran and Bull moved to Sullyan's side.

"Is it true that you are well acquainted with the effects of spellsilver, Colonel?" asked Corbyn, a hint of contempt in his voice.

"What do you mean by that, Corbyn?" demanded Anjer.

Corbyn's reply was sullen. "Only that I have heard she is able to thwart its numbing effects. She found our lads easily, wouldn't you say? It was very convenient."

Taran and Bull both gasped at Corbyn's nasty implication. Luckily, Anjer found it as distasteful as they did. He advanced on Corbyn, who retreated. Not many men were capable of facing Anjer down.

"My Lord, you are understandably distressed by what has happened," he snapped, sounding not at all sympathetic. "I suggest you take Kethro to the healer halls and allow Deshan to give you something to counter the shock. I am sure the Colonel will forgive your rashness in the light of your... condition."

Anjer's black eyes were fierce and his mouth a thin line. Corbyn swallowed, not wanting to back down yet having no choice. To avoid being forced to apologize, he turned on his heel and stalked away. Anjer sighed irritably.

Tikhal approached him. "You must forgive him, Majesty, Lord General. I am sure he meant no real offense. His lands have suffered badly at the hands of raiding Albians, and he is determined to have satisfaction." He turned to Sullyan. "Colonel, we are both very distressed at this dreadful occurrence. Allow me to tender our thanks for your assistance today. My son, for one, will show his gratitude when he wakes."

Sullyan smiled gently. "There is no need for gratitude, my Lord. I only wish I could have done more." She glanced at Pharikian, who was pale and trembling.

"Majesty," said Tikhal, "you ought to go and rest. I am sure Prince Aeyron will not be harmed. He is too valuable for that. We will do everything we can to recover him safely."

Pharikian nodded, although there was no comfort in Tikhal's words.

"Go with your son, my Lord," advised Sullyan quietly. "We will care for the Hierarch."

As Tikhal left with the unconscious Rand, Taran felt Sullyan touch Pharikian's flagging psyche to bolster his strength. He was alarmed by the monarch's frailty, as was she. "Lord General, we should get him inside," she urged. Anjer took Pharikian's unresisting arm and led him to the palace doors.

They had nearly reached his private chambers when they heard a commotion behind them. Princess Idrimar came running toward them and flung herself sobbing into her father's arms. He buried his face in her hair and they wept together. Embarrassed, Taran, Bull, and Ozella stood a little way off.

"They need privacy, Anjer," murmured Sullyan, and the Lord General steered the royal pair into the Hierarch's chambers. "Tell Timar I am at his command should he need me."

Anjer nodded as the door of the suite closed behind him.

✤ ✤ ✤ ✤ ✤

Making their way to her rooms, the men followed Sullyan inside. She collapsed onto one of the settles, worried and puzzled. She noticed Taran looking concerned, and remembered her panic on the hill. He would be wondering which of the two recent shocks had affected her most.

"So, what do you make of that?" rumbled Bull, crossing to the fire and automatically setting water for fellan. She didn't immediately answer and he glanced over sharply.

"We must wait for the boys to recover their senses," she eventually said. "I will not speculate until then. Is that fellan ready yet?"

They were on their second cup when a tap at the door heralded the arrival of Baron Gaslek, the Hierarch's secretary. Taran opened the door and ushered the little man in. Bull offered the Baron fellan, which he accepted, and Ozella made room for him on the couch.

Gaslek was carrying a thick and ancient-looking book. Seating himself, he placed the book on the table and took a few appreciative sips of Bull's evilly strong fellan. "Bad business this," he said.

Sullyan nodded. "Have you heard whether Rand or Kethro have recovered consciousness yet, my Lord?"

Gaslek shook his head. "I've been in the archives all morning. I only heard the news as I was coming to see you. I gather it was you who found them?"

"I was able to locate them, yes," she replied, not wanting to dwell on the morning's events. "Did you find anything of interest in the archives?"

"Perhaps." Gaslek's tone was cautious as he placed his cup on the table. "His Majesty asked me to look this out for you."

He passed her the book, which was a loosely bound collection of manuscripts, all written in differing hands. It recorded the lives of various long-dead Artesans, including their rank and the characteristics of their power. Sullyan stared at it, captivated.

"How old is this, Baron?" She turned the old and brittle pages carefully.

"Centuries. It's the only one of its kind, to my knowledge. The parchment you want is nearer the front." He put out a hand and turned the pages, finally tapping one with his forefinger.

She bent her head and read aloud: "Liyan Tamilane, Supreme Master, Hierarch of Andaryon, 7002-7080." She raised her head. "Baron, that is well over three hundred years ago!"

The secretary nodded. "There has not been another to our knowledge since Tamilane died. He was the last."

"I wonder why?" she mused, continuing to read.

She was fascinated to learn that the achievement which most distinguished the Supreme Master from her own rank was the ability to influence the so-called fifth element of Spirit. She knew there were those who denied the existence of Spirit as a tangible element, consigning it to the realms of the hypothetical. Personally, she had always suspected that it did, in fact, exist and could be manipulated. Interesting though her speculations were, there was nothing particularly enlightening about Tamilane's talents recorded in the parchment. The text did mention, however, that a Supreme Master was able to conceal his imprint within the substrate so that only another Supreme Master could detect his working. She didn't know whether to be relieved or disappointed that there was no mention of him being able to communicate with non-gifted minds or intercept private conversations without the knowledge of those concerned.

She glanced up at Gaslek. "Is that all?"

He shook his head. "If you turn to the very last of the manuscripts, you will find records of two natural sports, the most recent of which occurred only thirty years ago."

She found the much newer parchments where he indicated, and her eyes widened as she read them through. Both sports, one of Master rank, the other Master-elite, had the ability to tap into elemental forces directly and instinctively, without recourse to the substrate. Neither had needed any training, and because the substrate was unaffected, no other Artesan had been able to detect their working. They could also, apparently, read the thoughts of those close to them, gifted or ungifted, and it was by this means that the sport who was of Master rank was finally discovered.

He was six years old before his parents became suspicious. Before that they merely thought him accident prone, and he was certainly subject to tantrums. But the instances of minor earth tremors and violent storms which occurred whenever he was upset soon aroused their fears.

His father, an Artesan of Adept rank, had probed his son at the appropriate times for emerging Artesan talent, with no success. The father's remarks were recorded, the case being so unusual.

My probing left me with a sense of disquiet, although I could not at the time have said why. Instead of the slowly-developing pattern of the fledgling Artesan or the barren but naturally shielded mind of the ungifted, all I sensed from my son was blankness, as if a void of darkness lived in his soul. It was most unnatural and I shied from it. After my first probe, the experience was so imprinted on my mind that I was reluctant to conduct the next test. When I finally did so in his sixth year and found the same disturbing vacuity, I resolved never to probe him again.

Sullyan had been reading the parchment aloud so they could all hear, but when she reached this point she raised her head and fell silent, her eyes unfocused. The words struck a chord in her mind, but try as she might she could not pin it down.

"What happened to him?" asked Taran.

She came back to herself with a shake and scanned the parchment. Her expression grew sad. "He was killed."

The others were shocked. "Why?" demanded Taran. "He was only six years old!"

She nodded. "Yes, but imagine the damage a six-year-old child could do with a Master's powers. How many young children do you know who have any concept of how easily people can be hurt? And if he was prone to tantrums...."

"But couldn't he be controlled?" protested the Adept. "Couldn't his parents—"

"They tried, Taran," she murmured. "His mother tried."

"What happened?" he asked, clearly sensing it wasn't successful.

"He killed her. He read her intentions, threw a tantrum, and collapsed a ceiling on top of her. She was crushed instantly."

Taran fell silent.

When no one else seemed willing to speak, Bull asked, "So, how did they deal with him?"

"They waited until he was asleep so he would not detect their thoughts, and ran him through." Her tone was dispassionate. "They could not risk him harming anyone else. It was fortunate he had not killed before. Or maybe he had and they did not realize."

Gaslek cleared his throat, gathering the book to his chest. "Does this information help you at all, Lady?"

Coming out of her sad reflections, Sullyan gave him a grateful smile. "I thank you for your trouble, Baron. You must have spent many long hours searching those parchments out."

"No, not really. I know most of what's in the archives. It didn't take me long to find these."

He stood up, pausing when they heard another tap at the door. When Taran answered it, Norkis was standing there. The young page looked pale and frightened.

"What is it, Norkis?" asked Sullyan.

His voice hoarse with weeping, the lad said, "The Hierarch bade me tell you that the young lords Rand and Kethro have regained consciousness, Lady. His Majesty awaits you in the infirmary, if you will come."

"Of course we will come," she replied, laying a soothing hand on his shoulder. "Do not weep, Norkis. We will find the Heir."

He smiled wanly as they followed him. When they reached the healers' wing, he showed them to the room where the two young lords lay.

Rand and Kethro occupied a small private room with space for only two beds. The Master Physician, the Hierarch, and their fathers were already there when Sullyan and the others arrived.

Lord Corbyn looked up with a hostile glare. He had obviously calmed since his earlier outburst and his son's recovery had helped dampen his anger, but he was clearly far from pleased to see her there. He dismissed her presence, pointedly turning back to his son.

Both young men appeared pale and apprehensive. Kethro, the younger of the two, seemed especially nervous. Rand, who at eighteen was a year older than Kethro, was dealing better with his fear and was attempting to answer his father's questions. Lord Tikhal was sitting on the bed beside his son with one arm around the young man's shoulders for support. Pharikian stood at the foot of the bed, still alarmingly pale, and Deshan was at Rand's other side, trying to persuade the youth to take one of his restorative potions.

Rand drank off the potion. Kethro was subjected to the same treatment, and a measure of color came back to the boys' pale faces.

"Do you feel up to telling us what happened out there?" Tikhal asked quietly. "His Majesty is very concerned for Prince Aeyron. Anything you can tell us might be helpful."

Rand closed pale eyes and his brow creased in pain. "He fought them so well," he whispered, and Pharikian leaned closer.

"Tell me, Rand," he urged.

"We were asleep, sir," the youth began, glancing at Kethro for support. "We'd had a good hunt and celebrated our catch that evening. We didn't retire until late and so we were all sound asleep. There were two sentries on duty. There should have been four, but Prince Aeyron changed the orders, saying it wasn't really necessary to have four on watch as we were so near the Citadel."

Sullyan frowned and shook her head. They might have been in friendly territory, but having only two sentries was risky, especially during the dawn watch. This was the worst watch, the duty most dreaded by soldiers. Their bodies were naturally at their lowest ebb in the small hours before sunrise, and it was easy to slip into the mistake of thinking yourself safe. The Prince's escort would have been grateful for his thoughtfulness, but they should have overridden his orders.

Rand went on. "We planned to spend another day hunting, after which we hoped to return to the palace with enough meat for a feast." He stopped again and swallowed, his father encouraging him with a squeeze of his shoulders. Rand shot an uneasy look at Kethro before he continued.

"We were woken before dawn by shouting, but it was already too late. There were twelve in our escort, as well as the three of us, but we were still outnumbered. The sentries yelled as soon as they saw the raiders coming, but they burst out of the substrate practically on top of us."

Sullyan gave a small gasp.

"Two of the raiders came straight for me, and two went for Kethro. We were still in our blankets and didn't even have time to stand up, let alone grab weapons. They leaped on top of us and pinned us down, then they used spellsilver cord to tie us up. Two others went for Prince Aeyron, but he was faster than us."

Rand glanced at his father, shamefaced. "Kethro and I had drunk quite a lot of brandy the night before, but Prince Aeyron didn't drink as much. He was more alert than we were, and he killed the two men who were trying to subdue him. But the Guards had been taken by surprise and the camp was overrun, and he was being attacked on all sides. He just wasn't able to concentrate for long enough to get a call through the substrate.

"The raiders slaughtered the Guards. They fell all around us. They fought like heroes and Prince Aeyron was defended to the last, but then one of the raiders threw a knife at him and it caught his sword arm."

Pharikian went paler still and Sullyan could see him

trembling. Without a second thought she reached out and lent him some strength. She saw him straighten slightly in response. Rand was still speaking, his eyes distant and his voice rough as he relived the terrifying ordeal. Kethro had his head bowed and stared silently at his tightly clasped hands.

"When Prince Aeyron went down, there were only about five of the Guard left. It didn't take the raiders long to finish them off, and then they stood over the Prince, laughing. They tied him up with the spellsilver cord. He was lying very quiet, but he was definitely alive. They wanted him alive. I heard them say so. I don't think the knife wound was too serious. The raiders bound it with a cloth, and then they dragged him to his feet and slung him over one of the Guards' horses.

"I didn't see much more. Kethro and I were bundled onto horses too, but I passed out before I heard what they intended to do. I was dizzy from the effects of the spellsilver and the shock, and I don't suppose the brandy helped either. I was terrified they were going to kill us."

Rand looked full at the Hierarch, the first time he had been able to do so. His eyes were full of shame.

"I'm so sorry we couldn't protect Prince Aeyron, Majesty. If only we hadn't drunk so much the night before, we might have been more use. Both of us can use our swords, but we just didn't get the chance."

Pharikian shook his head, unable to find it in his heart to blame either boy.

"They were so quick, Father," continued Rand, turning to Tikhal. "They must have known exactly where we were, and who we were. They knew Kethro and I were Artesans, and they knew which of us was the Prince. They were human, all of them, and they knew exactly what they were doing."

"My Lord Rand," put in Sullyan, "you said you heard them

say they wanted the Heir alive. Did you hear anything that might help us discover where they have taken him?"

Rand stared at her. He knew who she was and that his father thought well of her, but she could see the suspicion in his eyes. Kethro stirred uneasily and glanced at his father. Corbyn's eyes were fastened on Sullyan's face and she could sense his hostility. Kethro quickly looked away again.

"Answer the Colonel, Rand," said Tikhal.

Rand closed his eyes, trying to remember.

"I was feeling very strange by the time the Prince was overpowered," he said, "and I can't remember exactly what happened. There was a lot of noise and it was difficult to hear. But one of the men said something like, 'We've got him, lads, we've earned our pay. All we have to do now is deliver him alive to the King's man and collect our reward.'"

"The King's man?" Corbyn's voice cut across Rand's like a sword thrust, making Kethro jump. "Did you hear that, Majesty?" He rounded on Tikhal. "I told you Elias Rovannon was behind all this, but would you believe me? You heard your son. They were all human and they knew exactly who the Heir was! Who else would have the authority and resources to arrange something like this? And he has Artesans who serve him!" He turned a vicious look on Sullyan and spat at her feet. "What do you say to that, Colonel?"

He had gone too far for the Hierarch. Now that he knew for sure his son was alive and likely to stay that way until whoever had taken him chose to reveal their demands, Pharikian was more himself. He loomed over the enraged Corbyn and faced him down.

"That's enough!" he snapped, his yellow eyes fierce. "I will forgive your appalling manners because I share your distress, but I will not hear accusations against my ally, King Elias, and I will not tolerate you abusing Colonel Sullyan. Might I remind you that it was she who found your son? You would do well to reflect on how fortunate you are that he is not still in the raiders' hands. We will not indulge in useless and unmannerly defamation, Lord Corbyn, and I will have no more of this disgraceful behavior toward a guest under my roof. Do not forget she is a King's ambassador! If you cannot control yourself better than this, you can leave."

Corbyn went white, realizing he had gone too far. Even his son was looking at him with an expression of frightened anxiety, and this caught Sullyan's attention more than Corbyn's bile. Was Kethro's fear for his father, she wondered, or himself?

The black-haired lord subsided, mumbled an apology to his monarch, and sat back down on his son's bed. Kethro had uttered not one word throughout the proceedings, and Sullyan's musings now led her to wonder whether the son shared his father's views. Was Kethro keeping his counsel until they were alone?

The Hierarch then gave Kethro the opportunity to add his recollections to Rand's. His questions brought a flush of color to the boy's pale face, but he didn't tell them anything new. Pharikian studied his drained appearance and didn't press him. He turned back to Rand.

"I thank you for recounting this morning's attack and for reassuring me that Aeyron is still alive. It can't have been easy for you, and I regret you were caught up in it. It appears we can do no more for the moment other than wait for my son's captors to make their demands. I suggest that you and Kethro get some rest."

He turned to Tikhal and Corbyn, although he refused to look Corbyn in the eye. "My Lords, you were invited here to present certain concerns to me. In the light of these events, do you still wish to do so?"

"Of course, Majesty!" stated Corbyn, denying Tikhal, as senior noble, his right to reply. Aeyron's abduction notwithstanding, Corbyn clearly wasn't going to lose the chance of voicing his displeasure and demanding satisfaction for his losses.

Tikhal shot a look of disgust at the unrepentant Corbyn and sighed. "We don't want to burden you further, Majesty, but it is why we came, after all. To my mind, today's events only serve to reinforce the necessity."

Pharikian inclined his head. "Very well, gentlemen. I will receive you in the lesser audience chamber this afternoon. Colonel Sullyan, as ambassador to King Elias, will you also attend?"

Corbyn started angrily, but subsided under Pharikian's hard stare. Sullyan merely nodded and the Hierarch left the room. Deshan herded everyone but the two lords out also, saying his patients needed rest.

Taran, Bull, and Ozella followed Sullyan back to their rooms, where she instructed them all to fetch their weapons. She had decided that after the morning's distressing events what they needed was distraction. She found that nothing concentrated the mind as well as having someone come at her with cold, sharp steel. She eyed Ozella thoughtfully as the men returned with their blades.

"You will partner me, Ozella," she told him, frowning at the sudden paling of his olive skin. Fear crept into his eyes as she said, "You need sharpening up. You have not been paying attention of late."

She caught Bull smiling privately. He knew she really meant that *she* required sharpening up. It took much skill and concentration to fence effectively with novices without doing them harm, and it would require all her attention. She had thought to help Ozella by giving him some personal instruction, yet he seemed terrified by the suggestion. She had noticed his earlier strange distraction and wondered if he was sickening. She was beginning to wish she had not brought him after all.

As they reached the training ground, Taran, who had been mulling over what Rand had told them, said, "Colonel, the raiders this morning may have been Albian, but surely Prince Aeyron is still in Andaryon?"

"I seriously doubt it. Why do you say that?"

"Because he was wounded. Doesn't that mean he couldn't have crossed the Veils?"

"Ah, I see what you mean. No, it is my belief that the Heir was taken through the Veils immediately. The adverse effect of the substrate on a wound is transmitted mainly through the psyche, and spellsilver blocks access to the psyche. Prince Aeyron was not the one manipulating the substrate, and so would not have suffered its full effects. Lord Rand did say that it was not a particularly serious wound, so whoever opened the Veils would only have had to shield Aeyron, as you and Robin did for Bulldog when he had that shoulder wound before Marik's banquet, remember?"

Taran nodded.

"The only real risk Aeyron faces from his injury," she continued, "is infection. It is too soon for that to have set in yet, but if the wound is not tended and healed, then he will be unable to return until the infection is dealt with." She eyed the Adept meaningfully. "Let us hope his captors understand his worth and the importance of keeping him healthy."

After two hours of weapons practice, she finally released them to return to their rooms. She had been as gentle and understanding with Ozella as she could, spending much time in coaching and guiding, yet by the end of their session he seemed more distressed than ever. At one point, she thought he was going to burst into tears. It was very puzzling, yet she could not spare the time to discover its cause. They all needed to wash and change and take a little refreshment before attending the Hierarch.

At the appointed time they were shown into the lesser audience chamber, finding the Lords Tikhal and Corbyn already there, along with Anjer and Ephan. The two Generals and Lord Tikhal greeted the Albians cordially, but Corbyn refused to acknowledge them, staring covertly at Sullyan through baleful eyes.

She directed Taran, Bull, and Ozella to seats at the edge of the chamber, and they all stood in homage as Pharikian entered the room. Baron Gaslek accompanied him. Sullyan was pleased to see that the elderly ruler appeared more rested and in control of himself. Rand's assurance that Aeyron was alive had done much to ease his heart. He took the chair at the head of the table with Gaslek beside him. Anjer and Ephan took seats to his right, with Tikhal and Corbyn to his left. Sullyan took her place opposite him, at the bottom of the table.

Pharikian placed his hands on the polished wood before him and looked around them all.

"My Lords, General Ephan, Ambassador Sullyan. The purpose of this meeting is to discuss the state of relations between the realms of Andaryon and Albia and the effects of raiding into our lands by parties of unknown humans."

"Unknown?" interjected Corbyn rudely. "We all know who sent them!"

Gaslek rapped on the table. "You will have your chance to speak, my Lord, when his Majesty invites you to do so. Pray keep silent until then."

Sullyan silently applauded Gaslek, who rarely emerged from his fussy exterior to show the steel beneath.

Pharikian glared at Corbyn but refused to be ruffled. "I deliberately postponed this meeting in order to include Ambassador Sullyan among our number. Albia has also experienced outland raiding, and King Elias himself has been put at risk of his life. This is of deep concern to me, as it was my express command that the terms of the Pact brokered twenty-four years ago by Morgan Sullyan should be honored and that raiding into Albia would remain forbidden. High King Elias and I have entered into a treaty of trade and cooperation, and anything that damages this also damages our realm. If any of you have any knowledge or suspicions as to who is behind these hostile activities, I charge you to voice them."

He turned to Tikhal, forestalling Corbyn's rush to speak. "My Lord Tikhal, would you begin by telling us what depredations your province has suffered?"

Tikhal glanced at each person in turn, his eyes resting longest on Sullyan. "Majesty, I first began hearing reports of raiding around three months ago. They were only small raids and did no real damage. Groups of five or six men would descend on a village or manor in the dead of night and carry off what they could. There were no fatalities and no wanton destruction."

"Three months, my Lord?" said Ephan. "Why didn't you mention something sooner?"

"Because, General, I was unaware that the raiders were human. They came at night and none were killed, so I assumed it was only the young bloods." He spread his hands. "In common with most provinces, many of my nobles have younger sons who are hot-headed, and they yearn for an outlet for their energies." He smiled indulgently over the vagaries of younger sons. "With the realm of Albia denied them, they have been amusing themselves by raiding their neighbors' lands."

Ephan snorted and Sullyan smiled inwardly. Andaryans were well known for their love of dueling and warfare, and she was not at all surprised to learn that they still routinely predated on each another. It was a characteristic of the race.

Tikhal went on. "However, about a month ago I received a visit from Lord Corbyn. He informed me that he had recently repulsed two raiding parties that had been terrorizing some of his smaller settlements. In doing so, some of the raiders were killed. I regret to tell you"—he looked at Sullyan—"they were all human."

"They did a lot of damage, Majesty, and many of my people were left homeless," said Corbyn. He cast Sullyan a look of pure hatred. "My vassals have had enough, Majesty. They are demanding action."

Anjer glared at the black-haired lord. "Just what are you saying, Corbyn?"

Corbyn chose to ignore Anjer, continuing to address the Hierarch. "I'm only telling you how they feel, Majesty. They want revenge for what they've suffered, they want to retaliate, and I for one don't blame them!"

Tikhal looked worried. "Calm down, Corbyn."

Sullyan watched the two lords with interest. It was evident that although Tikhal was of higher rank than the black-haired Corbyn he had little or no control over his fellow lord. She wondered how Tikhal would cope if Corbyn decided to challenge him.

Pharikian appealed to the commander in charge of the Velletian Guard. "Ephan, what is your opinion?"

"The situation is serious, Majesty. I can't deny that. But condoning wholesale raids into Albia is not the answer. We need to establish who our enemy is, and, in the light of this morning's events, sooner rather than later."

Pharikian turned his yellow eyes on Sullyan. "What do you say, Colonel?"

She regarded him openly. "I agree with General Ephan, Majesty. We can do nothing at present for fear of endangering the Heir, but even once he is safely returned, there is nothing to be gained from unconsidered retaliation. It would only engender more of the same, and both our realms would suffer. My Lord Corbyn, would you see the progress made so far, and the obvious benefits to both our races, swept away by one prejudiced faction?"

Their eyes turned to Corbyn. "All I know," he said hotly, "is that my lands and people are suffering at human hands! I find it highly suspicious that no sooner do we have agreements in place to trade with Albia and stop our young men from raiding than Albians start to raid us. It's too convenient, too coincidental, for my liking!"

"But if you're convinced Elias Rovannon is behind these raids," growled Anjer, "how do you explain the fact that he has also been threatened?"

Corbyn shrugged. "Perhaps one of his nobles has decided to take advantage of his preoccupation, Lord General. Such challenges to a sovereign are hardly unknown." He looked pointedly at Sullyan. "After all, someone provided Rykan with backing, didn't they? Who's to say they were Andaryan? And just because their coup here failed doesn't mean they wouldn't try elsewhere."

Corbyn's shrewdness unsettled Sullyan. He was right, of course. If only she knew for certain that this was what Reen and his backers were after. But something told her it wasn't that simple.

Pharikian stirred. "Gentlemen, I have no intention whatsoever of sanctioning military action against Albia. Even, and especially, after what has happened to my son. I will do nothing to jeopardize his safe return. And I warn you, Corbyn," he fixed the fuming Lord with a baleful eye, "if I hear your name, or any of your vassals names, mentioned in connection with retaliatory raids, I will have no compunction in asking the Lord General here to enforce my decree. I trust both Colonel Sullyan and King Elias to do everything in their power to resolve this situation and uncover those responsible. Until we either hear from my son's captors or apprehend them, Andaryon will not respond."

Corbyn surged to his feet. "Then what am I to do? What am I to tell my nobles? That they are to sit and let these humans"—he spat the word—"do what they want with my lands? That we're to let them rape our women and kill our men and rampage at will across the countryside? I tell you now, Majesty, they will not stand for it! I will not stand for it! This meeting is a travesty. You had no intention of acting on my grievances. King Elias has you in his pocket, and the whole of Andaryon will suffer for it!"

Purple with rage, Corbyn turned on his heel and stalked from the audience chamber. Anjer rose to his feet roaring, "Corbyn!" but the noble ignored him.

"Let him go, Anjer," sighed the Hierarch, running a hand over his face. "He's always been impetuous. He was never going to listen to reason after what happened to Kethro this morning."

"That's no excuse for ill-manners. He needs to remember who he is," Anjer growled. "If it's military action he wants, I can give him some. I'll soon bring him back into line."

"Sit down, Anjer," commanded Pharikian. Anjer's bluster faded. He was far from happy, but he obeyed his monarch and subsided, muttering under his mustache.

"Majesty, I apologize for Lord Corbyn's rudeness," said Tikhal. "The truth is, most of his vassals are intent on war and they've been badgering him for action. I've done my best to stall him, but I don't know how much longer I can hold him off. He's been much more determined of late, which isn't like him."

Sullyan didn't like the sound of that. Nor did Anjer, although for different reasons. He spoke bluntly.

"If they try to overthrow you, Tikhal, what will you do?"

Tikhal frowned. "It won't come to that."

"But if it does, what will you do?"

Tikhal swallowed. "Try to stop him, of course. But if all his vassals stand with him, they may well defeat me."

Pharikian sighed deeply. "I thought we were past all these petty feuds, gentlemen. I have worked all my adult life toward a more stable society. Have I wasted all that time? Did Morgan

Sullyan's selflessness acheive nothing after all?"

Sullyan bowed her head on hearing her sire's name. He had sacrificed himself to broker the Pact that had seen an end to the constant raiding into Albia and the civil strife among Andaryon's nobles. Now it looked as though he had died in vain.

She spoke softly. "Was Lord Corbyn party to the Pact?"

Pharikian shot her a glance. "His father was."

"And was it binding on his descendants?"

Gaslek stirred. "Yes, Colonel, it was. If Lord Corbyn breaks the terms of the Pact, then he forfeits his lands and wealth, both for himself and his Heirs."

"But if he gets enough backing from his supporters," put in Tikhal, "the terms of the Pact will count for nothing."

"And what of all the other lords who signed their rights away?" demanded Gaslek, swinging on Tikhal. "Your father included, may I remind you, my Lord! You are all sworn to uphold the terms of the Pact. You are honor bound to come together against Corbyn and his followers, to defend the Hierarch's will."

"I am aware of that, Baron, and I would do my duty, believe me," said Tikhal. "But, forgive me, Majesty, if Prince Aeyron's captors use him to force the Hierarch to abdicate, what authority will the Pact command then?"

Chapter Twenty-Three

The meeting broke up after Tikhal's disquieting statement. Pharikian remained seated as the Andaryans took their leave, his eyes unfocused. Sullyan signaled to Bull, and he drew the others away. Ozella looked as if he wanted to stay, but he didn't resist Bull's hand on his shoulder.

Once the chamber door had closed, Sullyan moved round the table to Pharikian's side. He still looked pale and old, and she knew how keenly he was feeling the loss of his son. She covered his cold hand with hers. He didn't respond. His head was bowed, his eyes had closed, and his face was lined and gray.

Very gently, she touched his psyche and offered him comfort. He clung to it like a drowning man, the ferocity of his need taking her by surprise. In a flash of shared pain, she saw the decades of struggle he had endured simply to hold on to his rule, and she understood the sheer effort of will he had poured into controlling the innate hostility and competitiveness that was an Andaryan's natural instinct. She saw how deeply he missed the loyalty and support her father had given him, and how intently he wished Morgan were still alive. Tears sprang into her eyes and her own heart ached with grief.

"Ah, child," he groaned, "I did not mean to inflict that on you. I'm so sorry. It's just that without Morgan and my beloved Idriana I am so very alone. I couldn't bear to lose Aeyron too."

She had never seen him break down so thoroughly before. Greatly daring, she took him into her arms and he suddenly let himself go, clutching at her like a child bereft, allowing his fear and emotion free rein. She gave him time to purge before lending him a measure of strength to ease the trembling of his aged frame.

He finally found some stability and released his tight grip. She gave him a watery smile. He managed to return it, albeit fleetingly. His voice rough with emotion, he said, "You are like a daughter to me, do you know that, Brynne?"

"And you are the nearest I shall ever have to a father, Timar."

His eyes misted over. "I often wish you had decided to stay here instead of returning to Albia once you defeated Rykan. You will always have a home here, my child."

The longing in his words touched her heart. "Thank you, Timar. That means more to me than I could ever say. I was sorely tempted to take your offer, believe me. Yet despite my part-Andaryan blood, I am essentially human and my place is in Albia. Besides, I had feelings other than my own to consider when I made my decision. Half my heart may reside here with you, but the other half, like my duty, lies elsewhere."

She paused and took a breath. She had to do this now, although she hated to burden him further. "Timar, I have something to tell you about what happened today. Forgive me, but I have not been completely open with you."

His eyes widened and he leaned back, the better to see her face. "Oh?"

"I decided to wait until we were alone, partly because I fear what it might mean, and partly because of my suspicions about our adversary being able to overhear us. After I located Rand and Kethro this morning, I used the circle to do a detailed sweep of the substrate."

"I know. I felt you."

She closed her eyes and took another deep breath. "I need to show you what I found."

She offered him what she had shown Taran. His reaction was similar to the Adept's at first, but Pharikian was more experienced than Taran, and shrewder. He saw her concern.

"But how can that be?" he said, puzzling over the familiar pattern in the substrate. "You didn't enter Andaryon through the Forest, did you? You came out on the Plain."

"Precisely. So how did my pattern become imprinted on the substrate right over the place where the Prince was attacked?"

✤ ✤ ✤ ✤ ✤

By the time Baron Reen arrived at the Queen's solar the morning was nearly over. She was waiting for him, an expression of concern on her face. He entered her presence confidently and went down on one knee, clasping her cold hand.

"We've done it, Madam," he gloated. "It went even better than I hoped! I'll give them some time to think about it and wonder what we want, and then I'll send the messenger."

"And what of the... hostage?" Sofira's voice held a note of fear. "I trust he is held securely?"

"I have not seen him yet, Madam, but rest assured, he poses no threat. Izack had strict instructions and I would have heard if anything was amiss. Even if he proved troublesome, it would not affect our plans if we had to incapacitate him, or even kill him. I would rather wait until the deal is done before dispensing with him, though. He may still prove useful as a means of persuading the demon King, should he be reluctant to answer our demands."

"Do you think he will, Hezra?" she asked, anxiety still evident in her eyes.

"Oh no, my Queen, he will do exactly what we want. How could he not? Think, Madam. What lengths would you go to in his position, if it was your son?"

"Don't," she begged. "I don't even want to think of that! I don't know what I'll do if this doesn't work and we have to resort to the second part of your plan."

His eyes narrowed and he rose. She looked up at him, suddenly unsure. He spoke sternly. "Madam, I have already told you that we may well have to implement it. And I have also assured you that you have absolutely nothing to fear. Do you not trust me?"

A frown appeared on her face. "Of course I do!"

He gave her a smile. "Then trust me to know what's best."

He reveled in the power he held over her, but had to be careful how far he went with it. She was no weak and feeble woman to need a man to make her decisions, no matter how she felt about him. Time enough to exert his authority when she was Regent. He took up one of her hands and kissed it, noting the faint flush of pleasure on her cheek. Women held no amorous interest for Reen, but he was more than content to have her look that way upon him.

"I know what I'm doing, my Lady. Nothing can now go wrong. You may have to be strong for a while, but I know you can bear it. Your understandable reactions will do much to lend credence to the tale, so do not try to hide them. For now, though, I must leave you. I must check on our guest and make myself known to him. It is only polite for the host to welcome his visitor, after all."

"Is that wise, Hezra? Wouldn't it be best if he never knows who we are? What if he should escape or be rescued?"

Reen laughed unpleasantly. "Rescue? Oh, there's no chance of that, Madam! I have him secure in more ways than one. He will never live to return home, no matter what his demon father does. But I have to see him. There is a small task I need him to perform for me."

There was a slight noise by the door and Reen turned his head. Furious, he whipped round. "Huw," he roared, "what in Perdition's name are you doing here? Get out!"

His menacing tone and threatening gesture made Huw yelp and sent him scuttling away. Huw had good reason to be terrified of Reen.

Sofira sent him a disapproving look. "I wish you would be gentler with him, Hezra. There's no need to be so rough."

Reen glared at the vacant doorway, his pounding heart beginning to slow. "He has to know whom to obey. You give him too much freedom, and we may regret that one day. You know what a mimic he is. What if he were to repeat what we say?" Reen shook his head, dismissing the lad from his mind. "Now, Madam, if you will excuse me, I must see to our guest. I will return to you afterward, for we must discuss our plans for keeping our admirable military forces occupied over the next few days."

He bowed to her and Queen Sofira inclined her head. Anxiety still showed in her eyes.

The Baron returned swiftly to his chambers and called for Seth, ordering him to summon the Commander of Reen's personal bodyguard. Seth bowed himself out of the room, and Reen collected the few items he needed while he waited for the Commander to appear. He knew it would take a while. The castle's ancient dungeons were deep below the earth. Reen had no intention of going down there unescorted, as the passageways were dank, odious, and slippery. The Commander, however, must have been anticipating his master's call, as it was not long before he arrived. Seth showed him in and he halted before the Baron, grinning.

Reen smiled back. "I take it all went well?"

The pale, stocky man grinned wider. "It went well for us, my Lord, but perhaps not so well for our guest!"

"I trust you didn't hurt him?" There was mock concern in Reen's tone.

Commander Izack's eyes widened with innocence. "We

treated him respectfully, my Lord, just like you said. I'm afraid he was less than cooperative, however, and I had to protect my men. You understand."

"I understand perfectly. Is he more inclined to be helpful now?"

"Perhaps you would like to come and see for yourself, my Lord? He has been complaining about the facilities and I would hate unfavorable reports of my hospitality to reach your ears."

Reen chuckled, a guttural sound. "Lead on, Commander! You have more than earned your reward. I trust you paid our associates well?"

"They got what they were promised, my Lord. You should receive the other item you requested very soon now."

"Well done, Izack. With any luck we won't need it, but I prefer to be cautious. You never know when these things will prove useful."

The Baron followed Izack as they began their descent to the dungeon levels. He was obliged to hold a scented cloth to his nose long before they reached the deeper cells. Sunlight never touched these damp and noisome caverns with their dripping walls, iron-studded doors, chains, and instruments of pain. They had been constructed many hundreds of years ago and had once seen extensive use in the days before King Kandaran established the High Kingship. In those days, the petty-kings and nobles held their power by might of arms and fear alone. The dungeons had been abandoned since Kandaran's time, however, and were now in disrepair. Few people even knew of their existence, as wrongdoers were now held either in the civic cells or in the lock-ups of the Minster's beadle.

Ironically, it was through the Minster's records that the Baron first learned of the dungeons. After his arrival in Loxton with the Queen, he spent some time in the Minster's library researching

Loxton's theological history, keen to find out why the Church held so little authority here in the north. What he found angered him, and the people's lack of respect for their Matria Church was something he intended to address once this heretical Artesan nonsense was dealt with.

The Commander led him to a stout oak door, quite new, and produced a bunch of keys, inserting the shiniest one into the huge iron lock. It turned with a satisfying *clunk,* and Reen heard the faintest scrape of movement. Izack pushed the door open. By the light of the lamp he held, Reen could just make out a man half-lying on the filthy floor.

Long and lean, the man raised his head to the light, trying to make out who stood there. The outlandishness of his pale yellow, slit-pupiled eyes made Reen shudder, and he noted the bruises on the man's face and the soiled cloth covering the wound on his arm. Both arms were bound tightly behind the man's back, the soft gleam of silver just visible among the cords. There was pain and discomfort on his face, and Reen was pleased to see it. He stepped forward, attracting the demon's attention.

"Who are you?" the prisoner asked, his voice husky with pain and fear. "What do you want with me?"

Reen removed his scented cloth, nearly gagging on the stench in the cell. He didn't attempt to hide his revulsion and lashed out with his foot, catching Aeyron on his wounded arm. The Prince hissed with pain.

"Do not speak unless I command it!" spat Reen. "You are lucky to be alive, demon, and if you want to stay that way, you'll do as I say."

Aeyron stared at Reen as he walked around his prisoner, studying him. His past dealings with such unnatural beings had been conducted under a veneer of respect. He had needed something from them and was unable to show his true feelings.

287

This one, however, was powerless, and as he had no intention of releasing it alive, it hardly mattered what he did or said to it. It was less than human, after all, less even than an animal, and no guilt would accrue should he treat it cruelly.

"You have been brought here for a reason," stated Reen. He had not intended to tell the demon anything, but the satisfaction of his success was too intense. He wanted to gloat. After all, the demon wouldn't live to repeat what it heard.

"There is something I want, something only your father can procure for me. Once I have it, you will be released. If you refuse to do as I ask, you will be killed, and not swiftly. My Commander here has no love for your kind, as I'm sure you have discovered, and he will be happy to carry out my instructions."

The Prince shot Izack a fear-filled glance. Izack smiled nastily, showing his teeth.

The Baron carried on. "If you do decide to refuse us and force us to kill you, know that we will not deprive your father of your body. We will send it back to him piece by piece, just to show our good intentions. He can then conduct whatever meaningless rite you outlanders use."

Aeyron blanched. "What do you want me to do?" he asked hoarsely.

That insolence earned him a violent blow which slammed his head against the wall. Groaning, he struggled to retain consciousness.

Izack stepped back, massaging his right hand. "You were told not to speak," he grated.

Aeyron glared at him, hatred showing through his pain.

The Baron smiled and said casually, "Since you ask, I only require you to write me a letter."

"Wh—?" Aeyron quickly closed his bleeding mouth.

The Baron gestured and Izack unballed his fist, kneeling down beside their captive. He grinned as Aeyron flinched. Releasing one of Aeyron's hands, Izack held the point of his knife painfully to the Prince's throat. The Baron laid parchment on the floor of the cell.

✤ ✤ ✤ ✤ ✤

Robin had been hearing some very ugly rumors and was growing heartily sick of coming across groups of off-duty men who broke guiltily apart when they saw him. Never one for gossip, Robin had no patience with those who indulged in damaging speculation. He had rank to uphold, and could not allow a few nasty remarks to interfere in his relationship with those under his command. Nevertheless, this situation could not continue. Determined to get to the bottom of the rumors, he decided to talk to Denny.

He made his way to the infirmary as soon as he was free. It was mid-afternoon, lunch was over, and the healers had already made their rounds changing dressings. There were few people about when Robin entered the room where Denny lay in his bed, half-propped by pillows and looking very sorry for himself.

He looked up disinterestedly as Robin approached him. Not knowing the other officer, Robin was unsure how to proceed. He stopped a few paces away and smiled tentatively. Denny, who had an easy-going and friendly disposition, smiled back.

He broke the clumsy silence. "Major Tamsen, isn't it? To what do I owe this honor?"

His cheerful manner eased the tension. Receiving his nod of permission, Robin perched on the edge of the bed.

"I don't know about honor," he said. "I just thought you might appreciate some company. I know what it's like being stuck in here, and most of your men are out on duty with ours. I thought you might appreciate a friendly face."

Denny grinned. "Shall I tell you what I'd really appreciate?" he murmured, leaning as far forward as his stiff body would allow.

"Let me guess," chuckled Robin. "Food."

Denny's eyes went innocently wide. "How did you know?"

Robin laughed. "Because Healer Arlen is a personal friend of mine and I know what she's like. But I warn you," Robin lowered his voice, "if she finds out you've asked me to smuggle food it won't only be your hide she nails to the door."

Denny's face fell. "So you won't do it?"

He looked so woebegone that Robin laughed again. "I didn't say that. I'll do what I can. There's a young cadet who can sometimes be persuaded to run errands for me. His name's Tad and he used to be a kitchen boy. If anyone knows how to smuggle food in here, it'll be Tad. He's not above taking the odd risk or two, especially for me. And Rienne likes him, so that might help. But if you say anything to get him caught, we'll show you no mercy. Rienne's a demon when she's angry."

Denny held up his good hand in a parody of the King's Oath. "On my honor," he grinned, "only food shall pass my lips."

"It had better!"

The two men eyed each other, Denny clearly aware that this was not the reason for Robin's visit. Now the ice was broken, the Major felt he could address the subject.

"Lieutenant," he began, but Denny interrupted him.

"Please, Major, my name's Denny, or Owyn, if you like. I don't feel much like a lieutenant in here."

"Very well," the other man agreed. "I'm Robin when I'm off-duty. Owyn, I wanted to ask you what you know about the rumors going round. You know what I mean, the ones about Colonel Sullyan and Captain Elijah."

Denny's eyes widened in shock. "I *knew* he was lying when he said you knew about it!" There was vindication in his tone. "I couldn't see how you could possibly condone what they were doing right under your nose. And once I'd seen you... well, there's no comparison, is there?"

Robin felt his heart clench suddenly. "What do you mean, 'condone what they were doing?'"

"You mean you still don't know? I thought everyone knew by now. They weren't exactly discreet." Seeing Robin's look of shock, Denny added, "Oh, sorry! Do you really want me to tell you, or would you rather wait and ask them yourself?"

Robin tried to compose himself. His heart was hammering strangely. He wasn't prepared for this. Despite his irritation and growing concern over the rumors, his own common sense had told him he would find only spurious nonsense, something and nothing blown out of all proportion. He knew he ought to hear what Denny had to say before jumping to any conclusions, but the Lieutenant was clearly convinced he was right. If that was the case, then Robin's whole world was about to shatter around him.

He swallowed, his throat unnaturally dry. He was grateful for Denny's thoughtfulness, giving him the choice of whom to ask, but he had to have the full story now. Something deep within, some strange disembodied voice, was nagging him and it would not be stilled. Hearing the tale from Denny would give him time to consider his reactions, and maybe allow him the upper hand if he was forced to confront the miscreants.

"Tell me," he said, his voice rough with emotion.

"You sure?"

Robin felt hot with confusion, but he nodded.

"All right, then." Denny proceeded to tell him, unemotionally, what he had seen and heard at Port Loxton.

Robin listened dispassionately, his eyes hard and unseeing, his hands clamped together, his white knuckles the only indication of his inner turmoil. It was a mercy that no one else entered the room. Robin's fragile heart could not have borne that. When Denny came to the part about Taran telling him that Robin knew about him and Sullyan, the Major's eyes sharpened on the young Lieutenant's

291

face.

"Tell me exactly what he said," he demanded.

Denny considered a moment. "He'd been acting very strangely. He was clearly worried about something, and he kept glancing over at the Colonel while we rode. You must remember that I was wounded and not at my best. I'd been watching Captain Elijah because it was something to do, and to be perfectly honest, I was amusing myself wondering how they concealed the affair from everyone else here.

"Anyway, along you came to relieve the Colonel, and the Captain's face was a picture. He was horrified to see it was you, and he was really squirming when you thanked him for 'looking after her.' I just couldn't believe his nerve. And when I saw you, and realized that you were exactly suited to Sullyan, I—" He broke off, flushing with embarrassment.

"What?"

"Oh, it's only that Captain Elijah isn't the first to have fallen inappropriately for Sullyan. I trained with her, you know, and I was foolish enough to try my luck more than once. Came to nothing, of course. I always knew I didn't stand a chance. With her looks and talents, she was always going to go for someone like you. But I never really expected to succeed. Not like Parren did."

"Don't mention that man's name to me!" The force of Robin's anger startled him as much as it did Denny. "He's been the cause of most of my problems over the past three years! If I find out he's got anything to do with this—"

"No, no," said Denny hastily, "he only gave me background information. He was as incredulous as you are."

"Yes, I bet he was." Robin's heart pounded all the harder. The strange inner sensation was beginning to make him nauseous. All he needed was Parren's vicious tongue adding to this. "Go on."

"Well," continued Denny, "once I'd seen you, I found it even more incredible that Sullyan had allowed Captain Elijah's infatuation to develop into an affair. He told me you knew all about it, that it had been going on since before you and Sullyan were wed. He even told me it didn't matter, because you were all friends! I can tell you, it was the most shocking thing I've ever heard, and I'm no prude."

Robin felt his face, his entire body, it seemed, drain of blood. He was struggling for breath. "Let me get this straight," he rasped. "You're saying Taran Elijah told you he'd been sleeping with my wife?"

"I had it from his own lips, Robin. And that's not all." Denny was warming to his theme, ignoring or not noticing the tears in Robin's eyes. "While they were at Port Loxton, he was also carrying on with Baron Reen's niece, Lady Jinella. She was very taken with him, by all accounts, and was broken-hearted when she caught him sneaking out of the Colonel's room in the middle of the night, both of them half-naked from her bed!"

Robin couldn't speak. He was trembling, his eyes feverishly bright and his face ashen. His heart had turned to stone and he wanted to vomit. He rose unsteadily from the bed.

Denny frowned in concern. "Robin, are you all right? Gods, you look awful!"

Robin didn't respond. He wasn't in control of his thoughts. All he could see were images of the two of them together, and he couldn't push them out of his mind. All he could hear was the soft sound of Sullyan's voice speaking her vows on their wedding day. His blood froze. What a sham that had been! He thought of the many times she had been alone with Taran when Robin was on duty, often late into the night. He remembered her strange moods lately and her reluctance to share her body, how cold she had been toward him since her return from Port Loxton. And, most damning of all, how Taran had avoided him since, and how he flushed red with embarrassment whenever he saw Robin.

The Major put a hand on the wall to steady himself, his thoughts uncontrolled, chaotic. He remembered, with grim irony, how he had given Taran his trust before they left for Port Loxton. How thoroughly that trust had been betrayed! He only just choked down the sobs that welled into his throat.

Denny was watching him closely. Fearful of breaking down in front of the wounded officer, Robin pushed away from the wall. He had to get out. He made for the door, stumbling blindly through it, tears filling his eyes. He nearly collided with one of the junior healers coming to check on the patients. The man didn't speak, but Robin felt the weight of his gaze as he left.

Chapter Twenty-Four

Taran, Bull, and Ozella took their evening meal in their rooms while Sullyan dined privately with the Hierarch and his daughter. The Princess was still very shocked by her brother's abduction, and her condition made her prone to weeping. Deshan had provided restorative treatments for them both, but Idrimar's face, naturally pale, was still ashen.

Since her marriage to Marik, Idrimar had blossomed out of her melancholy nature, but she had already lost one sibling—her twin—and this threat to her brother plunged her deep into gloom. She hardly touched her food and sat with her hands clasped protectively over her belly.

Pharikian made an effort for his daughter's sake but his heart wasn't in it. Sullyan, who had made a full report to General Blaine via the substrate, sat lost in her own thoughts, replaying the General's angry concern in her mind. At least she knew he would protect Elias from similar danger.

They moved on to the brandy, which Sullyan refused, and Norkis began clearing away the exquisite but largely untouched meal. There was a commotion in the corridor and the sound of running feet. Pharikian and Idrimar both blanched in fear and Sullyan's first thought was, *No, not again!*

She moved to stand protectively in front of the Hierarch and the Princess. They clung to each other as the door slammed violently open. Sullyan stared in amazement at the tall man standing stock-still in the doorway.

Relief and irritation coursed through her. "Ty!"

Ty Marik grinned apologetically as his racing breaths slowed. He moved past her toward the sobbing Princess, who rushed blindly into his arms. Sullyan glanced at the Hierarch. He was smiling gently at his daughter's husband, and Sullyan was glad to see a lighter expression on his careworn face. She wondered suddenly whether he fully appreciated that, should Aeyron not survive, the lean man embracing his daughter would be the next ruler of Andaryon.

Once they were calm, Marik freed himself from Idrimar's arms and greeted his father-by-marriage. He conveyed his sympathies and assured Pharikian of his total and unconditional support in the efforts to find the Prince.

"Oh, but I nearly forgot," he exclaimed, reaching into his doublet and drawing out a sealed parchment. "As I was coming through the Forest I met a messenger. He saw I was headed this way and gave me this for you." He passed Pharikian the parchment.

The Hierarch frowned as he broke the seal and opened the message. At once he gasped and let the parchment fall to the table.

"What is it, Timar?" Sullyan asked with deep concern.

His face had gone gray and he was trembling. He pushed the parchment shakily across to her and she took it and read. Marik looked over her shoulder, an expression of shock on his long face.

The Prince is unharmed, for now. If you wish him to remain so, you will accede to our demands. You have three days in which to procure thirty pounds of reverse polarity spellsilver. If you fail, your son will be killed. We will send him back to you piece by piece. You will be contacted again in three days to arrange delivery.

There was no signature and Sullyan did not recognize the writing. She raised her eyes to Pharikian's horror-stuck face.

"Thirty pounds!" she said. "What on earth can they want with so much?"

No one had an answer. Dreading what she would find, she turned the parchment over. Her worst fears were confirmed and her heart turned to ice when she saw the broken seal.

"Whose is it?" asked Marik, not able to see it clearly. Her eyes huge, Sullyan stared at Pharikian. He glanced away.

"It is the seal of King Elias," she whispered, letting the parchment fall to the table.

"Then the rumors are true!" exclaimed Marik.

"Of course they are not true!" she snapped. "Can you truly think of a reason why King Elias would kidnap Prince Aeyron? If he had a need for spellsilver, he would trade for it."

"But the seal—"

"Anyone can reproduce or steal a seal," she said.

He stared at her. "I suppose so." He sat, pulling the Princess down with him. "I'm sorry, Brynne, I should have thought."

"What can you tell us of the messenger, Ty? Was he human?"

"Of course not. Do you think I would accept a message thrust at me by a strange human? No, he was an Andaryan messenger."

"Whose livery did he wear?"

Marik had the grace to look shamed. "Do you know, I never thought to look? It happened so fast. He rode up to us, asked me if I'd take the thing, and then galloped off." He saw the look she was giving him and added defensively, "It was getting dark, you know, and he was cloaked!"

Sullyan sighed. "The next time something unexpected happens, keep your wits about you, will you?"

Idrimar was about to leap to her husband's defense, but he soothed her, saying, "It's all right, Idri, don't upset yourself, not in your condition. Brynne's right, I should have taken more notice."

He looked over at the Hierarch, who hadn't moved, his eyes still fixed on the parchment. "What will you do, Timar?"

Pharikian raised his head and Sullyan saw the hopelessness in his eyes. Her heart ached with grief. "What do you think, Brynne?" he asked, unable even to consider a decision.

She shrugged. "Pay the ransom, if you can."

Marik drew a shocked breath. "Do you know how much thirty pounds of that kind of spellsilver is worth?"

"As much as the Prince's life?" she snapped.

He subsided at once. "Oh, gods, of course not. Forgive me, Timar."

Pharikian made no response. Sullyan watched him with sympathy, reading pain and despair in the lines on his face. She spoke gently. "Can you pay it, Timar?"

He looked blindly at her, unable to think straight. "I really don't know at this moment, Brynne. Reverse polarity spellsilver is rare enough and its uses few, so it is not a commodity I keep to hand. I have mines, of course, and they will have stockpiles, but how quickly I could gather such a large amount, I cannot say."

"Well," she said briskly, "at least this message tells us one thing for certain." He frowned at her. "We now know that our enemy has Andaryan allies, or Andaryans in his pay, at the very least. I thought this was so after the attack on King Elias, but it was just possible that the raid was an unconnected incident, unlikely though that seemed. This confirms it was not. And I have an instant suspicion as to who those allies might be."

The Princess, who had slipped the parchment toward her and was reading it, gave a gasp. "It tells us something else, Father. Look!"

She thrust the message back under Pharikian's nose. He stared blankly at it for a few seconds, and then he too gave a gasp. "Yes,

Idri, you're right, I don't know why I didn't see it before. Brynne, this was written by my son. I'm sure of it."

"Then that is a comfort, is it not? For he could not have done so unless he was fully conscious and unharmed, as the message says."

The Hierarch nodded. "The writing is shaky. That must be why I didn't recognize it at first. Yes, we must let ourselves be encouraged by this. Aeyron is strong and will conduct himself with dignity through this ordeal. He will be relying on us, so we must not fail to secure his release. Gaslek will find out how much spellsilver we have to hand."

Relieved to see him more himself, Sullyan made a decision. "Timar, with your permission, I should return to Albia tomorrow. I will inform the General and King Elias of this latest development tonight, but as I am certain Prince Aeyron is being held in Albia, I can be more use to you there. You have Ty to help you now. He and Idrimar will look after you and support you. If there are any other developments, you know I am at your command. I assure you, I will do everything in my power to find the Prince, but I believe I can best achieve that by returning to Albia."

Pharikian hesitated, plainly torn between begging her to stay and the knowledge that she could not. He sighed. "Very well, Brynne, you may go. But you will inform me the minute you discover anything of importance? Anything at all?"

The plaintive note in his voice gave her a pang of grief for this man she had come to love as a father. She hated to see him so vulnerable. She could only nod her assurance, as her voice would have given her away. She turned to Marik.

"Ty, would you grant me a private word? I can explain the situation to you and some of our suspicions, and there are one or two questions I would like to ask you."

Idrimar wasn't pleased to lose her husband's comforting

presence so soon, but he quickly reassured her and accompanied Sullyan back to her rooms. Once there, she saw the fresh fellan Bull had left brewing on the hearth. Smiling in grateful affection, she poured two cups. She and Marik sat together on the couch while she told him in detail what had happened. She also told him what she had not told Pharikian; that her suspicions concerning their enemy's allies centered on the disgruntled and warlike Corbyn.

"What do you know of him, Ty?"

"Not much." Marik's expression was somber as he watched her over his cup. "He's a northern noble, Tikhal's immediate neighbor. He's supposedly subordinate to Tikhal, but he's been growing stronger of late and gathering support from other discontented nobles. It wouldn't surprise me if he challenged Tikhal for supremacy in the north one day."

She nodded. "He as good as threatened it today."

Marik's eyes widened. "Did he? By the gods, that was precocious. I wouldn't have thought him strong enough yet."

Sullyan told him what Corbyn had said, and Marik whistled.

"We'd be back to where we were before the Pact," he exclaimed. "And if what Tikhal said about them killing Aeyron or forcing Timar to abdicate came to pass, then the Pact really would be dead."

She cocked her head at him. "If Prince Aeyron is killed or Timar forced to abdicate, to whom will the Crown fall?"

The stunned and horrified look on his face would have amused her had the situation not been so serious.

"Bloody hell, Brynne," he whispered, "you'd better find him quick, for all our sakes!"

Once the shock of his situation had faded, Sullyan asked Marik about Rykan's palace.

"I destroyed it as soon as I could," he told her, his pale eyes darkening at the memory. "After what happened to both of us there, I could hardly bear to look at it."

She ducked her head. "Oh, Ty. I try to remember only that you helped me when no one else could and kept me alive long enough for my friends to find me. I will always be grateful for that. You risked your life for me and that can never be repaid."

He smiled. "Well, if not for you, I wouldn't be allied to the Andaryan ruling House and be anticipating the birth of twins. It is I who should be thanking you. Having said that," he added casually, "I am rather disappointed in you."

"What do you mean?"

"I mean I think you could have told me rather than waiting for me to work it out for myself. We have both been wed the same amount of time, you know. I presume Timar knows?"

She frowned, completely puzzled. "Knows what, Ty? I do not understand you."

He looked hurt. "Oh, come on, Brynne! I thought we were friends."

"We are, which is why I am trying not to get angry! Just what is it you think I have not told you? It can be nothing of great importance."

He stood up, deeply upset now. She could see it in his eyes.

"How can you say that? You don't consider it important telling me you're pregnant?"

She felt her face go white and stared at him, dumbstruck. He waited for her response, his expression becoming more unsure as the wait went on. Recovering from her shock, she smiled sadly. "Ty, whatever made you think that? I am not pregnant. Rykan made very sure I would never be able to carry a child. I am sorry, my friend. I thought you knew that."

Marik stared hard at her, studying her pale face and slender form minutely. His face reddened and he sat down.

"Brynne... oh, I'm so sorry. I just thought... you looked... oh, gods, I didn't know. I'm sorry."

She moved closer, taking his hands in hers. "There is no need for sorrow. I have come to terms with it now. You are not to blame. I only thought you might have guessed as you were the first to be aware of the danger Rykan's... abuse placed me in. But tell me. What made you think I was pregnant?"

He was thoroughly embarrassed now, plainly wanted to forget the whole thing. "You have that look about you," he mumbled. "I guessed before Idri did that she was carrying, and I was right. I just didn't think. Will you forgive me?"

She leaned forward and kissed him, causing his lean face to redden further. "There is nothing to forgive, my friend. Let us forget it. Now, shall we get back to business?"

"Of course," he said, grateful for the change of subject. "What do you want to know?"

She smiled. "Before you destroyed it, did you find anything at all in Rykan's palace to suggest who was backing him?"

He shook his head. "There was nothing in any of his written records."

"Do you still have those records?"

"Yes. I didn't think we should destroy them."

"Quite right. Could you send for them and let Gaslek go over them? No, I am not suggesting you did not look properly," she said, seeing his indignant expression, "but Gaslek is used to reading these things, and the smallest reference may be a clue which could easily be missed. Now, what of Sonten's holdings? I believe you bestowed them on Nazir?"

"Yes," he said, leaning back and taking more fellan. "I was going to give him my old manor of Cardon, but Idri wants me to pass that to our son."

Sullyan nodded. "Very appropriate. Would Nazir have gone

through Sonten's records?"

"I doubt it. What's Sonten's relevance? It wasn't him they were interested in, it was Rykan."

"Granted, but Sonten was as ambitious as Rykan, although fortunately not as ruthless. We may never know for sure, but I suspect he intended to challenge Rykan through Jaskin once the boy had mastered the Staff. Why else would they steal it? And if that is the case, then Sonten may have had contact with whoever was financing Rykan. It will definitely be worth looking into Sonten's records, if Nazir still has them."

"Oh, he has them. Nazir hasn't done anything to Sonten's manor. It's far more luxurious than anything he's ever seen. I expect he's still trying to find his way round all the rooms."

"Then please get him to send everything to Gaslek. I am sure Timar will not object. I just hope Gaslek will forgive me all this extra work."

Marik snorted. "Gaslek adores trawling through old records. He'll love you forever!"

She smiled. "One last question, Ty, and then you can return to Idrimar. I realize you were not on close terms with Rykan"— Marik made a strangled noise, choking on his fellan—"but I need to know whether any of his commanders or higher-ranking nobles were Artesans."

Marik frowned and Sullyan went on. "I ask because when Sonten captured Taran, Cal, Bull, and Robin, he had two Artesans with him. One was Commander Heron, but he perished with Sonten at Hyecombe. Would you know who the other might have been?"

Marik's frown deepened. "Are you sure about this?"

"Of course. When Vanyr, Ky-shan, and I found them, I distinctly saw the impressions of two trained psyche patterns in Sonten's band."

"Then they were both Sonten's men," said the Duke confidently. "They certainly weren't Rykan's. The only gifted noble who was allowed to get close to Rykan was Jaskin, and that was only because he was thinking of making the boy his Heir. Rykan didn't trust anyone. He was far too concerned about protecting his status to permit anyone with power anywhere near him. He simply wouldn't have tolerated the potential threat. How do you think Sonten managed to rise to the position he held? Giftless as he was, no one else would have elevated him. Mind you, there was an Artesan in Rykan's forces, a commander named Verris. Rykan had some kind of hold over him, but I never knew what it was. Anyway, Verris got himself killed during the Albian invasion.

"Rykan didn't encourage his nobles to develop their powers. I only held on to my manor because of the weakness of my gift, and Sonten would never even have become Rykan's general had he been born with the power he craved."

Sullyan considered this, not doubting Marik for a second. She had never fully appreciated his dilemma, thankful on the one hand that he had little in the way of talent yet powerless to resist Rykan and ally himself with the Hierarch, as his heart would have led him to do.

She turned back to the matter in hand. "Then if the Artesan I sensed was Sonten's, there may be mention of him in the Durkos records. Please ask Nazir to send them as swiftly as he can. This is one lead that might prove to be immensely important, especially if the man is still alive."

She let him go, seeing how he fretted after Idrimar. She was weary herself. Despite the abatement of her intermittent sickness, she seemed to tire easily these days. Standing and stretching an aching back, she prepared herself for another difficult communication with General Blaine before seeking her rest.

✤ ✤ ✤ ✤ ✤

On returning to the Manor early the next morning, Sullyan and her companions were greeted by signs of frantic activity. At least two companies were being readied for action, one of them Sullyan's own. Seeing this, she leaped from Drum's back and accosted Captain Dexter, who was issuing hasty orders. He turned a relieved look on her.

"Colonel, thank the gods you're back. The General wants you to attend him immediately. There have been several serious demon raids overnight, and patrols are being sent out to deal with them. The Major left before first light with half our men, and we're to leave as soon as you're ready. But the General wants to see you first."

"Very well, Captain," she replied, already moving off. "I will be back directly. Carry on with your orders and make sure all are ready to ride on my return."

She left at a run, leaving Bull, Taran, and Ozella to their own devices. When she arrived at Blaine's door, Elias was with him. Both men appeared strained and careworn. The General had already told Elias about Aeyron's abduction and the ransom demand, and the King's face showed his concern. Both men looked up as she entered, Elias acknowledging her hasty salute.

"Captain Dexter says there have been more raids," she said.

Elias scowled as Blaine made his report. "Our scouts brought word in the predawn hours of two serious incursions only a few miles south of here," he said. "Villages are burning and people are being killed, seemingly at random. One of Vassa's companies has gone to deal with one group, and Major Tamsen took half his men to run off the second. I didn't call for you as I knew you were returning early, but a few minutes before you arrived I received word of a third raid, this one to the north. Vassa's organizing a rota of patrols, but Captain Dexter offered to ready the rest of your company so you could leave immediately."

Blaine's expression was bleak as he watched her face. "Just what is going on here, Sullyan? Didn't you manage to convince Pharikian of our innocence over those raids?"

She raised her brows. "Of course I did, General. Timar is well aware that we had nothing to do with the raids in Andaryon. He has the threat of civil strife in his own lands to contend with, as many of his nobles are discontented with what they see as his failure to retaliate. Some of them want him to break with us. He fears another attempt on his crown, and with good reason. I can assure you, these latest attacks were neither instigated nor authorized by the Hierarch.

"There is more to this than we know at present, but the abduction of Prince Aeyron is a serious escalation. I am convinced all these events are linked, and this ransom demand of spellsilver may give us a clue to our enemy's ultimate purpose. Although, for the moment, neither Pharikian nor I can guess what it might be."

"How is Pharikian?" asked the King, a hint of dark shadows under his eyes.

Sullyan regarded him openly. "Heartsick, your Majesty. Aeyron is his Heir and his only son. I am sure you can imagine how he feels."

Elias winced, dropping his eyes. Sullyan turned back to Blaine. "A thought occurs to me, General. Two attempts have already been made on the King's life. Might these raids so near to home be a ploy to empty the Manor of its forces? Loath as I am to suggest we leave the people to fend for themselves, we must not allow ourselves to be fooled into leaving the King with too few defenders."

Blaine's expression tightened, as if he considered her words an implied criticism. Elias, however, wasn't concerned with that. "You surely don't think they'd attack here?" he asked.

She stared at him and brutally pointed out, "They tried within the very boundaries of your own stronghold, your Majesty. What makes you think they would balk at trying here?"

Neither Blaine nor Elias could answer her, and it was clear that even the General had not seriously considered this possibility. She left them then, returning to Dexter and the men of her command. She led them out into the morning, riding swiftly with her senses alert, always aware that this could be a ruse to cover another attempt on the life of her King.

✤ ✤ ✤ ✤ ✤

Cal was surprised but pleased that morning when Robin took him along as Acting Captain when he left the Manor with his company of fifty men. Rienne, proud but worried, had Cal make many promises to be careful: not that he needed reminding of what he stood to lose if he was not. They rode out into darkness and quickly covered the miles to the reported site of the raid. Robin sent Cal and another man forward to scout the area.

Cal was determined not to let Robin's strangely irritable mood distract him from this chance to show his mettle. Still, the dark-skinned young man couldn't imagine what had caused it. Robin could be hot-headed, but he had never shown the kind of temper he was in of late.

The men were puzzled too. The Major's mood was so out of character that they were dismayed, thinking there must be some military reason for it; impending war, maybe. Most of them had heard the rumors, of course, but none of them gave the gossip any credence, and Robin had never been one to bother with it, so his ill temper remained a troubling mystery.

Cal and his companion checked the area carefully on foot and soon came across a group of about twenty Andaryans systematically firing and looting a small farming settlement. It was totally senseless; the farmstead was a poor place and held nothing of value. From what Cal could see, the raiders were bent on wanton destruction and nothing else. He reported swiftly back to Robin, whose foul mood was still much in evidence.

"Right, lads, no holding back. Let's teach these demons that they can't raid wholesale into our lands without encountering our steel!"

Cal was surprised to hear Robin refer to the Andaryans as demons, but he had no time to ponder. The men gave Robin their eager agreement, and the Major led them at a gallop straight toward the farmstead, where the cries and screams of the little community could be heard above the crackle and roar of burning buildings.

Dawn's light was only just breaking across the sky, but the light from flaming barns and cottages illuminated the stark shapes of the raiders, outlining targets for the men. The fight was short, bloody, and brutal.

When it was over and they had tended their own wounded, Cal risked a quiet word with Robin.

"Major, shouldn't we have tried to take prisoners? We might have been able to find out who's behind this."

To his shock, Robin rounded furiously on him.

"Are you criticizing me?"

Cal stepped back a pace, his face falling. Robin continued angrily. "You're only Acting Captain, remember! Don't get above yourself. Go and see what you can do for those poor farmers. Leave the strategy to those who know what they're doing."

Hurt and stunned by this unjust reaction, Cal didn't mention that he thought he had recognized one of the Andaryan raiders. He couldn't remember where he had seen the man, and he wasn't among those they had killed. Disinclined to brave Robin's foul mood a second time, Cal dismissed it from his mind.

He received sympathetic looks from some of the men, none of

whom dared speak out in his defense. They went about trying to help the farmers put out the fires and tend their wounded and dying, of whom there were many. The raiders had been merciless and the greasy smoke, reeking of charred wood and burned flesh, stuck in everyone's throats.

✠ ✠ ✠ ✠ ✠

Had Cal but known it, Robin's fury was directed more at himself than the younger man. Sure that his black mood was justified, he nevertheless knew he shouldn't have allowed it to affect his professional judgment. He was horrified that he might now be responsible for letting vital information slip through their fingers. Cal was right. He should have given orders to take prisoners at all costs. Instead, he had taken out his feelings of betrayal on the raiders.

Yet he was damned if he would take a reminder from a subordinate. He had made what could turn out to be a grave mistake, and this knowledge fueled his fury at what Sullyan and Taran had made him do. Instead of apologizing to Cal and forcing his anger down, he moved among the dead in a mounting rage, looking for colors of allegiance, anything to lessen the magnitude of his error.

He found nothing.

Chapter Twenty-Five

Sullyan rode shoulder to shoulder with Captain Dexter as she led her company to a rendezvous with the scouts who had reported the raid to the north. She was aware of Dexter watching her, and surmised the rumors were behind his scrutiny. Well, he would find no fault with her focus. She didn't mind his concern. They all trusted each other with their lives every time they went out, and a good captain always had the best interests of his men at heart. Dexter would never believe such tales as those spread by the men of Port Loxton, but he was right to be wary.

After half an hour's hard ride they met up with the scouts, who led Sullyan's command unerringly toward the trouble. The raiders had spent some time here, and most of the buildings were well alight. Sullyan gave swift orders for her men to surround the village and cut off any route of escape. She held them back from a rushed assault despite the pitiful cries of wounded villagers.

They closed their circle warily, alert for ambush or attack. The outer houses were either deserted or inhabited only by the dead. The sounds of combat came from farther in, and Sullyan prepared to order a charge. When they neared the center of the village, she saw that the people had gathered there in desperate defense of their lives, opposing the raiders with whatever weapons they had to hand, most of which were useless against swords and crossbows.

"Remember, men," she yelled, "we need one or two alive at least. Do the best you can."

One of the raiders heard her and turned just as the charge

began. He roared at his men, who immediately broke off the attack, falling back before the Albians' rush. The raiders aimed a determined wedge of fighting men at one portion of Sullyan's cordon, and, with some loss of life, forced a way through and fled for the woods. The men from the Manor galloped hard in pursuit.

Sullyan didn't stay for the villagers. They would have to wait until she had leisure to return. A captive was her objective, and she urged her men to greater speed. Just when she thought she was gaining on her quarry, she felt a familiar prickle in her mind. Someone was breaching the substrate! Torn between the desire to search for the Artesan responsible and the need to block her prey's escape, she opted for the latter and set her opposing will against the opening of the tunnel.

It turned out to be a serious mistake.

When she opened her eyes, it was to a blinding headache and the sight of Captain Dexter looking anxiously down on her. She sat up shakily, wondering what on earth she was doing lying on the ground. Dexter put out a hand and helped her up.

"Are you all right, Colonel?"

The question made no sense. Her eyes wouldn't focus and she swayed on her feet. She heard Dexter call urgently over his shoulder.

"Wil, bring that liquor here, will you?"

The Corporal came over, holding out a small leather flask. Dexter took it and removed the cork.

"Now, Colonel," he said kindly, "I know you don't normally drink, but I think you ought to take a sip of this. It'll help clear your head."

He sounded very worried. She stared vacantly, but obediently swallowed when he helped her to a mouthful of the fiery liquid. It made her cough, but had the desired effect. When her eyes decided to function again, she frowned at him.

"What happened, Captain?"

His concern deepened. "You don't remember?"

She ran a hand across her face, becoming aware of the men clustered around her and the comforting presence of Drum at her shoulder. She gathered her wits slowly, her head pounding.

"We were pursuing the raiders," she said, her thoughts clearing. "I felt someone open the substrate and reached out to stop them. What happened next?"

The Captain snorted. "What happened was that for no apparent reason, you fell off that great black beast!"

"Fell off?" she repeated faintly. "I have never fallen from a horse in my life."

"Well, you have now. I nearly rode over you."

She shook her head, trying to order her thoughts. "I take it they all got away?"

He nodded. "We did try. I left one of the lads with you and went after them, but they had already disappeared. Must have gone through that tunnel you mentioned." Dexter had no Artesan power, but he had been around Sullyan long enough to understand it.

She sighed. Despite the pain in her head, she would have to search. Rubbing her back, she said, "Help me mount, will you? I think I must have landed on a tree root."

He linked his hands under her foot and boosted her up onto Drum. He was still concerned. She had never needed such help before. He watched her warily to check she was all right.

"Mount the men, Captain," she said, her voice sounding more normal. "Lead them back to the village and do what you can for those poor people. I will follow soon."

He obeyed, but she saw his whispered order to Wil. The Corporal lagged behind to keep an eye on her.

She didn't mind; he had the right. Sitting Drum quietly, she explored her aching head. There was pain when she expended her power, and this worried her. Things were becoming clearer now, although it had happened so fast. When she had reached out to oppose the tunnel's opening, there was an instant and violent backlash so unexpected that it threw her physically from Drum's back. She had never experienced its like before.

Apprehensive as to what she would find, she probed the substrate. Her worst fears were soon realized. The reason her power had backfired so totally was that it had met its twin. The faint psyche imprint embedded in the substrate was hers. She had effectively blocked her own power.

Something very terrible was happening here, and she didn't have a clue what it was.

Hugging herself in fear, she smiled to reassure Wil. Still shaky, she followed him back to the village where they spent what time they could with the panicked inhabitants.

✣ ✣ ✣ ✣ ✣

On receiving Sullyan's terse report through the substrate, Blaine issued orders for those already in the field to stay out for a tour of duty. It was impossible for the Manor's forces to reach stricken villages as quickly as the raiders could move through the Veils, but if they were already in the area they stood a better chance of a swift response.

Robin's company were nearly back by the time Blaine's message reached them. As he had wounded with him, Robin gave the order to continue to the Manor. He intended to collect fresh men and then go back out to finish his tour.

His mood hadn't improved, and all his men were wary of speaking to him. Cal rode behind him, scowling unhappily and wondering what on earth could be causing such uncharacteristic bad temper.

Cal couldn't recall seeing him in such a state before, and decided to mention it to Bull. Apart from Sullyan, Bull knew

Robin best and might be able to help him deal with whatever was troubling him. Yet that would have to wait, as they would be off again once they had delivered their wounded to the infirmary.

✣ ✣ ✣ ✣ ✣

Robin allowed his men a brief respite while he reported to the General. If his mood was black when he approached the interview, it was ten times worse when he came out. The General didn't accuse him outright of dereliction of duty, but Robin's excuse that the raiders had refused to surrender simply didn't satisfy Blaine. He delivered a stinging admonition and told Robin to buck his ideas up, using the tone he generally reserved for junior officers. The fact that Elias was also present compounded the Major's humiliation.

When he left Blaine's office, Robin's face was flushed with shame. The General's dressing down rang in his ears as he stalked through the Manor. It was Taran's great misfortune to step out of his room right into Robin's path.

As if it were some hidden trigger buried deep inside Robin just waiting to ignite his fury, the sight of Taran caused a meltdown. The Major hadn't intended to confront Taran about the rumors before speaking to Sullyan, but in his present mood the opportunity could not be missed. His rage had been building ever since his talk with Denny, and seeing Taran made him lose all control.

He lunged abruptly and grabbed Taran by the jacket, forcing him violently back into his room. Slamming the door shut with his foot, he thrust his furious face into Taran's.

Utterly shocked, Taran was unable to resist. Robin's muscular strength was too much for him. Taran stared at him fearfully, beginning to tremble.

"So, you thought you could get away with it, did you?" snarled Robin, his hands bunched in the leather at Taran's throat, his breath hot on the Adept's face. "Thought I wouldn't realize, wouldn't notice? Well, you've not been very clever, have you? You were seen, both of you, and now I know all about it."

"I don't—" began Taran, but Robin was squeezing his throat and Taran could hardly get the words out.

"Oh, no you don't," spat Robin. "Don't you dare try to deny it. I've heard all about your treacherous affair! Did you think that because we were friends you could do what you liked?" He shook the Adept roughly. "Well? How many times has it been, Taran? Whenever I was on duty? Whenever I was out of the way?"

The horror that appeared on Taran's face told Robin he understood what he was being accused of. Humiliation and shame flooded Taran's psyche, and tears pricked his eyes. His face turned crimson.

"I haven't—" he tried, but Robin was beyond hearing.

"You've been laughing at me!" he yelled, spitting the words in Taran's face. Taran's mortified expression only increased Robin's rage. "The whole place is laughing at me! Everyone knows now. Why couldn't you keep your dirty little hands to yourself? Why couldn't you leave her alone? You've been itching to try it on with her ever since you came here. You knew how much she meant to me. She was my life! But you've destroyed all that. All that agony I went through last year, all that heartache and soul-searching, all that pain and terror. All for nothing… nothing!"

He shook Taran again and the Adept looked frightened, as if he doubted Robin's sanity.

"Robin," he gasped, alarm in his tone. "It's not true. We did nothing wrong."

"*NOTHING WRONG?*" screamed Robin, his handsome features savagely twisted. "Yes, you would think that! You told Denny I knew all about it, didn't you?"

"No, I… well, yes, but I didn't mean—"

It was no use. Robin's voice fell to a menacing whisper, and the pain in his eyes was horrible to see. "You thought you had the right to do what you wanted. Well, my friend, I'm here to tell you you're wrong. Very wrong. If you want to keep your health, if you don't want your brains fried in your head, you'll pack your bags and get out. I don't want you here when I return, do you understand? You've forfeited your place. You're not wanted. I don't care where you go, just make it far away. Do I make myself clear?"

The Adept shivered. He made no further attempt at speech. Robin was beyond reason. The Major was a Master Artesan; quite capable of frying someone's brain if he lost control. Taran tried to nod his acceptance, but Robin's hands remained clamped about his throat.

"I'm warning you, Taran Elijah," he continued, his eyes hot and full of pain, "and I don't want you to mistake me. If I ever come across you again, wherever it may be, I won't hesitate to kill you for what you've done. You've ruined my life, and I can see no good reason not to ruin yours. Remember that!"

He slammed Taran's body so hard against the wall that the Adept was momentarily stunned. Released from Robin's grip and shaking uncontrollably, Taran slumped to the floor. Tears ran down his face. Robin stared at him in disgust before stalking out, violently slamming the door.

✣ ✣ ✣ ✣ ✣

The Major's pounding footsteps retreated down the corridor like a fading heartbeat. His head spinning and his heart sick, Taran buried his face in his hands. He wept. He stayed where he was, slowly mastering his thumping heart and trembling body until he felt able to stand.

Climbing shakily to his feet, Taran tried to order his thoughts. How could he have been so stupid? Only now did he realize what Denny had been hinting at on the journey to the Manor. When he thought further back, he understood what had caused the men's mutterings and furtive glances when they left Port Loxton with the King. He also recalled Jinella steadfastly ignoring him that morning, and suddenly wondered whether she had been the one to see him coming out of Sullyan's room that night. It made sense of the Baron's behavior and some of his acid comments that day. Taran shook his head in remorse.

It was all his fault. If he had gone to Robin immediately and told him what had happened, this would have been averted. He should have taken Rienne's advice. Taran had been a coward, trusting that his friendship with Robin would prove stronger than the rumors. There was no one to blame but himself that it hadn't.

He had no option but to do as Robin said. He was not going to involve Sullyan in this. She had other worries to concern her, and she and Robin would mend their fences far easier if Taran was out of the way.

With a heavy heart, he began to pack.

✠ ✠ ✠ ✠ ✠

Rienne spent the morning in the infirmary treating the wounded men from Robin's company. None were gravely injured, but she was kept so busy that she hardly had a moment to think. Once the men were settled and things had died down, she decided to take her noon break. Humming to herself and wondering if the baby inside her could hear her or recognize her voice, she pushed open the door to the rooms she shared with Cal and Taran.

She stopped. A pack lay on the floor, stuffed full. Sounds were coming from Taran's room. He never took this much with him when he went off with Sullyan or one of the companies into the field, so this must be something unusual. She closed the door behind her and the sounds of movement ceased.

"Taran?"

The silence continued for a short while longer, and then his door slowly opened. He stood there looking at her. She took in the pallor of his face and the dejected line of his shoulders. Then she saw the second pack lying on his bed. His traveling cloak was beside it. She stared at him and he turned away.

"Taran? What's going on?"

Her first thought, irrational though it was, was that something had happened to Cal. It couldn't have, though. Taran wouldn't be skulking in his room if he had bad news for her. Something else had happened, something that had affected him deeply, but she couldn't imagine what it might be.

"Tell me what's going on!"

Taran's shoulders sagged even more and he sat abruptly on the bed. "I'm going away, Rienne."

His words stunned her. It was the last thing she expected to hear.

"Going away? Where? Why?"

He avoided her gaze. "I don't know yet. Don't ask me, Rienne. Just let me be. I'm going, and that's an end to it."

Her gray eyes widened and she sat beside him, laying a hand on his arm.

"Oh, no you don't. That's not good enough. Come on, you know you'll have to tell me. I'm not going to let you leave until you do. I can see you're upset, so out with it. What's happened to make you consider giving up everything you've ever wanted?"

Now Taran did look at her, and the weight of unhappiness in his hazel eyes caused her to hiss in shock.

"Oh, Taran, it must be something dreadful! You're frightening me. Please tell me what it is."

Taking up her hands, whether for his comfort or hers she couldn't tell, Taran told her everything.

She sat stunned when he was done, unable to speak, seeing only the pain in his eyes and feeling the trembling of his hands.

She could scarcely believe Robin had gone to such lengths. Why would he react like this? It wasn't like him to let such feeble gossip get under his skin.

Rage welled abruptly inside her for Denny's vicious, gossiping tongue. She felt like slapping him senseless.

"Taran," she said firmly, giving his hands a shake, "this is all wrong. You can't leave like this. You have to tell Brynne."

He stood up, shaking her off. "No. I won't involve her in this. It's my fault and my responsibility. I'm not going to go bearing tales to her, especially with all these raids going on. She has enough on her mind. It's time I stood on my own feet and made my own decisions. I won't tell Sullyan and neither will you, if you have any respect for me at all. The best thing I can do is go away and remove part of the problem. Robin made it very clear he doesn't want me around, and I won't cause him more pain than I already have. They'll stand a better chance of reconciling if I'm not here. Once they have, well, then we'll see."

"But running away like this will make everyone think you're guilty!"

"Most of them already do, and I am guilty, in a way." He sighed. "Not of what Robin thinks, I'll grant you, but near enough. I'm guilty of letting things go too far. It's my fault he believes what he does. I've made up my mind to go, and I'm going now, before Robin finishes his tour of duty." He turned and put the final items into the pack on his bed.

Rienne's eyes filled with tears. "But what about Cal? You can't leave without saying goodbye! He's your Apprentice. What will he do without you?"

Taran smiled sadly and replied in a calmer tone. "Cal has his own place now. He's gaining respect as a captain and he's sure to be promoted soon. He has the College behind him, with all the coaching he could need. Far better than anything I could give him.

And he has you."

Rienne couldn't hold back the sobs. Taran turned back to her and placed his hands on her shoulders. "Oh, Rienne! I wish this hadn't happened, believe me. I don't want to go, of course I don't, and I'll miss you and Cal terribly. But don't you see it's the only thing I can do? I've brought this on myself and I have to do what I can to put it right. If it'll make you feel better, tell Cal I'll stay a couple of days at Milo's inn—you remember, the one we stayed at when we first came here? I'll wait until he comes before I go away for good. I wouldn't want him to think I'd abandoned him. Will that suit you?"

It suited her not at all, but she saw how determined he was and realized it was the best she would get. She nodded unhappily and watched as he fastened his pack.

She couldn't watch him leave, he was distressed enough without seeing her break down before him, so she accompanied him only as far as the infirmary. They embraced in emotional turmoil before finally breaking apart.

✣ ✣ ✣ ✣ ✣

Taran didn't look back as he walked to the horse lines. He had sent a runner to Solet earlier asking for his gelding to be saddled. It was the same horse he had brought from Hyecombe, so Taran didn't have to worry about taking one of the Manor horses. Still, he hadn't ridden his own beast since coming here, and it would feel very small and unfamiliar compared to Thunder, the Manor stallion he usually rode.

The stablemaster regarded him sourly as he mounted the gelding, eyeing the full packs pointedly. Taran ignored his unsubtle curiosity and rode slowly out of the yard and down the lane. He approached the blocky gatehouse where they had waited to meet Robin on that first fateful day, and couldn't suppress his emotions as he passed it. The swordsman on guard duty raised the barrier for him, and Taran left the confines of the Manor, not expecting to ever return. He rode despondently away from the only life and people he had ever truly loved.

✤ ✤ ✤ ✤ ✤

*D*amn, thought Rienne angrily, she still hadn't told Taran her news! All this upset had robbed her of the opportunity, as well as the pleasure of seeing his reaction. Someone was going to pay for that.

Dashing tears from her eyes, she marched into the infirmary. A great anger was boiling inside her. Aware that it was probably her pregnancy intensifying her emotions, she nevertheless made purposely for a certain room. The room where Lieutenant-Major Denny lay, blissfully unaware of the misery he had caused or the storm he had unleashed with his gossip.

The few healers who saw Rienne stared in concern at her pale face and glaring eyes. She was usually the gentlest of people, although they were all aware of the steel that could rise to the surface when needed. None of them had ever seen her truly angry, though, and they marveled at her furious countenance.

Reaching Denny's room, she ignored his smile of greeting as she stalked toward his bed.

"Get out," she snapped.

His smile faded. "What?"

"Get out of my infirmary. I am no longer willing to treat you. You've been on at me for days to let you up. Well, now you've got your chance. Go on. You're not welcome here and I want you out."

"But—"

Her fury boiled over. "You've been nothing but trouble since Taran first met you! You've been spreading your vicious lies, and now you've ruined the lives of three good people, and maybe more! Well, I hope you're pleased with yourself. Taran is leaving because of you and I'm losing one of the best friends I ever had!

I'll never forgive you for that, and I want you out of my sight."

He had the grace to look sheepish. "I only said what I saw and heard—"

"You twisted what was seen and heard out of all proportion!" she raged. "You don't deserve it, but I'm going to explain it to you. Yes, Taran's in love with Sullyan. He has been ever since he first set eyes on her. Everyone knows it and has always known it. He made no secret of it. That's what he meant when he told you Robin knew about them. But Taran would never do anything to cause either of them pain. He's the most honorable man I know. Unlike some I could mention!"

Denny winced. "But what about Lady Jinella seeing him leave Sullyan's room half-naked in the middle of the night?"

She nearly screamed. "You took the word of a silly young girl who considered herself slighted and made an issue of it! If Sullyan had heard serious news, she would have called any one of us into her room, no matter what the hour of day or night. And she never worries about modesty. You should know that if you trained with her like you say!"

Denny reddened and hung his head.

His contrition only incensed Rienne further. "Oh, don't bother being ashamed of yourself now," she cried, "it's too late! Robin nearly fought with Taran over your malicious rumors, and now Taran has left rather than be the cause of more pain!"

Denny gave a guilty start.

"Yes," she yelled, "he's gone! I don't know where he's going and neither does he. You've destroyed the life he's built here, and you have no idea how precious it was. Not to mention what you've done to Robin. What Sullyan will say when she finds out, I can't guess, but I wouldn't be you for all the gold in the King's Treasury! And I won't harbor you here anymore. You've forfeited your right to healing, as far as I'm concerned. Take yourself off and get out of my sight. I don't ever want to see you again. You can be crippled for life for all I care. It's no more than you deserve!"

Rienne was sobbing now and there were concerned faces at the door. The whole infirmary had heard her tirade. No one had ever been thrown out by a healer before, but no one dared come near as Denny slowly and painfully rose from the bed, wrapping a robe about him as best he could, holding his sore arm awkwardly. Rienne watched him with burning eyes.

"If you care about what you've done," she hissed, "if you want to put things right, then you'll find Robin as soon as he returns and tell him you were mistaken. I doubt he'll believe you, but it's the least you can do. Now get out of my sight before I do something I'll regret!"

She collapsed, sobbing, to the rumpled bed while Denny limped painfully out of the door.

Chapter Twenty-Six

Ozella watched Taran leave the stable yard. The young foreigner was hiding, taking comfort in the care of his horse again. He wasn't ready to face Parren and didn't want to return to the barracks until he knew for certain where Parren was. He couldn't ask someone about the Captain's whereabouts without arousing suspicion, and he didn't know enough about the Manor's duty rosters to work it out for himself.

He knew that Parren reported to Colonel Vassa, and he was aware that one of Vassa's companies was in the field, but Parren led one company and Lieutenant-Major Baily led the other. Ozella didn't know which one was out. He hung around the stables, currying his horse and cleaning harness, hoping to hear what he wanted to know before finishing his work or falling foul of Solet. The rumors and the strange mood of the men had soured the stablemaster's temper even more than usual. He had been prowling around the stable yard, finding fault with his stable lads' work. Eventually, he came to where Ozella was brushing out Felika's mane for at least the hundredth time.

"Are you still here?" he demanded, making Ozella jump. "You must have finished that by now. Leave the poor beast alone, let him rest. Haven't you anything better to do? Go on, be off with you!"

Ozella had no choice but to obey, and looked anxiously

around for Parren as he emerged onto the yard. There was still no sign of him, so Ozella made his way back to the barracks.

When he had first arrived at the Manor, he had expected his rooms to be in the main building. He was a Lord, after all. But he was soon disabused of that notion. It was Blaine's policy not to foster favoritism, and as Ozella would be training with the cadets, the General thought it best if the Beraxian also lived with them. He told Ozella that this arrangement would help him fit in and make friends.

It hadn't.

Ozella slouched morosely along, his eyes on the ground. Because of this, he failed to see the dark shape lounging just around the corner of the barracks wall until it was too late. Parren, grinning, stepped into Ozella's path.

"Trying to avoid me, were you?"

The low, menacing voice made Ozella's heart falter. His head came up in fright. "Of course not!"

The lie was plain and Parren studied him, looking pleased with the fear he saw. "I should have thought you'd want to seek me out," he drawled, "seeing as the safety of your sisters depends on you delivering what I asked for." He stared meaningfully at Ozella while jingling something his pocket.

His sisters' rings! Ozella went white. "Are they all right?" he hissed. "If you've hurt them, I'll—"

"Yes? You'll what? Come on, Ozella, I'd be very interested to hear what you'd do."

Ozella felt sick, and Parren grinned. "It was a close thing," he said. "Another half-hour and I would have given an order you might have regretted. You're only just in time. Provided, that is," he grabbed Ozella's shirt, leaning in close so the youth could smell his unsavory breath, "the information you bring me is worth hearing."

Ozella swallowed, remembering the strange lassitude that had affected his concentration over the past two days. "I'll tell you everything I know," he said hopelessly.

Parren smiled. "Oh, you will. Indeed you will. Come with me."

Feeling sick, trapped, and very alone, Ozella obeyed.

✣ ✣ ✣ ✣ ✣

Sullyan's company finished their tour of duty with no further incident. She led them back to the Manor, feeling weary and troubled. Dexter watched her carefully, plainly fearing another fall, but she couldn't be irritated with him. The pounding in her skull was testament to the trauma she had suffered. She used her powers to draw out the bruise, but the sick pain in her head only intensified. Now she had to report to a healer immediately and be declared either fit or infirm. It was inescapable. Sullyan was duty-bound to submit to Rienne's examination.

In truth, she didn't really mind. The headache alone told her all was not well, and the pain of expending power to deal with it worried her further. Not to mention the shock of finding, yet again, the imprint of her own psyche in the substrate where it had no right to be.

Leaving Drum in the care of Solet's stable boys, she made her way to the infirmary. Sullyan always felt more comfortable dealing with Rienne, as they shared a special bond and Sullyan could always sense Rienne's deep empathy. She headed for the small, comfortable office Rienne occupied when not doing her rounds.

On entering the room, she immediately caught the flavor of Rienne's unhappiness, and frowned to see her careworn face.

"What is it, Rienne?"

"It can wait," the healer replied, causing Sullyan to narrow her eyes. "What can I do for you?"

Allowing Rienne her way, Sullyan explained what had

happened. Rienne was alarmed and her professional instincts came immediately into play. She asked Sullyan to sit in the easy chair before her desk and came to stand beside her. Sullyan submitted wordlessly to Rienne's examination, affording the healer access to her powers in order to assist her.

After a short while, during which several unexplained expressions crossed Rienne's face, the healer handed Sullyan some willow extract. "Drink this. It will help with the pain. There's no permanent damage, I'm glad to say. You were lucky, Brynne. What caused you to fall from Drum, anyway? I can't recall such a thing ever happening before."

"It never has." Sullyan drank the potion before giving Rienne a brief account of how she had come to be thrown. "I should have been more careful," she finished.

Rienne shook her head. "How could you have known? It's not as if you expected it."

"Maybe not, but it seems to be something I must look for in the future." She shot Rienne a shrewd glance. "Now, are you going to tell me what has upset you?"

Rienne sighed. "I could never hide anything from you, could I?"

Sullyan smiled faintly and Rienne went back to her chair. She remained silent for a moment and seemed to be struggling with some internal quandary. Sullyan waited her out, but her patience wouldn't hold for long. She needed to report to Blaine.

As if realizing this, Rienne spoke abruptly. "Taran's gone."

Whatever Sullyan had thought might be upsetting Rienne, it wasn't this. "Gone? What do you mean? Gone where?"

"He's left the Manor. He went about two hours ago. I think he's gone to that inn on the Tolk road. At least, that's what he said he'd do. As to the why, I'm afraid you'll have to ask him."

Sullyan's eyes narrowed. "I do not have time for this."

"I know you don't. That was one of the reasons he left. He asked me not to tell you, and I can't go against his wishes any more than I already have. But I had to tell you he's gone. I didn't want to take the risk that you might suddenly need him."

Sullyan frowned. "Are you saying he has gone for good?" She was finding this hard to take with all her other worries. Damn the man! What was he playing at?

"He believes he has," said Rienne. "I can't say any more, Brynne. He promised to wait at the inn until Cal goes to say goodbye, but where he'll go after that, I don't think even he knows."

"And you will not tell me his reasons?"

Rienne closed her eyes. "I can't. Please don't ask me."

Sullyan rose, an expletive on her lips for the inconsiderate timing of Taran's departure. But it died unsaid when she saw Rienne's distress.

Hands on hips, she said, "I suppose this has to do with the rumors that have been spreading about here lately?"

Unable to lie, Rienne nodded. Now the expletive did escape and Rienne's eyes widened. Sullyan was normally so softly spoken and polite that the vicious curses she sometimes gave vent to still took Rienne by surprise.

Sullyan refused to apologize for her language. "When do you expect Cal back?"

Faint hope appeared in Rienne's eyes. "Before the evening meal."

Sullyan saw it and smiled. "I will do my best to find time to speak with Taran. But now, I really must report to the General. I thank you for telling me. I understand your loyalty to Taran and I will not press you for details. But I wish he had chosen a more convenient time to let his honor get the better of him!"

Putting Taran out of her mind, Sullyan made her way to

Blaine's office. She entered without ceremony and found the General and the King occupying the inner room behind the purely functional office, where the seating was more comfortable. The welcome aroma of fellan wafted out, and Blaine indicated a vacant chair as he poured a mugful. She accepted it gratefully and the bitter liquid, aided by Rienne's potion, began its healing work on the pounding in her skull.

She made her report, Blaine and Elias listening intently to the details. Blaine narrowed his eyes as she explained about her fall. He already knew she had found her own imprint at the site of Aeyron's abduction and was as perplexed as she was. Elias was even more so, not being an Artesan.

"But isn't that impossible?" he asked. "Isn't everyone's pattern unique?"

"Indeed, Elias," she said, "although it is possible for them to be similar in structure, especially if you compare the areas relating to the mastery of the various elements. My psyche, for example, would closely match the General's if you compared the portions relating to the element of Earth. And if you could see my pattern laid out beside Pharikian's, you would detect startling similarities, as we are the same rank. But they would not be identical."

"Then how do you explain it?"

She shook her head. "I cannot. Not yet. On both occasions the imprint was very faint, and maybe I did not see the whole pattern. Were I to see it fresh and complete, maybe then I could find those subtle differences. They must be there, for it certainly is not mine, that much I can state with certainty! But it has to be a very close match to have had such a strong effect on my power."

Neither man had any suggestions. Unless Pharikian could come up with some, this was one mystery she would have to solve on her own. It frightened her, knowing there was an unknown Artesan with powers that matched or perhaps even surpassed her own. Especially as he was either committed to harming his own kind or was being coerced into it.

They moved on to discussing how they could best counter the increased threat from raiding, for if it continued much longer it would stretch the resources of the Manor and Elias's other garrisons around the country. He had already received reports of similar problems from three other provinces, although on a lighter scale. Indeed, Elias's messenger service was also being stretched to its limits, as messages came and went at an alarming rate.

This was exactly the kind of problem Elias had set up his College to alleviate. If only they had enough trained Artesans right now!

"I am beginning to wonder," mused Sullyan, "whether the true purpose of these raids might be to keep us fully occupied and prevent us from looking for Prince Aeyron and his abductors. The timing is suspiciously coincidental."

"Perhaps," Elias agreed. "It would certainly explain why they're selecting such poor and random targets. But if, as you say, there are rebels among Pharikian's nobility who oppose his treaty with us, then surely these petty tactics are just what they would employ to goad us into breaking with him?"

"I agree," she said, "but there is no reason why they could not achieve both objectives with the same ploy. And if that is their desire, does it not strengthen the likelihood of there being collaboration between dissidents of both realms? Those who desire Pharikian's removal and those who are working both against your rule and the legitimization of the Artesan craft would benefit equally from unrest in our lands. How convenient that those best equipped to hunt them have their hands very effectively tied!"

She gazed openly into Elias's piercing blue eyes. "Do you not think, your Majesty, that it might now be prudent to detail someone specifically to search for whoever is behind all this? I am convinced that the Prince is being held in Albia, and Pharikian is beside himself with fear. He cannot come and search himself, nor can he send someone to do it for him. As your ambassador, I as good as promised we would do all we could to find his son, and I would not have my word proved false. Such a search would also benefit us, as I am certain that when we find Prince Aeyron we will also find our traitor."

Blaine nodded in agreement, but Elias was less than convinced.

"When you say 'detail someone,' I take it you are offering yourself?"

She inclined her head. "I am yours to command, Elias. I will do as you bid me."

He regarded her levelly and she returned his gaze. "No, I can't spare you. The current situation is too delicate for me to feel comfortable sending you off on what is bound to be a very dangerous mission. Sympathetic as I am to Timar's pain, have you considered that this abduction might have been staged in order to lure you into their clutches? Whoever 'they' are?"

"I doubt it. I do not think I am their primary target. They have had plenty of opportunity to attack me without resorting to such an elaborate and risky trap. The incident at Port Loxton might have left their intended victim unclear, but they were definitely trying to kill you during the ambush on our journey here. I cannot think that the elimination of just one powerful Artesan is their goal. If it was, why not just kill Aeyron, a Master Artesan, rather than holding him for ransom?

"And we must also consider their demand for thirty pounds of reverse polarity spellsilver. Rather than blocking it, that kind of spellsilver actually amplifies metaphysical power. So how could it be used against us?"

"It might be intended to augment the powers of whoever is

opposing us," put in Blaine. "We know there's at least one Artesan involved in this plot, willing or no."

"Thirty pounds is a vast amount, far too much to simply be needed for augmenting metaforce. But I take your point, General, for I am sure the Staff was created for just such a purpose. Remember, though, the spellsilver used in the Staff was encased in silicon-ceramic, so if some of this silver is intended for a similar purpose, why was no ceramic included in the demand?"

"What's the significance of the ceramic?" Elias asked.

"When an Artesan wants to channel or shape the power he raises rather than using it in its raw state, he has to contain it," Sullyan explained. "Otherwise it just leaks away. For example, when we open portways we construct them where there is a natural or artificial boundary so the power can be anchored and will stand alone long enough to be used. For spellsilver to function as an amplifier, the forces it absorbs must be contained, or they will simply run straight through. The silicon-ceramic is a light but strong Earth-element barrier which can contain huge quantities of power before becoming overloaded. However, you would only need about a pound of silver to make such a Staff as Rykan's, and I simply cannot understand the significance of the enormous amount specified in the ransom demand. Surely this is all the more reason to set someone to search for our enemy?"

The King's mouth set in a firm line. "No, Brynne, and this is a command! You are not to go looking for trouble, do you hear me? I can't spare you while we still don't know what's going on. We will counter these raids as they occur, but otherwise we will watch and wait. Maybe they will make a mistake. But don't worry, I'll not give them the satisfaction of seeing what I have built up crumble to pieces at the merest hint of trouble. If a breach of our trade alliance is what they hope for, then for my part they will remain disappointed!

"We will wait for the time limit on the ransom to expire, and then consider the instructions for payment once Pharikian receives them. They will have to send someone to collect the silver. They will be vulnerable then, and we will have our chance to apprehend them."

Sullyan felt frustrated by what she saw as Elias's failure to fully appreciate the situation. "And if they make no mistakes? What if they manage to take the silver and still hold on to the Prince? What if they kill him, Elias? What will you say to Timar then? Do you think he will consider your trade alliance worth his son's life?"

Elias bridled at her challenging tone. Blaine, clearly realizing the King was on the verge of losing his temper, sent Sullyan a message through the substrate. He was inclined to agree with her, he said, but he wouldn't antagonize Elias in front of her. With the conflict still unresolved, Blaine sent her to her rest. He told her he would work on Elias in private.

Chapter Twenty-Seven

Rest was the last thing on Sullyan's mind. She had unwisely allowed her temper to rise at Elias's refusal to send her in search of the Prince, and now she felt torn between her duty to the King and her love for Pharikian. Obedience to her monarch should be her primary concern, but how should she react when she knew he was wrong? It was an unfamiliar experience to believe she knew better than Elias, but in matters concerning Artesans she probably did. She knew the General agreed with her, but despite having more influence over Elias, he was under the same constraints as she. She could only hope he would use that influence to convince the King.

Knowing there was nothing more she could do to sway Elias, she decided to attend to the matter of Taran. She had intended to spend some private time with Robin that evening. They had not seen much of each other since her return from Port Loxton and she felt it keenly. Now, even he would have to wait. If she rode swiftly, she should be able to reach the inn, talk with Taran, and return before the night was too far advanced. She would try to persuade him that he need not be absent from the Manor until the rumors died down, and she was damned if she would allow him to depart on the strength of some misguided gossip.

Allowing her frustration with Elias and with Taran's over-developed sense of honor to irritate her, she was curt with Solet when he objected to her taking Drum out again so soon.

"Just saddle him, Stablemaster," she snapped. "When I want

your advice on my horse's stamina, I will ask for it!"

Solet stumped off to do her bidding, muttering under his breath. Yet he had the black harnessed in minutes, and Drum was as eager as ever to respond to his rider's commands. Once she was mounted, he cantered out of the yard with his ears pricked.

Sullyan cut across the Manor grounds on her way to the inn. She knew many short cuts that would reduce her journey time by half. If she was lucky, she could grab a bite there before she returned. She had taken only fellan since before dawn.

It was twilight when she finally reached the inn, and a light rain was falling. She was thankful she had brought her cloak. If she had not, she might have been more inclined to irritation when she walked into the warm and convivial inn. It was busy; being summer, all the roads were open and there were many travelers about. News of the raids had spread, though, and there were not as many groups of visiting families as usual. The inn's patrons were mostly merchants and tradesmen who could not afford to let outlanders ruin their livelihoods.

As she walked over to the bar, the innkeeper noticed her.

"Colonel Sullyan, we don't often see you in here! Can I get you something to drink?"

"Maybe later, Milo. I am looking for a friend of mine. He arrived a couple of hours ago. Tall, brown hair, hazel eyes? He was probably a little distracted."

"Oh, him!" Milo made a sour face. "He's one of yours, is he? What's he done then, deserted? I thought there was something funny about him. He looked sort of... furtive, if you know what I mean. I hope he can pay for his room and board."

"He is a friend," she snapped, glaring at the man, "and he has done nothing wrong. The King will pay for his lodgings. Now, where is he, if you please? I have little time to waste bandying words with you. I have been out keeping your business safe from marauders all day!"

Milo was taken aback by her commanding manner and her reprimand. He replied hastily. "He's in the private snug, Colonel. Shall I send you in some supper? It's been raining out there and you've had a long ride."

His fawning tone earned him a hard stare. "I thank you, Milo. Some food would be most welcome."

As the relieved innkeeper bustled off to organize their supper, Sullyan hung her damp cloak on the hooks provided. Crossing the crowded commons toward the half-open door to the private snug, she saw that Taran was alone. She was not surprised. Most of the inn's patrons went there for news and company, not solitude. She could also see how profoundly unhappy he was. The five empty tankards on his table were testament to that, and he was nursing another as he stared blankly at the floor.

Her voice was sharper than she intended when she spoke.

"I suppose you think getting drunk will help?"

He gave a guilty start as his eyes found hers. She was lounging nonchalantly in the doorway, leaning against the jamb, her arms folded. Her gaze assessed him, noting the embarrassed flush on his face. Irritated, she wished he would stop being so diffident.

"Brynne," he exclaimed, glancing at the empty tankards in front of him. "I asked Rienne not to tell you where I was."

"Oh, you did, did you? And did you really think she would let you leave like that, with no word to me? That was hardly fair on her, especially in her condition. Or did you think I would not notice your absence? Come on, Taran! You know me better than that. You are a friend and I care about you."

His brow creased. "What do you mean, 'in her condition?'"

Sullyan sighed. "She was so distressed by your going that she forgot to tell you her news. Rienne is pregnant, my friend. She is carrying Cal's child."

She had not moved from the doorway, but even from there she could see the gleam of tears in his eyes. His misery wiped away all trace of annoyance. He was the way he was; it was one of the reasons she loved him so well. She could not fault his actions in the light of his sensibilities. Sighing again, she moved closer.

He refused to meet her gaze. Taking the chair opposite, she leaned forward, seeing how he flinched as she wrapped her fingers around his hands. She almost thought he would draw back, but he did not.

"Taran."

He tried hard not to look at her, but her presence was too compelling. When he finally met her gaze, the sympathy and warmth in her eyes nearly undid his resolve.

"Tell me what has troubled you so," she said. "I cannot believe you have let yourself be driven out by a few malicious stories. Have I not told you to ignore such petty jealousies?"

He answered reluctantly. "It wasn't the stories that drove me out."

She could sense his determination not to tell her, and gave his psyche a subtle nudge. Like Rienne, he found it hard to resist her and was unable to lie to her. If he did attempt to conceal the truth, or only reveal parts of it, she would know, and he wouldn't want such deception to hurt her. Nevertheless, he did the best he could.

"My presence was upsetting Robin, so I thought it would help if I wasn't around for a while. The rumors will die the sooner without me there to fuel them. You and Robin have enough to worry about without me adding to the problem."

"What made you think Robin was upset?" Her tone was neutral but her attitude sharp.

Still Taran tried to dissemble. "Well, he wouldn't have made that mistake otherwise, would he?"

Her sharply indrawn breath made him flush again as he

realized she didn't know.

"What mistake?"

He answered feebly. "You really ought to ask Robin."

She wasn't having that, and gripped his hand tightly. "I am asking you, Taran. What mistake?"

He turned his head away, misery plain on his face. "He told his men to kill all the invaders. He forgot about taking captives. I heard the General was furious and gave him a dressing down in front of the King."

"And?" She was merciless, well aware there was more.

Taran grew increasingly distressed and she began to fear what he might tell her. "I was in the wrong place at the wrong time," he said, desperate for her to let it go. "He was just letting off steam."

Sullyan watched him carefully, seeing the passage of painful memories and not liking the implications of the sweat on his brow. She released his hands. Leaning back in her chair, she spoke as gently as her mounting unease would allow.

"Taran, you have to tell me exactly what occurred between you."

He shook his head. "I can't, Brynne. It wasn't his fault. Please don't make me speak of it."

She pursed her lips. "I must. I am sorry. It pains me to cause you further upset, but I must know what was said. If Robin has allowed the rumors to affect his professional judgment, then I have to know. I am still his commanding officer, and anything that has a bearing on the security of the Manor, the King, or the execution of our duties cannot remain concealed. You have to tell me, no matter how painful it might be."

She was being gentle with him despite the steel beneath her words. He was still reluctant, and Sullyan could not afford to wait until he found the strength to cope with his guilt. Much as she despised herself for doing it, she applied a touch more pressure to his psyche. His eyes grew wide with disbelief.

"Do not make me do this," she said softly.

Defeated, he haltingly told her what had occurred between them, even repeating Robin's exact words. He held nothing back, knowing she wasn't going to leave him even a shred of dignity. He disclosed everything, even his innermost feelings. Tears came again as he related his shame, and when he was done he fell silent, his eyes fixed blankly on her unmoving form.

She dropped her head to her hands, unable to recognize the man she thought of as her soul mate in Taran's words. How could this be true? How could the man she adored have done this? Yet she could hear the truth in Taran's voice. She sat silent even after he was done, until a movement by the door heralded the arrival of Milo, bearing two plates of hot food. He came hesitantly into the room and laid the plates on the table. He departed hastily.

Taran allowed the delicious aroma of roasted meat to distract him, absently toying with his eating knife and picking at a few choice morsels. Sullyan raised her head at Milo's entrance, but her eyes were tear-filled and unfocused. She sat in silence, leaving the food untouched. Taran, not knowing what to say, concentrated on the meal.

When he had nearly finished and Sullyan's plate was quite cold, she stood. Her body was trembling and she addressed him coldly, but he knew the frost was not for him.

"Taran, I want your sworn word that you will not leave this inn. I understand your wish to be absent from the Manor, and I respect it. You have not taken a formal oath, and I cannot command you in a military sense. As a Master Artesan, however, you owe me your allegiance. I will not release you from that and you will obey me."

He hesitated, and her eyes narrowed. She would use force if she had to, but she would rather have his willing obedience.

Finally, he nodded.

"Good. Rienne will tell Cal of your decision to leave, and he may ride out and see you when he is at liberty to do so. I will also have to inform the King and the General, but I will do my best to keep the reason private. They have worries enough at present, so that should pose no problem."

Taran hung his head. He would be mortified to be the cause of yet more trouble to the General, who had been more than generous in letting Taran stay at the Manor when he wasn't a member of the military. Seeing his chagrin, some of her sternness melted. She came to his side and kneeled by his chair, taking one of his hands.

"I am so sorry you have been put through this. You have been such a good friend to both Robin and I, and I cannot bear that there should be enmity or awkwardness between us. I will do all I can to resolve it."

She forestalled his attempt to speak. "No, my friend, you will not take any blame for this. You and I are innocent of everything but a strong and abiding friendship, and I would be sorely grieved if anything damaged that. Robin's behavior was extreme and uncalled for, and he will answer for it to me. He shall apologize to you, or I will know the reason why!

"Now, I must return to the Manor. You will stay here and you can keep your gold in your pocket. You are still a member of the King's College, do not forget that. I have already told Milo that your lodgings are covered, so you can take that pained expression from your face. Come, Taran, smile for me and lighten your heart. You have suffered a grave shock and you have been wronged, but you are not without friends. All will be well."

She gave his cheek a light kiss and he reddened, doubtless wondering when he would cease being a burden and be able to repay her kindness and support. He made a start by finding a small smile of gratitude as she stood and left the room.

When she glanced back, he had the tankard of Milo's best ale in his hand, his expression dark and sad.

✤ ✤ ✤ ✤ ✤

Cal was anxious by the time Rienne returned to their chambers. His mood wasn't helped by his failure to find Taran, with whom he had hoped to discuss Robin's harsh words. Cal didn't want to bring his raw emotions to Rienne, not in her condition. Registering her inner turmoil as she entered the room, however, he forgot his own troubles and listened in dismay while she related what had happened between Robin and Taran.

"But he can't leave," he exclaimed. "Where will he go, what will he do? We can't just let him go off like this."

"I couldn't stop him, Cal. You should have seen him. He was in a dreadful state. I've never seen him so shocked and upset. But I made him promise to wait at that inn on the Tolk road at least until you had been to see him.

"And then Brynne got the story out of me. I had as good as promised Taran not to tell her, but you know I can't keep secrets from her. I didn't tell her the reason, only that he had gone. Hopefully she'll find some time this evening to speak with him, but whether even she can persuade him to return, I don't know.

"Oh, Cal, this is such a mess! And there was I thinking we were settled here. After last year, and once the weddings were over, I thought life couldn't get much better. And then becoming pregnant...."

The tears that had been threatening suddenly broke free. Cal held her close while she sobbed, trying vainly to comfort her. Eventually, she calmed and he released her.

"I had better go and see Taran, love," he said, looking down into her red-rimmed eyes. "Will you be all right?"

She nodded. "It's getting late, and it's still raining. You'll never get there and back tonight and still get some sleep. You had better stay over with Taran until you're due back on patrol. I'll be all right. An undisturbed night's sleep will do me good. Go on now, or it'll be too late."

✤ ✤ ✤ ✤ ✤

Rienne's eyes would have widened in shock and her hands would have covered her ears had she heard the string of profanities Sullyan muttered as she galloped Drum back to the Manor. She was shocked to the core and distressed by what Taran had told her. The incomprehensible thought that Robin had allowed a few unfounded stories to jeopardize not only a strong friendship but also the life of his King, not to mention the men of his command and his own life, set her mercurial temper well and truly alight. Yet what distressed and hurt her more was that Robin had believed and acted upon such stories without ever speaking to her. This caused a cold, hard fury to burn within her as she rode.

It was deep into the evening when she finally parted from Drum at the stable yard. Her back was stiff as she strode through the rain up to the Manor.

As she expected, Robin's company had returned. The men were lounging in the commons, talking of the day's events. From what she could hear, most of the conversation revolved around the Major's uncharacteristically bad mood and his unprecedented error of judgment. Unseen, Sullyan stood at the door and listened to the men condemning Robin's harsh treatment of Cal. Her heart grew stony and her eyes glittered with rage as she withdrew. She had gone to the commons hoping to find Cal, only he was not there. Hearing the men's comments, she guessed he would be taking comfort in Rienne's arms. She would not disturb him there.

Instead, she made her way to the senior officers' hall. All eyes turned to her as she threw the door open. Robin was seated in a corner, sipping from a glass of amber-colored liquor. Baily was there, along with Vassa, Dexter, and a few of the other captains.

Parren was there too, and her fury grew as she caught the self-satisfied gleam in his eye and the smirk on his lips.

Ignoring the others, she snapped, "Major Tamsen, a word in private, if you please."

He must have been expecting some kind of backlash, at least on the subject of his error. Rising slowly, a carefully neutral expression on his face, he followed her from the room. Sullyan stalked silently ahead, leaving him to read her anger from the rigidity of her back. He followed her down the marble stairs and into their shared office. He turned to face her as she shut the door and leaned back against it.

"Would you care to explain to me what the Void you thought you were doing?"

She could sense his guilt, and her curt tone and frosty eyes fanned it into smoldering anger.

"All right," he snapped, "so I made a mistake! I'm not perfect. Did you think I was? Then I'm very sorry to have disappointed you. Of course, you've never made an error in your life, have you?"

His immediate defensiveness and spite only fuelled her fury. She was in no mood for pertness or insubordination, but his lapse of judgment was not uppermost in her mind. She was hurting on a more personal level.

Her voice was hoarse with ire as she retorted, "I was not referring to your reprehensible lack of foresight and loss of self-command in the field, Major, although that was bad enough!" He bridled at her show of temper, but she plowed on regardless. "I meant your unforgivable treatment and condemnation of an innocent man, a trusted friend, one who has wished you nothing but good since he has known you! What gave you the right to abuse Taran so thoroughly? Why should you bother with the idle gossip of malicious tongues that concoct stories out of thin air? I thought better of you than that, Robin."

Shockingly, his eyes blazed with uncontrolled anger. "And I thought better of you! You're my wife, Sullyan, or have you forgotten that? Did your vows mean nothing to you? Was our wedding just a sham?"

Her eyes widened and she felt her blood freeze. She had scarcely been able to credit Taran's story, but Robin's reactions confirmed it beyond any doubt. She grew cold with fear, her wounded heart limping.

"Is that really what you think? How can you doubt me, Robin? What has happened to the trust we shared? You know very well how I feel about you. How could you possibly believe I would betray you?"

The tension in the room ratcheted up a notch, like some unseen hand priming a crossbow. It felt strange... almost tangible. Robin moved menacingly forward, his hands raised, his fury mounting. She frowned. He was so out of control that she saw a brief flash of his memories as he remembered the sly glances, knowing smiles, and vulgar gestures some of the Loxton men still gave when they thought he wasn't looking. His voice trembled with anger.

"Don't take me for a fool. I've spoken to those who saw you! 'They weren't very discreet' were the words I heard. You thought you were far enough away, thought no one at the capital would notice, didn't you? Well, they did notice. It's no use trying to deny it. I don't know why I didn't see it sooner. I must have been blind all these months. And to think he even had the gall to tell me he was in love with you! I must be such an idiot. I thought you cared so deeply for me that it wouldn't matter.

"You've been so cold to me recently. Did you think I wouldn't care, wouldn't notice you didn't want me? Why couldn't you have told me it was him you wanted? Why did you let me find out like this? I'm a laughing stock now, do you realize that? All because you couldn't keep your hands off each other once you got away from me!"

Sullyan couldn't understand where this depth of fury had come from. Her body started to tremble. She couldn't take her stricken gaze from Robin's face. She hadn't realized he had been so affected by her recent loss of enthusiasm for love-making. She had tried so hard not to let the sickness affect her, and it simply hadn't occurred to her that he might think she had lost her feelings for him. The attacks on the King and the recent raids had filled her waking thoughts, and she had assumed he understood. Now, she saw how wrong she was. Yet he had not come to her with his worries, and she was deeply hurt that he should bottle them up and allow them to damage the trust they shared. Although their depth and strength were beyond comprehension, this angry jealousy and unreasoning suspicion were the result. Despite an earlier resolve to deal with him calmly, the tension in the air and the injustice of his allegations suddenly filled her with fury. She felt wounded to the core of her heart. Her voice was cold and harsh as she responded.

"What gives you the right to make these vicious accusations? Are you so jealous that you cannot allow me a little free space now and then? You were not always so suspicious. Hot-headed and juvenile sometimes, yes, but never stupid! How can you believe I would want Taran over you? How many times have I told you I do not love him that way? I would not have taken him to Port Loxton had I been able to go with you, but you had duties to attend to! Should I have gone alone? You trusted Taran! You even helped persuade him to go when he was so concerned over your feelings! Do you not remember that?"

"Of course I remember!" yelled Robin, the violence in his tone shocking her anew. "How you must have laughed about that! It was a very underhanded trick, getting me to beg him to go, to look after you. What a joke! He'd been 'looking after' you for months already, hadn't he? That's why you were so cool toward me!"

He swung his back to her and she could see the tremor in his shoulders. He stood there in fury, his hands clenched into fists as if that was the only way he could stop himself from striking her. If he had been like this when confronting Taran, then she could understand the Adept's rush to leave. She had to weather the storm, but for reasons she couldn't fathom, Robin was beyond control. She was growing fearful of the outcome.

Then he went too far.

"When did it start? Tell me that." His voice was unrecognizable in his anguish. "Was it before Marik's banquet? Were you sleeping with him even then? Was that how you got over Rykan's rape so easily? I often wondered how you did that. But that's the answer, isn't it? Rykan wasn't the first, was he?"

Sullyan gasped and froze, her pounding blood congealing to ice in her veins. A pain began, deep in her chest. Her stomach lurched as if she had been kicked from the inside, and she felt sick and dizzy. But even then Robin wasn't done. He was unaware, or uncaring of the terrible damage his words were inflicting.

"You were just using me afterward, weren't you? You made me believe I was so special, the only one who could help you forget what Rykan did to you and replace the pain and fear with love and tenderness. Yet all the time you were comparing us! Well, which one did you prefer? Which of us satisfied you most?"

She simply couldn't believe she was hearing this. She couldn't move to leave or react. She was stunned and shocked to her very soul and could hardly breathe. Did he really believe what he was saying? Where had all this venom come from? If he really thought her capable of such base deception, then they didn't have what she thought they did. His words injured her deeply, cutting her heart like a knife. He could not have hurt her more if he had raped her himself.

Her volition returned abruptly, her self-control destroyed by his stream of vicious anger, and she knew she could take no more.

"How dare you?" she screamed. "Stop it, STOP IT!"

Tormented beyond endurance, she used her powers on him, gripping him body and mind in the unbreakable sphere of her power. In the sudden, tension-ridden silence, anguished disbelief, sheer incomprehension that she could actually use her forces against him blazed in an agony of betrayal from Robin's pain-darkened eyes.

She could scarcely believe it herself. How had she lost control so completely? Appalled at what he had driven her to do, she instantly released him. But the damage was done. He panted in distress and she had to turn away. Her eyes were burning, her chest was tight. She was unable to face him.

Tears of remorse stung Robin's eyes as the realization of what he had said punched through his fury. He staggered, hardly able to believe he had uttered such dreadful accusations. He had no idea why he had said them. They had never entered his head before, but it was no use telling her that. Even if the rest of it was true, he knew perfectly well that Rykan's abuse had scarred her physically as well as spiritually, and she would never be completely free of it. And in his anger at her betrayal he had thrown that terrible experience back in her face.

Still angry, still distressed at her use of power, the shame of what he had said nevertheless acted as a cold drench to his passion. He was about to try to undo some of the damage, but she spoke first.

"Get out."

The words were soft but held icy contempt. They were like a slap in the face, and his intended apology died unborn. His outrage at her double betrayal stiffened his back, and he turned on his heel. Grasping the doorknob, he prepared to wrench it open when her voice came again, still in that icy, unfeeling tone.

"I could make you hear me, Robin. I could use my power to convince you once and for all that I am innocent of every accusation you have flung at me. Yet I will not. If you cannot believe me, if you cannot hear the honesty in my voice, then no use of power will sway you. And I have already abused my power tonight. I have committed the most basic sin one Artesan can perpetrate on another, and it fills me with horror. You drove me to lose my control, something that has never happened before. I can never forgive myself, and I will not leave myself open that way again.

"So go. Go somewhere quiet and think long and hard about what has occurred between us. Cruel words have been uttered, and trust has been betrayed on both sides. Think very carefully about your feelings, Robin. You risk throwing away something young and precious if you do not.

"Now go."

She returned the stare he gave her over his shoulder. There was an unfathomable look in his pain-filled eyes and his face was pinched and white. For herself, she felt nauseous, dizzy. Some of it was due, no doubt, to lack of food, yet her appetite had faded and the very thought of eating brought bile up into her throat. She watched coldly as Robin stood by the door. He hesitated a fraction as his hand moved to turn the knob, and she thought, with heart-wrenching hope, that he might turn, apologize, and run to her arms.

He did not. Silently, he left her.

Sullyan stayed where she was once the door had closed, her mind endlessly replaying the dreadful events of the last half hour. She still could not believe it. Didn't they share the deepest and most precious love anyone could ever wish for? Didn't they both trust one another implicitly with no room for doubt? So she had always thought. How then had it come to this? How had it been so thoroughly poisoned, so easily overset? How could he even think it of her, let alone come to believe it so completely that he would physically assault one of his closest friends?

Thoughts of Taran's pain, Robin's fury, and her own anguish caused a great welling of grief and despair to wash over her. Burying her face in her hands, she wept.

Chapter Twenty-Eight

Sullyan lay wakeful all the dark night long, waiting for Robin's step in the corridor, longing for his presence in their bed. He didn't come. She didn't know where he passed the night, but he chose to pass it alone.

Hope died in her breast when dawn came and there was still no sign of him. She rose, weary and heartsick. With no other choice, she met with her command and made ready to go out on patrol. She accepted a pack of supplies from Tad and knew that even he noted the dark circles under her eyes and the pallor of her face. She led her company out under leaden, weeping skies. Dawn brought no cheerful sunshine to lighten her mood.

✤ ✤ ✤ ✤ ✤

Cal rode back to the Manor a couple of hours later, his own heart heavy. He was thoroughly reluctant to face Robin in the light of what he had learned from Taran, but he would just have to grit his teeth and try to forget it, at least while they were on duty. Robin was his commanding officer, although Cal might consider transferring to one of Vassa's companies if things didn't improve.

There was no time to see Rienne before riding out, so Cal waited at the horse lines until the Major arrived with the rest of the men. Robin glanced at him but otherwise ignored him, for which Cal was grateful. They could all see the strain on Robin's face, but due to his recent moodiness, no one commented. Cal was spared the trouble of hiding what he knew. Mounting his horse, he fell in behind Robin, determined to push the whole affair to the back of his mind.

✦ ✦ ✦ ✦ ✦

Vassa's companies weren't due out until later that afternoon, so Parren took the opportunity to pen another message to the Baron. He knew Reen would relish the news that a wedge had finally been driven between Robin and Sullyan. Although he had promised as much, Parren had been dubious of the Baron's ability to influence the Artesans at the Manor. These latest events had erased those doubts. Parren's enemies were suffering, and Parren was pleased.

Once his message was on its way, unremarked among the many going from the King to the capital, the sallow Captain began to plan how best to compound his enemies' misery and heighten his own long-anticipated victory over them. Grinning as he replayed what he had overheard while eavesdropping outside the door to their office last night, he sauntered back from the runner station toward his own chambers. He directed a mocking bow in Ozella's direction when he chanced to see the young foreigner on his way to a lesson with Bull. Ozella's suddenly white face and expression of terror made him smile.

Parren hadn't yet given Ozella any new instructions. Neither had he given the Beraxian any assurances of his sisters' safety. All he gave in response to Ozella's frantic pleas for their release was an enigmatic smile and admonitions to "be good." Parren knew Ozella was finding it increasingly difficult to hide his distress, and his current training regime was more of a hindrance than a help.

Parren could not have cared less.

✦ ✦ ✦ ✦ ✦

There had been a puzzling change in Ozella's behavior lately, and

Bull was worried. The young Lord was less enthusiastic than ever about his cadet training, but he was suddenly desperate to improve his talents as an Artesan.

He started by seeking Bull out and requesting instruction, asking all sorts of detailed questions and cajoling Bull into giving him strengthening exercises as well as extra instruction. When Bull asked the reason for this abrupt about face, Ozella was evasive. To cap it all, thought Bull, today he was even stranger. For although he seemed to take in what he was told and appeared to be trying to do what was asked, his powers of attention were suffering and he often lost the thread of what he was doing. This reminded Bull uncomfortably of Ozella's peculiar lethargy during the recent trip to Andaryon.

Today they were working with gems, and Bull had tasked Ozella and Tad with calling power through several stones in turn so they could experience the difference in the power levels each one produced. Tad had successfully called Earth through a progression of gems, but Ozella couldn't seem to grasp the process at all.

Bull gathered the gems into a leather pouch and took one into his hand so Ozella couldn't see which it was. He instructed the youth to call Earth from the stone, identifying it by the level of force it produced. Ozella narrowed his almond eyes, trying to concentrate. Unfortunately for him, he hadn't paid attention to Tad's efforts. It was apparent the youth was distracted by something, though Bull had no idea what it could be.

Frowning hard, Ozella tried to focus his will. Because he had no idea which gemstone Bull held and no recollection of which gem had produced what level of force, he failed to identify the stone. Yet his touch was tentative at best, and the power he raised feeble, and Bull would have challenged even Robin to identify the source with such lack of effort. Exasperated, he told Ozella to try again.

"Use your senses, lad," he commanded gruffly. "You're not concentrating. Come on, a baby could do this."

Stung by Bull's scornful tone, and spurred on by Tad's inquisitive gaze, Ozella tried harder. Unfortunately, he tried too hard. Bull roared with pain as Ozella's frustration caused him to call too harshly, overloading the gem until it shattered. Sharp slivers of crystal pierced Bull's hand, driving deep into the flesh.

Cursing, Bull used his own powers to numb the pain and a cloth to mop the blood while Ozella, flushed and deeply embarrassed, muttered abject apologies.

Bull regarded him coldly. "I don't know what's got into you lately! First you show no signs of wanting to learn, then you plead with Sullyan to take you to Andaryon, where you promptly fall asleep. Then you as good as beg me to teach you, and now you've lost all pretense of concentration! What's going on, Ozella? If you carry on like this, you'll give me no option but to recommend you for dismissal."

To Bull's shock, Ozella's face drained to white and he looked as though he might faint. "No, don't do that!" he cried. "Please! I'm sorry, I can't help it sometimes. I'll try harder, Bull, I promise. Just don't let them throw me out! You don't know... you don't know how important it is for me to be here."

Bowing his head to his hands, Ozella burst into uncontrollable sobs.

"All right, all right," said Bull hurriedly, exchanging a puzzled look with Tad. "Calm down, lad. There's no need to take on so. It was an accident, I know. But you must realize you can cause all sorts of damage if you don't learn to control yourself. You'll never be able to channel metaforce effectively if you can't master your emotions.

"Look, I've got to go to the infirmary and get these shards out.

Tad, you practice what you were doing earlier with the cornelian and the diamond. Ozella, if you really want to make progress, you can start by learning to channel through the amber. I want to see you pass metaforce through it without melting it. All right?"

Ozella nodded and wiped his eyes. Bull shook his head and left the room.

He made his way to the infirmary, where the noon meals had just been cleared away. He hadn't realized it was so late. He would miss second servings in the commons if this took too long. He found Rienne, who had just returned after her own meal, and she exclaimed over his lacerated hand.

"That looks nasty, Bull. What on earth happened?"

"Yes, that's it. Earth happened," he quipped, explaining when she didn't understand.

Taking him into one of the treatment rooms, she made sure he had numbed his hand before she probed for the crystal splinters with fine tweezers. It didn't take long. Treating conscious Artesans was an easy task, for not only could they deal with their own pain, they could also tell their healer where any foreign bodies were and when they were all removed.

Having extracted all the shards, she waited while Bull stopped the bleeding and began to close the wounds. Then she gently bound the hand, as he would have to keep it covered while the newly knitted flesh strengthened. Some of the shards had driven to the bone.

He watched her while she worked and noticed the hint of bruising beneath her eyes and the pallor of her face.

"What's the matter, Rienne? I know there's something."

Tying off the bandage, she sighed and sat on the table beside him. "You haven't heard, then?"

"Heard what? I gather you don't mean those ridiculous rumors."

She hesitated, clearly not knowing where to start. Then she told him all she knew, and his honest brown eyes were wide when the tale was over.

"I can't believe this!" he muttered. "So that's why Denny left his bed so early when he clearly wasn't fit. I just assumed he'd had enough cosseting, although I thought he was running a risk. That arm's nowhere near healed."

Rienne turned away, shame on her face. "I couldn't trust myself to treat him anymore. Whenever I looked at him, I felt sick. He's done such damage. I just couldn't bear him near me."

"I'm not blaming you, dear heart!" Bull took her hand. "He's lucky you didn't break his other arm. But what I really can't credit is Robin reacting so badly to gossip. What could have got into him? Poor Taran! He must have been scared witless to leave like that."

"You should have seen him. He was in a terrible state. I do hope Brynne has been able to talk him round. She said she would try to see him yesterday. Cal went over there last night, but I don't know what happened. He went out on patrol as soon as he got back. Oh, I do hope he and Robin don't come to blows again! Cal was furious when I told him, and talking to Taran won't have calmed him any."

"Come to blows again?" repeated Bull. "Are you telling me Robin had a go at Cal too?"

"Oh, not physically," she said. "But he chewed Cal out in front of the men for daring to question his lack of orders about taking captives on that first raid. Cal was very upset. He said Robin was almost savage about it."

"What is going on?" puzzled Bull. "This isn't like Robin at all. I know he can be hot-headed, but I thought he had it under control now. I'll have to have a word with him. He can't go on like this."

"You might want to speak with Brynne first," said Rienne.

"She's his superior officer. It's really up to her to deal with any backlash over these rumors. I doubt she has any notion of how damaging they've become."

"No," Bull snorted. "She wouldn't have. You know how little she worries over things like that. She's lived with rumors all her life and she takes less notice of them than what she eats. She won't have any patience with Robin if he's taken any of this to heart. Perhaps I ought to try to speak with him before she does, just to let him know what he's in for if she gets her famous temper up."

Rienne shook her head. "You might already be too late. I don't suppose she will have kept quiet if they spent any time together last night."

"Damn," he said, "you're probably right. Then I'll have a case of wounded pride to deal with. Remember what he was like after she chewed him out over that stupid duel with Parren?"

Rienne's face paled further. That incident had marked the start of a painful time for all of them.

Bull regarded her narrowly. He could see she was deeply worried, but something told him she hadn't given him all the facts.

"There's something else, isn't there? Come on now, holding out won't do you any good. If there's any more bad news, you'd better let me have it."

To his surprise, Rienne smiled. Her gray eyes lost their strained appearance and her face fell back into its usual softness.

"You're right, as usual, but it's not bad news." She took a breath. "Bull, Cal and I are going to be parents."

His mouth dropped open and he sat stunned for a few moments. Then his florid face broke into a delighted smile. "Oh, Rienne!" He leaned forward and gathered her into a warm bear hug. "That's wonderful news. What did Cal say? When is it due? Taran will be so proud of you both! Have you told Sully yet? She'll be over the moon!"

Rienne laughed at Bull's jumble of words and did her best to answer him. "Cal was as pleased as you could imagine. It's due in around six months' time. I didn't get round to telling Taran before he left. Yes, Brynne knows about it. I asked her to confirm it for me. I felt a little guilty about it, but you're right, she was very pleased for us."

"Guilty? Why on earth should you feel guilty?"

"Isn't it obvious? Remember, she can't have children of her own."

Bull snorted again. "Gods, Rienne, don't ever think she wouldn't be as pleased as anyone for you and Cal! In fact, this could be the best thing for her. She'll be able to cosset and play with your baby without the responsibility of having her own. She'd find it very hard giving up her current way of life to look after a baby, you know, even for a short time."

Rienne smiled sadly. "Yes, that's true, and I appreciate what you're saying. Brynne can spend as much time as she likes with my baby, but if you think that loving someone else's child could possibly make up for being unable to bear your own, then you're very much mistaken. It could even cause her to feel worse about her barrenness rather than better."

Bull frowned. "Do you really think so? Has she said something to you?"

"Of course not." Rienne sighed and rose. "You know she never talks about things she has no control over. She says she's accepted it, and I believe her up to a point. But I don't think even she realizes how deeply these feelings can run. I'm sure her recent health worries are all rooted in the same problem, although every time I examine her I can find nothing really wrong. We're going to have to support her over the next few months. It could be a very difficult time for her."

Bull rose too, thinking he ought to check on Tad and Ozella

before releasing them to their meals. His own stomach was growling for food. "It's going to be a difficult time all round," he agreed, "especially if this situation with the raiding worsens."

"Do you think it will?"

Bull heard the note of fear in her voice. "I don't honestly know, dear heart. But you can rely on Blaine and Sullyan getting to the bottom of it soon. We've had to play a waiting game over these past few months, but now our enemy has finally made a move it's only a matter of time before we discover who he is. Elias won't see his treaty with Andaryon threatened, and he won't easily be pushed into an escalation. Once we know who's really behind all this, we'll find a way to stop him, you'll see."

Bull didn't voice his opinion that little progress had been made so far toward uncovering who was behind the raids. The previous months of careful searching for the creator of the Staff were as frustrating as they were futile. Now that the attacks were intensifying, how would any of them find time to search? And now there was Prince Aeyron to consider, whose plight must be causing Pharikian terrible pain. Bull had an uneasy feeling that things were going to get much worse before they got better.

Chapter Twenty-Nine

Sullyan and Dexter led their exhausted company back to the Manor in the middle of the afternoon. The weather had deteriorated, and they were wet as well as weary. The raiders' sporadic attacks had sent them scurrying from village to small town to hamlet, always one step behind, as the raiders used the Veils to evade patrols before the Albians got close enough to engage them. The raiders were wreaking mayhem on the villagers, and unless the Albians could stop them, there would be widespread disruption of the vital work in the fields. Many of the farmers were understandably reluctant to leave their homes and families undefended.

Sullyan and her men advised each community on how to protect itself, promising aid and support where they could. Yet she knew they stood little chance of putting an end to the damaging assaults unless they could identify the source of, and reason for, the raiding.

Many of the village Elders muttered about war and the necessity for retaliation. She could have done without these protests, but she couldn't blame the villagers. Their livelihoods and families were being torn apart by demons. She supposed she would feel the same in their shoes and reluctantly agreed to carry their messages to Elias.

Riding at the head of her command back toward the Manor, she contacted Ty Marik for an update on the situation in Andaryon. Marik's feeble Artesan powers meant that Sullyan had to exert herself in order to reach him. The strain of doing so only added to the weariness in her bones. Weariness caused by fears for her country and the pain of her rift from Robin.

Marik's news was depressingly familiar.

Yes, we're experiencing raiding too. Small groups of humans appear from nowhere, cause as much damage as possible, and then vanish before we can deal with them. It's driving Anjer mad. No prisoners have been taken, and any injured raiders are dispatched by their own comrades before they cross the Veils. They obviously don't want to risk capture.

Sullyan cursed under her breath.

What is the mood of your people, Ty? How is Timar bearing up?

She heard Marik's mental sigh.

The mood's turning ugly. Corbyn's still pouring poison on everything and demanding the right to respond in kind. I wouldn't be at all surprised if some of his men are responsible for the attacks in your realm. He's said nothing on the subject, but I think he has enough support in the north to act on his own. Timar fears to send him packing in case we lose what little control we have. Anjer can cow him for the moment, but it won't hold forever.

Timar's taking it badly, Brynne. Aeyron was a great source of strength and support, and Timar feels his son's loss deeply. Idri's beside herself with worry for them both. I think Timar's hanging on the hope that you'll be back soon.

Sullyan's heart clenched in sorrow for her foster father's pain.

You must be Timar's strength for now, Ty. I am not free to come. I am needed here and I cannot desert my duty, no matter how much I wish to be with you. Tell Timar and Idri that my thoughts are with them, and remind them they can bespeak me any time they wish. When I have the liberty to come I will be there, believe me. Have you made any progress with Rykan's or Sonten's records?

She heard Marik's dry chuckle in her mind, a genuine sound of mirth amid the gloom.

Gaslek's in his element. He's probably the only cheerful person here right now. Nazir sent him a trunkful of papers from Sonten's mansion, and I managed to get hold of all the rest of Rykan's archives. Gaslek's buried under a ton of parchment and he's as happy as a pig in poop! Timar ordered him to concentrate on that to the exclusion of all else. If there's anything to find, the Baron will find it, never fear.

Sullyan gave a small smile.

Keep me informed, will you? Especially if there are any developments concerning Aeyron's ransom. The three days expire tomorrow. Stay close to Timar and be ready to support him when he needs you.

Breaking the link with relief, she rode the rest of the way in somber mood, wondering whether the chances had improved of convincing Elias to send her in search of their enemy. She doubted it, but in the light of Marik's news she felt she had to try again.

Once she had washed off the grime and made herself presentable, she gave her report to Blaine and the King. Both men appeared more careworn than before, and neither had had anything like enough sleep. She dutifully handed over the messages of protest entrusted to her by the village Elders. Drinking fellan while the King read the messages, she gauged his mood before deciding what to say.

"Your Majesty, just before I returned today I took the liberty of bespeaking Duke Marik for an update on the situation in Andaryon."

Elias fixed her with his piercing gaze. "And?"

She faced him openly. Now was not the time to show her frustration.

"The news is not good. They have been subject to raiding on the same scale as us, and the Albian raiders use the same tactics. Surprise attacks on outlying villages, doing as much damage as possible before vanishing through the Veils at the first sign of organized resistance. They also kill any wounded who are in danger of capture. Your Majesty, some of Pharikian's nobles are pressing him to break with you and declare war."

Blaine shook his head, but Elias's gaze never left hers. "And will he?"

Sullyan dropped her eyes. "That is not for me to say, your Majesty. He is overcome with grief and worry for his son, and I do not care to think what this will do to him. He will be most reluctant to accede to their demands, and for the moment Lord General Anjer is keeping the rebels at bay. How long that will last, I cannot say. But if enough of the higher-ranking nobles experience such raiding, they may well band together, gainsay the Hierarch, and act on their own."

"I would say they already are," retorted Elias. "They are doing untold damage, Colonel, and I can't allow it to go on indefinitely." He eyed her with unconcealed frustration. "Brynne, why can't you use your powers to slip through the Veils and catch these raiders before they escape? Use their own tactics against them?"

She had expected such a question, but thought the General might have informed the King why he was asking the impossible. She shook her head ruefully.

"I wish it were that simple, your Majesty. So far, neither you nor Timar has broached the subject of an agreement to transfer troops through the other's realm. Not only would it be a serious breach of protocol, but it is also impossible on a more practical level. First, I would have to focus all my energies on continually scanning the substrate for any openings large enough to admit a raiding party. Then I would have to construct not only a tunnel into

Andaryon, but immediately another back into our own lands, to where the raiders were. You have heard me say before that working the substrate drains our energies, and only those of us who are Adept-elite and above could do as I have described more than once or twice in a day. If I were to spend myself like that, I would be fit for nothing in a very short space of time. I am truly sorry, your Majesty, but in this case the raiders have the advantage."

Elias's eyes blazed in anger, not at her but at the untenable situation in which he found himself. He was trapped and he knew it.

"I cannot just sit by and watch my people being systematically plundered of their homes and livelihoods!" he thundered. "It's intolerable."

"All the more reason, then, to spend more effort in searching for those responsible," she urged. "War is what they want. We must not let them force it on us. Please, your Majesty, give me leave to concentrate on finding them before they succeed in their plan."

Elias slapped his hand on the table. "No, Colonel! I've already told you, I can't spare you."

He stared her down when she tried to protest, and she looked to Blaine in appeal. The General's expression was closed, but she was sure he shared her views.

Her tacit request for backup angered Elias, and he snapped at her. "It's no good looking at Mathias! He, at least, will obey his King."

She flinched and drew a sharp breath at this unfair reprimand, then kneeled before the angry monarch. "As will I, your Majesty."

Her submissive gesture mollified Elias, and she felt his twinge of shame. He was not usually disposed toward bad temper, but he was in danger of losing control of this situation. Deeply committed to the fair rule of his country, he bitterly resented this most personal of attacks on his policies. He was helpless to make any real contribution to the battle being waged, as his opposers had access to powers that he did not. His own deep-seated envy of those who did was beginning to surface.

"Oh, get up, Brynne, I wasn't questioning your loyalty. But I need those I trust to stay by me. Despite what you may think, I took note of your advice and sent a message to Lord Levant, asking him to instruct the garrison to watch for any signs of our enemy. We don't have much to go on, I know, but they'll ask questions and report anything suspicious. If you have any specific suggestions as to what they should look for, you should give them to the General."

It was not what Sullyan wanted, and she doubted it would do much good, but it was the best she would get. "I will," she replied, seating herself once more, "and my first recommendation is that they should watch Baron Reen most closely. May I ask who receives the messages you send to the capital?"

Elias narrowed his eyes at the unexpected question. "Why do you ask? You surely don't suspect my messengers?"

She shrugged. "In such uncertain times, your Majesty, I would discount nothing. I have no reason to suspect them. I merely wondered whether your dispatches went directly to the recipient or through your office first?"

"They go through my Chamberlain, Lord Kinsey, of course," said Elias. "He passes them on."

Via a servant, no doubt, thought Sullyan. She gathered her strength before voicing her next question. She was risking Elias's anger again, but she had to ask.

"And if, in your absence, Lord Kinsey was... directed... to hand the messages to someone with higher authority? Would he do so?"

Elias scowled. "Only Sofira has the authority to intercept my messages, and you already know what I think of your suspicions concerning my Queen."

"But what about her closest confidante? What about the Baron? If she bestowed her authority on him in a time of conflict, who would dare gainsay him?"

Elias considered this, his irritation arrested.

"Yes," he mused, "it is possible he could use his influence to further his own ends without Sofira's knowledge."

"Then may I respectfully suggest that any runners you send to the castle are instructed by you personally to bypass Lord Kinsey and hand the dispatches directly to the recipient? If we are right and the Baron is involved in some way, then your absence means he is ideally placed to control what happens at the capital. Were it not for this escalation of hostilities I would suggest you return there, but it is out of the question."

"It certainly is," put in Blaine. "And if the Baron is responsible for this unrest, then sending his Majesty unprotected into his sphere of influence is an invitation to murder, considering the two attempts on his life so far."

"I agree, General. I merely point out that we have no authoritative vantage at the castle now, save through his Majesty's letters. It would be risky to involve the Queen in our suspicions, for if Reen is guilty of treason and she is unaware, we would be placing her in great jeopardy by informing her of our speculations."

She heard Elias draw a breath and guessed what he was thinking. He had not considered that his Queen or his children might be in danger. If Sullyan was right and Reen was behind all this or in league with whoever was, then how safe were they? Their adversary would hardly balk at taking them hostage. What had happened to Prince Aeyron was testament to that.

Elias stared at Blaine. "Perhaps I ought to move Sofira and the children."

Sullyan knew that Blaine had already considered this and decided against it. He wasn't completely convinced by her argument that the Queen had to be involved in the plot, but neither would he dismiss the possibility out of hand. However, there was no firm evidence on which to act, and with the King so far from the capital, Sofira was necessary to the administration of Albia. Blaine temporized.

"Where would you send them, Elias? Don't forget, it's too dangerous to travel the countryside right now. They're safest where they are. I've already sent a runner to the garrison with instructions to increase the royal guard. Our men will defend them well should any raiders be bold enough to attempt an attack. And if Sullyan is right and Reen is involved, you would not want him knowing where they were. How would you explain that to the Queen without informing her of our suspicions?"

Elias cursed. Sullyan knew he despised feeling so helpless. He barely acknowledged her respectful salute as she rose to leave.

The General followed her to the door. She regarded him in surprise when he stepped outside with her. He seemed unsure of himself, a rare thing. She waited him out.

"I suppose you've heard about Major Tamsen's error yesterday?" he said finally.

Her expression hardened. "I have, General."

"And have you also heard the rumors being bandied about by the men from Port Loxton?"

Her hands clenched. "Yes."

"Then do something about it, will you? We can do without dissention among our own, Colonel! If the rumors have affected the Major's ability to carry out his duties, then it's up to you to sort it out. I was afraid this might happen if I allowed you both to remain here once you were wed. It's not an ideal situation to have married partners stationed together. Why do you think the men are discouraged from courting the healers? Look how Healer Arlen worries when Cal is on patrol! It leads to too much friction, and I don't like it. If you and Robin can't come to some agreement, one of you will have to transfer."

Sullyan froze. Blaine saw the pain in her eyes.

"You know I don't want to lose either of you," he said, his tone gentler. "You assured me before you were wed that your private life would not affect your professional duties. Now it has. Elias has caught no hint of it yet, but he will unless you sort it out. I don't want to give him an excuse to move one of you to the capital, but he will if he believes it necessary. I don't suppose you want that either, so do something about it."

"Yes, General."

Sullyan saluted stiffly, remaining rooted to the spot once Blaine had reentered his rooms.

She didn't need this. Curse Robin for believing those stupid tales! How could he let her down like this? But then she remembered her own betrayal, her loss of control and use of power against the one she loved above everyone else. How could she have done that? They were both at fault, and she didn't know how to put it right. Damage had been done and hurt given, but the time needed for healing might not be to hand.

She headed back to her rooms, hoping desperately to see Robin. She was sure his command would have returned by now, but there was no sign of him. Some of his clothes were missing. Sullyan sighed and collapsed onto the couch, too distressed even to brew fellan.

The sound of the outer office door opening brought her to her feet, her heart racing with hope and fear. Yet even before the knock came at her chamber door, she knew it wasn't Robin.

"Come in, Bull," she called listlessly, and sank back onto the couch.

The big man radiated anxiety. He came straight over to her and kneeled on the floor. She gazed into his worried eyes and found a wan smile for him.

"What the Void's going on, Sully? What's all this about Robin and Taran? Have you managed to calm things down?"

The tears that welled in her eyes dismayed him, and he caught her in his arms. He held her silently, and worried while she worked some of the hurt out of her system. Once she was calmer, he handed her a cloth to dry her eyes. In a firm but gentle tone, he demanded the whole story. Unable to hold back in his comforting presence, she told him. She withheld the hugely hurtful remarks Robin had made concerning Rykan, not trusting herself to speak of them. Nevertheless, Bull was fuming when she was done.

"The stupid idiot! What the Void does he think he's playing at? You wait until I get my hands on him. I'll give him a story to believe!"

Her release had restored Sullyan's sense of control. "You will do nothing of the sort, Bull. There has been enough of that kind of thing already. This is between Robin and me. It is about trust, and you will only make matters worse if you interfere. Robin's pride is at stake here, and his confidence. I will not have that undermined. He will come to his senses, given time."

Bull was unconvinced. "Will he? And can you afford to wait for him to realize what a fool he's been? What on earth possessed him to believe those rumors, anyway? Has he listened to nothing he's been told over the past three years?"

Sullyan couldn't stop fresh tears appearing, and Bull shook his head in disgust. He changed the subject. "Have you spoken to Taran yet?"

Composing herself with an effort, she nodded. As he brewed fellan, she told him what had transpired between her and the

Adept.

"So, he's not coming back, then?" Bull asked, handing her a steaming mug. "There are many who will miss him, Rienne not least."

Sullyan didn't miss Bull's veiled reference to Rienne's condition. The memory of her friend's happy news caused Sullyan to smile, and Bull was glad to see some of the strain disappear from her face.

"We will all be here for Rienne," she murmured. "I am sure Taran will return once things have settled."

Sipping his fellan, Bull gazed speculatively at her. "I probably shouldn't bother you with this just now, but I'm a little concerned about Ozella."

"Oh?"

"He's been acting very strangely lately." Bull sprawled in the chair opposite her. "You know how lazy he's been since he came here, and how Robin, Taran, and I have all tried to convince him of the need to work harder? Well, none of us really got through to him. I couldn't believe it when he suddenly begged you to take him to Andaryon. I thought maybe he'd finally seen sense. But he never paid attention to what was happening around him, despite saying he wanted to observe the workings of diplomacy. He was really depressed when we got back.

"Then I had him in my rooms the other day, practically on his knees, pleading to be given extra instruction. He even asked for strengthening exercises! But today he completely lost it and a simple exercise turned into total disaster."

"Is that what happened to your hand?"

Bull nodded. "It's not too bad. I've healed the worst bits. But the injury isn't what concerns me. There's something wrong with the boy. Something's troubling him, and he's not going to get anywhere until he tells us what it is."

Sullyan sighed. She had too many responsibilities these days, too many calls on her time and too little energy to deal with them. Where was her stamina when she needed it? Just lately, it seemed to have deserted her.

Bull gazed at her, sensing her unease. "Look, just forget I said anything. You don't have time for this. I'll keep an eye on the boy and see if I can get through to him. But if he won't talk to me, I don't know what else I can do."

She smiled gratefully at the huge man sitting across from her. "What would I do without you, Bull? If I can spare the time, I will speak with Ozella. Be sure to tell him he can approach me any time if he needs to. Now, how is Tad doing?"

They spent some time discussing less vital matters. The mere familiarity of their talk served to soothe and relax Sullyan and lend an air of normality to an otherwise fraught situation. By the time Bull rose to leave, she was feeling better.

She hugged him affectionately, reflecting, not for the first time, that he would have made her the ideal partner had he only been younger. Her love for him ran deep and true.

"I can sleep now, Bull," she assured him, and despite not being totally convinced, he left her to rest. He was right to doubt, for as soon as she was alone in the big bed, the absence of her life mate caused her to lie wakeful far into the night.

Chapter Thirty

"Wake up!"

The man's boot slammed painfully into his ribs. Semi-conscious, his wrists circled tightly with spellsilver, Aeyron could only groan. His whole body was one vast bruise, some ribs were surely cracked, and he was parched and starved. His captors had offered him neither food nor water, and he feared his usefulness to them was nearly at an end.

He opened his eyes slowly. He could hardly focus. He was barely capable of feeling now, although some of Izack's persuasive methods would have drawn responses from a corpse. When he was finally able to see, the Prince vaguely registered the Baron's unwelcome presence, crouched beside him like a hungry spider.

Aeyron still occupied the dank, dark cell in the otherwise deserted dungeons. His only company, when left mercifully alone by his captors, were rats, and the only sound other than his own labored breathing was the far-off drip of water. This had driven him nearly mad when he was aware enough to register thirst. Now, he was too far gone to care.

He saw the Baron wrinkle his nose at the dreadful odors in the cell. No one had bothered to clear away the ordure from Aeyron's body. Combined with the reek of infection, this made the cell a very unpleasant place. Reen clutched a scented cloth to the lower half of his face and looked as if he was on the verge of gagging.

Izack, standing menacingly to one side, seemed unaffected.

"Well, my fine Prince," mocked the Baron, "how do you like our hospitality? Has Izack been treating you well? Are the beds to your satisfaction?"

Aeyron stared blankly at him. He had learned not to make a sound on the rare occasions when the Baron appeared, for Izack needed no encouragement in his brutality. The sadistic Commander had paid his captive frequent visits of his own, and their only purpose, as far as the Andaryan could make out, was to satisfy his lust for violence. Aeyron's half-naked body bore ample evidence of Izack's gratification.

Reen stood, gazing smugly at his helpless prisoner. "You will be glad to know that your ordeal is nearly over," he announced, smiling with malicious pleasure when Aeyron failed to suppress a feeble start. "Oh, yes. Your royal father should have acceded to my demands by now. The time has come to send him my final message. What do you think, my fine Prince? Shall we send him a message from you, too?"

A flare of hope rose unbidden into Aeyron's eyes. It died almost instantly. The Prince had no energy to sustain it even had he truly believed he would be set free.

Reen cocked his head to one side. "What, you don't want to let him know you're alive? To send him some hope, some token, from his son? Come now, what kind of man are you?"

The Baron took a step forward, towering over Aeyron, daring him to reply. Aeyron watched in sick despair, fully convinced the hour of his death had come. Reen, however, hadn't finished gloating.

"Ah, but of course," he snarled, "you're not a man at all, are you? You're nothing but a creature, and an unnatural one at that. All of Albia will thank me when I have put an end to traffic with such as you. Our Matria Church will regain her rightful place and finally succeed in stamping out those who profess to arcane arts.

"Izack, hold him!"

The Commander kneeled, laying hold of Aeyron with strong and heavy hands. The Prince astonished himself, for the fear of what was coming released strength he didn't know he possessed. He struggled violently. His half-starved efforts, however, were no match for the fit Commander. His resistance was futile.

The knife flashed in the guttering torchlight and Aeyron's harsh scream of agony rang through the deserted dungeons. He fell into black oblivion and knew no more.

✤ ✤ ✤ ✤ ✤

"Well, Madam, I have to tell you that I believe the time has come."

Baron Reen stood in Queen Sofira's private solar, waiting for the storm. His Lady's reaction was typically intense, and just as he had expected.

"No, Hezra!" Tears started in her eyes. Her bleached face turned even paler and two spots of color burned high in her cheeks. "I implore you, I beg you! It's not necessary. There has to be another way."

"Now, Madam, calm yourself. We have already discussed this. You knew it was a possibility if the demons didn't declare war."

Reen had to be cautious. His next two moves were vital to his plans. He couldn't afford for Sofira to weaken or the whole scheme could be compromised. War was a very necessary part of his plans, for not only would it occupy the very powerful Artesan minds which might otherwise interfere with his goal, but it would also discredit Elias. A realm-war would show the populace how ill-advised the King's tolerant policies were, and how fragile was his loyalty to Albia. Reen intended that the war, together with the ongoing and highly damaging raids, should be seen as a direct consequence of trafficking with outlanders. Then, when he finally abolished such blasphemous intercourse, he would be seen as the savior of humankind.

He would gain the acclaim and trust of the people, as well as having Sofira's backing and endorsement. When Elias fell from grace, given, of course, that he survived the war, he, Hezra Reen, would be uniquely placed to bring about a new era not only in the governing of Albia, but also in the spiritual welfare of its people.

His soul swelled at the thought. Such high ideals, so selflessly conceived! He congratulated himself on his nobility and purity of purpose. Once Elias was deposed or dead, he would become the benevolent and fatherly influence behind the throne. He would guide the steps and mold the morality of young Prince Eadan, and then they would finally have a true monarch of the Faith. How the people would revere him!

First, though, he had to pacify the Queen.

"Everything is in place, Madam. My associate in Andaryon has finally sent me the item I requested, so my final message to the demon ruler is on its way. Soon, the silver will be in our possession. Yet, as I have already explained, that in itself is not enough. There is still the possibility that one of Elias's so-called Artesans"—he nearly spat the word—"could interfere with our plans, although I doubt even his favored Colonel Sullyan could stop us now. I need them all to be fully occupied and kept out of our way. The concluding phase of my plan is delicate and will require time to be fully effective, so this final stage is vital. I know it distresses you, but just consider the rewards."

Reen came closer and took Sofira's cold hands in his. He stared compellingly into her hard gray eyes, softened slightly by her tears, and willed away her selfish fear.

"Just think what we stand to achieve! And it is not such a great sacrifice on your part. It will only be for a few days, and there is no danger. He will be quite safe. I have put all the arrangements in place, and you may trust me implicitly. I would never do anything to imperil him. You have my sworn word on that.

"But this is the only way to ensure that Elias is as committed to war as the demons. Once we have succeeded, just imagine how the people will love you! You will be seen as the greatest champion of humankind that has ever lived. You will be the mother of a new age, a glorious age, an age of the Church and great spiritual healing! Just think of that, Madam, and let it sustain you through these few days of sacrifice."

His rhetoric skill warmed Reen's core. Sofira sat entranced, her eyes fixed on his face. His zeal and utter belief in what he was doing, the sheer necessity of it, always captivated her. His self-commitment spoke to her soul, and he knew it.

Sensing Sofira's defiance beginning to crumble, Reen smiled winningly and clasped her hands. "You are truly one of the great Queens, Madam," he declared. "There will be ballads made of your noble sacrifice and selfless devotion to your people. Your name will go down in the archives as one of the principal architects of a new era in Albia's history. I am so proud of you."

Sofira's last vestige of protest wilted under Reen's flattery. Her expression resigned, she said, "Do what you must, Hezra. I am in your hands. But I warn you"—suddenly, the lioness instinct of a mother's love bared its fangs at the Baron—"if any harm comes to him, you will pay dearly!"

He must never forget she was a Queen, he thought as he left her presence. Yet that was just as it should be, and he was quietly satisfied with his day's work.

✣ ✣ ✣ ✣ ✣

Sullyan lay wakeful in the gloomy predawn light. She was not due out on patrol until late afternoon and would normally have welcomed the few hours respite. The last two days had been exhausting both physically and mentally. However, the necessity of facing Robin again and obeying Blaine's command to put things right between them, at least to enable them to function without friction, consumed most of her waking energy. She felt drained and soulweary.

Never one to lie long abed, she sighed and slipped from the comforter. Padding into the living space, she put water to heat for fellan. In the small washroom, she refreshed her body, if not her mind. Once dressed in her usual combat leathers, she sat on the couch by the window and drank her morning fellan, devoid of enthusiasm. She had lost all sense of taste lately and took no pleasure in the bitter brew. It was normally the only thing that revived her, but today she doubted if standing under an icy waterfall could wash away the staleness pervading her mind. She fervently hoped she wasn't sickening again. Certainly, she felt very odd.

Steeling herself, she searched for the right words to offer Robin. Tears came to her eyes. To think that the implicit trust they had shared could be so easily shattered. Had she really been so naïve at Port Loxton? Had she behaved so recklessly as to give rise to these vicious rumors? She didn't think so. As far as she could recall, the only occasion when an observer might have been given cause to wonder was when Taran had entered her room late at night. Apart from that, they had hardly been alone. She had spent most of her time with the King, and Taran had been busy escorting Jinella about the fair.

Her stomach lurched as a piece of the puzzle suddenly fell into place. Why had she not seen it before? Jinella was Baron Reen's niece, and her general behavior indicated that she shared her uncle's haughty nature. As Taran had agreed to be her escort, she would have taken his undivided attention as a right. If she had suspected him of hiding a prior attachment to Sullyan, she would not have hesitated to run to her uncle. And Reen would have swiftly spread such a juicy tale.

Sullyan sighed, wishing she had warned Taran to be on his guard when dealing with Jinella. She cursed her own dismissive attitudes. It was all very well developing a tough skin against rumor when there was only herself to consider, but she ought to have been more mindful of the possible effects on her friends.

So much for her supposed diplomatic skills! Slow tears coursed down her cheeks as she realized that she alone was responsible for her current situation. How could she blame Robin for believing the rumors when she had allowed them to breed and circulate? His barbed words concerning Rykan were obviously born of insecurity, brought on by her failure to deal with the rumors.

Fully prepared to humble herself and beg his pardon, she rose to leave. Robin also was not due out again until later that day, but as she had no idea where he had spent the last two nights, she would have to seek him out. The delicacy of the situation forbade her from summoning him through the substrate. They only did that when there was no other choice.

Wrapped up in her thoughts as she was, the desperate call which suddenly crashed into her mind sent her reeling against the wall. She didn't immediately recognize who it was, but once she removed her hands from her aching head and dulled the pain, she realized that the call was comprised of two signatures, not one. Both were distraught, both in urgent need of her.

Oh gods, Ty, whatever is it?

Marik's tone was flustered, his thoughts disorganized. Anjer, who had linked with Marik to allow him to reach Sullyan, was no less agitated. She felt a cold grip of fear tighten about her heart.

We need you, Brynne, Timar needs you! He's collapsed, and Deshan fears for his mind. He's calling for you. You have to come!

She was already moving; the desperation in Marik's tone

could not be refused. It didn't take her long to reach the horse lines. She didn't bother with Drum's saddle, merely slipping the light bridle over his ears and vaulting to his back as soon as he was clear of the stable. Showering earth behind him, he responded to his rider's need and charged recklessly down the lane.

She opened a trans-Veil corridor even as she rode. It was risky, as she didn't intend to anchor it. She had only done this once before and would not have attempted it now but for the urgent pounding of her blood. She blessed Drum's strange inborn sense that allowed him to cross the Veils by himself at need. It meant he would not spook at what she intended to do.

The tunnel's shimmer opened before her and raced through the Veils only a couple of feet ahead of Drum's coal black nose. She allowed it to close a few feet behind his streaming tail. She burst out onto the Citadel Plain not fifty yards from Caer Vellet's southern gate.

The sentries were understandably startled, and one let fly a crossbow bolt before recognizing her. The current state of unrest and the morning's cataclysmic events had made them all jumpy, and a huge black warhorse bursting out of nowhere was not to be tolerated without defensive action. Drum slithered to a halt before the gates and she identified herself to the sentries before he had fully stopped.

Once through, she raced Drum up the Processional Way, calling to Marik as she went. The palace gates were opened to her and she dismounted even as Drum barreled through them. She thrust his reins at a white-faced groom before her feet had touched the ground. Marik was at the doors to meet her. He looked dreadful. His face was a peculiar shade of gray, he was wringing his long hands, and it was almost more than he could do to keep from tugging her arm to hurry her. As they strode through the corridors toward Pharikian's private apartments, he finally calmed sufficiently to tell her what was wrong.

"It's the ransom, Brynne," he panted. "Timar ordered his mine foremen to gather it at one of the northern mines prior to shipping it down here. They only just managed to scrape together the full amount, even though they've had the miners working nonstop. Yesterday, we heard they had filled the request and had it ready for shipping. Timar told them to bring it overnight and to make sure it was guarded well. He was desperate to have it here today for when the final instructions came."

Marik glanced at her from red-rimmed eyes. "He's been so distraught. He's not been eating or sleeping, although Deshan's tried his best. He's been on the verge of breakdown ever since Aeyron was taken. And then, early this morning...."

He faltered.

Sullyan halted him with a gentle hand. "Tell me, Ty."

Swallowing painfully, he said, "There was a message. At first light, the sentries saw a riderless horse bearing Tikhal's colors come galloping out of the Forest. Timar's largest and most profitable mine is on Tikhal's land, and that's where the ransom was being accumulated. The sentries caught the horse and saw that its saddle was smeared with fresh blood. Attached to the saddle rings was a pouch containing a small box and a parchment, both addressed to the Hierarch."

Marik fell silent again, too overwrought to speak. But then he took a deep breath and carried on.

"The parchment was a letter, written in an unknown hand. There were only two lines of script. It read, '*We have the silver. In return, we have sent you what remains of your son.*'"

Sullyan felt tight bands clamp about her laboring heart.

"That's when Timar collapsed," continued Marik, his voice full of pain. "Deshan was already with him, as was Anjer. Idri and I had been called, and we arrived just as he opened the box. Idri's in a bad way too, although she's doing her best for her father. I'm so frightened for them, Brynne! Idri could lose the twins if we can't calm her. And Deshan fears for Timar's mind. He really needs your help."

"Then let us go to them, Ty. The rest can keep."

Forcing down her grief, Sullyan tried to marshal her strength. She wasn't in perfect health after the exhaustions of the past few days, but she could not worry about that now. As they entered Pharikian's rooms, the Master Physician glanced up from the Hierarch's side. His expression was one of unfeigned relief.

Sullyan stopped cold, shocked by Pharikian's condition. He was lying in his bed and his tall, lean form seemed shrunken and old. He had lost weight, and his unresponsive face was more lined and gray than ever. His years, the burden of his responsibility, and the recent terrors of his son's abduction were written plain on the papery skin. His cheeks were sunken and his lips blue.

Princess Idrimar sat next to the bed, tears tracking down her face as she clasped her father's hand. She too glanced up at the younger woman, but with no great hope in her eyes.

Sullyan turned quietly to Marik.

"See if you can persuade her Highness to leave, Ty. She needs rest and can do no more here. Deshan and I are best left alone. We will call you if there is any news."

Marik wrung his hands. "It's no use, Brynne. I've already tried. She just won't leave him."

Sullyan pursed her lips and approached the Princess. Standing by her side, she looked down at the man she thought of as her foster father. She reached out to gently caress his cheek. He stirred slightly, causing the Princess to exclaim.

"Highness," said Sullyan gently, "you must leave now. Deshan and I need room to work. Your father is exhausted and needs peace and quiet. He will be aware of your presence and also your distress. This is helping neither of you. You both need to allow your bodies to rest. Go with Ty. Trust me. Let your husband comfort you."

Idrimar stared up at Sullyan and opened her mouth to protest. Sullyan played her trump card.

"Think of your unborns, Highness. They too can sense your upset, and it will do them no good. You know you can trust Deshan and me to do everything we can for your father. We can help him more than you at present. He will need you strong and calm when he recovers, so please let Ty take you to your rooms and help you sleep. Rest assured, we will call you if your father wakes."

Unable to gainsay her, Idrimar reluctantly rose, giving her father's hand a final squeeze. Tears still sliding down her face, she allowed Marik to lead her away, the Duke casting a grateful look at Sullyan over his shoulder. She turned her attention back to Pharikian, taking Idri's place by the bed. With Deshan watching silently, she placed a hand on either side of Pharikian's face and probed his psyche deeply.

She expected to find shock and exhaustion. She knew from personal experience what the mind could do to protect itself from assault. On two separate occasions she had walled herself away from friends who could have helped her, and one of those situations nearly proved irreversible. Instead of retreating to a place of safety and darkness within, however, Pharikian was doing something far more destructive. His mind, overloaded with grief, shock, and despair, was flailing toward annihilation. The jumble of chaotic thoughts and threats of self-injury almost drove Sullyan out when she sought to identify herself to him.

Eventually, defeated, she pulled out. She had been unable to reach him or make him hear her. He had even attacked her once or twice, although his powers, fluctuating in a maelstrom of self-recrimination, were directed primarily against himself.

She raised weary eyes to the Master Physician. "He refuses to hear me, Deshan. There is only one way to help him now. We must wall him off from his power."

The healer shook his head, his expression betraying his dismay.

She glanced back down at the figure in the bed. "It will require every Artesan in the palace, and it has to be soon. He is beginning to burn up. If we leave him, he will destroy first his body and then his mind. He is caught in a loop of self-blame, and I could not break through it. To block off his power is our only option if we are to save him."

Deshan stared at her. "I don't think we can do it. There aren't enough of us."

"There have to be. The alternative is to watch him destroy himself, and I am not prepared to do that without a fight! Come now, you and Anjer are Masters, Ephan is Adept-elite, Barrin is a Journeyman, and I am Pharikian's equal. We have to be enough. Call the others, get them here quickly. We do not have much time."

Deshan did so, and they all arrived swiftly, save Barrin who had only just returned to the Citadel from patrol. While they waited for him, Sullyan told the others what to expect.

"I need your strength to be passive and available. No resistance, no suggestions. Just be open to my needs. I will do the work and I will shield you. I will also bear the brunt of his anger should he try to stop us. I warn you, he is very far gone and bent on destruction. It may take me some time, but once I gain entry I shall take your energies swiftly in order to seal his power.

"I know this is extreme, but once it is done Deshan will be able to treat his body as he would any ungifted patient. He will be able to concentrate on healing Timar without the constant threat of him committing suicide."

The moment Barrin arrived he was sucked into the group with no explanations other than to do as he was told. Gathering them round the bed, Sullyan reached out to each man in turn, linking their psyches together. Once they were all present in her mind, she turned to the Hierarch. Stilling her own fears, suffusing her thoughts with serenity, she approached his consciousness once more. As before, he refused to acknowledge her. This time Sullyan ignored the frantic rush of self-blame and destructive desires which threatened to swamp her. She slipped around his attention to seek the seat of his power.

She had done this once before, and the memory almost broke her concentration. Compelled to take Rykan's life force once she had defeated him, she had extracted the very essence of his metaphysical powers against his will. Although this time the source was very different, her avenue of access to Pharikian's power was much the same. Years ago, Pharikian had donated lifeblood to her mother, blood which was somehow passed on to Sullyan in the womb. She already carried part of his essence within her, and this prevented him from denying her by sheer will alone.

The strength of his power, however, was something else.

As soon as his tormented psyche realized what she meant to do, his full and frightening might was unleashed against her. She was ready for him. Forming a barrier of her own forces, which were the equal of his, she set herself against his will, refusing to be overcome. Frustrated anger shrieked around her, battering her shield. Then, while his whole attention was bent on fighting her, she called on the combined strength of those gathered in her mind and swiftly cast a net of force around his psyche, sealing it away before he could divert power to thwart her.

She steeled herself to ignore the frantic howls of betrayal coming from the depths of Pharikian's soul. Deprived of what he so desperately sought, his psyche thrashed and writhed. Without the strength of his metaforce to sustain this destructive resistance, though, the sedatives Deshan had given him earlier were able to take effect. His anguished mental tones gradually faded into drugged sleep.

As the awful pressure of Pharikian's powerful will was snuffed out, Sullyan almost fainted with relief. Despite her mighty shield, he had burned her. She slumped to the bed, releasing the captive minds that had provided her with strength. Each man sagged with the shock of the ordeal. Their labored breathing was loud in the chamber.

Deshan was the first to move, and he wasted no time in checking Pharikian's body. No one had to ask whether Sullyan had been successful. They could all sense the unnatural quiet within the silent man on the bed. The absence of such a fundamental part of the ruler they all loved was deeply disturbing.

"You will be able to get him back?"

It was Barrin, voicing the one question no one wanted to ask. Sullyan couldn't be irritable at his implied lack of trust. It was love that drove his fears, not suspicion. She smiled at him.

"Once he has had time to heal, I will release him. For now, he needs rest. With strength of the body comes strength of the mind, and he will be well."

She rose wearily and Deshan grasped her hand in grateful thanks. The others filed from the room to leave their ruler in peace.

"I will go to the Princess," Sullyan told Deshan. "I need to tell her what has occurred. I expect Marik will be along to see you later."

Deshan nodded and Sullyan turned to go, pausing briefly to caress Pharikian's lined face with tender fingers. She was very sore where his betrayed fury had burned her mind, and she could only hope he would forgive what she had done.

Making her way to the Princess's apartments, she gained access once the guard on the door sent a maid for Marik. She was ushered into a finely appointed sitting room and smiled at the welcome aroma that greeted her. She felt drained, and fellan was just what she needed. When Marik appeared, he handed her a steaming cup and indicated a chair. She sank gratefully into it, and he sat opposite.

"I finally got Idri to sleep," he said. "Deshan gave me some pills and I managed to slip one into her drink. She'll never forgive me, but it's done now."

"It was necessary, Ty." Already, Sullyan could feel the bitter fellan beginning to ease the throbbing in her head.

"How is he?" asked the Duke, stretching his long legs in front of him.

Sullyan spent a few minutes describing what had taken place in Pharikian's chambers. When she was through, she found the courage to ask Marik what Pharikian had seen to cause his collapse, although she dreaded what he might tell her. "What was in the box, Ty? What was it that sent him over the edge?"

Marik dropped his eyes and didn't immediately reply. Then he rose to his feet and crossed to a low fruitwood table set against one wall. He returned with a small wooden box and a piece of parchment and handed them to her. She briefly scanned the note. It read exactly as Marik had told her. He had only omitted one detail. On the bottom of the note, in place of a signature, was the unmistakable sun-circled seal of King Elias Rovannon.

Shaking her head, she set the parchment down, turning her attention to the box. It was quite small, rectangular in shape, about five inches long by two wide. It had simple spiral designs carved into it and was quite unremarkable. She thought she knew what she would see when she opened the lid.

Resting on a cloth which had once been white was the royal

signet ring of Andaryon, the crest depicting a tangwyr clutching a four-starred crown in its talons. Sullyan had seen it before. Pharikian wore one like it, and Aeyron had worn his on the little finger of his right hand. If he was still alive—and she seriously doubted it—he would wear it there no more, for the ring was still on the finger within the bloody box.

She blanched, sensing the agony and hearing the screams of the Prince as his right hand was maimed. Whether he had survived the taking of the ring she couldn't tell, but she knew Pharikian was convinced he had not. The note seemed to bear that out. She closed the lid over its grisly contents and bowed her head.

Some few moments passed before Marik said, "Gods, Brynne, what the Void do we do now?"

Sullyan raised her head and regarded him steadily. His eyes widened in understanding and he shook his head. Sullyan held his gaze, refusing to let him escape. "My friend," she said softly, "you must assume command of the throne."

Marik's eyes betrayed his fear. "But I know so little about governing a country."

"Then learn! Anjer will assist you, and so will Idri. They will steer you through it and see that you make no serious mistakes. You were a good lord to the people of Cardon, and you have already impressed those of Kymer. Governing Andaryon is much the same as ruling your own lands. Only the scale is larger."

He nodded slowly, deep in thought.

"We must act quickly," she continued, giving him no time to brood. "You told me the mine where the ransom was being gathered is on Tikhal's lands. Who knew the arrangements for shipping the silver?"

"Idri and I, Anjer, Ephan, Tikhal, and Corbyn."

"Are Tikhal and Corbyn still here?"

He shrugged. "As far as I know. They were yesterday."

"Find them, Ty. Question them as to the loyalty of their people, especially the miners. Someone must have passed information to Aeyron's abductors. Blood was spilled. Instruct Tikhal to find out who was detailed to guard the shipment and what has happened to them. Find out as much about the theft as possible, and then instruct Anjer and Tikhal to take any disciplinary action you deem necessary.

"Whoever took his Highness obviously never intended to exchange him for the ransom, which means plans to steal the silver were in place before the abduction. This implies it was an Andaryan ally of our enemy who carried out the theft. Tikhal must be instructed to make detailed enquiries to see what may be learned. Has Gaslek made any progress with the records you sent him?"

Marik shook his head. He told Sullyan that he hadn't spoken to the Hierarch's secretary since delivering Rykan's and Sonten's archives to him. Gaslek had given instructions for meals to be delivered to his rooms and had locked himself away with the mountain of papers in order to work undisturbed.

Sullyan rose. "We should pay him a visit. He may not yet know of the day's events, and his work is even more vital now."

Marik followed her from the room, but they didn't get far before they met Baron Gaslek hurrying along the corridor, his robes flapping about his legs, his spectacles slipping off the end of his nose, and his arms clasped protectively around a sheaf of papers. He saw them approaching and stopped.

"I have to see Pharikian," he panted.

"Have you found something, my Lord?" asked Sullyan.

"I have, Lady, but I ought to see Pharikian first."

"I'm afraid that won't be possible, Baron," said Marik, his firm tone causing Sullyan to raise her brows approvingly. "His Majesty received distressing news concerning Prince Aeyron this morning and is currently indisposed. In fact, he is unable to rule at present. In the absence of the Heir, I am assuming command. You may bring your news to me."

Gaslek gaped, both for the content of Marik's words and the manner of his speech. The gravity of the situation had clearly come home to the Duke, and he was determined to make the best showing he could. Sullyan knew that Pharikian had been more than good to Marik since he had married Idrimar, and considering he had once been branded a traitor due to his enforced support of Rykan, Marik owed the Hierarch much more than mere allegiance.

Gaslek swallowed. "Is his Highness...?"

Sullyan touched his arm. "We do not yet know, my Lord, but his Majesty fears the worst. He was so distraught Deshan and I have had to seal him away from his powers. We will keep him asleep for the present, for his own good. The Duke of Kymer will assume the throne until his Majesty recovers. You had best tell him what you have found."

"Well then," fussed Gaslek, concern plain on his face, "we had better go in here and I'll show you."

He ushered them into an empty office and closed the door. Moving to the desk, he placed his papers on it and sorted them into orderly stacks. Sullyan and Marik tried to hide their impatience.

"These papers," the Baron began, "are payment records from Rykan's palace. They go back quite some time. Now, there may be a perfectly innocent explanation for this, but I thought it worthy of notice."

He pointed out various passages in Rykan's records detailing payments made to his elite guard. They were dry and boring lists, and Sullyan couldn't blame Marik for not having read them before. When she saw what Gaslek had discovered, she frowned. The entries were always at the bottom, and the amount of gold bestowed, and the person named as recipient, were both a surprise.

She glanced at Marik. The date on the most recent parchment was about two months before Rykan issued his ill-fated challenge to Pharikian's rule.

"Blackmail?" suggested Marik.

"Quite possibly," she agreed. "But how, and why, would Lord Corbyn be blackmailing Rykan? And if it was not blackmail, then why would Rykan pay a northern lord more than one of his own generals?"

Congratulating Gaslek on such efficient detective work, Marik sent him back to his studies with instructions to continue the search and to let him know immediately if he found any more references to Lord Corbyn.

"Or his son," added Sullyan abruptly. Gaslek raised a brow but forbore to comment.

Marik's expression was hard and his pale eyes flinty as he and Sullyan hastened to the guest wing where Tikhal and Corbyn were housed.

It was no great surprise to find Corbyn's suite empty.

Chapter Thirty-One

When questioned, Tikhal professed ignorance of his fellow lord's departure. Sullyan believed him. However, she also noted the hastily covered start of surprise given by his son when he heard the news.

Marik gave Tikhal a brief outline of the day's events and left the Lord of the North in no doubt as to his expectations. Tikhal agreed to send someone to question the mine workers, but was of the opinion that they were probably blameless. They were all handpicked and loyal men. He was also apprised of the circumstances surrounding Marik's assumption of command, both he and his son showing genuine fear for the probable fate of the Heir. In fact, Rand turned positively green when he learned the grisly nature of the message, and Sullyan thought it might benefit Marik to get Rand alone for an intimate chat.

Leaving Tikhal and Rand to their thoughts, Sullyan accompanied Marik as he sought out Anjer and told the huge man that he was assuming temporary command of the throne. She didn't miss the look Anjer cast her as he formally accepted Marik as Regent. He had clearly expected the development.

"I will have the necessary proclamations issued at once, your Grace," he said, giving the Duke a respectful bow. Marik smoothly made the appropriate responses.

Having done everything she reasonably could under the circumstances, Sullyan had to return to the Manor. She was due out on patrol in a couple of hours and could not afford to be late.

Before she left, she decided to pay Pharikian one last visit to satisfy herself of his condition.

She never made it.

For the second time that day, a furious summons crashed into her burned and aching psyche. The harsh tones of General Blaine, suffused with such anger as she had rarely known from him, swamped her mind.

Sullyan! Where the Void are you? Get back here now! Elias's son has been abducted and he's beside himself with rage. All patrols have been canceled and an emergency council called.

His tone oozing betrayed hurt, he added, *How* dare *you be absent when I need you? I'm very disappointed in you, Sullyan. I never thought you'd desert us at a time like this.*

Her eyes pricking with the shock of his unjust accusation, Sullyan traveled as swiftly as she could back to Albia, being as reckless as before in crossing the Veils. Wondering how much more grief she could take in one day, she berated herself for not anticipating this tragic occurrence.

✤ ✤ ✤ ✤ ✤

Bull had spent some time thinking over Sullyan's words the night before, both concerning her situation with Robin and also the problem of Ozella. He would obey her command not to interfere, but he had no intention of keeping quiet should he come across the Major in the course of his duties. He also came to a decision over Ozella, and young Tad was the key to his plan.

Bull made his way toward the College in search of the young cadet. To reach the College, he had to pass the barracks, and he was rather surprised to see Lieutenant-Major Denny and Robin walking together outside the low building, deep in conversation. Guessing that Robin had spent the last two nights in the barracks, he wondered what the men thought. He must see if he could get some of them talking over supper. Robin would be out on patrol by then, so the men wouldn't be wary of his overhearing.

As he watched, the two men finished their conversation. Denny went back into the barracks, walking slowly and awkwardly as he was still very weak and sore. Robin turned in Bull's direction. His pale face was set and his eyes downcast, so he didn't see the big man leaning against the corner of the building. When he came abreast of Bull, Robin looked up, startled.

"Bull! I didn't see you there."

Bull stared at the young man. His usually fresh and handsome face was worn and strained. His indigo eyes were shadowed with worry, and his shoulders bowed. The ready smile he usually wore was missing. He returned Bull's stare and his expression quickly changed to one of irritation.

"If you've got something to say, big man, then say it. Otherwise, leave me alone."

"Oh, I've got something to say, all right," growled Bull. "I just don't know if I can keep my temper."

"Keep your mouth shut, then." Robin turned to walk on.

Bull wasn't going to take that. He planted himself in front of Robin. "You young idiot! What the Void do you think you're playing at?"

"Nothing," spat Robin, his own temper rising. "I'm playing at nothing, Bull. Ask Sullyan what she's playing at. Ask Taran!"

"I would, only you've driven him out, haven't you? Well, I hope you're proud of yourself. Oh, come on, Robin! Can't you see you're mistaken? If you believe for one minute that either of them would betray you like that, then you've no more sense than a mule's backside!"

Robin rounded on him. "What do you know about it? I've spoken to people who saw them, Bull! It's not just hearsay or gossip. This is fact."

"Oh, fact, is it? Says who? Denny? And what exactly did he

see, Robin? Two good friends working together, that's what. That's why she took Taran with her, for the gods' sake! What did you expect her to do, ignore him? She would have behaved the same way if I'd gone, do you realize that? Would you have believed the rumors if it had been me instead of Taran? Because I love her just as much as he does, I can tell you that! And I know for a fact that she loves me too, because she's told me often enough.

"But she doesn't feel the same way about either of us as she does about you, gods help her! You know that perfectly well, yet this is how you repay her. One stupid little rumor from a man who's bored out of his brain, a man who knows no better than to elaborate on some overheard, spiteful comment, and you throw away everything you've achieved over the last four years like a broken bowstring. Not to mention the love and trust of your life mate! What kind of a man does that make you?"

Robin looked as if he wanted to strike Bull, and the big man would almost have welcomed a fight. He thought he could probably still beat Robin in a fistfight, owing to his greater mass and size, but even if he couldn't, it would give the young man a chance to work some of the poison out of his system. The Major controlled his fury with a huge effort, although his fists remained balled. Ignoring Bull's question, he flung one of his own.

"If they're so innocent, Bull, why did she turn her powers on me? Tell me that, if you can! If that isn't a betrayal of trust, I don't know what is."

Bull shook his head. He was still dismayed at how overwrought Sullyan must have been to forget herself so thoroughly. He retorted forcefully. "You drove her to that! Something else to be proud of. You're the only one who's ever succeeded in making her lose control. That alone should tell you the depth of her feelings!"

He turned his head briefly before facing the furious young man again. Dropping the anger, he tried appealing to Robin through sadness. "Dammit, Robin, she's hurting so badly. She needs her friends around her right now. We all do. Artesans should stick together at times like this, not tear each other apart."

Robin's hand cut the air in a desperate gesture. "Well, I'm hurting too," he cried, a note of hysteria creeping into his voice. "Only no one seems to care about that! You're all turning against me and I've done nothing wrong. If all you can do is blame and berate me, then I'm better off without you. Just leave me alone in future."

He flung himself away and stalked off, but not before Bull saw the tears glittering in his eyes. The big man stood staring after Robin, only now realizing how deeply the rumors had sunk into the young man's soul. Thinking that he had better find out exactly what Robin had heard to make him believe them so completely, Bull resolved to talk with Denny at the first opportunity. For now, though, he needed to find Tad.

✠ ✠ ✠ ✠ ✠

Parren returned from patrol just after the noon meal. He was tired and sweaty, for his command had encountered two raiding parties and had pursued the second one for a good few miles before losing them through the Veils. He had formed the impression that the demons were desperate, as if the person who should have opened the Veils was unavailable or preoccupied.

When they did manage to escape, they left Parren furious. He had been so close! Given another ten minutes, he was sure he could have run them down and taken captives. Now that would have been a feather in his cap. No one else had succeeded in taking prisoners, not even the all-powerful Colonel Sullyan, and he would have given much to have seen her face if he had been the one to bring back prisoners.

Then he calmed himself, thinking through the situation. Would it actually be to his advantage to capture one of the raiders? What if it adversely affected the Baron's plans? Yet he had been given no instructions from the Baron concerning the subject, and soon he ceased to worry about it. Though he had not been successful, no one could doubt his devotion to duty or question his commitment, not this time. And anyway, didn't he already have a pocketful of gold from his patron, sent to him only the day before along with another message from the Baron? Although, by the sounds of it, there might not be many more such parcels.

In the message, Reen had intimated that his plans were nearing fruition. He added that their benefactress, whom Parren had no doubt was the Queen, was extremely pleased with his efforts so far and had already decided on his future reward. The gold was merely a token, although to Parren it represented a whole year's pay.

Reen also told Parren that Ozella's usefulness was probably over. The men guarding Ozella's sisters were needed elsewhere, and Reen had ordered the girls' release. They would be left to make their own way home or to a place of safety, and by the tone of the Baron's letter, they would not find this easy. He left it up to Parren to decide whether to tell Ozella or not, and upon reflection, Parren decided against telling him. At least, not until he was secure in his new position, where Ozella's denouncement could not hurt him. Parren smiled maliciously and fingered the two gold rings in his pocket.

He headed for his rooms, intending to wash away the grime of his labors and change his clothes before seeing what food was available in the commons. As luck would have it, he chanced across the young foreigner before reaching his chambers.

Parren saw Ozella's face go white as the Beraxian saw him approaching. Several expressions conveying murderous thoughts and desires flickered briefly across his face. He swallowed when he saw the knowing look Parren gave him.

Sauntering up to the younger man, Parren stopped in front of him, looking him over as if appraising his threat and discounting it.

"Killing me would be a grave mistake, my friend," he sneered, "even if you were capable of it, which you're not. You'd be signing your sisters' death warrants, and your own, if you tried. You're not that important to me, you know, so don't tempt me to remove you."

"When are you going to end this, Captain?" pleaded Ozella. "How long are you going to keep torturing me?"

"For as long as you're useful!" Parren stepped abruptly close to Ozella. The olive-skinned youth took a backward pace, as if slapped, and sweat broke out on his brow.

Parren smiled. He had just decided that even if the Baron had no further need of Ozella's services, Parren could still make use of him to further his own vengeful ends. He was deeply satisfied by Robin's reactions to Denny's scandalmongering and wondered if the Lieutenant had any idea of the tremendous damage he had caused. Parren remembered Denny well from their days as cadets, and had always suspected Sullyan had helped him through their final tests. Although Denny had never done Parren any actual harm, he had refused to join Parren's schemes to discredit her back then. The scarred Captain's soul was gratified to think he had used another of her friends against her.

Now that he had managed to create the rift between her and Robin, it was time to drive the wedge in further and cause as much grief to them both as he could. His smile turned sadistic and Ozella winced.

"I have a task for you, my fine lord," purred Parren. "I know how hard you have found it to fit in here, and I feel sorry for you." Ozella made a choking sound. "I want to help you. You need a friend, Ozella. Someone to confide in, someone to share moments of uncertainty with, someone to bolster your spirits. You have been feeling a bit depressed lately, haven't you?"

"You evil bastard," rasped Ozella, staring at the flash of pleasure in Parren's flat eyes. The Captain was aware how deeply Ozella wished he had the courage to put his hands about Parren's throat and squeeze the life out of him.

Staring back at him, Parren brought the two gold rings out of his pocket. He held them up before Ozella's dark eyes and slowly closed his fist about them, leaving Ozella in no doubt of his meaning. The fire in those almond eyes died and the sick despair returned.

"Better," approved the Captain. "Don't push me too often, Ozella. You have two sisters, remember. I only need one to keep you in line."

Ozella gasped like a stranded fish. He had clearly never considered that point.

Parren saw the unhealthy pallor of Ozella's skin deepen as the Beraxian's shoulders slumped. He fervently wished he had the man's sisters in reality. Reen should have offered to let Parren guard them. He would have enjoyed that.

"What I want you to do," he continued, reveling in Ozella's air of submission, "is to make friends with that runt of a cadet. What's his name... Tad, isn't it? The one who has the pathetic crush on Major Tamsen. He doesn't have many friends here either, I believe, so you should be ideally suited. I want you to become his shadow, his confidante. I want you to get him to tell you everything he knows or hears about Major Tamsen or any of the other Artesans. Do you understand? Make yourself indispensable to him. Be a brother to him, Ozella!"

The young lord swallowed. There was something depraved about Parren's tone and Ozella clearly didn't like it, but Parren knew there was nothing he could do. He was trapped and helpless, with no hope of an end to his torture. Parren saw the tears that pricked his eyes and smiled. Ozella slowly nodded his acceptance and Parren turned away, pleased with his own little scheme.

✤ ✤ ✤ ✤ ✤

Bull found Tad practicing training exercises in the College.

"How's the hand, sir?" the lad asked when Bull entered the room.

"Mending fine," said Bull, giving Tad a genuine smile and allowing the lad's cheerfulness to dispel the frustration and sorrow resulting from his row with Robin. He lowered his bulk onto one of the tables. "Another day or so and it'll be back to normal."

"Is there something I can do for you?" Tad seated himself on a table opposite Bull. It wasn't lost on the older man that Tad's habit of perching on the corner of a table or desk, one leg swinging, was copied exactly from Robin. He wondered if Tad was even aware of the imitation. Tad's infatuation was born of respect and love, and he could have had far worse role models than Robin. Current situation excepted, of course.

"I want to ask you to do something, lad, and it could be fairly important, although you might not agree with me when you hear what it is."

Tad frowned and cocked his head.

"We're all a little concerned about Ozella," continued Bull. "I expect you've noticed that he doesn't mix much with the rest of us, and he has no friends among the men, from what I've seen."

Tad nodded.

"Well, he's been acting strangely of late, and I've come to the conclusion there's something wrong. But I don't think he'll talk to me, and with things the way they are right now, no one else can spare the time to win him over."

Tad's face cleared. "I see, sir! You want me to make a friend of him and see if I can find out what's troubling him, is that it?"

Bull smiled. "You're very quick, lad. That's it exactly. I don't know what your chances are, but you're the only one who might be able to get through to him. I can't offer you much advice, but I do know he's very keen on that desert-bred horse of his. You might try starting there. You know a lot about horses now. Tell him how much you admire the animal, or something like that. If you can get him talking about his horse, he might open up about other things."

Tad looked dubious. "I agree it's a good place to start, sir. I just hope I can be a good liar. Because that skinny animal of his is useless for anything except desert racing. It's certainly no match for our beasts."

Bull chuckled. "I happen to agree with you, but we don't have to tell Ozella that, do we? Just do your best."

✤ ✤ ✤ ✤ ✤

Sullyan's mind was in turmoil as she raced up to the Manor. She could understand Blaine's anger at her absence and wished she had been here when the news of Eadan's abduction arrived. She realized how her presence in Andaryon would look to the King, but then wondered whether Blaine would have told him. Well, she would soon know.

She cursed silently as she ran. Their enemy was growing strong and bold indeed if he could reach within the castle and abduct the Prince from under his guards' noses. Yet this merely added weight to her theory that their enemy was within their own walls. Her prime suspect would be perfectly placed to carry out the deed without anyone being the wiser.

Her suspicions of the Queen's involvement grew stronger than ever.

Blaine's door was ajar and she could hear angry voices within. She didn't bother to knock as she pushed it open. The room was full. Colonel Vassa stood by the window, his arms folded across his chest, his face reflecting extreme concern at this latest development. Robin stood by him, resolutely refusing to meet her gaze. Captain Dexter and Lieutenant-Major Baily were also there, as were some of the other captains. General Blaine was standing beside the King, who was sitting slumped in his chair, his head bowed over a parchment which he clenched in white fingers. His face was flushed.

Blaine stared at her, clearly still angry over her absence. Vassa's expression was neutral. Not being an Artesan, he usually withheld his opinion except over military matters. Robin watched her covertly, frowning as if he too couldn't believe where she had been. She felt a pang of grief. He of all people should have understood the debt of gratitude and love she owed Timar Pharikian. Baily and Dexter, along with the other captains, simply looked worried and confused.

In the silence that greeted her arrival, King Elias stood slowly. He trembled and his eyes, when they met hers, were almost inhuman; cold and savage. He didn't speak, but thrust the parchment toward her. She saw how his hand shook. He appeared to have aged by twenty years. Her heart filled with pity for him and she wanted to throw her arms about him for comfort. His hostile gaze held her back, however, and she could see now was not the time to display familiarity. He needed her professional skills more. She took the parchment and scanned it.

Fair exchange, Elias, since you are so keen on a trade-alliance. You attack our villages, we raid yours. You kill our people, we have killed yours. Yet still you weren't satisfied. You took my son, my only Heir.

Fair exchange, then. Your son for mine. Until you return Prince Aeyron, whole and unharmed, you

will not see your little boy. And if Aeyron is harmed
in any way, your son will suffer the same. Think on
that, Elias, and decide if it is not a fair trade.

At the bottom of the parchment, in place of a signature, was the royal seal of Pharikian's House.

Sullyan raised her head from the note and looked straight into the cold fury of Elias's stare. Her eyes filled with tears. Eadan was only just over a year old.

"Oh, Elias!" she breathed, her own hand trembling as she held the parchment.

The men were still watching her. The King took a step forward. She felt once more that strange tension that had filled the room while she and Robin argued.

"Where were you?" His voice was low and cold, quite unlike his usual tones.

She frowned. "I was not on duty, your Majesty. I was—"

"I said, where the Void were you?" His voice increased in volume and he took another step closer.

"I was attending the Hierarch, your Majesty. He received some bad news about his son and collapsed. He needed me."

Elias's unnatural stillness exploded into shocking fury. "How *dare* you? *He* needed you? What about me? *I* needed you, but when we searched for you, we found you were dancing attendance on the abductor of my son! You're supposed to be *my* subject, Colonel. You're supposed to serve me! Or have you forgotten that?"

Sullyan blanched in the face of his fury and fell to her knees before him. "Never, your Majesty! I would never forget that I serve you. I am yours to command, you know that. Yet how could I refuse the call of a dear friend in distress? Should I have left him to die when I could save him? Timar had nothing to do with the abduction of your son, you have my sworn word on that."

Elias's face flushed deeper and his eyes glittered feverishly. He appeared not to have heard her last words. "Is he dying?"

"I believe he will live, Majesty, given time to heal."

"Then I pray he does not get it!"

She stared in consternation, thinking she had never seen a man in such extreme distress. Pharikian's own reaction was no less violent, but the two men differed in that the Hierarch's anger turned inward, whereas Elias wanted to smash something.

"He will pay for this," snarled the King, turning away.

Sullyan was still on her knees. He hadn't bothered to raise her. She watched him carefully, a dreadful suspicion forming in her mind.

"Mathias," he snapped, "raise the militia. Get word to every village. They are to arm and send here every able-bodied man they have. Send runners to the garrisons. They are to march here immediately. I will send word to Kinsey to mobilize the Loxton garrison and raise the city. I need every man I can get."

"Your Majesty!" protested Sullyan before Blaine could speak. She rose unbidden, her eyes full of horror. "What are you doing?"

Elias rounded on her. "What do you think I'm doing? Would you have me just sit here and twiddle my thumbs when that treacherous demon has stolen my son?"

"Timar does not have your son!" she insisted. "You are not thinking clearly. You are doing exactly what our enemy wants you to do. You are playing into his hands!"

Her exasperated tone caused Elias to freeze. He stood so still, she could almost hear the pounding of his blood.

"What did you say?"

His voice was frigid and he advanced on her menacingly. She glanced in appeal at the General. Surely he could see this was a complete overreaction? Surely he could feel something was wrong? Yet Blaine had closed his eyes. She was on her own.

Trying to stall him, Sullyan chose to misinterpret her monarch's words. "Timar Pharikian does not have your son, your Majesty," she repeated, hoping her soft tone would cut through the red mist of Elias's fury. The situation was lost if she could not halt this desperate and unthinking rush for revenge. "He has no reason to abduct your son since he knows you were not responsible for taking Aeyron. How would Timar gain access to Prince Eadan? He was guarded too well. No, your Majesty. We must look within our own walls for the culprit."

Refusing to be sidetracked, Elias shouted, "Then how do you explain the letter? How do you explain his seal?"

"Your Majesty, the letter Timar received early this morning, together with Aeyron's ring, was signed with your seal. Did you send that letter to him? Did you sever Aeyron's finger and send it with his royal signet to his father? Of course not!"

She stopped. Elias had turned bone-white and his trembling body would no longer hold him erect. He collapsed into a chair, breathing heavily; his blue eyes, hot with pain, fixed on her face. Blaine stared at her in open-mouthed horror while the other men muttered among themselves. Even Robin shook his head in despair.

Elias raised his face to the ceiling, two spots of color flaming high in his cheeks. His eyes darkened with terror and pain. "Oh, gods! Eadan!"

Too late, Sullyan recalled the passage in the note warning that Prince Eadan would be maimed to match any injury Aeyron suffered. She cursed herself for the slip.

"Your Majesty," she began, moving toward the King. She had to lessen the damage, but it was too late. He was too far gone. He had been pushed beyond hearing, beyond reason. He stared mindlessly at her, all rage gone, all feeling walled away. She

403

quailed at the alien nature of his expression.

"Your Majesty," she tried again, "allow me to take some men and search for Prince Eadan. He has not crossed the Veils. He is here in Albia still, I would swear it. Whoever has taken Prince Aeyron also has your son. Timar Pharikian has nothing to do with this. He is as distraught as you are, and even now lies powerless in his bed, stricken with grief. His utter desolation may even prove too much for him. I beg you, do not attack Andaryon. You will be playing into the hands of your enemies, and I dread to think what that could mean. Give me leave, your Majesty. Send me to search for your son."

Life returned to Elias's dead eyes. His expression changed subtly, and she didn't like what she saw. It was as if he had suddenly become a different person. She glanced at Blaine, who was watching his monarch.

Elias spoke sharply. "Do you serve me, Colonel Sullyan?"

She replied fervently. "Yes, your Majesty. You know I do."

The King rose, all traces of distress vanished. He was fully, coldly, and unnaturally in control of himself. His voice, when he spoke, was strong and clear, yet oddly altered.

"Then I command you to lead my forces against the Hierarch, Timar Pharikian. As of now, we are at war with the realm of Andaryon."

The End

Glossary

Albian Characters

Ardoch, Master. Elias's legendary swordmaster.

Baily. A Major at the Manor under Colonel Vassa.

Brynne Sullyan. A Colonel at the Manor under General Blaine.

Bull, aka Bulldog, aka Hal Bullen. Colonel Sullyan's aide.

Cal Tyler. Taran's friend, and life mate of Rienne Arlen.

Devis. Son of Jed, landlord of the Hazel Tree.

Dexter. A Captain at the Manor under Major Tamsen.

Eaden, Prince. Son of King Elias and Queen Sofira.

Elias Rovannon. Albia's High King.

Fiann. A master bard from the Second Realm, Sinnia.

Fergus. A Kingsman at Port Loxton.

Goran. Master cook at the Manor.

Hal Bullen. See 'Bull.'

Hallian. A Captain at Port Loxton.

Hezra Reen. An Albian Baron from High King Elias's court.

Huw. A disabled youth living at Loxton Castle.

Hyram. General Blaine's valet.

Izack. Baron Reen's personal Commander.

Jed. Landlord of the Hazel Tree, an inn on the way to Port Loxton.

Jerrim Vassa. A Colonel at the Manor.

Jessy. Deceased sister of Robin Tamsen.

Jinella, Lady. The niece of Baron Reen.

Josh. Stablemaster at Port Loxton.

Kandaran. High King Elias's father, murdered during Albia's civil war.

Kinsey, Lord. Chamberlain to High King Elias.

Lerric. Client-king of Bordenn Province, father of Queen Sofira.

Lily. Lady Jinella's maid.

Lyanda. Female member of King Elias's runner service.

Mathias Blaine. The Manor's senior officer and General-in-Command to High King Elias.

Milo. Landlord of an inn close to the Manor.

Morgan Sullyan. Deceased father of Brynne Sullyan.

Owyn Denny. A Lieutenant-Major at Port Loxton.

Ozella. A young Lord from Beraxia, sent to study at the Manor.

Parren, Glinn. A Captain at the Manor under Colonel Vassa.

Rendan Levant, Lord. First Minister to High King Elias.

Rienne Arlen. A healer, and Cal Tyler's life mate.

Robin Tamsen. A Major at the Manor under Colonel Sullyan.

Seline, Princess. Daughter of King Elias and Queen Sofira.

Seth. Baron Reen's manservant.

Sofira. Queen to High King Elias Rovannon.

Solet. The Manor's stablemaster.

Tad Greylin. A cadet and Apprentice Artesan at the Manor.

Taran Elijah. Artesan-Adept and close friend of Brynne Sullyan.

Wil. A Corporal at the Manor.

Zane. Son of Jed, landlord of the Hazel Tree.

Andaryan Characters

Aeyron Pharikian. Timar Pharikian's son and Heir.

Anjer, Lord General. Officer in overall command of the Hierarch's forces.

Barrin. A Commander in the Hierarch's forces.

Brianne. Baby daughter of Anjer and Torien.

Corbyn, Lord. A northerner, one of Lord Tikhal's nobles.

Deshan. The Hierarch's Master Healer, also a Master Artesan.

Ephan. General in the Hierarch's forces, overall commander of the Velletian Guard.

Gaslek. An Andaryan Baron, secretary to the Hierarch.

Heron. Sonten's Artesan Commander who perished at the siege of Hyecombe.

Idriana. Deceased wife of Timar Pharikian.

Idrimar Pharikian. Daughter of Timar Pharikian.

Jaskin. Sonten's nephew, killed by Taran.

Kethro. Artesan son of Lord Corbyn.

Ky-shan. The leader of a band of pirates from Andaryon's eastern seaboard.

Liyan Tamilane. One-time Hierarch and the last known Supreme Master Artesan.

Nazir, Lord. One of Duke Marik's nobles, made Lord of Durkos after Sonten's demise.

Norkis. Senior page to the Hierarch of Andaryon.

Rand. Artesan son of Lord Tikhal.

Rykan. Deceased Lord of Kymer province, one time aspirant to the Andaryan throne.

Sonten. Deceased general to Duke Rykan. Former Lord of Durkos Province.

Tikhal. An Andaryan Lord, also known as the Lord of the North. Pharikian's premier noble.

Timar Pharikian. The Hierarch, Supreme Ruler of Andaryon.

Torien, Lady. The wife of Lord General Anjer.

Torman Vanyr. Deceased commander of the Velletian Guard.

Ty Marik. Former Count of Cardon Province, now Duke of Cardon and Kymer.

Verris. Deceased commander of Rykan's forces.

Realms of the World

First Realm—Endormir

Endormirians are sometimes known as 'Roamerlings' because of their itinerant habits. They are small and slim, dark skinned, with brown or black eyes showing hardly any whites. The Artesan gift runs only through the males, and gifted males always become clan-leaders. As Endomir suffers from severe winter conditions, its people cross the Veils into the other realms for the winter months, where they are well known as traders.

Second Realm—Sinnia

Sinnians are tall and milk-haired, with pale skin. They live in clans and were once nomadic but now live in settlements. All are born able to control their metaforce up to the rank of Adept and are thus considered 'sports'. Their race often produces highly gifted musicians and storytellers.

Third Realm—Relkor

Relkorians are small, fierce and stocky, notorious for raiding the other realms for slaves to work their mines and quarries. Their Artesans, both male and female, invariably become slave-lords.

Fourth Realm—Albia

Albia is the human realm. The Artesan gift runs through both male and female lines, each gender being equal in potential. The craft is currently out of favour due to raiding by both Relkorian and Andaryan Artesans. Albians widely believe that all Artesans use their powers only for gain and control.

Fifth Realm—Andaryon

A warlike race characterised by eyes with slit pupils. They fight constantly amongst themselves, vying for position within the Hierocracy. The Artesan gift passes only through the male line and females play a minor and downtrodden role. Only the most powerful Artesan can become and hold the rank of Hierarch. Their battles for supremacy are governed by strict, ritualistic laws.

Terms

Artesan. A person born with the ability to control metaforce and master the four primal elements.

Brine-rum. Strong liquor, drunk by pirates on Andaryon's eastern seaboard.

Codes of Combat. Strict laws governing any conflict between Andaryan nobles.

Demons. Derogatory term used in Albia to describe those of the Andaryan race.

Earth ball. An explosive sphere of Earth element formed by an Artesan for use as a weapon.

Fellan. A dark, aromatic and bitter beverage brewed from the seeds of the fellan-plant.

Firefield. A barrier formed from the primal element of Fire, through which only Artesans can pass. Firefields formed by those of inferior Artesan rank can easily be destroyed by those of a higher rank.

Firewater. Incredibly strong liquor.

Free traders. Another term for pirate.

Kingsman. Term used to describe members of the High King's fighting forces.

Matria Church. The Minster in Port Loxton, seat of Albia's primary faith, the Faith of the Wheel.

Metaforce (also called life force). The force of existence pertaining to all things, both animate and inanimate.

Perdition. A state of non-being for the soul—a place where souls with no ultimate destination reside.

Primal elements. Earth, Water, Fire, and Air.

Primal Sacrament. Andaryan name for the Pact, an agreement brokered between Andaryan nobles. Used to settle wars ending in stalemate, it involves the willing suicide of a powerful Artesan.

Portway. Structure formed by an Artesan from a primal element, usually Earth or Water, which gives its creator access through the Veils.

Psyche. An Artesan's unique and personal pattern through which they can manipulate metaforce and channel the primal elements.

Roamerling. Slightly derogatory term for the nomads of Endormir.

Sally port. A small door within a larger fortified barrier, allowing only one person to pass through at a time.

Substrate. The medium in which the primal elements reside, and in which the world and all things have their being.

Tangwyr. Monstrous Andaryan raptor trained to hunt men.

The Pact. (See Primal Sacrament).

The Staff. Mysterious and terrible weapon capable of stealing and storing metaforce. Can only be used by Artesans.

The Veils. Misty barriers separating the five Realms of the World. Only Artesans have the power to move through the Veils.

The Void. Dark abyss at the end of life into which all souls pass before reaching their final destination.

The Wheel. Central principle of Albian faith.

Velletian Guard. Personal guard of the Hierarch of Andaryon.

Witch. Derogatory term for an Artesan.

Artesan ranks and their attributes

Level one: Apprentice. Person born with the Artesan gift and the ability to influence the first primal element of Earth. Able to hear other Artesans speaking telepathically but unable to initiate such speech.

Level two: Apprentice-elite. Has some skill in influencing their own metaforce. Has attained mastery over the element of Earth. Able to initiate telepathic speech but only with Artesans already known to them. Able to build substrate structures, identify a person by the pattern of their psyche, and counter metaphysical attack to some degree.

Level three: Journeyman. Has mastery over Earth and is able to influence Water. Able to build portways and travel through the Veils. Has some skill in using metaforce for offense. Also able to initiate psyche-overlay and converse telepathically with any other Artesan. Possesses some self-healing potential.

Level four: Adept. Has mastery over both Earth and Water. Able to build more complex substrate structures such as corridors. Able to influence where such structures emerge. Possesses stronger offensive and defensive capabilities. Able to merge psyche fully with other Artesans. Increased healing abilities.

Level five: Adept-elite. Has mastery over Earth and Water and is able to influence Fire. Possesses great healing powers which can even aid the ungifted (with their permission). Able to initiate powersinks and merges of psyche. Able to construct such structures as Firefields.

Level six: Master. Has mastery over Earth, Water and Fire. Able to control the power of an inferior Artesan against their will. Control over personal metaforce now almost total. Possesses incredible healing powers.

Level seven: Master-elite. Has mastery over Earth, Water and Fire and is able to influence Air, the most capricious primal element. Able to absorb a lesser or even equal-ranked Artesan's power and metaforce provided some link or permission (however tenuous) can be found.

Level eight: Senior Master. Has complete mastery over all four primal elements. Is able to absorb another Artesan's power by force, even sometimes without a link. Possesses a high degree of metaphysical (and usually spiritual) strength.

Level nine: Supreme Master. It has never been fully established whether this rank actually exists. Supreme Masters are supposedly able to influence Spirit - largely regarded as the mythical 'fifth element.' Ancient texts refer only to the possibility; no mention has ever been found of a being attaining Supreme Masterhood.

Sport or lay-Artesan. Freaks of nature, sports are thought to be able to control their own metaforce from birth, to whatever level of strength they inherently possess. As they receive no training their working is often undetectable. They are also believed to be able to 'hear' the thoughts of those around them; gifted or ungifted, and directly, not through the substrate.

Cas Peace was born and brought up in the lovely county of Hampshire, in the UK, where she still lives. On leaving school, she trained for two years before qualifying as a teacher of equitation. During this time she also learned to carriage-drive. She spent thirteen years in the British Civil Service before moving to Rome, where she and her husband, Dave, lived for three years. They return whenever they can.

As well as her love of horses, Cas is mad about dogs, especially Lurchers. She enjoys dog agility training and currently owns two rescue Lurchers, Milly and Milo. Cas loves country walks, working in stained glass, and folk singing. She is currently working on writing and recording songs for each of her fantasy books. The song associated with King's Envoy is "The Wheel Will Turn"; for King's Champion it is "The Ballad of Tallimore"; and for King's Artesan it is "Morgan's Song (All That We Are)." For The Challenge it is "Meadowsweet". All Cas's book songs can be found at and downloaded from her website, see below.

Cas has also written a nonfiction book, "For the Love of Daisy," which tells the life story of her mischievous and beautiful Dalmatian. Details and other information can be found on her website:

www.caspeace.com.

Other Books by Cas Peace:

Artesans of Albia Fantasy Series:

Trilogy One: *Artesans of Albia*

Book One: *King's Envoy*

Book Two: *King's Champion*

Book Three: *King's Artesan*

Trilogy Two: *Circle of Conspiracy*

Book One: *The Challenge*

Book Two: *The Circle* (Winter 2014)

Book Three: *Full Circle* (Spring 2015)

Non-Fiction

For the Love of Daisy

9 781939 993311